The Boy Who Made God Smile

To Weave a Rainbow

Beneath Napoleon's Hat Volume 1: Eagles without a Cliff

Beneath Napoleon's Hat Volume 2: A Black Violet

Beneath Napoleon's Hat Volume 3: Sylvia Beach and the Melancholy Jesus

Patchwork

The Boy Who Made God Smile

G.J. Martin

Colley Books

First published in 2016
By Colley Books Ltd
All rights reserved
© G.J. Martin 2016
The right of G.J. Martin to be identified as author of this work has been
asserted in accordance with Section 77 of the Copyright, Designs and
Patents Act 1988
Hardback ISBN 978-0-9931892-9-6
Paperback ISBN 978-0-9955320-0-7

British Library Cataloguing in Publication Data.
A catalogue record for this book is available from the British Library.

Printed in Garamond 11/12

Hardback limited to 50 numbered copies.

Colley Books Ltd
c/o Brown McLeod Ltd
51 Clarkegrove Road
Sheffield S10 2NH
www.colleybooks.com

This novel is dedicated to my two daughters, Ellen and Alice and to the memory of Noel Fox.

Sai Baba's Ashram

Preface

In the spring of 1994 I went to India to follow the path of the gods. For a long time I had been preparing to write a book about avatars, God-Men and God-Woman (I only knew of one), but instead I created a myth called *The Boy Who Made God Smile*. It was a novella that described the startling world of Sai Baba's ashram at Whitefield in southern India. I went on to visit calmer spaces, particularly the Red Mountain retreat of Sri Ramana Maharshi, and many more avatars, the touchable God-Men of India who seem to offer instant solutions, both practical and spiritual, to lives that are troubled or lack purpose. Whilst there I met Noel Fox, the documentary film maker. He became my Boswell—his description and at his insistence —I'd planned to travel alone. Together we joined the spiritual tourists and later we would write a film about these experiences. It was to be called *God Incorporated*. Despite being funded and sponsored by two television networks, Noel's deteriorating health meant the film was never made. In its stead, I have given him this book.

Acknowledgements

Many people helped with my researches before I visited India. Several organizations and their leaders, a number of members of an influential Russian family, and returning pilgrims readily told their stories, but at that time, they wished to remain anonymous. The character Rita is a composite of several women who feared for their lives after the assassination attempt on Sai Baba. They will remain anonymous despite Sai Baba's death. Controversy still surrounds him.

The support and involvement of Henderson Mullin and Aimee Wilkinson of Writing East Midlands have been exemplary. Their interest and encouragement have been invaluable throughout the development of this novel.

Writing East Midlands awarded me a mentoring prize. The chair of the final panel of judges was Anne Zouroudi. She became my mentor and loved the story of the boy Hari who made his God smile. Over a period of eighteen months, three new narratives were developed, interwoven and finally, this full-length novel appeared.

I particularly thank Anne Zouroudi for her professionalism, her insight into the world of commercial publishing and her careful criticism, always tempered with reassurance and praise. All these people together have made this book possible and my ingenious and tireless publisher, Dr John Basford, has made it real.

We have included some of the drawings I made during my visit. Travelling with a sketchbook always seems less intrusive than pointing a camera and the resultant scenes are often more spontaneous.

Contents

CHAPTER ONE
Beggars and Cheats

Hari had been in India only four days when the beggar woman arrived singing. His father and mother and some of their friends were waiting for his grandfather's taxi to arrive from the city, to take them back to Bangalore. They were sipping tea in a café called 'Sai Deep', outside the main gateway of the ashram. The tops of its fairy-tale buildings, painted in gaudy greens and pinks, peeped over high walls that were garlanded with dangerous barbed wire.

A ditch had appeared in-between the café and the walls. It was already a metre deep, a metre wide and the dirt that had been dug to make it was piled as loose mounds at its edges. It was full of garbage. All manner of debris littered its margins and depths. Waste food, human waste, twisted metal, screwed paper: a vile mound and pit that shocked Hari's eyes and offended his nose. It wasn't just the flies that buzzed and hovered. Dirty, knickerless children played on its verges; more purposeful adults sifted for discarded prizes. The surprise was the beggar woman. Hari stole forbidden glances. He was enthralled. She was still singing.

She crouched on the brink, feet pressed deep into the barrier mound, and began a careful inspection of the pieces of paper, bits of tin and piles of ashes within her immediate reach. She slithered easefully into the bottom of the pit. She unwrapped her sari and began to smear her naked body with all the unspeakable filth she sat in. She was thorough. She matted her hair, smeared her face, embraced and wrapped herself in the dregs of the midden.

Hari stared, fascinated.

"Why is she doing that father?"

"It is disgusting, child. I forbid you to look."

"But why is she washing in rubbish?"

"Because she is mad."

"I think she is very beautiful, father."

"I told you to look away."

With a clumsy lunge, Ajay Sarnhi snapped his son's head round, averting the improper gaze in an instant. It was a surprisingly violent and unexpected act. The moment it was done, the father looked to his father for approval. Ramu Sarnhi gave none. His face was impassive, betraying little. Ajay could read nothing there.

Hari was stunned. His father rarely touched him, even with affection. The ten-year-old boy was further confused when his usually passive mother spoke angrily to his father.

"That was uncalled for. What has got into you?"

Ajay looked away, shamefaced.

There was no mistaking Ramu Sarnhi's expression after this outburst.

It was one of disapproval and contempt. To his mind, Esther Sarnhi's comments were as unacceptable as her husband's tolerance of them. The family fell silent.

A child with chopped hair and odd eyes that stared, rushed into the café. She made strange guttural sounds, gags and grunts and gestured towards her mouth implying food, imagining eating, miming morsels of rolled up pieces of rice, invisible, in her clutching finger ends. The child had a child, a long-limbed baby that clutched like a monkey with a tousle of black hair and gigantic, sad, black eyes, the normal white surround a pale grey. Child and child tapped the shoulder of a middle-aged Western woman with growing-back shaven head, gaping sari and red spot spiritual eye smeared at the top of her nose. She waved them away.

"No more! I already gave you ten rupees today. Go and feed your baby. Don't beg!"

Absent-mindedly, the Western woman played with the baby's toes and chucked its chin with a bent forefinger. The baby did not smile. It kept its hangdog look, pleading, innocent against all comforting odds.

The café owner scurried them away, angry on behalf of his customers. Hari didn't know what he said, but it seemed to work for a few moments; then, the ever-present beggars would seep back.

Hari could not get used to the eight and nine-year-old boys and girls with elfin babies riding their hips. They were younger than him and already seemed lost, with nothing to look forward to. Every morsel of food he lifted to his mouth seemed to have been eaten by six or eight wanting eyes. Four thirsty faces thrust into his, begrudged each sip of tea.

"Sai Ram! Sai Ram!"

It meant 'Mother', his grandfather explained, it meant, 'Father', it meant, 'Give!'

"Why do they do this, Grandfather?"

"They choose to, Hari. It is a life they seek."

Hari's grandfather was an impressive man. He had swept-back, silver-grey hair, gold spectacles and a delicately embroidered, white, silk tunic. He looked as wealthy as he was and spoke with accustomed authority. Nevertheless, Hari found it difficult to believe what he said.

"But they look so sad."

"It comes with practice." The grandfather smiled. Hari frowned.

"Do I sound harsh, young man? I don't mean to. I have lived with the beggars all my years. I learn not to see them. Many will tell you stories of the fabulous, secret wealth of some beggars. They will say, 'Hari, look there!' "

Hari didn't move.

"Do it! Look there!" Hari followed his grandfather's pointing finger and his gaze came to rest on the shining head of a seated beggar who had no legs.

2

To reinforce this loss, crossed neatly, next to his ugly stumps, were the even uglier man-made replacements that served as artificial legs when he wished to walk.

"You see him?"

"Yes."

"At night, when he has begged his fill, he puts on his legs and walks to his chauffeur-driven car. Then, he is delivered to the best restaurant in Bangalore for his dinner. I have seen him there often. He always eats fish cooked in a French sauce. After dinner he drinks American beer in a bar near the restaurant, then goes to his hotel. He has a whole suite to himself. I understand that one of his many pairs of legs has diamonds in the knees. He also has a house on the coast in Kerala … And not a word of this is true!" He laughed. Hari lowered his eyes. He had begun to believe the story.

"We tell each other such stories so we don't feel guilty. But it is very hard to help beggars."

"Why? I don't understand."

"Because," Ramu Sarnhi sighed, "because, begging works. To be a beggar is to be part of a whole caste. You cannot choose to beg. You have to be born to it. A beggar is very proud. I will tell you a real story. Not far from here, I have been building a small house. It will be for visitors to the ashram and for me. There is a tree near to where the house will be. There are four or five families of beggars who have come to live in its shade. They have a tarpaulin for a roof and some stone slabs for a hearth. So they sleep and cook and live. I asked my builder to give them work. I pay good rates. 'Too high!' according to my builder. 'We don't pay as much in the country as you do in Bangalore,' he says to me. 'Still,' I say, 'pay city rates and feed them, I can't stand to see the children starve.' He offers them twenty-five rupees a day, food and clean water. They should be happy. Were they?" The grandfather leaned towards Hari. "Well?"

"I don't know, Grandfather. Yes?" Hari thought no, but waited.

"No!" The grandfather beamed.

"Do you know what they said?" Hari wasn't meant to answer.

"They said: 'You insult us. We are not workers; we are beggars. Keep your twenty-five rupees.'" He sighed, raised his shoulders and spread the palms of his hands in a gesture of sad, certain knowing.

"So, there you are. Beggars are proud, beggars are born, none are rich, but they are always, always here."

And they were.

"Sai Ram! Sai Ram!"

The beautiful beggar woman had stopped singing. She was clothed and walking towards the café. There was an instant and extreme reaction. The proprietor stooped, clutched a handful of earth and flung it towards her.

3

He missed, but she changed her path and walked away.

Other customers, unknown to Hari, congratulated the proprietor, reassured him of their approval with smiles, kind words and handshakes.

"Why do they hate her so, Grandfather?" Hari asked, anxious and perplexed.

"She is a beggar and everything she has done is inappropriate." His grandfather scowled in disapproval.

"She has a name!" the Western lady declared.

No one responded.

"She has a name!"

It was Hari who dared to ask, "What is the beggar woman's name?"

Pleased to be acknowledged, the Western lady replied in a gentler tone for Hari than the one she had assumed in her startling assertion.

"Lunasha. That is her name. She has been much wronged."

Embarrassed by her sudden anger, the lady from the West felt the need to explain herself. She began with an introduction.

"I'm Joan, by the way, from Winchester, at least, I was there once upon a time. This is where I live now. I have a house in the village, here in Whitefield."

The customers in the café shuffled in their seats and whispered greetings and nodded in acknowledgement.

Hari was frustrated. He wanted to know more about Lunasha than her name.

"It's a beautiful name." He thought he'd whispered this to himself but Joan overheard him.

"It means the beauty and brightness of flowers," she explained.

This idea delighted Hari.

"But all withered now."

"Do you know her story?" asked Hari's mother, newly emboldened and daring to be noticed.

"Yes. Everybody here does. Perhaps everybody in India may or should know what happened to her."

"Is it proper?" asked Ramu Sarnhi, already implying his disapproval.

"It's very improper but it can be tactfully told." She glanced towards Hari and the other women listening in. "Lunasha is cursed by her beauty. It led to marriage when she was very young. The brother of her husband became besotted with her. He stalked her. Trod every step she took. Spied from the shadows. His courage grew and he gave her flowers, then chocolates, then beatings." She paused as her story darkened. "On one occasion he threatened to kill himself."

"What with?" Hari's father asked. The sneer in his voice registered his disbelief. His interruption annoyed all those listening.

"Rat poison," Joan replied instantly. The speed and certainty of her answer silenced any doubts. "He even promised marriage."

"But that was impossible," Hari's mother stated with quiet certainty.

"Precisely. That is why, with no stratagems left, he violated her."

To Hari, the word sounded vile and violent. To the adult listeners, it conveyed its precise meaning.

Hari's grandfather ended the short silence.

"It is a common enough story. I read such tales almost every day in *The Hindu* newspaper." He was dismissive. The other men nodded wisely; the women sighed, ashamed of the men, ashamed equally of their enforced muteness.

"They are not tales, sir," Joan declared. "They are tragedies and daily occurrences, as you so coldly say." She paused, took a careful breath, and stated with a calm certainty that shocked her listeners. "The men are to blame."

Her declaration sparked an instant debate. A dozen unidentified voices offered their thoughts.

"Hardly. It is always the women," said a man. "They provoke us constantly."

"What with?" asked Joan in disbelief.

"Their clothing. Their talk," said the same man.

"What talk?" asked Hari's mother.

"They talk to men. What can they expect?"

Smugly satisfied, his argument won, he was prepared to make concessions.

"I will accept men are to blame only because they have failed to control their women."

"Do they need controlling?" asked Joan.

"Most certainly. That is according to the *Laws of Manu*," explained a cultured, new male voice. "All is contained in the *Manusmriti*." He was obviously a scholar. "It says, with the authority of the ages, written in a sacred text, that the male controls the female because she is dangerous to men."

"It is surely the opposite." Joan was perplexed by these cultural certainties.

"Widows must devote their lives to the austere pursuits of religion," Ramu Sarnhi proclaimed.

"Lunasha is not a widow," Joan replied.

"A pity, then she could atone for her behaviour by throwing herself on her husband's funeral pyre."

"The good old ritual of suttee."

This declaration from the scholar seemed to meet with the concerted agreement of all the men.

Hari was still thinking of Lunasha. Tentatively he asked Joan, hoping he'd not entirely misunderstood, "If the beggar woman was hurt, why is she here, like she is?"

"Don't concern yourself, my son. This is not your business and you are still a child. You cannot understand." Hari's father was uncomfortable with this discussion and didn't welcome Hari's interest.

"He can understand injustice," Joan interceded. "It was a good question to ask, young man. She is here, like this, as you put it, because her husband sent her away. His greater loyalty lay with his brother. Her mother's family felt she had disgraced them, so they also sent her away."

"What happened was a sort of punishment," the scholar began to explain. "Now she must make amends."

Hari was going to speak but caught the chilling glare in his father's eyes and fell into a confused silence.

Hari didn't like his father in India. It changed him.

They'd arrived at Mumbai airport in the dark of the very early morning. The heat was improbable, the mass of people impenetrable, the smells and sounds new and strange.

Through the knot of milling people a placard was waving overhead with the name 'Sarnhi' scribbled on it.

"There's our man. He is for us." Hari's father, a neat little man with a sullen look, managed a smile. He was more relieved than he'd dare to admit. He'd failed to make contact with the hotel during the past week and hoped against hope he would be met.

They were driven into town in a white minibus, empty except for Hari and his parents. The door wouldn't stay closed and the driver was a maniac, swerving and cursing and weaving a way through a city as busy in the night as Birmingham was at midday.

Along the sides of the roads were the fabled slums—a structural mess of people and things that thrived according to evolutionary rules all their own. The smell was fecal, the scale beyond imagining.

Their hotel was grand but crumbling. They'd been given the whole of the top floor. There was a huge lounge with ornate settees elaborately carved out of extinct hardwoods. There was a dining room that was waiting to seat eight and a walk-in shower room bigger than any of the rooms in their house in England. Everything was wonderful. Hari was thrilled, his father amazed.

"Pennies for pounds!" Ajay Sarnhi kept chanting. "Pennies for pounds!"

He already knew India was cheap. He warned Hari and his mother not to 'play the Raj', whatever that meant, but even he couldn't believe how far his elastic currency would stretch.

All was well until breakfast. And then there was the row.

Hari tried to remember the sequence. It was innocuous enough in the beginning, he remembered. There was a simple question.

6

"Would you like fresh orange juice?" the waiter had asked of his father.
"Whatever comes with our all-in breakfast," had been his father's reply.
"So, you would like three orange juices?"
"Yes, of course."
They ate. They rose to leave. Then Hari's father was stopped.
"You have to pay your bill, sir."
"It has already been paid," explained Hari's father. "I paid by credit card many, many weeks ago. You have had my money for several weeks already." Hari's father was instantly aggressive. He tried to usher the waiter away. He turned to Hari and his mother, smiled and explained, "I hoped to avoid any difficulty by paying in advance. I have all my receipts. I was warned. There will be no problem. Don't worry."
The waiter returned with a leather-bound pouch that was half-open to display the bill in question.
"Your room is paid for," explained the waiter, "but not your breakfast."
"It was all inclusive. I have the necessary papers somewhere. Must I seek them to prove you wrong?"
"You had breakfast off the menu. This was not included."
"Let me see." Hari's father snatched the bill. Every item had been charged separately, especially the orange juice.
"I don't understand. I will not pay this."
"How much is it?" asked Hari's mother, concerned now.
"It is only a few pennies, but that is not the point. I will not be cheated. Ah! Ah! Now I see. Come here!"
He summoned the waiter.
"It was the orange juice that caused this, yes?"
Shamefaced, the waiter, head bowed, replied to his shoes.
"You ordered orange juice."
"No. You forced it on us. You misled us. I said whatever comes with the deal. Are you on commission if you can mislead your guests? You have cheated me. I will not pay. See." Hari's father tore up the bill and dropped the pieces on the floor.
The waiter scrabbled to pick them up.
"But if you do not pay I must. It will come from my wages. I will not eat."
"It's your punishment for cheating. Now you must pay, not me."
Hari's mother interceded. She was usually quiet and deferential but was always alert and possessed an intelligence she kept secret.
"Surely we can give him something. It's nothing to us, everything to him."
Hari's father was fuming. He was trapped in his rage.
"Please help him," Hari's mother pleaded.
"Come here," Hari's father commanded. "There." He gave the waiter

a few rupees. "That is for the orange juice. I will not pay twice for my breakfast. Now go!"

The waiter bowed constantly, edging backwards out of sight.

"Why must they do this?" Hari's father asked of no one in particular. "The room was splendid and ridiculously cheap. They were on time at the airport. The breakfast was good. Then, the one last final detail goes hopelessly wrong and destroys all that has gone before. That is so typical of India. Why must Indians cheat?"

Hari had never seen his father so angry. It was possible he might be cross with his employees. He might be a different man at his place of work but, in the home, the only place he and Hari ever met, he was always quietly and calmly in control, of the household and himself.

How had India made his father so cruel?

Hari could hear his father's raised voice, noisy amongst the other men in the Sai Deep Café. He moved closer to his mother.

"May I go for a walk? I don't like all this shouting."

"Of course. Would you like me to come with you?"

"No. I'll be happy alone."

He was.

He began to saunter along the road away from Whitefield. The noise of the café, the bustle of the bazaar, the crowd of people that had invaded what was only a small village, quickly receded. At first, trees at ample intervals lined his way. Then came little houses with painted directions: 'Way to Rita Conveni' to the left, to the right, 'Jeannie's House'. The shutters were up.

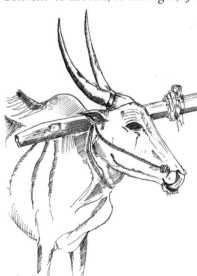

Beyond the roadside bushes the rice paddies spread. Squares of water trapped inside earth-pile boundaries criss-crossed into an endless, flat valley distance. Hari could see clusters of coconut palm trees, unnecessary oases in a desert of wet. The tips of grasses poked through the surface of the lagoons. Beyond, brown gooey bogs squelched and oozed and beyond these, the fields looked entirely green.

A skinny ploughman, in white-sleeved shirt and tea-towel skirt, high-stepped through the clinging mud that the buffalo-pulled plough cut into shiny slices. The cattle had sad, distant eyes. Hari hoped they were focussed somewhere restful. Their elegant,

The cattle had sad, distant eyes

curved horns had been painted a tasteful shade of blue. They were sag-skinned and scrawny. Their protruding backbones were narrow enough to be sharp. Hari marvelled at their improbably thin legs and delicately shown, split hooves. He was startled as a long, pink tongue curled to lick nostrils that were painfully laced with a controlling orange rope, the same length that tied them to the linking wooden harness. Despite their labour, they still seemed elegant, oddly aristocratic.

There was a bridge at the edge of the village. It was just two lorries or four buffalo wide, tarmacked at the centre, with sand for pavements. Simple, two-bar gate sides of yellowing concrete stopped the crossers falling into the green river beneath. The river's surface floated with a scum of soapsuds. It didn't seem to mind. It was used to this, and had many more purposes to fulfil than an English river.

The slap, slapping, slap noise came from the hefty swipes of the dhobi wallahs, human washing machines, half-submerged in the slow-flowing water and beating their laundry pieces onto now smooth rocks with such violent anger that Hari jumped, even when expecting the sudden, wet, cotton crack.

Hari was distracted by three sounds: the squeal of a frog stabbed in an instant by a heron, now still with guilt, the screech of something flying in bright green feathers surrounded by a trio of circling red kites, and the angry shouting of the launderers in the river at the approach of someone strange.

Stepping absent-mindedly, with the deliberate, toe-stretched walk of a ballerina, the filthy young beggar woman drifted towards the river's shore. In her outstretched right hand she balanced an un-gripped, uneaten chapatti. This precious gift of food, this vegetable-filled, tightly-rolled pancake, the generous present of someone's pity, was entirely ignored, treated with disdain. It wasn't even certain that she knew it was there. A muddy stone thrown in anger hit her arm and the food fell. She didn't notice. Noisy shouting and armfuls of water splashed from the river drove her further away from the bridge. She picked a slippery way between purple-flowered bushes that grew out of the river and knelt, melting into the water. She ducked her head, unwrapped her sari and began an elaborate washing of garment and body that was almost a dance.

"It is Lunasha," Hari declared. The dhobi wallahs were still intent on their prey. Water, rocks and mud, even scrunched-up bits of laundry, missiles of sodden cotton were hurled towards the beggar woman. Her bathing desecrated their river. Her being polluted the water that should cleanse. They were angry but never aimed to hit. They would drive her away.

"Leave her alone!" shouted Hari. "Why won't you leave her alone?"

Only one of the men looked his way. Seeing a boy, waving frantically, he waved in turn and resumed his splashing.

The beggar woman drifted out of range and left the river further downstream, much to the relief of the washer men. They chatted as friends and exchanged moments of remembered heroism in their rebuttal of the beggar. Hari was hurt and puzzled. He could find no easy meaning to their hostility or Lunasha's contradictory washing rituals.

A hooting lorry crowded the bridge. Its clatter alerted Hari to the need to return. People were leaving. The beggars were waking. A tall, grey-bearded man with a sad stance but eyes glittering with hope swept the road with a worn-down broom. He cupped his hand for thanks. He felt official but no one had asked. The next lorry undid his cleaning. Another, with skeleton thin legs permanently veed into lameness, shuffled on his bottom to the middle of the road. Nothing stopped.

... skeleton thin legs permanently veed into lameness

Now was the time for noise. People began to travel the road. Taxis sped past and dozens of rickshaws, motorised bikes with seats for one or two, wiggled and wove dangerous passages through people, livestock and other rickshaws. The shops had opened, the bazaar was awake, and the vendors were amassing. Hari began to run. He could not be late. It was nearly time to meet God.

CHAPTER TWO
The Family

Hari's grandfather, Ramu Sarnhi, was a Hindu. His ancestors hailed from the Swat Valley way to the north of India. Even in that ancient past they were involved in the silk trade. Moslem invaders drove them from their fertile valley over into Jammu and Kashmir. More modern disputes over territory drove them to the south of India where they could feel entirely at home amongst a land overflowing with Hindus. They were always a silk family.

Ramu's childhood was scarred by poverty. His memories shamed him. How could his mother constantly dip her hands into scalding water to palpate the cocoons of the worms? Nothing she did could remove Ramu's sense of sympathetic pain. Not even the beauty of her skill in teasing a single thread to unravel itself to its full, remarkable length (more than a mile, she once claimed) and who could doubt her? A strand so thin she would match it to others, three, four, perhaps five, and twist them all into a workable thread to be guided onto a winding frame. Sometimes he would dare himself to mimic her. He would dip his hand into water so hot he couldn't bear it for more than a few seconds. His sore, red fingers bore testimony to his weakness and his mother's fortitude.

Hari's father, Ajay, had been born in Bangalore and bred into the family business. By then the Sarnhis owned a huge emporium in Mahatma Gandhi Road, the Oxford Street of Bangalore. Ramu Sarnhi dealt in the most exquisite silks and embroidered materials. He traded throughout the world, sending his eldest son, Ajay, to England to be educated, integrated and finally to be the British extension of the Sarnhi silk empire.

Hari had been overwhelmed at the sheer size and content of his grandfather's store. On his first visit, there was a sale of saris. Dozens of beautiful Indian girls paraded in front of the huge store, each wearing the most elegant samples of stock, proffering invitations, giving one-to-one service with smiling persuasion. The colours were dazzling: shining purples, greens and reds, the fabric so fine and so perfect it seemed to shimmer with a life and light of its own.

"It is made with love. That is why it shines so," explained Hari's grandfather.

They had visited the small village near Whitefield where the weaving process began. It was noon and so hot Hari wanted to laugh. The earth road they were walking down was baked so hard it had shrunk to cracking. Three-or-four-inch fissures had opened up, gaping holes that swallowed lizards whole and seemed too deep to believe. Hari hung behind with his mother, while his father, grandfather and other male colleagues strode ahead talking business. He chatted happily. His mother was very shy, but kept a special laughter and a whispered talkativeness just for Hari. She and all her family were from Birmingham. They too were in the 'rag trade', as she called it. Her people were market traders, low end, mostly passing on the unwanted remnants of materials: half, quarter, or one eighth bales that others could not profitably use. Her father, mother and two brothers were noisy, confident, loud-laughing people. She feared she lacked the skill to shout and sell. She kept the accounts and kept quiet.

Their stall was a permanent fixture in the covered Rag Market at the heart of the Bull Ring shopping centre. Beneath a latticework of Victorian ironmongery that supported a vast metal roof, a network of narrow aisles laced together row on row of shops and stands with an improbable collection of brightly coloured goods for sale. It was tawdry and cheap but Esther loved it. It had an unabashed honesty. Hanging high on one wall she remembered a row of miniature dresses made of chiffon and lace in the brightest reds and pinks that only little girls could think pretty. There were skeins of cotton and balls of wool in all the colours of many rainbows and in a basket there were zips selling at ten for a pound. There were shoes, bags and plastic combs for the hair and a dire warning that stood on the stall next to theirs. 'We do not give refunds on any costume wigs or gloves.' She had been warned.

Their stall was cluttered and gaudy, piled high with swathes and rolls of material. They'd draped samples of cloth across the lowest stanchion of the metal roof and used every inch of space to display their goods. A large cardboard sign, clumsily written in marker pen, bullet pointed their range.

- Bridal Wear Crystal organza
- Satins
- Taffeta
- Silk PVC
- Crêpe Satin
- Duchess
- Cotton

It was the PVC after the silk that was the only family embarrassment. Ancient Brummies, as tolerant as they were outspoken, they had no problem with Ajay Sarnhi's race, colour or creed when he began to pursue Esther. Their only prejudice was against the quality of the product he once tried to sell them. Ajay had produced samples of the finest silk shipped from Bangalore by his father. They'd rarely touched such exquisite fabric.

Ajay was just leaning his trade in The Fancy Silk Store, a four-storey emporium outside the Rag Market proper, where he was exposed to thousands of the finest cloths. He had ambitions to stay at the luxury end of even those, if he could. He lived in an Aladdin's cave where money was sucked through metal pipes to be deposited, counted and checked on the official desk of the presiding patriarch. It was haberdashers' heaven. No one in Esther's family thought to inhabit such a space.

Even though this was Esther's first visit to India, there was much that she recognised, much that was familiar. The liberal, highly Westernised culture of Bangalore, the most fashionable of south Indian cities, could bridge the gap with certain areas of central Birmingham, that most Indian of Western cities.

But England was never this hot. A group of women and children beckoned Hari and his mother to the well in the centre of the village. The men folk had disappeared into a hut. Hari's father had waved that they should wait. Skinny, naked children giggled and hid behind a splendid cast iron pump. They peeped and waited till Hari came close then swung in unison on the metal armature until spurts of cool water burst at his feet. They crowded round, splashed and showered and spotted Hari's legs with mud. A mother filled a purple metal mug and gave it to Esther, who bowed gracefully and sipped slowly. Hari, with less dignity, stuck his head in the way of the spout and happily drenched his head and shoulders. In the few moments it took to evaporate in the 40° temperature, he felt cool.

They waited in the humming heat. Hari wandered off into the farm area of the village. A lone woman tended a lone cow. A hand bell rang to his left. He peered into the dark doorway of a windowless barn and startled a classroom of schoolchildren. By the time his eyes had adjusted to the dim interior, the whole class of shining eyes had leapt to its feet and wished him, "Good morning, Sir!" in shouted, jubilant English. Hari thanked them and their teacher, a young girl of eighteen or so, standing by a chalkboard at the extremity of the interior gloom. To his delight and embarrassment, they all applauded his English. He slipped away, acknowledging their enthusiasm and clapping at them in return.

Hari was beckoned to the hut his father and grandfather had entered. Inside was a handloom that seemed to fill the room entirely. Half-made, emerging by a mysterious, almost magical process, was a beautiful, iridescent green sari, with an intricate and delicate pattern in gold along its border. The weaver bowed and his assistant withdrew into an open cupboard that was a doorway into a small store. He quickly re-emerged with his arms laden with silk cloth whose sheen and depth of colour caught the breath. Hari was bewitched. His grandfather broke the spell.

"This was me, fifty years ago. I made the cloth that I now sell. These men still produce the finest silk saris in all of southern India. I buy everything they make. The whole village works for me and for your husband, Esther, and for your father and grandfather, Hari. Isn't that amazing? That one man could make one garment, sell it for a profit, save and sell, then save more and sell more, until he need only buy and sell, until he has built an

13

emporium and a worldwide business and now all this could be lost because he is to die."

There was a shocked silence. Ajay shook his head at his father, as if to say 'not in front of the boy'.

Hari clutched his mother's hand and looked up at her to see if it was true. There was a pause whilst he looked. It was true. No one caught anyone else's gaze. All eyes were turned inward, embarrassed, pondering. Hari left his mother's side and took hold of his grandfather's unoffered hand.

"Are you really going to die?" He spoke boldly. There was an air of challenge in his voice.

"I'm not sure, son." Grandfather Sarnhi seemed confused, as if found out in a mean act.

"Not if God has anything to do with it," whispered Esther, coming to the rescue.

"Right! Right!" Hari's father suddenly brightened. "That's the way. Sai Baba is the way. Of course. Now I'm happy again. Be happy too, Hari. Grandfather and the business will be fine." He clasped Hari on the shoulder, squeezed and ushered him from the workroom, where his forced jollity met the afternoon heat.

The family party walked slowly back to Whitefield. Grandfather and father remained stubbornly animated, busy with facts and futures. Hari straggled. His mother slowed to comfort him, to help him understand.

"Your grandfather is an elderly man. He works much too hard. He stays awake much too long. It has put a terrible strain on his heart. The doctors have told him that he could die on any morning that he chooses."

"Is there no cure?"

"Possibly. I'm not sure. I do know that your grandfather has put enormous faith in Sai Baba. That is why he is in Whitefield. That is why we wait to see God every morning and every afternoon."

"Sai Baba is Grandfather's God?"

"Yes."

"Is he mine?"

"Yes, if you believe in him."

"Of course I do. Can He save grandfather?" Hari spoke with a capital 'H'.

"He can, but it's not certain that he will."

"What can make Him?"

"Nothing can make him, but your father and I have come to India to create a family group to increase your grandfather's chance of an interview."

"What kind of an interview?"

"A meeting with Sai Baba, in private. Your grandfather believes he can persuade him to help him if only they can meet face to face. I think he just might."

"How do you get an interview? What do you have to do?"

"No one knows. When you see Sai Baba's helpers tap people on the shoulder and send them away, it is to those few that he has granted an interview. But no one knows who will be chosen. Let us hope it will be this family."

"Yes, indeed," interrupted Hari's father, "we need Grandfather to be well. There is so much to be done." He lightly embraced his father and son and gently nudged the arc of three generations forward. Esther followed behind.

Ramu Sarnhi turned to Ajay and confessed, "It is entirely my fault that there remains so much to be done."

"No, no. I won't hear such things." Ajay beamed his reassurance but Ramu Sarnhi, unconvinced, turned to his grandson. "But it is true, Hari. I thought I would live forever. I am a private man. Because I had to make everything for myself I learned only to trust myself. So, no one knows my business except me. That was a mistake. When the doctors said I was very ill, I knew I had to act quickly. I have to pass all the secrets of my affairs to your father. He had to come here. He had to see with his own eyes and hear directly from me with his own ears, all that I know, all that he must know, to enable the whole complex empire I have made in my head to live on in his head, and one day in yours. Do you see, Hari?"

"Yes, Grandfather." Hari didn't understand, but he knew it was important.

"And so, Sai Baba must grant me this time. There are so many secrets," Ramu Sarnhi added in a whisper, somewhat shamefaced.

"Don't forget the hospital," Ajay added, hoping to reassure his father.

"No, I don't forget." But he had.

"You see Hari, Sai Baba has built an amazing hospital." Ajay over-emphasized the word 'amazing' wishing to lift Hari's mood of gloom.

"A miraculous hospital," interrupted the grandfather, adding to the superlatives. "It is not far from here, at Puttaparthi. There is nowhere like it anywhere in the world, let alone in India, and it is an hour's private plane flight away. I am sure Sai Baba will grant me a bed. I know it. I am certain. Today, there will be an interview. Come, we must hurry, it is nearly time for darshan."

CHAPTER THREE
Darshan

In response to Hari's question, Ramu Sarnhi was carefully explaining that: "'Darshan' is a word that doesn't translate easily into English. It is to do with being granted an audience, being in a presence, letting someone or something be seen. Most straightforwardly, it means the viewing of a God. The trouble for most Europeans though, Hari, is that India seems to have many kinds of God."

On their journey to Whitefield, Hari and his family had stopped at a vast temple to the Hindu God, Shiva. There, Hari had been beckoned to a darshan, but what he saw, as 'God', was strange and shocking. Deep in the incense-rich bowels of a cave-dark temple—even Hari needed to stoop on entering—they were confronted by an ugly outcropping of stone: a flattened, granite snake-head, wrapped in a white cotton bib and dangled with garlands of flowers. It was crude and frightened with an ancient fear and was Shiva.

It was explained to Hari that Shiva had argued with Brahma, the Hindu God of Gods, and the source of all existence. Indeed, Brahma literally lost his head (happily, he still had four left) over the disagreement and swore that Shiva would never be worshipped on earth in his own likeness. Instead, Shiva would appear, suddenly and spontaneously extruding from the earth, in the form of the 'lingam', the ugly headstone, rock-snake that Hari had seen.

But Sathya Sai Baba was not made of stone. He appeared at darshan as living, breathing, moving flesh. He gestured and touched, sang and performed miracles.

"What is Sai Baba?" Hari asked his mother.

"Don't you mean 'who'?" returned his mother, as they bumped their way by taxi from Bangalore to Whitefield that first morning for that first darshan.

"I think I know who he is. He is God?" Hari offered.

"Yes. He is 'Baba', 'Father'." This was Ramu Sarnhi talking. "I call him 'Swami' in my head, 'Holy One'. I have become a devotee."

But only recently. It was barely three months ago that Ramu Sarnhi left for his office in Bangalore but arrived at its main hospital instead. Walking purposefully along Mahatma Gandhi Road his legs buckled, his heart failed and his head bounced on the pavement. For a few seconds he was conscious that he might actually be dying. There was no pain, that would come later, but his ears filled with the rushing sound of water, a roar of flooding that rose to a climax that flashed not light but blackness. He was woken by pain. His head throbbed, his chest burnt and his heart fluttered. It wasn't up to its task. No act of will could increase the flow of blood to a brain that was anxious to think and scheme.

Ramu Sarnhi felt vulnerable for the first time in his life. He always appeared 'tough', his authority asserted rather than natural, but penetrate the surface, delve beneath to the inner man, and that was tough as well— through and through. Even when as young as Hari, Ramu Sarnhi had dependants. He learnt to thrive in a difficult world, living on his wits, expecting no help, evolving a poker face that would not betray what he truly thought. He learnt to suppress his nervousness. Fear and excitement appeared the same.

His first thoughts when in a comfortable consciousness, pain lulled by morphine and his sense of importance restored by the ingratiating presence of his own and the hospital staff, were: "How do I survive? How will I thrive? This is not a convenient time to die."

He needed information. Honest truths. Lackeys and sycophants were all well and good but now he must have real answers to facts he might not wish to face. He invited his own displeasure.

"Tell me the honest truth, will I die, Doctor?" he demanded of a young surgeon who was nervous in Ramu Sarnhi's presence.

"Yes," was the curt reply. Not nervous enough it seemed.

"I will?"

"Yes. I just said so."

"How long have I got?"

"I'm amazed you're still alive," was the alarming reply.

An urgent plan was needed. Ramu Sarnhi's mind raced to find a solution.

"Is there no cure?" he asked, calmer now he knew.

"No. I'm afraid not. There may be places in the USA that could explore the full extent of the damage to the valves of your heart. They could replace the heart altogether in California but you'll not live long enough to find a match. From the tests we've done, I think the arteries are damaged too and as a consequence, your lungs are not at their best. Do you experience difficulty breathing?"

"I do now," was Ramu Sarnhi's curt reply.

The doctor was clinically correct, diagnostically secure, but Ramu Sarnhi wished he might sugar the pill just a little, despite demanding the opposite. It was a bitter centre to swallow whole with no sweet coating. He needed a miracle either of science or religion; he didn't mind which. A wonderful technician or a pliable God must extend his life.

To his delight and relief, he realized there was a man being God on his very doorstep. For many years now, Sai Baba had spent his summer months at his ashram in Whitefield. Ramu Sarnhi knew of the hospital and college and the hullabaloo and the razzamatazz but he'd thought the whole thing was bogus and fit only for his semi-literate workers from the nearby villages. They dutifully worshipped their God, twice a day, when He deigned to be in residence.

Ramu Sarnhi must learn more. His need was urgent. He had no defined span of life left. Each day could be his last. The thought frightened him at first, and then it thrilled him. He found an access of energy and pestered and interrogated the silk families he employed to gain some understanding of their beliefs and the significance of the avatar they were convinced was a god.

"Can he perform miracles?" Ramu Sarnhi asked.

"Yes, sir. Every day."

That was satisfactory. Then, visiting the ashram, he wooed the officials beyond reproach; bribed those beneath contempt and evolved a strategy. It would be two-pronged: science and God. He'd studied the brochures describing the wonders of the Super Speciality Hospital in Puttaparthi with its Cardiac Catheterisation Laboratories, Heart Bypass specialists and a stack of modern technical devices that just might provide enough clever science to put him back together. He needed a bed. Annoyingly, treatment was free. It couldn't be bought, at any price. He'd tried. All was in Sai Baba's gift.

If a miracle was needed he must get close to God. That meant an interview and they were hard to come by. It was proving very difficult to buy his way out of heaven. He needed a few months, at least, to unravel the skeins of his complicated business life. He summoned his family from England to create a group that might be more easily noticed. He began building a house in Whitefield to signal the permanence and depth of his new belief. He was prepared to shoulder his pride, bend his knee and worship this god called Sai Baba, his Swami.

Proud and excited at the prospect of his first darshan, Ramu Sarnhi leapt out of the taxi and readily paid the fare.

"I will wait," offered the driver, refusing the given rupees.

"I won't pay for your waiting." Ramu Sarnhi was frustrated. His thoughts were benign. He didn't want to barter, other than with God.

"It is all in the price. You pay what you think is right. But you are not prepared. You will need cushions. I will take you." Eagerly, the taxi driver pointed to the newly installed bazaar.

"Why would I need cushions?" The grandfather accentuated the 'I'.

"To sit on. It is uncomfortable on the ground." The driver was perplexed. Did this know-all man not understand the ritual of darshan?

"I don't sit on the ground. I sit on chairs or settees." Ramu Sarnhi spoke this truth calmly.

"There are no settees. This is an ashram." The driver was confident and convincing.

"Are there chairs?" asked Ramu Sarnhi, more tentative now.

"For the VIPs." If this was meant to discourage his passenger, it didn't.

"Then, I shall arrange for chairs."

The grandfather waved him away. Undaunted the young taxi driver tagged onto the Sarnhi family train.

"But what about the child? He won't get a chair."

"True. Take the boy. How much?"

"One hundred rupees."

"I will give you fifty."

The taxi driver sulked but accepted. Leading Hari to the bustling bazaar opposite the wrought-iron gates to the ashram, he quickly offered Hari a choice of brightly coloured cushions that neatly folded in two, with carrying handles that were instantly torn. It had cost two grimaces, two false exits, a smile and thirty rupees. Hari was quickly dismissed and left to pick his hazardous way through mountains of coconuts, armfuls of flower-garlands, books, bananas, photographs, sandals, tea, water, beggars and ash. A crazy circus surrounded the gates as thousands of the faithful ran the many gauntlets of this million-fingered crowd.

The Bazaar

Now inside, there was no sudden silence. The vast courtyard was busy with chatter, divisions and groupings and thousands of discarded shoes. Hari's mother waved him close to say goodbye.

"Your father has gone with Grandfather to make the necessary arrangements." Such arrangements were made in the vast buildings straight ahead, a fairy-tale palace with pale blue domes, pink and orange walls and icing-white decorations. "I must leave you now and sit with the women away from you, over there."

What had once been a huge tree providing shade was now Sai Ramesh Hall, a vast marble-floored structure of girders and steel trellises shaded by panels of dark-green and cream corrugated plastic. The men and women were divided. Hari's mother made her way to join all the other women on the left hand side of the hall. Outside, in the full sun, hundreds of men began to sit in neat rows behind posts that prevented entry to the hall. Silent and content, they stared at their toes. Some in Full Lotus postures rested their knuckles on the inside of their wide spread knees, touched first fingertip and thumb in perfect letter 'O' s and hummed in a closed-eye trance.

Hari joined a queue and sat expectantly on his new cushion. It provided no comfort. The hard concrete floor pushed upwards, the risen morning sun pushed downwards. Hari wriggled in-between. There were twenty people in front of Hari. His was the third of more than twenty lines of seated men. There were thirty or more in each line and still they kept coming. To his immediate right a blonde-haired European, as beautiful as an angel, sat quietly reading a very complex book. Hari glimpsed charts and figures and indecipherable squiggles that were clearly understood once but had been hidden for so long that only a few determined scholars dared to guess their meaning now. In a moment of sudden insight, Jean Paul said, "Ah!"

Hari said, "Pardon?"

And so a friendship began.

Jean Paul

Jean Paul was a young Frenchman from Lyons. There, he had worked in an orchard but for the past three months he had been following Sai Baba, first at the main ashram or monastery in Puttaparthi, and now in Whitefield.

"And you?" Jean Paul looked into Hari with a steady gaze of his startling blue eyes.

"I've only just arrived. I'm with my family. I'm only a schoolboy. My father keeps me. It was his father, my grandfather—they are from here, they are Indian—it was he who asked us all to come here."

"Why?"

"I'm not sure. He is making arrangements."

"Ah! Is he Very Important?"

"I suppose so. Does that matter?"

"It shouldn't but it does. We all wait in the sun. Soon, all the side courtyards will fill. The ladies will also spill into the sun and sit, uncomfortably. That is important; the lack of comfort is deliberate. Then, the people at the front of all their lines take part in a special lottery."

"Lottery?"

"Yes. They draw a number from a bag, from one to whatever. That number decides where, or even whether, you get to sit inside the hall. Yesterday, my line was number two. We all thought this blessed. It means you sit close enough to the aisle that Sai Baba may walk down. You may be near enough to be touched. But, some days, you sit out in the sun at the edge. You never know if you will even catch a glimpse of his robe. We all stretch to see. He will come from there." Hari rose to look and was frowned at by his fellow squatters and a very officious man in a white shirt, with a blue scarf and authoritative finger.

"No. It is etiquette to stay seated."

"Sorry."

"It is not a problem. You will soon know what to do."

"Where will he come from?"

"The top left hand corner. When you explore the ashram, go to the other side and you will see a huge ornamental gate with a clock and statues. Beyond the gates and out of sight of the drive are the houses where Sai Baba and his helpers live. He will walk down that drive. Then he will suddenly emerge from the gate into the courtyard."

"What does he look like?"

"You don't know?"

"No, I'm sorry."

"Wait and see. You will be surprised."

Hari thought quietly while Jean Paul mused.

"Jean Paul?"

"Yes, Hari?"

"Who is Sai Baba? Is He God?"

"He is *a* God, not . . . God."

"I think Grandfather thinks he is . . . " Hari paused, "God."

"Then, for your grandfather He is."

"Doesn't Sai Baba claim to be God?"

"Sometimes. Yes, sometimes, and when he does, of course, He is."

"I don't understand."

"Sai Baba is an avatar."

"What is an avatar?"

"It is not very easy to explain, Hari. There are many ancient books that describe all the qualities necessary to be called 'avatar'. Most of those called such in south India today fulfil very few of those requirements.

"Can there be more than one avatar?"

"Oh yes, there are many. There are three, no, four within a hundred miles of here. Their followers worship each as God. An avatar is a very special being, a human, apparently, but with godlike powers. They are God-Men, or in the case of Mata Amritanandamaj, God-Women."

"There is a lady avatar?"

"Yes, the Mother, further south, in Kerala. She has a huge following, all over the world. Sai Baba won't leave India but, nevertheless, he has hundreds of thousands, some claim millions of believers who worship and follow him. As a child called Sathya, in the small village, as it was then, of Puttaparthi, he threw a handful of jasmine flowers onto the ground and as they fell they formed a name. It was to be his name, Sai Baba. Even as a child he knew or believed himself to be the reborn Saint of Shirdi, a long dead miracle worker, whose name was the original Sai Baba. And there will be a third who will be called 'Prema' to replace this Sai Baba when he dies."

"Can God die?"

"Only his human shape."

"Is Sai Baba the best God-Man?"

"Some say so. They believe he is the Kalki Avatar. And before you ask, it is not easy to explain, hence books like these."

"Is that what those strange diagrams mean?"

"Partly. Do you know anything about astronomy?"

"A little bit. We did a project on the planets at school. I chose Mars."

"Okay. You know that Mars has moons that revolve around that planet and that planets revolve around themselves and they, with their moons revolve around the Sun and that the Sun, with its planets and their moons revolves around what?"

"I don't know." Hari was still trying to remember the name of the moons of Mars. He should have known. There were two.

"The Grand Centre, the space where Brahma lives, the seat of creative power. It is from there that he controls the way men think, the way they feel and act towards each other, what they value. Our Sun moves to and from this centre in a giant spin that takes twenty-four thousand years. That huge time span is broken down into smaller units called Yugas. The nearest point to the centre is called the Sathya Yuga and lasts four thousand years. Look." Jean Paul pointed Hari to that part of the complex astrological chart drawn in his book. "When we are that close to God we find it easy to be spiritual, easy to be good."

"Where are we now?"

"Here. At the furthest point from God that is possible, in the Kali Yuga. We are in the middle of a cycle that lasts twelve hundred years and so far from grace that most men can understand nothing but the obvious, value nothing but the material, trust nothing they cannot touch or physically grasp. We are in a dark age. We are at our worst. We need help. At such times Brahma sends us a special being, a God-Man. This is the Kalki Avatar. In the distant past there was Rama, then Krishna and now? The legend says, the writings state that the next Kalki Avatar has already reincarnated, been born again, but he has not yet revealed himself. Two thousand years ago, the sages thought it was Christ. It is a big time scale. No one is sure when year one was. The writer of this book claims that Kali Yuga has passed and we are moving back towards the centre. Others believe it has only just begun and that Sai Baba is the Kalki Avatar in waiting, poised to reveal his true powers and lead mankind to some kind of safety, some belief in values that matter to a God."

"What do you believe, Jean Paul?

"I don't know. I waver."

Hari's name was being called. In the line standing in the tree-shade by the wall, Hari's father was calling and his grandfather was beckoning him to join them.

"So, you are important."

"Why do you say that?" asked Hari, rising and folding his cushion as a dozen men shuffled to close the gap that he was leaving.

"You are going to join the VIP line, those who do not wait."

"Do they sit on chairs?"

"Some do."

"I think that was what Grandfather was arranging."

"Is he ill?"

"Yes, he is, but he just doesn't sit on the floor."

"I see. Well, I am happy to, and I am also happy to have met you, Hari. Enjoy your first darshan."

"Thank you. Goodbye."

Jean Paul was already deep in thought.

"There will be no need to sit and wait now, Hari, I have the necessary document," explained Ramu Sarnhi, waving a handwritten note scribbled on a scrap of paper, an official scrap of paper. "Your father and I will sit to the side and you must be near, so that we remain a party. There were no promises but enough was said."

"Yes, Grandfather."

"We can go in soon. There is no need for people like us to wait."

"No, Grandfather."

But they did wait, for a long time. The important people shuffled and tutted their impatience; the unimportant whispered their prayers, quiet and compact, seated on the hard ground. By now even the side courtyard was full, mostly of cross-legged, cushionless peasants. The shaded hall remained annoyingly empty when suddenly the line of VIPs began to move. Hari was beckoned towards a wobbly doorway, a gabled pillbox that was the only entrance to the inner compound. Before stepping through, two officials, signalled by a white tunic and blue scarf that sported an ornate golden clasp at the front and a perfect 'V' pointing down the back, grabbed Hari.

Without bending to speak, one asked, high above Hari's head, "Do you have a knife?"

Then the other, "Or a gun?"

Across the vast expanse of empty marble floor was a raised dais

CHAPTER FOUR
Seeing God

The incongruous doorway in the rope cordon was a metal detector: primitive, almost ridiculous, but apparently necessary.

"Why are they searching us, Father?" Hari asked, nervously.

"I'm not sure," was the father's honest reply.

"There was an incident. Last year. Not here," explained Grandfather Sarnhi in a fierce whisper.

"Well, where was it then?"

"I said, not here. We will discuss this elsewhere. Come, we are being called."

Polite but firmly guiding hands delivered the well dressed to selected parts of the floor. Ramu Sarnhi wriggled free of his guide and pointed himself and his family retinue to the seats at the edge.

"No! This way, please!" Hands at prayer and bows of humility only thinly disguised the hostility.

"I am to sit here." Ramu Sarnhi proffered the scrap of paper authority. Saddened, the usher was walking away, but kept the paper.

"I need that, for the future." Ramu Sarnhi declared with a note of annoyance. His rights of comfortable access had been tediously won.

"It is only for today," explained the usher, clearly pleased to have bested this man.

"It is for all days." Ramu Sarnhi extended his hand for the return of the scrap of paper that secured his ongoing privilege.

"Do not worry. I will remember you." The official crushed the contentious piece of paper and pushed it into the side pocket of his tunic.

"My thanks. We will remember each other, I'm sure." Prayer bows signalled a truce. Honour was satisfied and Hari was soon left free to stare.

Across the vast expanse of empty marble floor was a raised dais. A red carpet led to its middle and stopped in front of a large, black, elephant-headed figure garlanded with flowers. Hari already recognised this as the god Ganesh, the remover of obstacles. There were steps for entry at either side of the stage and an ornate canopy diamonded and crested in pink, blue and gold, was supported on four vast, candy-striped pillars. On the walls behind the stage were four long panels—two each side—with larger than life-sized photographs of what must be Sai Baba. Hari could only see the full image of one. Such an odd figure. He had never thought of God like this.

Centre stage was a throne, an ornately carved Victorian chair with matching foot stool, both upholstered in plush, maroon velvet. Behind the throne was a human sized goddess fashioned in bronze with too many arms outstretched. Two attendants, teenage boys, were draping these arms with flower bangles and strewing petals on the floor all around. One placed an electric fan, the sort that nods this way and that, before the throne and tested the flow of air for best effect. A box draped in satin provided a placement for a cup of water and two cotton napkins were placed, one on each of the velvet-cushioned arms of the throne. Bowing and kissing the green, petal-strewn carpet, the attendants backed away.

Hari watched the hall fill. An immensely aged man, an Indian with white hair and skin so thin that the light shone through, shuffled forwards, half-carried by the concerned relatives at each arm. He was left, clunk seated, in the middle of an empty row, red albino eyes glowing behind the tinted lenses of his glasses.

Straight ahead was a jack-in-the-box boy with aggressively spiked hair that had a fine dust dullness to it. He was unpleasant, surly looking, with hazel eyes and a dental brace so loose he kept flicking it onto his tongue, wiggling a front tooth that was already broken, then mouthing it back into ineffective place. He was waving for a friend to come to him and had been throughout the past, slow-passing hour.

To the left was an unimpressive, fifty-year-old European head, possibly German. Hollow-cheeked, eyes closed; he had big, oddly charismatic feet that drew Hari's attention. Beside him was another European. He wore a thin yellow wristband of twisted cotton and an intense, wise look.

There was a bustle, some activity. Hari strained to see into the corner. Nothing. This wasn't it. Instead, a group of musicians flooded in to fill the red carpet area in front of the stage. Technicians in ashram suits, loose fitting white tunics ballooning over the baggiest of white cotton trousers, wheeled in amplifiers, sought plugs and tapped squealing sound tests through wobbly microphones. Their sudden arrival raised the level of expectant tension in the hall.

But nothing happened. The sultry silence returned.

To Hari's right, a shorn-headed American, entirely correct and conscientiously Oriental, sat in Full Lotus on an elegant blue rug. He wore spectacles, stubble and lots of learnt intensity. He was clutching a book of the 'Sayings of Sai Baba' and staring into the middle distance, hoping to be thought spiritual.

To his side was another Westerner, in ashram gear, kerchief and American 'got it righteousness'. He had a limp beard, tightly shut eyes and a beatific calm. Beyond him was another Full Lotus with dirty long hair and careful self-denial. He looked like John Lennon in need of a bath and more flesh. Despite this, he stared at the throne through an expensive binocular camera.

Another group was being pushed into the gaps on the floor beside Hari. They were pale and strange, a party of five, with identifying silk kerchiefs in peacock green. Later, Hari would know they were from Iran. One of their number was hideously deformed. Hari wanted to look away but stared. The whole of the left-hand side of the jaw was stoved-in, the face appropriated by a mammoth, 'S' shaped scar. There was a tactful plaster spread across the deep channel and the upper lip to prevent the teeth from too shocking a cheekless snarl.

The hall was nearly full. Still a few arrived. An elderly civil-servant-seeming figure in a pale cocoa coloured linen suit and embroidered, collarless, silk shirt was ushered to a prime, instantly cleared area by the bowing officials. A tall, elegant man rushed forward and prostrated himself and eagerly tried but was prevented from kissing the feet of this alarmingly aloof man. Who was he?

Hari was distracted by the unexpected sound of music. There was singing. A voice. A choir. The rhythm was infectious. All the Westerners seemed to know the words. Few of the Indians in his area sang. There was a whispering. People shuffled. Heads began to turn. Over four thousand faced the corner, straining to see. Some stretched up and were ushered down by the orchestrating officials. There was a giant sigh.

He was there!

Head bowed, the glowing figure glided from view

Almost too far away to be in focus, Hari glimpsed the iridescent orange gown and frizzy ball of sculpted hair that imaged the distant God-Man, Sai Baba. Head bowed, the glowing figure glided from view, swallowed by the crowd and the perching, stretching, bobbing figures in between. Five minutes of strain and excitement passed. Between two distant pillars Hari caught momentary sight of an open face, soft-nosed, wide-lipped. Then suddenly, framed by the light from the courtyard, his teaselled hair a black halo, his orange robe on fire, He was there, on the edge, at the other side of the hall. Everything stopped. He stood, stared with a serious look, almost disapprovingly, at those within his gaze. In his left hand was a pack of letters; with his right hand, He gestured, a beckoning, lateral wave. Instead of people rising as this sign showed, they fell, self-flattened to the floor.

He moved forward, with a stumbling, slow shuffle, impossible to step out with the narrow orange robe tight to his ankles and brushing the floor.

The over-eager rose up on their knees and wriggled too close, pleading for notice, desperate to be seen. Two grey-haired men were stopped with a grimace. A shift of the gown and they kissed Baba's feet. With benign dismissal they crawled from the crowd and broke into gleeful chatter with an arranging official.

Letters waved in the air. Baba plucked out a few and when his hand was full, a waiting assistant whisked them away. Plates of sweets were raised to his eye. Most were ignored but almost turning away he would grasp a few and scatter them to the crowd with offhand indifference.

Close, so close now, Hari could see the lined face, the dark stare. He wanted to be seen but dare he look back? Like a judgmental lighthouse, Baba's look scanned the crowd. He almost perceived Hari but not quite. A flight of sweets landed in the corner. One bounced into Hari's lap. He placed it before him with care and turned to follow Sai Baba. A young Indian father offered scrolled photographs. Baba waited impatiently, distractedly, then concentrated to write on each one. With a sudden flurry, the man knelt and Baba clasped his head in a blessing but always looking around the while, always moving away.

Hari turned, and his sweet was gone.

Sai Baba mounted the stage. He stood beside his throne. The two attendants returned, crawled towards him and kissed his feet in turn. With slow deliberation, Baba sat, stretched out his legs, crossing one on the other, so the round, squat toes were all visible at once. He wiped his nose and looked down on the hall with a strange hauteur. He sat higher, withdrew one leg and left the other foot on its stool, the big toe obvious. With a glance, music started.

He beat time with the exposed big toe. Then, he tapped his right hand. Open and down then fist, knuckle, tap; open and down, then, fist, knuckle, tap. He invited everyone to sing with a papal wave of his free hand.

All stared intently into the inscrutable dark face of this powerful being. Every movement was watched. When He beat time everyone clapped; when He stopped, so did they. The hymns or bahjans were joyous and bright with happy rhythms.

Baba rose.

The music stopped mid-line. A bell rang. He collected the letters, fingered through a few, looking at names and shuffle-glided slowly to the left of the stage where a door opened itself and let in the sight of white-blue sky and the blossoming boughs of an orchard. The door slowly closed itself and he was gone.

The musicians struck up a farewell hymn. Everything ended in a unified hum, four thousand 'Om's' dwindling to silence.

28

CHAPTER FIVE
After Darshan

It was supposed that the time after darshan be filled with quiet contemplation and serious thought. Baba hoped his followers would devote this silent hiatus to thoughts of Him. Vain hope. The clatter and chatter of four thousand noisily departing pilgrims, eight thousand feet reuniting with as many shoes, sandals and slippers, the hailing of a thousand taxicabs and rickshaws, defied thinking.

"Hari! Hari! Don't dawdle. Over here!"

"Coming, Father!"

The family had reassembled by the main gates. Hari had left slowly, wondering at his lack of wonder. Worrying that there were so many questions in his head, so many puzzles. If Baba was God, why was he so sad? Why did he look so angry? So disappointed? So bored? Who on earth had stolen his sweet? Should he have eaten it straight away? Was that the thing to do? Had he been rude, ungrateful, in not accepting this gift thrown into his lap by God Himself? Had it then been made to disappear because spurned? Or, had the spiky-haired urchin from Iran snatched it while he turned away, fixing his gaze on Baba?

"Come on," coaxed Hari's mother, stretching out a hand.

Hari's legs responded slowly. Three and a half hours squatting on a marble floor had numbed his behind. The bones in his bottom, bones that he never knew he had, ached.

"They've gone to get a table at the café. We'd better hurry. Grandfather is in a bad mood. We mustn't keep him waiting. He says he's been kept waiting long enough for one day."

They braved the bazaar, hand in hand, as the traders and beggars pulled and nudged, offered and grasped, hoped then shrugged.

"Sit here, young man. I've ordered you a sandwich, a toasted sandwich with melted cheese and fresh tomatoes. He has shown me the tomatoes. And tea. Would you prefer soda?"

"I don't mind, Grandfather."

"Have both. Waiter, two more sodas. What flavour, Hari?"

"I ..."

"The waiter is waiting."

"Lemon, please."

"Thank you."

Grandfather Sarnhi waved the bowing man away with a flapping gesture from the back of his hand. They had not come far. The Sai Deep Café nestled in an alcove at the edge of the bazaar. With raised eyes, you could see a magnificent palm tree above the walls of the ashram, framing its pale blue domes. Looking to right and left, there were single table stalls piled high with technicolour wares. Shapeless dresses in shrill colours dangled from improvised cables stealing electricity for naked bulbs. Whole yellow stems sporting a hundred bananas, neatly curved in five clever rows, flanked waist-high piles of green coconuts, trepanned for a drink. If you looked down you would instantly look away. The waste from this market lay vilely exposed in an open sore of a ditch that didn't bear close scrutiny. Its dry, dark, vibrant smell was reminder enough.

There were five or six tables, a bench under a concrete staircase with an iron balustrade, more benches, stools, the odd chair that together let two dozen visitors sit and swap stories.

There was only one domestic sandwich maker that produced two toasted triangles when electricity, fuse and sheer nerve to switch power through a pyramid of plugs permitted. Food service was so slow that a completed order was greeted with delighted surprise rather than annoyance. Most customers fended for themselves. Rival food vendors were tolerated amongst the seated; the impatient popped to the next store and bought angel cakes, biscuits and bottles of cold water. No one seemed to mind. The foreign pilgrims had appropriated these seats as a place to meet, talk, question and share the stories of their lives. The proprietor seemed proud to be so used even if the purpose of his business was ignored.

"I don't know whether I was disappointed or not," began Hari's father. "The nearest thing I've ever experienced to it was going to a rock concert."

"I suppose it is similar," mused Esther Sarnhi. Hari had never been to a rock concert, so he couldn't compare. "You know, you get the support bands and the build up. The crazy tension: Will they come? Do they look like their picture? Are they good live? Then, just when you think they aren't coming, they come. And everybody is so relieved that they haven't been tricked that even if they can't see a thing or hear a word, they are happy." Hari's mother smiled at a private memory.

"I wasn't!" Ramu Sarnhi's annoyance interrupted her daydream.

"What's that, Grandfather?" asked Hari, always worried by a raised voice.

"Happy. I wasn't happy. If he knows what time he is coming, why does he make us wait?"

"We just need to learn the ropes, Father. The people that go to pop concerts regularly seem to know when the big band is going to play and arrive just in time. While the less sophisticated have been sweating and hoping, afraid they might miss it, the really knowing ones have been eating a good dinner. We'll get the hang of it."

"Jean Paul says that the waiting is part of it," offered Hari.

"Who?" asked the distracted grandfather.

"I think he has made a friend," suggested the mother.

30

"Yes?" The grandfather sighed, preoccupied. "Do you think they've put us in the best position? I mean, he didn't come anywhere near us. That wasn't meant to happen. How can we ask for an interview if we're not within earshot? We can hardly shout. It would be ill-mannered."

"Isn't it up to Sai Baba where he goes?" asked the mother.

"Well, of course. But, surely his route is organised. There were some pretty important characters arriving late today. And, as you intimated, Ajay, they know when to come. If I'm not mistaken, we weren't all that far from our prime minister."

Grandfather Sarnhi smiled at his proximity.

"So, that's who it was," thought Hari.

"The prime . . ." Hari's father was mightily impressed.

"Shush! I wonder how you get to sit next to him? Hey? Now, that would be a memory to treasure." Ramu Sarnhi let himself imagine the treasured memory.

The sodas arrived in clear, white bottles, hand-lettering in different colours distinguishing the flavours. The beer-bottle tops were half-lifted, revealing rust along their cracked centres, leaving similar brown traces around the glass lips of the bottles. Hari looked for a glass, hoped for a straw, but his father followed the fashion and drank from the bottle. Hari tried to scratch the top of his clean, failed, and, driven by thirst popped it in his mouth.

"Tea?" asked the proprietor, offering one mug for twenty.

"That's mine." Ramu Sarnhi reached over intervening heads. "There are three more needed here."

"Yes, sir, they are coming."

"One at a time?"

"Of course, sir, naturally, sir." The smiling proprietor failed to notice Ramu Sarnhi's sarcasm.

"Do you have a name? It would be easier if you had a name," suggested the grandfather.

"I am the proprietor, sir."

"Should I call you 'Proprietor'?" Ramu Sarnhi was pleased with his wit and softened his robust manner with the beginnings of a smile.

"That would be most kind, sir, thank you."

Defeated by politeness, the grandfather sipped his tea. Proprietor was a cheerful man of thirty with a mop of shiny hair and black sparkling eyes. He wore a Western style, short-sleeved shirt that must have once been white but was now grey yet clean, and neatly pressed slacks. He lived to please his often ungrateful customers. His efforts at efficiency were a distant dream. All of his ordered hopes could suddenly be dashed by disappearing electricity, uninvited insect swarms, missing fillings for his sandwiches; on some sad days there was even no bread. And still he smiled and patiently explained. He was never angry, except with the beggars.

Ajay Sarnhi was still smiling at the idea of having been so close to the prime minister of all India.

"No wonder there's a security nightmare. I mean, when men like that come here alone, without their own people, in their spare time, as it were. Can you imagine, in England, if ...?"

Hari was perplexed.

"I thought they were worried about Sai Baba, not his visitors. I thought they were afraid for Him, after what happened. What did happen, Grandfather? Can you tell me here?"

"Yes, I don't see why not."

Leaning forward to fully engage his listeners, Ramu Sarnhi started in a conspiratorial whisper: "In June of last year, at Prashanti Nilyayam, Sai Baba's main ashram in Puttaparthi, six men tried to murder Swami."

"They tried to kill God?" Hari asked in a loud voice.

CHAPTER SIX
God is a prisoner

"Yes Hari, they tried to kill God." Ramu Sarnhi wished to quieten his grandson, conscious that his sudden outburst had attracted the attention of the occupants of the tables next to theirs.

"Why?" asked an incredulous Hari.

"Yes, why?" demanded an authoritative voice from one of those neighbouring tables. "May I?"

A highly confident man, of middle years, sporting a splendid head of hair crafted to a point in the exact centre of his forehead, planted his chair beside the Sarnhi table and, uninvited, introduced himself.

"I am Bishnu. I have a particular interest in the shootings. I am almost official in that Mr Premanand, the head of the Indian Rationalist Association, has requested that I investigate these killings. I am a lawyer, you see, from Cochin and I will expose the truth. What is it you know? I must warn you, in the future, whatever you say may be ascribed to you and included in a book."

Intrigued and only slightly embarrassed by the sudden intrusion, Ramu Sarnhi introduced his family.

"I am new to all of this, I confess," Ramu Sarnhi began. "The information I have is second hand, reportage at best. I have been making a careful study of Sai Baba and have only recently elected to follow him."

"It may not be too late to dissuade you, then," interrupted Bishnu, with the beginnings of a smile.

"Perhaps not. What I was going to recount to my grandson were the contents of an apparently thorough, two-page newspaper article written last year, shortly after the assassination attempt. One of my managers gave it to me."

"I see." The lawyer had produced a notebook, an unimpressive, spiral-topped pad and began flipping through the used pages. On the first clear page he wrote down his first thoughts: 'I see.'

"He used the information to annoy the weavers in his charge. I am in the silk trade, you understand," was Ramu Sarnhi's explanation.

"Why would he annoy his workers?" asked the lawyer, puzzled.

"He was in danger of becoming popular. It is hard to manage men if they like you. He thought by casting doubt on the integrity of their god—they all worship Baba—that would aid his cause. And yours, perhaps."

"Indeed. Tell me about the article." The lawyer was alert, pencil poised.

"There were six men involved. Four were gunned down and there was a police dragnet across three of the southern states trying to find them. One was called Vijay. I can't remember the name of the other."

Ramu Sarnhi waited for a response from Bishnu. With none forthcoming, he added, " With such a search, it was surprising that they avoided capture. I wonder how did they manage to escape in the first place?"

Questioning tones still didn't elicit an immediate response, just grunts of disapproval. Looking up from his notebook, Bishnu explained, " No one escaped. The two missing men were already dead. The police search was a sham!"

'That's incredible," Ramu Sarnhi declared.

"Nevertheless, it happens to be the truth. Even Sai Baba acknowledged that his two servitors were the first to be killed in the plot. Being an all-seeing being, he claims to have warned them of their imminent death. They died in his interview room," Bishnu stated as a potentially damning afterthought.

"Who killed them there?" asked an astonished Ramu Sarnhi.

"Guess," was Bishnu's enigmatic reply.

Refusing to respond to or even entertain the idea of Sai Baba as a murderer, Ramu Sarnhi quickly returned to the version of events he thought he had understood.

"As I remember it, there was no intention to assassinate Baba. The plan, I must admit, sounded somewhat foolhardy. They hoped to take over the Mandir, the administrative building at Puttaparthi. They had been planning the coup for months in advance. They had weapons, explosives and anaesthetics."

"And what did they suggest they were going to do with anaesthetics?" asked Bishnu with a raised eyebrow.

"Immobilise anyone who resisted with ether. It was all very amateurish, clearly," Ramu Sarnhi conceded.

"Where would amateurs obtain Semtex and Central Intelligence Agency cyanide pills?" asked Bishnu, with an air of triumph.

"I've no idea," Ramu Sarnhi acknowledged.

"Did they actually have such things?" asked Ajay Sarnhi.

"Yes," Ramu Sarnhi admitted.

"Students? It's improbable, isn't it?" continued Ajay.

"I understand", began Ramu Sarnhi again, a little impatient, baulking at being treated as an expert when having such scant knowledge, " that the objective was a non-violent takeover of a few rooms on the ground floor. If the bid failed or Sai Baba disapproved of their action, they would take their own lives. They intended threatening the Trust 'henchmen', as they called them."

"Threatened with what?" asked Ajay.

"Exposure of all the murky goings on in the ashram. These weren't students, by the way. The Vijay character was in charge of security.

He was going to divert attention from their entry by an explosion near to the Poornachandra Auditorium. In the ensuing chaos they would wave their knives, take over the Mandir and immediately surrender to Sai Baba."

"So what went wrong?" Ajay asked his father.

"I don't know. All four men were killed inside the Mandir. The details are a mystery." The grandfather shrugged his shoulders to indicate his ignorance.

"There is no mystery," Bishnu stated. "Baba was supposedly alone in his bedroom, apart from a boy in his early teens called Subbappayya, a very useful witness of so many things, who has since been spirited away. Baba warned his two servitors that they were about to die. Incidentally, when asked about their demise his only comment was that death is a natural phenomenon and we should avoid worrying about it. As for himself, he would live as long as he pleased. A choice not offered those around him. To resume, Baba claimed he left his room to quell a commotion on the ground floor and went back inside. The intruders came to his door. He fled by a rear exit, setting off an alarm no one knew existed, locked the door from the outside and hid in his garage throughout the siege. The four men were trapped inside his bedroom. They only had knives as weapons but were gunned down by dozens of rifle bullets. According to the official police report, all four died of shock and haemorrhage due to firearms' injuries."

"So there was an official police report?" Ramu Sarnhi now realized.

"Yes. It was thrown out by the authorities," Bishnu said smugly. "It was dismissed out of hand. It was seen to be full of inaccuracies and falsifications. Good God, man, it was a cover-up."

Bishnu was finally angry.

"Don't you see? There are no eyewitnesses left alive. Any attempts at an inquiry have been quashed by government order. A home minister, several other authority figures, perhaps the prime minister himself—he is a devotee—have hushed it up. All investigations have been halted. According to a spokesman of the Sathya Sai Trust, the matter was purely internal and they did not wish to have any law enforcement agency investigating it. Those men, in a desperate attempt to expose the corruption at the heart of the Trust, were trapped, bound and executed by Sai Baba!"

"I protest!"

Standing tall over Bishnu, meaning to intimidate him, an outraged young woman with short, cropped hair and ice-green eyes declared her opposition.

"So do I!" attested her twin, husband or brother, they were certainly kin.

Bishnu was abashed and tried to stand but the woman bent towards him and shouted in his ear, "Baba is no murderer! He saves all our lives! He takes none!"

"Won't you join us?" offered Ramu Sarnhi, free to stand and eager to defuse the woman's fury.

"Please. We will. I apologise for my great anger but I couldn't remain quiet for another moment listening to this man's folly. He had to be challenged. I am Freja, this is my brother, Andreas. We are Danish and sworn devotees of Swami, who will not, could not, has not killed . . . anyone."

"I'm sure you're right, Freja. Please, pull up your table, ours is too small for all these chairs." Esther Sarnhi was happy to welcome another woman to the group, however unpromising the beginnings of their encounter.

"I did not mean to offend you, young lady, or you, Andreas?" Bishnu began in a conciliatory manner. "I cannot disguise my antipathy towards your chosen guru, yogi, god, whatever you may believe him to be, but I do concede my assertion was too extreme and unproven. I did not mean that Sai Baba himself in any way committed such an act. What I meant to imply, in an immoderate way, was that as head of the Trust then he must bear the final responsibility." A winning smile, a bow and a forehead heavily sweating signalled a sincere desire to please.

Before the Danish couple could respond, Ajay Sarnhi asked, " Could you please tell me something about this Trust, how it is corrupt, and what it is meant to do?"

There was a pause as the two Danes eyed first Bishnu, then each other. Freja was the first to respond.

"It is a charitable trust, made up of donations given by believers from all over the world. We have made offerings ourselves."

"And what are these offerings used for?" Ajay continued, tempering the mood.

"Good works. Good projects. There is a university, a major hospital."

"Is that Grandfather's hospital, Mother?" whispered Hari.

"The Super Speciality Hospital in Puttaparthi is a wonder of the world," Freja announced, turning her head towards Hari to make her declaration to him personally.

"Just how big is this Trust?" Ajay persisted, more interested in the economics of it all rather than the buildings.

Andreas explained that the hospital was started with a single donation of fifty million dollars.

"Who on earth has that sort of money?" asked Ajay, truly impressed.

"The owner of the 'Hard Rock Café' chain," Andreas instantly replied. "He is a follower of Sai Baba. He came here a number of years ago, was granted an interview and asked Swami's advice. He was proposing selling all his businesses and coming to stay with Sai Baba. Swami advised him to wait two more years before selling. He did, made one hundred million dollars more than he had originally hoped and split the difference with Swami. The money went to build the hospital. And do you know, those who accuse

Sai Baba of favouritism, it is now a long, long time since the owner of the cafés made his gift and he has not been granted another interview. No, not for fifty million dollars."

Ramu Sarnhi looked crestfallen.

Ajay Sarnhi giggled, "I think I'd be a little bit miffed, wouldn't you? I mean. I ask you. Fifty millions. Wow!"

"There was a letter of thanks. This is not a question of good manners," Andreas explained.

"Such sums are a fraction of the Trust's wealth," Bishnu added. "A reasonable estimate of its current value is five hundred crore."

"How much is a crore?" Hari asked his father.

"A crore is ten million rupees. That means the Trust has in it five billion rupees. Good God!" Ajay exclaimed in wonder.

"I hope so," Freja agreed.

Bishnu was persistent. "The corruption is widespread. The son-in-law of a Trust member runs a hotel in Puttaparthi. A Congress leader is involved, allegedly." Bishnu never forgot he was a lawyer. "Properties from abroad, instead of remaining within the Trust, are registered in the name of individual trustees or their appointed agents. There is a factory in Madras, flats in Bangalore and here in Whitefield and none of this can be exposed because Sai Baba refuses to co-operate. He in turn is protected by the highest in the land. It is a scandal!"

"Fifty million dollars. Five billion rupees." Ajay teased his mind with those improbable sums of money.

"Is the material world all you crave?" Freja demanded of Ajay, clearly frustrated at being surrounded by such secular beings.

"Not entirely but I am a man of business," Ajay asserted with some dignity.

"And I am seeking understanding," Ramu Sarnhi added, for some reason unknown to himself, hoping to win Freja's approval.

"And I am a man of science," Bishnu stated. "I cannot take seriously your man of cheap tricks, fake miracles and magical trinkets."

He'd thought he'd made his point. Freja did not agree.

"You do not believe and yet you arrogantly dismiss the believer without understanding the path she travels. You don't seem to realize that you are trapped in a world of action, condemned to this masquerade of a succession of lived lives, moving at a snail's pace to awareness. You think that your reason will free you, not recognizing that it is your gaoler. Your thinking ego, the centrepiece of this rational life you wish to celebrate, is like a magnet and the actions of your day-to-day living are iron filings that accrue to this ego. I can see the attractable filaments of metal dust like dandruff on your shoulders. You have a long, long way to go, my friend, until your rational mind stops your endless need to act in this world."

"For a Rationalist, there is no other," Bishnu asserted.

"Really? If you are a man of science, how do you cope with quantum physics, where matter will change to accommodate its measuring devices, where all logical rules end? If only Einstein had never lived. Leave explanations to Isaac Newton and his eighteenth century world when everything made sense. Click! Click! Click! This is the sound of equal and opposite pendulums clashing, dangling from a cradle and just as childish. Why would you scoff at truths beyond intellectual apprehension? Why don't you explore the science of yoga? It is a discipline. It is rigorous. It might even satisfy your need for facts."

"I doubt that." Bishnu was certain of his lack of belief.

"I know. Like Christ's Thomas, you need to touch the wounds. It saddens me that for people like you the materializations of the miraculous are your only focus. As always, you miss the point."

"I hadn't realized you'd made one," was Bishnu's riposte.

"You called Baba a trickster in faking the objects he gives to his guests. You mistrust the rings he asks them to wear, the chains for their necks and the watches for their wrists."

"If you're going to miracle up a watch, why not a Rolex instead of a common little Seiko?" Bishnu interjected, with scathing irony.

Ignoring this remark entirely, Freja continued with her argument. "Baba alone is the healer. He mends invisibly. He needs no intermediary objects to achieve a sense of wonder. So why would Baba use trinkets as gifts?"

"Enlighten us," Bishnu invited, with a wave of his hand.

"To divert attention from himself." Freja paused to let this idea settle. "Man, with all his limitations, simple and unsophisticated like you, can only put his trust in things he can handle. He prefers to believe that the God-given object is talismanic and that it contains within itself the magical power to heal or transform. In this interaction of a divine being with a physical man the object becomes the only point of interest. It is the source of power. But only God is effective, his healing unseen and lacking in drama. In the exchange, the trinket provides the necessary deflection to protect the divine privacy. Is this so hard to accept?"

After the intensity of the clash between Freja and Bishnu, the Sarnhi family was happy to leave, even if it meant arriving early for evening darshan. Ramu Sarnhi was not entirely disappointed by Bishnu's disturbing allegations. To trade in India offered daily opportunities to corrupt or be corrupted. Most employees assessed their worth not as facilitators but in their potential to annoy. The less trouble they caused, the greater would be their reward. Dealing in such a valued commodity as silk had led Ramu Sarnhi into worlds of privilege and rank where men of power wielded their

38

influence expensively. The lack of underlying principle was the same at all levels in the business community. If the Trust was corruptible then Ramu Sarnhi knew how to act. At what level and with whom he had yet to learn. If Sai Baba was bogus, his hospital wasn't. That was real enough. And if the Danish twins were right, then a miracle would be just as welcome.

Ajay Sarnhi marvelled at the extravagance of it all: the fortunes described were improbable, the structures and institutions immense, the influence far reaching and the glamour more Disney than Hollywood. He found the whole experience amusing and absurd.

His wife Esther was overwhelmed. She had enjoyed the sheer bluster of Freja—what confidence and nerve—and was secretly pleased to see Grandfather Sarnhi quelled.

Hari was utterly confused and just a little afraid. He thought monasteries were silent and worshippers whispered their prayers. This ashram was noisy and brash, full of rushing men and their money, a sulking God and such extreme versions of the truth that he didn't know who or what to believe.

The family rose but a nervous cough halted their leaving. Proprietor was rushing to their abandoned table: "Your cheese and tomato sandwiches, sir!"

"No! It's too late, isn't it? Hari, do you want this? We're about to go," Ramu Sarnhi explained.

"It is paid for, sir."

"Thank you. I'll take it and give it to . . ." He looked around, clutching the toasted triangles between mildly disapproving fingertips. With absent-minded disdain, he dropped the sandwiches onto the table. They spilt their contents there.

"You can never find a beggar when you want one."

CHAPTER SEVEN
Jean Paul ... then Borg

On most days, Hari found the tormented beggar woman, Lunasha. When not present she was in his thoughts. He was forbidden even to look at her but had decided to intercede in her troubled life, to find some way to help her. He was usually obedient and finding himself so often in the wrong, was accustomed to humility. Most of the world seemed wiser than him and certainly more competent to act. Alone he could do little but perhaps he might encourage another to accomplish what he could not. Before speaking out, before sharing even the vestige of his thoughts and concerns, he needed a guide to steer him through the maze of angers and the extremes of opinion that surrounded this controversial figure. The variety of responses confused and perplexed him.

Hari was alone on his bridge, an hour after evening darshan. It had been a disappointment. So many had been in the week following the excitement of that first seeing. Tonight's darshan had been particularly dispiriting. The family had waited patiently for more than two hours. Hari had fixed his gaze on the distant courtyard where Baba would usually appear to start his twice-daily progress. But suddenly he was standing by his throne, having inched through the stage door that normally provided his exit. It was a furtive and demeaning entrance. There was an audible moan as thousands of pilgrims realised that Baba would not be walking amongst them, that their particular missions could not succeed. The needed interview would not be given: the special journey was wasted. Baba sat heavily on his throne away from them all. With a tired gesture from Him the music began and hymns were sung. There was no clapping. Baba did not lead the way. To Hari, he looked tired and ill. Sad, certainly, and inward looking. He was not there, oddly minimal, not radiating any power. He seemed as small as His physical stature and Hari wept for his troubled God, ashamed of his own inability to help.

Ten minutes later Baba was gone.

Few people seemed to complain, not even the grandfather. But he had used the time to make some decisions. "Until my house is finished, I think we need to rent somewhere, here in Whitefield. Do you agree?"

"What exactly for, Father?" Ajay Sarnhi asked.

"I find the day is long and the gaps between morning and evening darshan is wasted time. The waiting makes me weary. It is too far to Bangalore to make four journeys by taxi. That, of course, is why I'm building a house here. We could obtain a place with a few rooms, somewhere to rest in the early afternoon, a kitchen and a cook to prepare luncheon and snacks. We could have meetings with business colleagues before leaving for dinner in Bangalore. I will need an agent for the house, to oversee lettings to foreign visitors. We can interview the 'possibles' in such rooms. I think the plan has much to recommend it."

The family agreed and went in search of rooms for rent. Hari was left alone. His opinion wasn't needed.

The ashram was an enclosed and safe area. Some of its inmates spilled into the few village houses that lined the road. Watchful eyes were everywhere and, apart from the beggars, it was a known and secure community. Hari was free to wander. He could shop in the bazaar, eat in the canteens, and spend his pocket money far less cautiously than he was used to in England. 'Pounds for pennies' as his father would gleefully claim.

But it was the peace of the river that Hari sought. Several times each day, usually before and after darshan, he would escape to the bridge from where he had witnessed the shameful actions of the dhobi wallahs as they threatened Lunasha, despite his crying out to stop them. It was on the outskirts of the village, beyond the houses, that Hari learnt to enjoy the really useful river and images of India that were recognisable from his school geography book.

Earlier, he'd visited the ashram canteen but found it full of banter, self-assertion, recognisable food and understandable languages. There were too many opinions too readily asserted and to Hari it felt familiar and intimidating. He knew his place and had no interest in the gossip. The red dot spiritual eyes at the centre of the frowning foreheads of so many excitable Western women seemed to beam with an intensity that cowed him and left him slightly wretched as more and more extravagant claims of miracles seen, voices heard, donations made, vows proclaimed and promises kept were bandied around in a competitive game of spiritual one-upmanship. It wasn't a peaceful place. And no one was hungry.

He sought Jean Paul and joined the queue a few places behind his wise friend in the Indian canteen. It was only a short walk away from the ashram but, culturally, the gap between the two was vast. It was Hari's first visit and the differences intrigued him.

People seemed to choose their food wisely in the Indian canteen. He wondered if the food was free, even though Hari knew to him the cost was immaterial. Most ate in silence. The skilful rolling of rice balls through the sauces that imparted so many subtle flavours was part of a ritual that made the act of eating an art. Food here seemed sacramental. It was not taken for granted. Without words, every mouthful, slowly and thoughtfully swallowed, seemed to contain a mute prayer of thanks. The people were hungry, nothing was left over, but the sense of composure and elegance eliminated all traces of greed.

"Hello, Hari." Jean Paul turned round and beckoned Hari to join him in the queue. It was an accepted practice. It took only one family member to secure a place and others would join at will to bring orders and additional trays to the food counters.

"You will need a tray. Should I help you choose? Are you not eating?" Jean Paul was concerned.

"No. Please. Get your meal." Hari was embarrassed. "We will go back to Bangalore for dinner. I have to meet my mother by the ashram gate a little later. Is this your restaurant?" Hari shuffled forward with the flow of the queue, anxious not to delay Jean Paul.

"Sort of. Yes, I suppose it is." Jean Paul smiled. He rarely thought of anything as his. "Here, Indian food is provided for residents of the ashram. And their guests." Jean Paul bowed gracefully towards Hari. "There is another canteen in the main building for the Europeans. But, to be frank, I am weary of eating spaghetti in tomato sauces. The food here at least changes occasionally."

Hari thought to tell Jean Paul of his recent visit but didn't want to interrupt his friend's meal.

"Is it free?" he thought to ask.

"Not quite, but nearly. We can buy tickets." Jean Paul showed Hari a multicoloured collection of what looked exactly like old-fashioned bus tickets: yellow, red, and purple.

"This is for drinking tea, that for pudding, that for rice and vegetables. It is a very complicated system to guarantee that many men are employed to operate it. This is how India thrives. There is always evidence of Indians at work when there is a queue. So, now tell me, Hari, why are you so sad?"

Hari was taken by surprise but answered instantly, "Because God is so sad and I don't understand why and I don't know what I can do. Suddenly, it all seems so complicated."

"One Holy Man said 'God is simple. Everything else is complex.'"

"Well, I don't understand everything else then. I don't understand why they would want to kill God, or keep Him prisoner. And I don't understand why He let them."

"Ah. The assassination attempt."

"You know about it?"

"Yes, I know about it. Come. It is our turn. Will you eat something?" Jean Paul ushered Hari to the row of desks where tickets were so carefully scrutinised and eventually swapped for precise items of food.

"It is all right just to drink some tea? It's just that my mother would be cross if I spoilt my appetite for my dinner."

"Are you hungry?"

"Erm . . . No."

"Why the pause? There is no need to be so polite."

"Oh, it's not that. I don't ever seem to be hungry. I forget and live in my thoughts and its only when I concentrate that I find out if I want to eat anything. I'm not hungry now but I am thirsty."

"Then I will get you some tea."

A brown plastic tray, with chipped edges and marbled scars, gradually filled with Jean Paul's supper. Standing and surveying the room he chose a quiet corner with meshed windows that would have overlooked the road, could you see through. Hari sat alongside and clutched his lukewarm, over-sweetened tea. Jean Paul fell silent and mouthed a prayer of thanks that Hari could follow, written in English in Sai Baba's handwriting on a scroll hanging above the window, garlanded with fresh flowers and other inscriptions in Telegu, the Indian language of the region around Puttaparthi, the version of Indian that Sai Baba himself spoke.

Jean Paul ate carefully. He would scoop a crescent of rice into his crooked little finger, tease it into a ball with his nervously busy finger tips, roll it through the scented liquid plopped onto the bare tray by the appropriate server, then would pop the moistened morsel into his mouth, where it seemed to dissolve. There was nothing to chew. The whole process was controlled, lacking in urgency.

"Tell me your thoughts, Hari. Why do you smile?" Jean Paul was gazing at the prayer scroll.

"One thought wasn't important."

"Tell me that one first."

"I was thinking that you didn't seem hungry either and that you were a very neat eater." Hari looked down, a little embarrassed.

"And the other thought?"

"I was wondering if the ashram was anything like Heaven."

"And if it were?"

"Heaven would be horrible. You sat and waited to see Him. We didn't. We jumped the queue and were given seats because my grandfather is wealthy."

"There is only one wealth, Hari, and that is spirituality. You cannot buy, sell or shuffle around that. It is the Soul, the untouchable, the private, the God-Part of us all."

"But, the wealth that is only money shouldn't be able to buy privileges from God." This was a statement that sounded like a question.

"What sort of privileges?"

"Interviews."

"I have no money, Hari, none, but I had an interview four years ago and another last year." Jean Paul turned to Hari to reinforce this startling confession. Hari was astonished.

"But …You? What happens?"

"There are a chosen number of us. Swami speaks. It is a kind of summary.

It is most impressive. It is all carefully staged, not false, just ordered. Each of us has a drama, a play. There is no end to the play and we choose the play. He knows where we all are in our drama. To be in such an interview is to see God at work, shaping our lives. But, now he will not talk to me any more. There is just silence. All I hear I hear internally. There will be no more spoken words. Ever."

"Why?"

"He says it is no longer needed. I am ready to go alone. He says."

"Are you?"

"I don't know, Hari. Swami is my teacher, my guru. And like any child that goes to school, you don't want to stop, especially visiting the lessons of your favourite teacher. I didn't want it to stop."

"Do you think you have lost him?"

"No. Not at all. I am joined to Baba. He is still my teacher."

"But, how does he teach you?"

"Invisibly."

"I don't really understand."

"I didn't want to, either. It was too grown-up a way." Jean Paul laughed at his next thought. "I read this exchange, once, it amuses me still, listen. A believer says 'I went to my teacher with nothing and came away with nothing.' Someone asks 'Why bother to go to the teacher then?' The reply is 'How otherwise would I know that I came away with nothing?' I have no less than anyone else who seeks God. I may have more, in that I believed I could see him."

"You can see Sai Baba. He exists. He's just there." Hari pointed through the window.

"The ashram is there." Jean Paul pulled Hari's arm to the right direction. Undaunted, Hari added, "You know what I mean. Just there." This time Hari only gestured with a waving finger.

"I didn't correct you to embarrass you. I meant for you to think that Baba cannot be in just one place. If Baba is there, then he is an object and somehow we have trapped him in our minds. And that is not good enough, and it is not the stuff of Gods. Mind is only a collection of thoughts and the thinker who thinks them. There is something behind the mind and that is where God is. We cannot think God. He begins when Mind stops. But Mind is afraid of its own death. And if you fight Mind with Mind then that just serves to make Mind stronger. Oh, it is hard, Hari, it is hard. I see your frowning and your worry and your fear. For someone like me to put aside 'Me' ..." He pointed at the spot between his own startled eyes with a hand shaped like a gun. "... is so difficult. Some believe it is not even possible. After all, without 'Me' ..." He shot himself, let his head slump to his chest then looked up slowly. "Who would be there to recognise or register what was happening?" Jean Paul paused, as if expecting Hari to be capable of answering his question. It was a few moments before Hari realised Jean Paul really was waiting for a response, his blue eyes looking, intently but gently, deep into Hari's.

"I can't answer you, Jean Paul, because I am not clever enough. Maybe when I'm older."

"No, you're wiser than me, Hari. You are still full of unquestioning love."

Hari fell silent with this thought.

Jean Paul asked, "Would you like something sweet to eat? I would."

Hari was happy to say yes. The queue for the honeyed and spiced cakes was happily short and Jean Paul returned quickly. Hari began his carefully reserved question before his friend had even sat down.

"Can I ask you about someone I have seen?"

Jean Paul nodded.

"Someone in trouble," Hari began. "Someone damaged," he added.

The pauses allowed Jean Paul to swallow the last of his sweetmeats. Hari ate his as Jean Paul answered.

"Yes. Of course you may. Who is this person you are so anxious about? He must be important to you. Not a member of your family, I hope?"

"No. No one of importance. Just a beggar woman. Yet, she is beautiful." Hari added quickly, feeling disloyal. "And because of her beauty she has been violated."

He confided this knowledge in a whisper that confirmed all the more his ignorance. Jean Paul suppressed a smile.

"She is called Lunasha," Hari added.

Jean Paul thought carefully before he replied.

"I have seen her, I believe. She is most certainly a tormented creature, at least, to all appearances. I have heard her story told. What is it you want to do for her, Hari?"

"What can be done? None of her family will help her and everyone else seems to hate her."

"The reactions you have seen surrounding this woman are very complex, Hari. They are not easy to understand, for anyone. To begin with, the anger and urgent need to be rid of her is more to do with guilt than hatred, or at least, not directed at the creature herself but towards a society that allows and condones such injustices. There are very few places in the world that value women, Hari. Our two countries do, but here in India, they do not. I will shock you. Every day unwanted daughters, newly-born, are cast aside, left to drown and drift down rivers, to die lonely deaths at the edge of forests or on the hidden sides of hills. A girl waits to become a wife: once a wife a widow and all her significance resides in her man. A few are accorded careers in enlightened cities like Bangalore but that merely adds value to the marriage trade."

"Can't she be a mother, like mine?" Hari interrupted, made insecure by Jean Paul's assertions. "Even if she's not important in the world?"

"Of course she can, Hari. She can be queen of all things domestic so long as she stays behind the veil. She must not challenge the male in his dominion over the world."

"Why?" Hari asked, simply.

"Why indeed? It is tradition and social practice. It is in the Scriptures. And yet, there are female forms of God, the Divine Feminine, Shakti. The *Mahabharata*, that great Hindu text, was written for women. There is even a living female avatar, The Mother, a rival for Sai Baba himself. But the Buddha, my great inspiration, thought women, as a rule, were scant in wisdom and deeply immersed in vanity. There was one notable exception. Would you like to hear her story, Hari? It is not dissimilar to that of your beggar woman."

"Yes. I would like to hear it, especially if ..." He didn't finish his sentence or his thought. He must remember he was forbidden to look at Lunasha, even in his mind's eye.

"My story is very ancient but still true. It took place at the time of the Buddha, five hundred years before the birth of Jesus Christ. A child was discovered at the foot of a mango tree. With no known parentage she was named after her birthplace, Ambapali. The name means the young leaves of the mango tree."

Hari thought Lunasha was a prettier name.

"She was beautiful, like your beggar woman."

Why didn't he use her name, Hari wondered?

"Many young noblemen desired her company, and why not? When aged only eleven she was declared the most beautiful child in the state of Bihar. In time she grew, if anything, more beautiful. She was betrothed to her childhood sweetheart. She was invited to Vaishali, a splendid city full of pleasure grounds and lotus ponds, there to dance before King Manudev. She enthralled him. He must possess her, whatever the cost. He waited, so cruelly, until the very day of her marriage. He killed her groom and claimed her as his bride. But a king could never marry a foundling. She became a courtesan, the privileged possession of a King and for seven years, she was given great wealth and a palace to live in."

"Why for only seven years?"

"Perhaps by then the king would turn his attentions to someone new, younger, fresher. His power put him beyond question or control. Then, one fateful day, the Buddha visited Vaishali. By chance he entered the garden of mangoes where Ambapali was found and where she discovered the Blessed One and his entourage of monks. She invited him to share a meal with her and her own retinue the following day. There was a silent agreement between

46

them. The king was outraged. He offered banquets to out-rival all other possible offerings, even tried to bribe Ambapali with gifts of gold but the Buddha returned to the garden of mangoes and ate a meal of sweet milk-rice and cakes in the cool shade of the trees.

"Ambapali intrigued the Buddha. Here was a woman who had moved successfully in worldly circles, who was the favourite of kings and princes, and yet she seemed composed and calm in her heart. Despite being constantly surrounded by riches and pleasure, she remained untainted, quiet and thoughtful.

"There were even more surprises. 'Holy one,' she is reported as saying to the Blessed One, 'I present this garden to your order. Accept it, if it be your will.' He did. And he accepted her. She entered holy orders and, in time, achieved the height of spiritual development. Isn't that a remarkable story?"

"Could that happen to Lunasha? Could she be saved?"

"Perhaps."

Hari was thoughtful once more.

"Jean Paul, why does Lunasha behave as she does?"

"In what way?"

"Why does she step into the ditch and cover herself in all that dirt and filth? It is so horrible to see." Hari screwed up his face in disgust.

"I cannot know what is in her mind but I can make a suggestion."

Hari nodded his approval.

"I think she is embracing the world's opinion of her. The victims of injustice often feel guilt that is not theirs. If she disgusts the world then she must be a valid object of disgust. The society of men sees her as dirty and besmirched, the ritual in the filth of the ditch confirms that opinion. She appears before the world as accused. She embraces and absorbs its opinion. It is an act of agreement. 'This is what you think. This is what I am.' Do you see?"

Hari was stubborn. He couldn't accept this version of the truth even if Lunasha could.

"No. She is beautiful."

"Not in the eyes of the world. Not in her eyes, not when they look at the world. Next time you see your beggar woman, Hari, look into her eyes. Tell me where they are looking. Then, I will try and explain what they are seeing and it will make you happy."

Jean Paul rested the open palm of his hand on Hari's slightly bowed head. He sensed the boy was near to tears, exhausted by the demands of a long, long day.

"Don't be troubled. As one wise man said, to try and contain God in words is like trying to put the ocean in a bucket. It doesn't stop men from trying. It doesn't stop many from believing they've actually succeeded.

I think another wise man's fears are justified. There really are fishes that believe they contain the sea. Come, I'll walk with you back to the ashram."

As Jean Paul lifted his hand away from Hari's head, another was lowered to replace it. A gnarled and witch-wizened hand, covered in an impossible number of silver rings shaped into forty or more human skulls with rubies and jet for red and black eyes. As Hari raised his head against the lifting pressure of this hand of death's-heads, he looked into an astonishing face.

"Hari," offered Jean Paul, mercifully not troubled by the new arrival, "I'd like you to meet my friend, Borg."

CHAPTER EIGHT
Borg and a miracle

Borg looked for all the world as if someone had just dug him up. His face was a patchwork of taut, then wrinkled skin. The immediate facial mask of eyes, nose and mouth had a boyish look to them, but the residue of past lifting and stretching had accumulated as withered skin behind the ears and at the edge of the chin. Deep rivulets permanently scarred the flesh of his neck. It reminded Hari of the giant tortoises of the Galapagos Islands when stretching to reach an overhanging leaf. Painfully thin, hollow-cheeked, with a mass of flyaway hair whose abundance merely accentuated the lack of flesh elsewhere, as Borg stood in the doorway, the evening sun appeared to shine through his translucent skin. He seemed vampiric, but not the fanged aggressor. Borg came after the vampire, its drained, bloodless victim. Wall-eyed, odd-toothed, yellow-nailed, Borg donned a pair of thick-framed Rayban sunglasses to protect some of him from the light, as he backed into the sunshine to let Jean Paul and Hari pass.

"Are you leaving?"

"Yes, Borg. Hari is to return to the ashram."

"I shall accompany you."

"Were you going to eat?"

"Never."

"Of course." Jean Paul smiled.

"Now, tell me young man." Borg placed his spindly hand of skulls onto Hari's shoulder. "Very young man. How many years?"

"I'm ten, Mr Borg. Ten years old."

"Just Borg. I've never been a mister. Well, to be precise, not for more than a century."

Hari looked nervously to Jean Paul for reassurance, guidance perhaps.

"Has Jean Paul been boring you? You may say we are friends. Did you know J. P. is our resident philosopher? Just bursting with wise things. Ferrighteningly intellectual. A fine mind, pretty face and totally likable. He's so nice; it makes you want to spit. Don't you agree?"

"Not really." Hari was losing his fear as he guessed Borg was playing.

"Pah! Contention. In one so young. You have corrupted him already, J. P. All this free-thinking you encourage. So unhealthy. So disrespectful. Has he been quoting his host of Wise Men at you? I do hope so."

"Take no notice of him, Hari. He is always complaining. It is because he is so very old."

"How old is he?" Hari tried to whisper but croaked.

"Excuse me. I am not deaf. All my faculties work. You may address yourself directly to me, if you will. Now, Stop." They did. Borg turned Hari to face him, then stooped to an uncomfortable closeness. "Ask me yourself. Speak slowly so I—can—read—your—lips."

Hari giggled.

"Well?" Hari glanced at Jean Paul who nodded his approval.

"How old are you?"

"Please, Borg," said Borg.

"Please, Borg. How old *are* you?" asked an obedient Hari.

"One hundred and twenty-one."

"Really?" This time Jean Paul merely shrugged his shoulders.

"I think so. Come, let's walk on." They did. "You see there is only one problem living to such a great age. You tend to forget. Certain things."

"What things?"

"Well, for instance, how old you are. How old did I say I was?"

"One hundred and twenty-one," Hari remembered.

"Now that is a great age, you must agree. You'd think by now one would

be shown equally great respect." Borg conducted each of his last three words with an extended forefinger wave. " A certain reverence. After all, I'm a century older than our pretty thinker here, and he shows me nothing but disrespect."

"It isn't true, Borg. You simply forget how respectful I have been."

"That is a possibility, I concede. Reluctantly." Borg slipped his hand into the ample pocket of his hugely baggy but immaculately ironed ashram trousers and produced a minute skull, carefully balanced at his upturned finger ends.

Borg produced a minute skull, carefully balanced at his upturned finger ends

"That thing is disgusting. Put it away, Borg."

Like a giant Hamlet with a miniature Yorick, Borg stared into the hollow eyes of the bone sphere with a gentle, puzzled affection.

"But, no one knew him, not this one, not even Horatio. It was only a child."

"Is it real?" asked Hari, disturbed but fascinated.

"Of course. See." The skull was offered—then withdrawn to almost touch the black lenses of the Raybans, in a short-sighted, close scrutiny.

"Very real. Very dead. An infant mortality. Dead before life. Charming isn't it?"

"It's gruesome," was Jean Paul's reaction.

"It's life," effused Borg.

"It's death," countered Jean Paul. "It's tasteless," was his afterthought.

"I've never licked it," was Borg's surreal counter. "Do you know that every skeleton that every doctor practises on in Europe has come from India? You're not allowed to dig up French and Germans, and certainly, an Englishman's bones are his jealously guarded castle. When they haven't been burnt, that is. This fashion for incineration only increases the Indian bone trade. I am merely a minor participant in a huge international enterprise."

"But why the skull of a child?" asked Hari, feeling oddly loyal to the unknown dead.

"I would like to give you all sorts of philosophical reasons. Clearly, the skull and the bones are to remind me of rats' alley, of fleshly death, of my own ridiculous mortality. A memento mori. A mediaeval reminder of a middle-aged death." Borg was speaking to his baby skull. "Mine! Reflected in his. I go on. He hardly began." He turned to Hari. "The truth is, I bought this one so it would go in my pocket. Like so. Invisible and discreet. You have no idea what an unsightly bulge a full-sized male skull creates in these ashram pants. Most vulgar. Take my word for it. Not at all acceptable."

Hari sniggered.

"The boy has sniggered, Jean Paul. He is past saving. You have done your work too well. He is a lost soul, beyond belief."

"He isn't."

"I'm not!"

"Such fierce loyalty. Ramakrishna would have been thrilled."

"Who?"

"What charming ignorance. Ramakrishna is one of J. P.'s wise men."

"One of the wisest, Hari," reassured Jean Paul.

"Where is he?"

"Long dead. He lived towards the end of the last century." Jean Paul began an explanation.

"I met him when I was a child," interrupted Borg, with some pride.

"Fascinating," was Jean Paul's uncritical response.

"He used to stammer, you know. Most endearing in a saint. But how he would have loved your fervour, Hari. And your certainty. I was a great waverer at your age. I think my father took me on a visit to the saint to instill a little certainty. I came away more confused, as I remember. The whole thing was rather disconcerting. Ramakrishna was nude. I fear my father thought it rather ungentlemanly of him not to cover up with a loincloth, a shawl or just something. It might have been suggested. In turn, Ramakrishna described my father as a 'householder devotee', which was rather amusing." Borg chuckled, an odd, throat-trapped sound. "The saint had scant regard for the scholar or the book-learned and had a wonderful way of asking the really obvious question."

"Such as?" asked Jean Paul.

"Such as: 'How badly do you want to see God?' 'How much does it grieve you to fail?' People like my father needed months of warning for such questions and as long as possible to frame impossible answers. The saint said something like: 'P-p-p-p-people grieve and sh-sh-sh-shed potfuls of tears at the death of their wives. D-d-d-d-did you?'

'She isn't dead,' replied my father, rather smugly.

'Will you?'

'Of course.'

'If you lost all your m-m-m-money, would you grieve?'

'Of course. Well … possibly.' The direct question caught him out in the truth, I would guess.

'B-b-but, do you grieve more than this because you cannot realise God?' And the answer, of course, was no, and always is. Except for saints and small boys."

Both Hari and Jean Paul felt included in Borg's last remark.

"What I liked best about the saintly Ramakrishna was that whenever he touched money his hands went numb. Which is more than can be said for every saint." Jean Paul tried to deflect Borg's cynicism from expression but Hari asked the invited question anyway.

"Don't you believe that Sai Baba is God?"

"A nicely phrased question, Hari. To answer you directly, I did. I think I still do but at times I waver. I'm not such a good person as Jean Paul. I find it hard to keep taking things on trust. I am into things material. I like to see wonders. I would have needed to stick my finger through the holes in Christ's hands. On this visit, I have spent thirteen months in Baba's ashrams, that is until I was evicted last year, and during that time I have seen nothing. There have been few talks, no meetings, fewer interviews, none for me. There have been no miracles, no healings. Hell, even I do healings."

"You ignore the vibhuti miracles, Borg. They occur daily," interceded Jean Paul.

52

"I don't count vibhuti. That's nothing." Borg swept the idea away with a dismissive swish of his hand.

"What is it?" asked Hari.

"Holy ash," Jean Paul explained. "Swami materializes vibhuti to help people with their illnesses."

"A pathetic trickle from his finger ends. They can all do it. Go and see Primananda in Trichy. He sprays it from his mouth, great clouds of the stuff. Poouf!" Borg mimed his description, pouting and blubbering his lips and billowing the invisible dust with his waving arms. "I mean clouds. It fills the hall at darshan, covers his audience. It's just a mantra. A spell. Say the words and hey presto, poouf!"

"Will I see this?" Hari asked Jean Paul, excited at the prospect.

"I will show you tomorrow. Watch Swami closely at morning darshan, especially when he is amongst the sick and seated."

"You won't see any 'poouf!'" added Borg, distancing himself, getting ready to leave.

"No, but you will see a miracle, Hari."

"A miracle?"

"Yes," reassured Jean Paul, leaving him quietly.

"No. Ha! Ha! Ha!" laughed Borg, leaving him noisily.

Hari stood waiting for his family.

Ramu Sarnhi had been full of excitement and self-congratulation concerning his immediate discovery of a perfect property to rent.

"That is not a sensible man. It must be the thin air in Kashmir. You need more oxygen than that to grow a good business brain. A hundred and fifty a month! It's worth twice that. Still, there will always be losers. And there will always be winners. On this occasion, we have won."

"Yes, Father, I would never have made such a low offer." Hari's father, was a little deflated.

"Ah! Well. You are not yet used to local conditions. You will learn. Quickly."

"Is the house nice, Father?" asked Hari. He was the only member of the family, business associate, or passing acquaintance who was yet to see inside or indeed outside the newly acquired property.

"It is very nice, Hari," assured his mother. "You will see it tomorrow. There are many rooms with beautiful carpets and cushions but no furniture, as yet. The kitchen is small but the main reception room is nearly as big as Sai Ramesh Hall, isn't it, Grandfather?"

The grandfather nodded his head sideways in agreement and delight at his daughter-in-law's flattery. It was her duty.

"Were the people that rented it silly?" Hari asked his mother.

"No, Hari, not silly. The owner is going back to Kashmir to get married.

I would guess he was pleased to be able to gain an income from his property whilst he was away. I don't think he was silly. I think he thought he was lucky to receive anything. That's most probably why he wasn't greedy."

Disgruntled at this far too reasonable explanation of his daughter-in-law's, Ramu Sarnhi steered his son away for serious talk, the kind that is only possible between men. "We will be a few moments. When you have finished your chatter meet us at the taxi rank," was his imperious parting comment.

"Yes, of course," Esther Sarnhi replied, dutifully.

"Is Grandfather cross?" Hari was concerned for his mother. In England she was never addressed so curtly.

"No, dear. He has lots of important things on his mind."

"Of course," remembered Hari. "There can be nothing more important than preparing to die."

"Did one of your friends tell you that?"

"No, I thought it."

Hari's mother hugged him close, made nervous by his accidental wisdom.

"You must be tired. Are you hungry?"

"Not really, mother."

"Would you like a snack?"

"It will spoil my dinner." He was trying to forget the spiced and honeyed cakes Jean Paul had given him.

"I don't think we'll be having any. Grandfather's new landlord gave us food. It was quite a banquet. Unfortunately its main ingredient was chicken."

"Meat?"

"Yes. The men ate it. I didn't, so we could find something together, a little vegetarian supper, perhaps."

"I would like that." Hari enjoyed being alone with his mother. Such time was always precious. It felt stolen, almost a conspiracy. Soon Hari would be expected to live amongst men. He would miss talking to his mother.

CHAPTER NINE
The Architectural Woman

Hari stood on the bridge at the edge of the village. He was as still as the heron beneath his gaze. He welcomed the silence of the river. The dhobi wallahs were chatting on its banks; their wash completed, the clean clothes and sheets were draped over the bushes, drying quickly in the 40° heat. One man dozed beneath their temporary shade.

Hari had been excused the noisy meeting of men of business in his grandfather's hired house. His father had wanted him there. As quickly as Ramu Sarnhi introduced colleagues, managers, trading partners and senior craftsmen to Hari's father, they were paraded before Hari as the next generation in waiting. Not even eleven years old, Hari thought this certain promise of continuity premature and the intensity of the greetings alarmed rather than reassured him. He'd never thought of his future; it was enough to realise he was about to change schools. That was challenging enough. Was he never to choose what happened next? Was he destined to be part of a silk family?

His mother peered into the noisy room, waiting for a signal to bring in refreshments for the excited guests. Ajay Sarnhi was busily important. He was clearly enjoying the attention and had never before heard himself praised by his father in such extravagant ways. He grinned. He preened. He embraced this transfer of power.

Nodded entry, Hari's mother led in a convoy of servants bearing silver trays of elegant cakes, savouries, glasses of sweet tea and sweeter juices. There was fruit in a basket and a tray piled high with puri, delicate spheres of air-filled bread, deep-fried and still warm, with piles of sugar and cinnamon to dip them in. She left with Hari, crooked in her protective arm.

"I'll take him out of your way, now. You can speak more freely. Say your goodbyes, Hari."

Bowing an exit, Hari was relieved to be free.

"Thank you, mother."

"It's no place for a boy, Hari." Nor for a man, the fleeting thought whispered as it passed through her mind. She hoped Hari might lead a different life, removed from the barter of markets, the pressure of trade, the authority of accounts and the insistent clatter of cash. Her closeness to Hari would diminish, her influence wane, and all final decisions would be her husband's not hers. But for a short while she might suggest other ways of being and introduce Hari to new worlds through the books he might read and the ideas she would license him to think.

In the distance, walking towards the bridge, Hari spied Lunasha. He looked to the river and her enemies on the shore. Dare he interrupt her journey, warn her, deflect her from the angry confrontation he knew she would face? As he dithered, she changed course and leaving the road, followed a raised mud track that shadowed the river then cut inland.

Where was she going? Hari wanted to know. He ran. He followed. He looked right and left. She bobbed in and out of focus as the impossible fissures cracked into the earth by the searing heat made walking a bobbing dance. He jumped and veered, careful to look down and up. The baked earth would snap an ankle on the instant. The dangerous mud edges were as rigid as iron.

He was approaching the edge of the village where his grandfather's workers weaved their beautiful silks. Lunasha had vanished. He crept into the square. All the house doors were closed and the courtyards of the compounds empty. Even the dogs were too lazy to bark in the crushing heat.

He heard the distant and muffled sound of singing. It was coming from the earth, not the air. It was buried beneath him. He stooped and crept towards the source. By the side of the grain barn and standing half a metre above ground, was a circle of red bricks three to four metres wide with an apparent entrance at ground level as each successive row shed a brick and neatly met on a stone threshold. Half the top was capped with a semi-circle of latticed wood, resting on a central wooden rail that had coiling rope secured then dangling down into the dark. The guttering of the barn was directed to a downpipe that ran into what was clearly a cistern, a giant man-made well to store precious water in defiance of the sun's heat.

The river was wide but it was shallow and Hari had already heard talk of its fickle nature, on occasion reduced to a trickle that could not sustain rice. This cistern, perhaps one of many, could provide what the river lacked.

At the edge Hari could see a row of steps cut into the circular wall and spiralling downwards to the water at its base. The singing echoed and with tentative steps, fingers spread to clutch any irregularities in the brick to steady his careful tread, Hari began his descent. He took less than a dozen steps. The water was much closer than he'd guessed. Two steps further down, it lapped over the brick. One step down, Lunasha had crumpled her sodden sari. It rested there. Hari stood very still, clamped to the wall, staring into the water beneath him.

Lunasha was floating on her back. Her arms were lifted above her head, her legs were splayed and she was spinning slowly in a circle. She was so light, seemingly supported by the meniscus, like the dozens of miniscule insects that trod the water's surface beside her, untroubled and unsinking companions in this cool, dark pool.

She reminded Hari of Leonardo da Vinci's Architectural Man.

He'd studied the drawing in art. The extra arms and legs had put him in mind of India and its many-limbed gods. He knew the head was one-eighth the size of the man: the length of his outstretched arms equal to his height. Hari never quite believed that. He learnt of palms and cubits and how the world could be measured in parts of a man. And now, before him was the perfection of woman. Light from above glittered on the water and lit its temporary guest. Hari stared.

She was a naked woman, of course, and Hari had had lessons in the classroom and more exciting gossip in the school yard, so knew more about woman and her sexuality than he let his parents believe—he didn't want to embarrass them. But Hari's gaze was dispassionate. Lunasha was an insubstantial creature. She was an idea, a dream, equally alive in imagination as in life.

Hari stumbled. Lunasha sank. Her head emerged and turned towards Hari but didn't seem to see him there. He backed away, edging his heel higher, feeling for each backward step. He stopped, half-in, half-out of the well. Lunasha was floating and spinning and singing once more. She looked straight at Hari. He could see her eyes but their focus went through and beyond him. They reflected the sky and the infinite; his particular being had no interest for her.

Hari left. He said goodbye, knowing she wouldn't hear. He must talk to Jean Paul. His anxiety was urgent. Lunasha's body had no flesh and little muscle to mask the bones. Her whole skeleton poked through. Hari was convinced she was going to die, and soon, if he didn't find a way to help her live.

CHAPTER TEN
A Saint?

Hari walked purposefully across an almost empty ashram. On the far side of the Great Hall a row of official buildings towered over the roadway that led to the private quarters of Sai Baba and his retinue. The entrance to this precious area, forbidden except to a chosen elite, was an elaborate construction of walls, pillars, plinths and statues, domes and clocks, trellis-works and plaster battlements. The gaudy of pink brick and primary coloured idols was softened by the pastel blue of the plastered recesses. The office areas, lining the approach to this ornate gateway, were equally grand. Orange walls tempered by salmon-pink and elaborate balconies beneath each blue window were balustraded and then crowned by a trio of cupolas, decorated all around like gigantic Wedgewood-patterned bowls upturned. Hari stared at the buildings, startled by their brash colours and overwrought designs.

"It is a little like a fairground, isn't it, Hari?" It was Jean Paul. Hari was delighted.

"I've been looking for you."

"I know," Jean Paul smiled. "The chain of whispers reached me a few minutes ago. I'm afraid you've missed your miracle. Perhaps it will happen this afternoon. Everyone was confused and distracted by the unsatisfactory darshan."

"What was wrong?" Hari frowned.

"Their taxis have yet to arrive and so they grumble and bemoan their need to wait and there is nowhere to dine well here, early or late."

"No. I meant with Sai Baba. Why didn't he stay with us?"

"I have no idea."

"He spoke to no one, except his own students and they were right next to the stage and his throne. He didn't even sit on it."

"I saw. He was distracted. Perhaps his mind was on other, more important things."

Hari thought for a moment about the kind of immense responsibilities a God might have. The scale of His obligations was beyond a human imagination. It was certainly beyond Hari's.

"I suppose. But to wait all those hours in the sun, to wheel in the sick and the dying and to offer letters and gifts and hope—all that hope—and then, such a disappointment. He took nothing, gave nothing, said nothing, sang no hymns and walked away after just a few minutes. Is he tired of us all, Jean Paul? Has God lost interest in us?"

"I don't think he can, even if he wanted to. We can choose to ignore him, even deny his existence, but he cannot overlook what he has made. He is stuck with us, Hari."

"Poor God."

"Poor God, indeed." Jean Paul smiled. "Tell me, what was it you wanted to see me about that couldn't wait until supper?" Jean Paul guided Hari to a raised step at the edge of a flower bed surrounded with a strip of ornamental lawn. He sat on the grass and leaned on the step, patting a place for Hari to sit. They were in a mysterious shade created by the sun filtering through the corrugated panels of turquoise plastic that protected the sides and the roof of the ashram from the intense heat. Hari sat beside Jean Paul and stared ahead.

"It is my beggar woman. I saw her earlier today, before darshan. She was swimming in a well, hidden underground, on the edge of the village that houses my grandfather's workers. I have never seen her eat even though she is given food."

"Have you fed her, Hari?"

"Yes. Well, no. Like I said ..." Hari was embarrassed. He felt discovered, exposed in something underhand. Jean Paul couldn't know of his father's prohibition. It had been repeated and reinforced with newly threatened sanctions only the day before. It was still in force.

"Yes, I have given her food but, no, she never eats it. She is dying, Jean Paul. Lunasha's life is hanging by a thread. She looked like a skeleton today and her thinness frightened me. Why won't she keep herself alive? Must she die? Is there any way to help her?"

"I'm not sure where to begin, Hari. But first, be reassured." Jean Paul touched Hari gently on the shoulder. Hari was reassured as promised. He felt an intense heat flow from the tips of Jean Paul's fingers. "We will not let Lunasha die."

"You named her," Hari whispered. He was oddly content, as if he'd achieved a significant victory.

"I don't use a name because I'm not quite sure who or where she is in the living of her life, but I will make one outrageous claim on her behalf." Jean Paul turned towards Hari. "I believe she is a saint."

Hari was dumbfounded. He sat in silence for several moments, suppressing tears.

"How can she be?" Relieved, delighted, perplexed and afraid, Hari ran the gamut of his emotions in tearful confusion.

"In India all the grandmasters appear in the form of beggars. It is perhaps why begging has never been a criminal offence here; you might be putting a god behind bars. Ramakrishna, the God-Man that Borg says he saw, possessed as little flesh as Lunasha and as few possessions. He warned us all not to spurn the abject and the poor; they might be almost perfect spiritual beings, as he was seen to be. So, this is a promising beginning for my claim for the beggar woman's sanctity. Do you understand the concept of reincarnation, Hari?"

"Probably not the 'concept'," Hari handled the word with care, suspicious of its meaning, "but I know the word means being reborn, to live a life again. I know the word."

"The early Christians also believed in reincarnation."

"They would have to do, because of Jesus Christ and Easter." Hari was quick to assert what he knew was true.

"Exactly. It was five centuries after the birth of Christ before a belief in reincarnation was declared a heresy. Suddenly what had been accepted was declared untrue."

"Do you believe in reincarnation, Jean Paul?"

"Entirely. Without question. But, there is a complex pattern and a hidden purpose to living a complete sequence of physical lives. In England and in France we happily talk about the soul as though its meaning were clearly defined. It is the immortal nature of man and all living things. Will that do for a definition? In India we use the name Self to mean Soul. Don't be confused; it's the same 'thing'. Have you ever seen a matryoshka doll? They're made of wood and come from Russia and are usually misnamed babushka? You separate the halves and a smaller doll lives inside the larger and so on in a lessening decline to a minute centre."

Hari nodded. "There's a miniature baby in the middle. I've got one," he said, reluctant to say so. He'd called his babushka and there was a man inside, nevertheless, only girls had dolls.

"Good. Well, in my belief, the Soul or Self is at the centre of three bodies, garments, dolls if you will, that shield and protect it. The first layer is the physical body. That body lives in the fractured and divided world of day-to-day. We call that ever-changing world Maya. It is a world where the vast majority of people on the earth always live, can only live. It is a world in which we act and do. The word 'to do' in India is Karma. It is a collection of all a man's actions and, annoyingly, a man's Karma follows him from incarnation to incarnation. All the past actions of all our former lives accumulate and press upon us and we can only influence that short and temporary life that you and I are living now. What we do within our current life will have an effect of our next life but we will not witness it, nor account for that future."

"That doesn't seem fair," Hari protested.

"Why not?" Jean Paul was surprised at Hari's intensity.

"Well, how can I be held responsible for somebody else's wrongdoing?"

"Hold that thought, for a while. But add another. How can you claim credit for somebody else's goodness? Let me go back to my dolls. The second layer is called the astral body. The word is full of stars and mystery. This body lights up the physical body like electricity makes a bulb shine. The astral world is a strange sphere, a universe of light and colour. It is composed of forces so infinitesimal, they are finer than the atom. This is a world that vibrates with the energy of life. I suppose a modern scientist would call it the quantum world, that impossible-to-see reality that exists beneath existence and seems to live by rules all of its own, often defying our usual processes and understanding."

Certainly Jean Paul was defying Hari's level of understanding at that moment.

"You've heard us all chant the word 'Om' or 'Aum'?" Jean Paul continued, hoping to find a way to unravel these teasing ideas for Hari.

Hari nodded. He'd never dared to ask why. Perhaps he'd come to understand that strange groaning now.

"It is the same as 'Amen'. It is the 'Word'—with a capital 'W'—of the Bible. Because in the beginning, as the apostle John claims, was the 'Word' and the 'Word' was God and the word was 'Om'. It is the whispered voice of the Holy Ghost, the cosmic murmurings of all the speaking gods. It is the sound of God sighing and it exists in the astral body."

"The sound of God sighing," Hari repeated, delighted with the idea. This he might understand. He was tempted to say 'Om' out loud, to test its power.

"Then finally," Jean Paul concluded, wishing to finish his exposition neatly, "the third layer is the causal body. This is the last of the soul's coverings. It is a complex of thought and ideas, a coming together and uniting of the physical and astral bodies. It is in using the causal body that we step from the physical world of Maya through to the astral world and all vibratory realms, on into the pure world of spirit."

Hari was utterly confused but mesmerised by Jean Paul's enthusiastic explanation.

"This is very hard, Hari, but I want you to at least understand that my claim that Lunasha may be a saint was not flippant and it wasn't untutored and it is highly probable when pursued within the systems of my belief. The fact I persistently call her beggar-woman is not to belittle her but to guarantee the possibility of her spiritual perfection. Remember, all grand masters and enlightened beings usually reside in the physical body of a beggar. Tell me, Hari, did you catch her eye? Could you intercept her gaze? Would she look at you?"

"No. Even when she turned her face towards mine, her eyes didn't stop at me. They looked ..." he paused, "... elsewhere."

"She no longer sees the physical world," Jean Paul was keen to explain. "She knows that it is an illusion. She sees beyond it and feeds off the energies of the astral world. I also think that because of the obvious injustice of her plight that this might be her final incarnation. Each physical rebirth is karmically predetermined. I think many who lived in her past had led spiritually good lives. Her suffering is the final act in the purification of her soul. I think very soon Lunasha will be pure spirit. One, two more lives perhaps. It is a long spiritual journey, many thousands of incarnations perhaps, but I think her journey is nearly complete. Soon she will be pure spirit: ever existing, ever conscious, ever new joy. We should be happy for her, Hari, but not careless. In her physical body she cannot experience her soul. None of us can. And no matter how far removed from our awareness of the world, she does suffer. Let's find her a home. And let's work together to find a fit and proper context where she can live out the rest of her life."

"Thank you for your help, Jean Paul." Hari was quiet and subdued.

"Did I baffle you?" asked Jean Paul, a little disappointed.

"Yes. But it doesn't matter. I know what you meant; even if I didn't understand all that you said. I'm glad she may be a saint because I have never seen her as a woman, even when naked, whether dirty or clean. I think I realise now why she washes in both dirt and water."

CHAPTER ELEVEN
A Miracle

From the shade of the VIP line Hari could just make out the figure of Jean Paul. It was late afternoon but still so hot that everyone standing was restless and everyone sitting seemed trapped in a quiet torpor of concentration as they used whatever means they could to overcame the humming heat of the day. Hari had tried to attract Jean Paul's attention. Calling was out of the question and eager waving didn't seem apt, so he settled on an intense stare that he felt sure would eventually be felt.

It wasn't necessary. Jean Paul knew where Hari was and quietly prayed to Sai Baba, asking that his young and devoted friend be granted the privilege of seeing a miracle. He tried to explain in the silence of his asking that Hari needed no proof and could believe without wonder but thought such loyalty might deserve or may have earned a gift, a token that his presence had been noted.

Hari and his family had already been shuffled into the inner compound before Jean Paul finished his prayer. Hari thought his stare had failed. He needed Jean Paul's help. Where on earth was he to look to see a miracle?

Sai Baba stood amongst women. Far to the left in the courtyard, beyond the hall, he lingered where he often walked by. He blessed bowed heads and, diminutive in size, stooped to those smaller and listened to their prayers. Made meek by their culture, the Indian peasant women, elegant in their saris, beautiful beyond their means, were startled by this privilege and beamed or wept their delight undisguised. Baba didn't speak but patted head after head, allowed crawling fingers to clutch at the hem of his orange gown as it dragged slowly by. He stepped onto the marble of the Sai Ramesh floor and stopped. Looking into the gloom of the chosen humanity inside, he frowned as his eyes became used to the lesser light.

A tall and elegant figure, the bespectacled, white silk clad warden of the ashram, who always hovered importantly within earshot and need of Baba, stepped closer, uninvited. In his shadow was an elderly man, balding and pale, clearly ill and in pain. To hear this unsolicited request, Baba turned his head away and the warden whispered into the black halo of wispy hair above Baba's shoulder. With a barely perceptible nod of acceptance, Baba turned as the warden bowed, striding carefully backwards and revealing the already kneeling object of his whispered concern.

Baba did not move. The kneeling, ailing man shuffled slowly forward, his head held high but his eyes deferentially low. Close enough, Baba signalled, and pointed to the floor. A painful bowing, a kissing of a toe, a gentle lifting and a hand encouraged to be held outstretched. Then it happened.

Jean Paul sought Hari who was correctly staring at Baba's hand.

High above the man's upturned head, Baba spun his wrist. He flicked his fingers against his own resisting thumb as if playing unseeable, silent castanets. Then, He lowered his hand with thumb and fingers coming to a delicate point until level with the waiting sufferer's face. Suddenly, inevitably, a gentle rain of grey ashen dust trickled and fell from around Baba's fingers into the waiting palm beneath. The tearful recipient, overcome, licked his palm free of the ash, always staring at Baba, as if for permission to eat. But Baba had already glided away. He flicked each finger in turn, from little to index, against his thumb, as if clearing away, cleaning off, the sticky residues of the miraculous vibhuti ash.

... a gentle rain of grey ashen dust trickled and fell from around Baba's fingers

Hari had seen it all.

Standing just inside the hall, back-lit by the courtyard sun, all the movements of Baba's hands, and sudden appearance of the trickling dust, had been clear, obvious, undeniable. Hari had seen a miracle.

Baba walked to the central aisle, cast a glance over his shoulder to the right where Hari and his family sat, lingered in a serious stare directed at no obvious object in the hall and waited, as if listening. Whatever diverting thing he saw or inaudible sound he heard seemed to distract and annoy him. He reached to swat an invisible fly with the swish of a wrist still held close to his body, turned, and walked purposefully down the central aisle. He stopped in the area reserved each day for his own students, from his own university. Relaxing a moment, the boys cleared a pathway that Baba followed and stood in their midst. He was lit from all directions by a dozen flashlights as he posed for the only cameras allowed inside the hall. The students would develop and then sell their photographs the following morning to any of fifty eager traders in these rare, close images. Many clever foreigners, hiding 'not-allowed' cameras with magical film and intricate lenses, had tried to photograph Baba without this permission. They tell stories that on developing their stolen pictures the space where Baba had stood was often found to be empty, or if a person was visible, the image was blurred beyond recognising.

Baba stopped the flashes of light and pointed across the students' space.

Diagonally, his chosen route avoided all waiting pilgrims and he arrived, unexpectedly, at the foot of the wrong stairs, or at least, so it seemed, for scurrying attendants quickly emerged to arrange and rearrange. By the time Baba had arrived, his throne was ready to be sat on.

Sitting, he sighed.

Afterwards, at the Sai Deep Café, Hari's musing on the source of Baba's sadness was overcome by his excitement at the miracle he had seen. He wanted to share it, excused himself from the family group, went in search of Jean Paul but found Borg instead.

"My young adamant friend, please, come and take tea with me." A smiling Borg waved Hari towards his table in the Indian Café, a native rival for Sai Deep, and mercifully free of Europeans, claimed Borg.

"Aren't you from Europe?" asked Hari.

"Only geographically. I was making a spiritual distinction. I consider my home to be Tibet. I have spent much of my life in a monastery there."

"What do you do in a monastery in Tibet? Thank you." Hari's tea had arrived. The service here was excellent.

"What do I do? It's more a question of what they do to me. For several thousand years the monks of the mountains have thought about death. Have you ever wondered why human beings grow old? Of course not, you're too young, barely a foetus. Would it surprise you to learn that it's not actually necessary? Well? Would it?"

"Er . . . yes." Hari hesitated.

"Does nobody ever talk to you? You don't appear to have picked up the knack of conversation. It's a little like tennis. I serve you a few words and if there's a question mark at the end of them then it's your turn to serve a few words back. Do you think you can master that?"

"Yes. I'm sorry, Borg. No, nobody does talk to me like this. But."

"But?"

"It's sometimes hard to know if you are really asking a question or whether you're going to answer it yourself. It would be rude to interrupt, wouldn't it?"

"The two words you need are 'rhetoric' and 'tone'. You should recognise a rhetorical question, that indeed needs no answer, by the tone of its asking. Clear?"

"Yes." Of course it wasn't. Hari envied the Indians their ability to nod their heads sideways, meaning neither yes nor no, agreement nor dissent, just a signal that they are paying attention, without opinion.

"Where was I?"

"Growing old."

"Not any more. Did you know that age is a decision of the body?"

"No."

"That each cell suddenly decides to end its own life?"

"No."

"That death is unnecessary? Now you may express wonder."

"Thank you. I find it hard to believe." Hari sipped his tea seriously.

"Yes. So did I. But, never underestimate monkish wisdom. These amazing men have developed medicines and ointments that persuade the body's cells to switch on again, and if you start early enough, not to switch off at all. I was a late starter. Nevertheless, for the past twenty years my face has been getting younger. Unfortunately, other parts of me have been ageing at the normal rate, so soon, I may have to face the prospect that bits of me will actually have died, whilst others are enjoying a second adolescence. Somewhat unnerving. If only I had started earlier. My principal healer is a hundred and fifty years old, and even he looks a little startled at times. He hasn't got a single wrinkle. Incredible. He puts it down to happiness, Oriental style. You know, living in a cave with absolutely no possessions and being endlessly thankful for it. I'm afraid I get a little bored, and at the risk of a suddenly ageing extremity, I have to escape. You see I also happen to know that happiness is a five star hotel. I have these urgent needs to be decadent and pampered. It is so ridiculously cheap here, that I decide to pretend to be obscenely rich for a few days. I demand air conditioning and a chauffeur driven car. When it comes to enjoyable living, it is not the Maharishi but the Maharaja who got it right. Well, well." Borg sighed. "But there is always a price to pay. Every time I indulge, some unguarded part of me starts dying."

"Hari! Hari!"

"Ah. Your guru is calling."

Hari liked to think of Jean Paul as being his teacher and was excited to have been found.

"I saw it! Jean Paul, I saw the miracle!"

"I'm so happy for you, Hari. It was out in the open. Easy for you to see. Swami has favoured you. Sometimes, the vibhuti is made and given so quickly, so privately, it is hard to see. I am happy that he has heard and honoured you."

"Tut! Tut! Tut!" Borg expressed his disapproval, but still smiled. "Would you little worshippers like tea? I feel bountiful today and may even buy you cake. Yes. It is decided." He clicked his fingers above his head. "Three teas and cake!"

"I haven't finished with this one yet."

"Soda?"

"Please."

Click!

"And a soda!"

"Won't we have one too many?"

66

"Someone will come to drink it."
And someone did. Immediately.
"Welcome good Doctor."
"Borg."

CHAPTER TWELVE
A Doctor

A round, boyish, Indian head of fifty something years, with a prep' school haircut and gentle brown eyes that seemed to have experienced far more  than the smooth cheeks beneath them, glanced across the table. Borg introduced: "Jean Paul, my wise young friend," and "Hari, his even younger friend, who I fear is becoming wise."

"I am most pleased to meet you." And the Doctor's delicate bow as he sat signalled a true interest. "Might I order some tea?"

"It is already ordered. See Hari, I also do miracles." Borg raised a single eyebrow.

"A devotee?" The Doctor spoke quietly through little lips as if sipping his words. He seemed most genteel, relaxed, with the social confidence of the highborn and the intellectual confidence of the highly educated.

The Doctor

"Hari was excited to see Swami perform a vibhuti miracle at darshan this morning," explained Jean Paul.

"It was marvellous. Did you see it? Were you there?" Hari showed his excitement.

"I no longer go to darshan. But certainly, I have seen Sathya perform this act many times."

"I fear the good Doctor shares my scepticism when it comes to miracles, Hari. He is a man of science."

"Medicine?" asked Hari.

"No. I cure minds not bodies," the Doctor explained.

"Is Borg a patient of yours?" Hari asked, in all innocence.

Everybody laughed, and Hari blushed.

"Yes!" claimed Jean Paul.

"No!" declared Borg and the Doctor together.

"I don't need a mind-doctor," Borg stated firmly.

"Yes, you do," Jean Paul contradicted.

"What on earth for?" Borg looked pained.

"Because you are crazy," explained the Doctor gently.

"Then, so is God," asserted Borg.

"Precisely," the Doctor concluded.

"But I saw it," interrupted Hari.

"I'm sorry, Hari. What did you see?" The Doctor gave Hari half of his attention.

"The miracle. I saw Baba make ash from the air. It came from nowhere. He created it from nothing."

"I ask you again, what did you see?" The Doctor was patient and gentle in his questioning.

Hari didn't really follow, so simply repeated himself.

"I saw a miracle."

"May we analyse this? You saw a man rub his fingers and a fine dust fell from them. Might you have seen a trick? A sleight of hand? A man who has painted a translucent suspension onto his fingers, an invisible varnish which, when released by friction, that is, the contrary motion of two fingers rubbing, degenerates into a fine powder? Might you have witnessed this? Might my description be equally valid and probably more acceptable?"

Hari had needed a moment to think before he replied: "But Sai Baba is not a man, He is a God. He doesn't need to trick people. Only ordinary men need to trick each other."

"You are right, Borg, your young friend is becoming wise." The Doctor smiled beyond Hari towards Jean Paul. "Let us assume, therefore, that we are dealing with an avatar, although of the sixty-four definable characteristics, I fear many are lacking. But, let us make that assumption. I would have problems with the notion of 'creation'. You claim that, and I quote, 'He created it, from nothing'—'it' being that most commonplace of substances, ash. Might it rather be that the substance, the 'it', already existed and that Sai Baba merely transported 'it' to where you saw 'it'? There have been examples of 'apportage', that is the correct term, that I find more acceptable than 'creation'." The Doctor spoke in measured tones that reflected the precision of his thoughts.

"Baba does not agree with you, good Doctor," offered Jean Paul. "He said, 'What I will, happens; what I order, materialises.' And more categorically, 'I do not transfer. I totally create.' So, he denies your 'apportage' theories. And, anyway, ash is one thing, but what about the rings and watches?"

"You've seen Him make watches?" asked a wide-eyed Hari.

"Only proprietary brands, Hari, " offered Borg. "He seems to have a particular fondness for 'Seiko'. Rather down market, I think. And as for copyright, well, that's a whole new can of worms, which as far as I know, he doesn't materialise. Don't you find the whole business rather tawdry, Jean Paul?"

"When the words are in your mouth, yes." Jean Paul was saddened by Borg's cynicism.

"But, why do it?" Borg asked.

"He has said, 'This is evidence of my divinity. For me, this is a kind of calling card to convince people of my love for them.'"

"But, cheap watches and silver rings?" Borg persisited.

"They may seem cheap to you. To the poor they have great value," claimed Jean Paul.

"But he only gives ash to the poor. It's the rich Westerners who get the solid goodies." Borg saw he'd found a flaw in his friend's argument.

"Of course." Apparently not.

"What do you mean, of course?" Borg expected further explanation.

"They need a special approach. The material minded have the greatest need of material comfort. Baba is not a fool. He calls such objects 'trinkets'. He knows their essential value and also how they are valued. If someone is wearing a ring Baba materialised for them, a ring that will grow with their fingers and often changes its inscription, then in times of trouble they can feel the grip of the ring and the instant memory of Baba. Those who wear Baba's 'trinkets' created from the air above their heads gain a continuous sense of security from them."

Reassured by a momentary silence, Jean Paul hoped he'd convinced Borg.

"But, might it not be argued, Jean Paul, that miracles and wonder workings are spiritually useless, mere entertainments, digressions from a serious search for God?" The Doctor had entered the argument.

"Christ performed miracles." Hari offered, thoughtfully. "Do you think that Christ was a charlatan, too, Doctor?"

"I don't think Sai Baba is a charlatan, Hari, and I certainly would never denigrate your Jesus Christ. But, as I remember, he was a reluctant user of miracles and only resorted to the miraculous as a last and disappointed resort, to point the secular minded towards God."

Hari wanted to explain that Jesus Christ wasn't his to defend or criticize, but he feared he might be questioned about his beliefs and he wasn't sure he could answer. He'd been taught to compare religions at school, to hold them as equals in a spiritual democracy. It was expedient. There were many different cultural groups in his school. The majority claimed to be Christian but didn't know why and never went to church. The Moslems were a significant minority in every class and were more assiduous followers. They seemed to know more certainly what they believed, so did the small number of Sikhs and Jews. Hari thought being Hindu was only marginally more significant than being pagan and those with no beliefs at all overwhelmed the numbers of his community. He began to listen once more to the discussion.

"Doctor, you especially must recognise that it takes a particularly sophisticated mind to love an abstraction," continued Jean Paul.

"Possibly, possibly, possibly." The Doctor's lips grew thinner as his thoughtful pauses grew wider. "But, whether we like it or not, a consciousness of God will necessarily have more than a hint of the abstract because its very nature lies outside the range of our psychological experiences. Isn't that the very point?"

"Maybe, Doctor, but we can only know God with our humanity." Jean Paul frowned.

"Surely, that is our limitation?" suggested the Doctor.

"It is as we are," Jean Paul concluded.

"True. But, shouldn't God-awareness tempt us to something better than we are?" The Doctor looked perplexed.

"Not better than, just other than. Thus!" Borg burst into the conversation by clanking his pocket-sized skull onto the table.

"What on earth is that, Borg?" complained the Doctor, turning his head half-sideways in melodramatic disgust, sniffing "Ugh!" and gesturing the pathetic object away.

"It doesn't smell. Not any more. But it is humanity." Borg prodded the troubling object through one eye and set it spinning on the axis of its own half-jaw bone. "To this favour we must come." Now balanced on the end of a finger, Borg turned the skull to look at each at the table in turn. "This is all humanity can manage. Premature death. And what died in there?" Borg placed the skull next to his nose and peered through an eye socket. "Hello! Anyone there? No. All that died was an 'I'. Excuse the pun. I wonder if this little creature was old enough to have a sense of itself. A sense of its separateness, that wonderful moment when 'I' is born and God dies. 'I!' 'I!' 'I!' 'Aye!' Such a devious thing is 'I'. Talk about the tail wagging the dog. 'I' has convinced us all, inside our own heads, the only space in which we think, that it is all of existence. But it isn't, it knows it, it fears the rest of consciousness ever finding out its awful secret, that 'I' lied because 'I'm' not all that is. So, to make sure you leave it alone, so it doesn't get demoted to just a part of knowing as opposed to all knowing, it creates a beautiful story. The story is called God, the Divine. But the mind's God, 'I''s creation is totally harmless, a bosom pal, always ready to answer our own prayers. 'I' has made a personal genie with endless wishes, every one granted and no demands in return. The whole thing sucks! It's for the fairies. It keeps the whole Divinity bit trapped inside the head, so it remains manageable. Garbage! This parental God stuff is for children. To step from 'I' to 'That' is a risky business. It takes nerve. It takes courage. It's scary. You have to let go of all you thought was certain." Borg let the skull plop into his lap. "People who try for a spiritual life are brave, courageous beings. They are not scrub-cheeked softies with happy-clappy grins but heroes with a sad-seriousness to their beings."

Hari was lost and not a little afraid. He didn't understand Borg's words but reacted to his passion and apparent anger. He wanted to leave, think his own thoughts. His mind was walking towards the bridge on the edge of the village, that peaceful place where Hari felt at ease. Would it be rude to just up and go there? He paused, ready. The Doctor's eyes focussed elsewhere and Jean Paul, as so often, looked inwards. It was left to Borg to break the silence he had created.

"Well, that's how I see it anyway. More tea? I'm being rich today."

"Not everyone can be a hero, Borg," offered Jean Paul, with a quiet assertion and Hari's nodded agreement.

"One in twenty," offered the Doctor.

"So precise a number," mused Jean Paul.

"Yes, so it seems."

"Who says?" asked a rather surly Borg.

"A number of men wiser than me. Oh, and the whole of the Chinese and Japanese and Far Eastern nations. Apparently, during the Korean War, the American prisoners were interrogated, the one in twenty removed for especial care, whilst the remaining majority never needed to be guarded. Oddly disappointing, isn't it?" The Doctor looked despondent.

"Maybe not. It merely shows that it is normal to be ordinary and that the rule should not be judged by the exception. For most people, religious worship calls for a personal God. They cannot pray to 'Nothingness'. And miraculous powers over the physical world are their proof of a God. I guess that most of us seem like children from your great age, Borg, and that it probably is intellectually unsound to seek for the absolute in this relative world of Nature, but the barely educated peasants that flock here are happy to love their physically manifest God." Jean Paul hoped he'd convinced Borg. It seemed he had.

"So am I, Jean Paul." Borg was sincere.

"But they do it without question," Jean Paul felt compelled to add.

"That I cannot do. That is my nature." Borg was apologetic.

"And to a lesser extent mine." So was the Doctor.

"We agree, good Doctor." Borg offered the Doctor his gnarled hand in recognition of a rare truce.

"I have no choice but to offer doubts, Jean Paul. I have seen so many changes in Sathya." The Doctor was thoughtful and fell silent.

"Doctor?"

"Yes, Hari?"

"Why don't you say Sai Baba like the rest of us. Don't you think He is real?"

"Oh, he is real, Hari, very real. He is my friend . . . was."

"You truly know Him?"

"Yes, I do. That is why I call him Sathya, because that was his proper name before, before all this." The Doctor waved at the ashram and its teeming life. "I have known Sathya Sai Baba for over thirty, no, probably now forty years." The very length of time seemed to sadden him. "When I first met him, he lived in such squalor that my father would not allow me to stay in his compound. In those days there was no such thing as 'interviews' or 'darshan', Sathya Sai Baba would talk to me ten even twenty times every day for as long as we both wanted. He was my friend and I loved him for that friendship. He became my teacher, my spiritual guru, and my guide. I was so happy then."

"What changed Him, Doctor? Did you just grow apart gradually?" asked Hari.

"No. The change was sudden and deliberate. Even in those days many foreigners would visit the otherwise insignificant village of Puttaparthi to be in the presence of this powerful, spiritual being. In 1968 an American woman born in Russia arrived. Almost immediately the whole God Business began. Suddenly Sathya was 'Avatar'. He had never claimed that status before, in fact, he vigorously denied such exaggerations of his powers, at least, that is how he saw it then. And suddenly, there is this. A huge, pointless hospital. Indians don't suffer from heart disease; it is a Westerner's problem. The region needed clinics to pull splinters from toes, not vast theatres for open-heart surgery. Any Indian that is knowledgeable enough to diagnose that he has a heart disease is likely to be wealthy enough to pay for his own surgery. And there are hotels, an airport, a university, just there." He pointed. "I suppose it would be hypocritical to criticise that. I benefited from its existence."

"You went to His university?" Hari was amazed by the Doctor's revelations.

"Yes. I was one of his students, one of his protégés." The Doctor smiled, remembering

"Has Sai Baba personally claimed Godhead?"

"Why do you ask, Jean Paul?"

"I just wondered if others had done so, supposedly in his name. For instance, Christ never claimed that he was the Son of God. Nowhere in the New Testament does he ever say this. The nearest he gets is when asked if he is, he replies 'Who do men say that I am?' I wondered if it was something like that?"

"Possibly, in the beginning. But I fear he loves all this now. He has become trapped by his own success and enshrined in his own fame."

"Isn't Baba God, then?" asked Hari, nervously. He already respected the Doctor.

"Baba is very, very special, Hari. I love him with all my heart. He is more than Man, but possibly less than God. He is more than the eye can see; more than the mind can think; he must be shown respect. Go to him. Learn, but you are entitled to keep your wits about you. For me he was a means, but I have found it hard to believe that he is the end. If he is that for you, then I honour that, but please excuse my sadness. You have found a God. I have lost a friend."

CHAPTER THIRTEEN
Jack

Hari was holding his breath. It was near to the end of afternoon darshan and Baba stood right next to him. There had been no spaces near his grandfather's seat so he had been tacked onto the Iranian party with the deformed man and green kerchiefs. Immediately to his left sat a large, heavy man with awkward, bending legs that stretched further forward than most officials allowed. His big toe bore a startling resemblance to the sacred toe of Baba that peeped out from the edge of his tunic. There were no more than a few inches between them. Hari wondered if they would touch.

Today's tunic was different. The usual iridescent orange had been changed for a less radiant red, a deep claret colour that seemed to absorb rather than emit light. Hari peered up at Baba's face. It was serious, concentrated with a deep, deep frown that made eagles' wings of his eyebrows and an angry stoop of his nose. Hari tried to follow Baba's gaze, but the eyes didn't finally focus. What were they seeing? Could he ignore faces and stare in at the souls? Why had he changed his gown? Did it mean a change of mood or was the other one dirty? Hari wondered how many he had and if any of the now familiar faces at the river did Baba's washing. Then he blushed, ashamed of such domestic thoughts when God stood at his feet.

Minute and almost inaudible, he caught the puttering sound of whispered words. He glimpsed the man to his left; saw lips moving, eyes glazed with staring, not at Baba's eyes, they were elsewhere (and who would dare to look into them?) but at the centre of Baba. What was being said? Hari stared, fascinated, as the large lips, sticking with nervousness and the urgency of the moment, quickened to finish as Baba budged and inched backwards. The lips stopped, incomplete, Hari guessed, for the mouth gaped without a word. The ever-attending warden reached to relieve Baba of a bulging pack of letters, absentmindedly, but no doubt purposefully plucked from the thousands of stretching hands. There was a fumble and Baba let the letters drop to the floor. He half-stooped and said in clearly audible words:

"Oh God!"

He straightened, left the warden and the other attendants to the task of retrieving the scattered messages and turned towards his throne. Hari laughed. He instantly stifled his noise, hopefully trapped in cupping hands and a mouthful of ashram suit. But the whispering man to his left noticed Hari's noise and winked in collusion. He opened his eyes wide and nodded towards the retreating Baba in immediate confirmation of what they had really heard.

Darshan over, Hari stood.

"Hey! You up there! Yes, you! Small, helpful, young man!"

It was the voice of the man to his left, the one with the noticeable toes and the whispered prayers. Hari had lingered, standing for a few moments after the long sitting, but oddly elated and inwardly chuckling at Baba's happy lapse.

"Excuse me! Have you forgotten me?"

"Sorry." Hari looked down and was greeted by a huge grin that smiled upwards with an American accent.

"I'm still down here and I'm stuck. Could you help me up?"

The almost round face was chubby and comfortable. The happy corners of the smiling mouth looked as if they ought to be chewing cigars, weren't but probably had. Every bit of the growing old body looked as if it had taken every opportunity for both pleasure and pain. It carried the sorrows as sad lines around the eyes, lines that vanished in a smile. And the happier moments as growing pounds round the proudly firm waist.

Hari knelt and looked at his problem. As bald as the Buddha, of similar shape and squatting on a cushion crushed to invisibility, how was he to help?

"If you don't mind my saying so, you could start by fully straightening my legs. I know they're there. I can see them. But, I haven't felt them since . . ." He pulled back the sagging sleeve of his brand new but already grubby ashram tunic and stared deliberately at his watch. "Since three-thirty, and that's ..." The watch strap broke. "... the end of that. Still, it hung on valiantly. He continued to read the time from his dangling watch, like a nurse taking a pulse. "Two hours since."

Jack

"All right. I'll help." Hari lifted the foot on top, with its magnificent yellow nails and widespread joints, and very carefully creaked it and then the ankle and then the very reluctant knee, nearly straight. As Hari reached for the other leg his hand was gripped in a firm shake that grew in wavelength until the whole of Hari's arm was waggling in time with the shaking.

"This is kind of intimate for strangers. We ought to be acquainted. I'm doing all right and my name's Jack. I'm an American from New York but living in Europe. Now it's your turn."

"I'm Hari." He was a little out of breath. There was nothing wrong with Jack's grip or his ability to shake. "From Birmingham. That's in England."

"It's really good to meet you, Harry. Now, I suggest you bend this other leg. No! Ow! It won't go that way. Towards my chin. Ow! Say, it does reach. Okay. Let's go for it!"

Hari stood astride the stretched-out leg and let Jack hold on to his lowered shoulder. By gripping tight biceps and elbow, with a timely stamp on the disastrously sliding cushion, Jack was prized upright. He stood, tottered, wobbled, grinned and said, "Gee, you're strong. Do you work out?"

"No. I . . ." Hari was flattered, embarrassed and knew for certain that he liked Jack. Probably, very much.

"Would you mind if I stayed leaning for a while?" Jack leaned. "Say if you would. I won't mind."

"No, please, lean." Hari was happy to oblige.

"Thank you. You see I'm fine once I get going. I kind of launch myself in a controlled stumble. I'm pretty efficient at it. But right now, I'm not certain there's any blood in my legs at all." Looking up instead of down, Hari saw into Jack's huge grin and was amused by the carefully arranged missing teeth. Turn and turn about, cheeky gaps of tooth-space-tooth looked like mini battlements or the carefully arranged stones of a dental Stonehenge.

"How long have you been here, Harry?" Jack pronounced Hari's name like all his friends at school in England. In India, somehow, it was clear his name ended in an 'i', not a 'y'.

"A few days now."

"Well, today is my first and I consider myself lucky to have made your acquaintance."

Hari was quiet. Somehow Jack made him feel important. And, he said nice things about him. Only his mother ever did that.

"Am I too heavy for you, young man?" They were shuffling across Sai Ramesh Hall.

"No. No, you're not."

"Then, why so serious?"

"Are you important, Jack?" Jack laughed.

"Why on earth do you ask me that?"

"You just seem important." Jack laughed again.

"Hell, no son. If I was, then I am no longer."

"What were you in the real world?"

"Many things. But, quickly, tell me, what is so 'unreal' about this place? Isn't this a part of the real world?"

"No." Hari lowered his eyes.

"Why not?" Jack was intrigued.

"Because God is here." Hari spoke in a respectful whisper, not that he feared being heard, but he didn't want his new friend—yes, he was a friend, thought Hari—he didn't want his new friend to embarrass himself.

"Yep." Jack nodded his thoughtful head. "I'll buy that. It's sure as Hell why I came."

"Is that why you stopped being what you were?"

"I guess so, Harry. There comes a time when only God will do."

Hari nodded in agreement.

"You've felt that too?" Jack smiled at the shared seriousness.

"Yes. Not just for me. For my grandfather and my father. And, I suppose, my mother as well. But she . . . "

"Are they all here?" Jack looked, rapidly, in several directions. "I'd sure like to meet them."

"They're here somewhere, probably with Grandfather. He has a house here. Two, really. One he's building and one he rents. He'll be with my father. They keep very busy. They have worries to share."

"What kind of worries are those, Harry? "

Hari sighed.

"Hey. There's no need to tell. Some other time, maybe. I'm real nosy. Excuse me." Jack patted Hari on the supporting shoulder. He wobbled and they both giggled."

"No, I would like to tell you, Jack," said Hari: "It's illness and business. Grandfather says he's dying and he needs God's help with his business. I didn't realise that God knew about such things, but I suppose if He knows everything then He must know about business as well."

"Guess so, Harry, but you might have thought that death's a wee bit more important than business. There's no real use for money in your coffin."

"They burn them over here. Grandfather is Hindu. He is an Indian. I'm sorry, I didn't explain."

"I kinda guessed."

"You are wise."

"Soon, I hope." Jack knew not to contradict Hari's simple statement. "But, I guess paper money rots as well as burns. Oooh!" Jack winced with a sudden pain. He had been trying to push his bare left foot towards where he thought he'd left his trainers. "You won't miss them. They're red. And size twelve. My feet aren't that big, but I like the space."

"Do you need to sit down, Jack?" asked an anxious Hari.

"No. Not wise. I may never get up again. Bad knees, bad back and really, really bad backside. You see, there's plenty of ballast here," Jack wobbled his bottom through his disguising, baggy, white trousers, "but I swear my bones are bruised from sitting on that marble floor."

"Couldn't you have a chair?"

"I don't think so. I'm not ill."

"Isn't that why you came?"

"No. Not that. I'm just old and curious and maybe just a little afraid."

"Of God?"

"No. Not of God. I'm afraid of seventy."

"Seventy what?" Hari's imagination flared.

"Seventy years."

"Oh." And was extinguished.

"I do believe they are my shoes." Alone and at right angles to each other, the huge white and red trainers refused to co-operate with Jack's probing big toe.

"Would you?" Hari knelt and guided each foot into its mightily cushioned shoe.

"Don't bother with the tying. Would you just stuff the laces inside, somewhere? I find it easier to flap. Then, when it's time to, I can just kick them off without needing to bend."

Jack took hold of Hari's wrist and looked deep into his eyes.

"Thank you for your help, young man. You've been kind to a very awkward body. Goodbye now." Jack took a deep breath, spread his arms as if embracing as invisible dancing partner, leaned forward far enough to begin to tumble, then stamped his right foot firmly on the ground. He was away and already waving over his shoulder but not turning.

"Goodbye!"

Hari watched him leave. After a moment's thought Hari shouted: "Jack! Jack!"

He ran to follow.

"Jack, there's something I must ask you!"

CHAPTER FOURTEEN
Jack, a bag and a train fare

Jack had made surprisingly quick progress into the bazaar. He had slowed to negotiate a bridge of wooden planks that crossed the rubbish ditch when Hari caught up to him.

"Jack! Jack! It's me, Hari."

Jack hadn't turned.

"Hello, Harry. Just look into that pit. I swear some of it is moving. It just might be alive. I want to be certain I'm not going to end up down there. Is there another route?" He pronounced it 'rowt'.

"There is, but all the ones into the bazaar are the same. It's safe. Let me." Hari wriggled by Jack, who clutched Hari's arm as he was let by. "Take care."

Hari strode across. Came back, walked to the middle, backwards, and grinned as he gently bowed the plank into a bouncing rhythm. The end behind his back slithered an inch and Hari, suddenly serious, scurried to Jack's side.

"Well, it was safe. Shall I lead?"

"Go on. I'll trust to you." Hari stepped forward with Jack's outstretched right hand resting for balance on Hari's shoulder. The rhythm of the gentle shuffle ended abruptly as Jack stamped onto solid earth.

"Hah! Made it! Thank you, Harry. Goodbye!" And off he went.

"Jack. There's . . ."

"Can't stop. This should see me straight to my room. Do you want to come along? It's through there." Jack pointed under an archway to a dirt track that led to a half-built white house with wooden scaffolding holding up an incomplete roof and over twenty leaning workers, resting in readiness for sudden activity.

"I'm not sure whether these guys are the builders or the building. It looks like a human pack of cards. Did you ever see so many overseers? Can you spot the worker? This is mine."

Jack's room was just beyond a pile of wet, red cement. It was on the edge of what would be a courtyard of a dozen or more rooms. As was clearly obvious, they weren't complete, despite being fully let.

"Apparently, I was really lucky to get this. God knows what bad luck brings. Wait. Wait. The key's here somewhere." Jack probed his pocket as deep as the knees whilst Hari nudged the huge padlock that held shut the already rusting bolt and obligingly it clicked open. Hari smiled his apology; they both shrugged their shoulders.

Jack's room was a mess. There was no attempt at order. A giant canvas bag with endless compartments spilt useful, improbable, and incongruous contents all over the beds—helpfully, there were three—the floor, the open-curtained hanging areas, the front and backs of open cupboard doors, and now Hari.

"Could you hold this a moment? And this? And? You know, Harry, I need a bag of some sort. This lot kinda scrunches up my pockets." There had been: a camera, extra films, a micro-cassette recorder, two guide books, diaries, an address book, a bottle of water, a wallet, a pair of pliers.

"Why do you ...?"

A device for phoning the answer machine, an orange . . .

"This place is chaotic, already." Jack nodded, wisely.

"How long have you been here?"

"Since this morning. You need to know, Harry, in case you missed it, I'm a bit of a slob. It seems that objects are beyond my control. I've become reconciled to it over the years. I have never lost anything; it's just that things, especially things that think they're really important, like airplane tickets and driver's licences, keep hiding from me. They think it's a game but it can be very frustrating. You learn to be philosophical. Things that get lost can just as easily get found. You just have to be patient. See! What was I saying?" Jack grinned in triumph as he jangled the keys to his padlock, retrieved from somewhere unknown to both of them.

Jack slumped on the bed, gaping for breath for a moment in the overwhelming heat.

"Is it always this hot?"

"I'm afraid so. When you first come it's all you talk about. I don't think people from Birmingham can really understand what this kind of hot is. Not until you're in it. I kept thinking it might go away, especially at night time."

"It doesn't?"

"No."

"Not even in the middle of the night?"

"No."

"Hell." Jack seemed truly concerned.

"Is that a problem for you, Jack?"

"Well, I don't know, we'll see. I have some medication. It may be a problem. But where do you get off with all this sweat?"

Hari giggled.

"It's horrible, isn't it? I kept wriggling at first, trying to stop my clothes sticking to my back. Father bought us all ashram suits. They're so thin that you hardly know you're wearing anything. But even a nice clean one, first thing after your shower, sticks like more skin in seconds. Yuck!" And Hari wriggled inside his newly recognised stickiness. "You just accept it after a while."

"Okay." Jack smiled. "Shall we get that bag?" Jack looked carefully at Hari. "Give me a pull?"

"Yes."

"What's on your mind?" Jack stopped looking to give Hari the space to think his answer in.

"What were you whispering to Sai Baba?" Hari's own voice tapered to a nervous whisper.

"Could you hear that?"

"Yes. I didn't mean to. I mean I wasn't listening. It's just that it sounded important."

"It was really kinda intimate, Harry. Do I have to tell you?"

"Of course not. I'm sorry. Please forgive me. I've been very rude."

"No. No. No. Hey. You come sit here. Clear some of this mess, that's it. You sit here." Hari did.

"We're friends, huh?"

"Yes, please."

"Shake on it?" They do.

"Okay. I can't swear it's word by word because I was pretty nervous and just overwhelmed but I wanted to know where I should go next. I don't mean new projects or new ventures, I meant, what could I best do with the rest of my life for the best. I've been lucky. I've been successful. I've been loved. I've had family, wonderful children. And, I just wondered how I could kinda say thank you for all this and do something half-useful in return."

"You didn't want anything from Him?"

"No. Just some advice, a nudge in the right direction."

"Did He nudge you? Your toes nearly met."

"The hell they did!" Jack laughed. "Is that right?"

"Yes. Didn't you know?"

"No. I had no idea." Jack was chuckling.

"Did Baba say anything?"

"Yes." Jack was oddly calm.

"He did?" Hari was excited.

"Yes. Not a voice. It wasn't words. It's hard to describe. As I sat there, at his feet, it was as though the ordinary physical barriers between two human bodies disappeared. I 'merged' with him. That's the only word that works 'merged'. I've tried others. That's the one. It felt easy and natural. I just felt a part of him, his being. I felt let into his presence. It was a good feeling, Harry. So calm, but very rich, very intense. So. Shall we go shopping?"

"Is that it?"

"Kinda undramatic, aren't I? It's not deliberate. I'm great at drama. I can make a crisis out of next to nothing and involve the whole neighbourhood in seconds. But this wasn't like that. It was like a huge, warm hug. I felt reassured and I felt welcome. And that's a good feeling."

"What are you to do?"

"That I'm not sure of, but I do know that I'm moving me the right way."

Jack was driving the Indian traders mad.

"No. You're not listening. I want the bag with the picture of Baba printed on it but I don't want this white bag, I want that orange bag but with this picture."

"But, orange bag has Shiva picture. Very beautiful picture."

"I don't want Shiva. I want Baba."

"Here is Baba. Beautiful bag."

"But it's white."

"Oh yes. Very white."

"But I want orange. Okay. Okay. That's enough." The Indian trader beamed. Now the object of purchase was decided, the real discussion could begin. The price. But Jack confused the issue by leaving.

"Where you going?" The trader was lost.

"To find the bag I want."

"Wait! Wait! It is coming. Very soon. They will make bag in twenty seconds time. Please wait." He exaggerated. It took thirty seconds, but there it was: an orange, cotton shoulder bag, a flimsy sack, with a picture of Sai Baba in the centre.

"How much?"

"Fifty rupees."

"Okay."

Now Jack had really confused the issue.

"You will pay fifty rupees?" Two or three skinny traders shuffled close to overhear.

"If that's what it costs."

"But is not fifty rupees a lot of money?"

"Well, you tell me. How much should I give you?"

"We will offer twenty five rupees," interrupted Hari, trying to be helpful.

"Oh! Not possible. This is a beautiful bag, specially commissioned. I must have forty rupees."

"But, I offered fifty. Why is he so cross?"

"It's how he makes his living, Jack. It's no fun unless you argue."

"Thirty!"

"Thirty five!"

"We accept." Hari lifted a crumpled fifty-rupee note from Jack's open palm. Given the new bag in exchange, Jack wandered happily away. "Tell him to keep the change."

It took several minutes and umpteen false starts to cross the busy dirt road. Jangling, whistling, hooting vehicles jostled to transport the day-tripping pilgrims back to their homes in Bangalore and beyond.

"Excuse me." A barely audible voice came from the shadow of a roadside tree.

"Excuse me!" It was more insistent as it feared Jack and Hari had passed by.

"Who spoke?" asked Hari, peering into the gloom.

"That was me. Excuse me." A small Indian, dressed like a businessman in lightweight suit, probably short-sleeved shirt and neatly knotted tie stepped warily into the early evening sunlight.

"I have a difficulty and I was told."

"Told what?" asked Jack, his New York accent tinged with aggression.

"I was told to stop you. It is your penance for not recognising Swami."

"I don't understand you, fella."

"That was Swami." His nervous, small hand pointed to the retreating, neat boot of a maroon Jaguar car. "In that car. That was Swami."

"In a Jaguar?" asked a surprised Hari.

"The big red car. It was Swami and you did not see him and he said I was to tell you that you didn't acknowledge him and that in penance for that absent-mindedness you were to help me. It is what Swami said. I have to." He seemed genuinely nervous, almost tearful, and hugely embarrassed.

"I have difficulty. I am separated from my family. They have all my money and I cannot return with them. To the north. I have no train ticket to return. They have taken it."

"Well, how much do you need?" asked Jack, becoming concerned.

"Two hundred rupees."

"That's a hell of a lot." Jack was beginning to understand the currency.

"It is a long way."

"Must be. Look. That's too much. I think this is a scam, Harry, what do you reckon?"

"I no cheat! I never cheat! I am an honest man. I work, with a job and money enough. Swami said. Come with me to the railway. Don't give me money. Swami said to ask for the ticket. I don't want your money. I don't want to ask. I never cheat."

"All right. All right. Calm down. Calm down. Hey!" Jack looked at Hari and shrugged his shoulders.

"What should I do? Do you believe him?"

"I don't cheat!"

"Okay. I hear you fella'. Just stay quiet while I consult my friend here. Well?"

"I don't know, Jack. It's up to you. I don't have any money. He seems genuine. He seems to be telling the truth."

"I reckon so too." Jack fumbled into his pocket. "I've no idea how much there is here." He opened his palm and amongst the crumpled colony of rupees lay two neatly folded one hundred rupee notes. Jack hadn't noticed. Hari was fascinated and carefully lifted them free.

"How much?"

"Two hundred rupees."

"Do I have that?"

"Yes, Jack. The notes are here." He offered them to Jack who steered them, still in Hari's fingers, towards the waiting man.

"Here you go."

"Thank you." With the crisp notes carefully gripped between the apexes of fingers that waved in prayer, the waiting man backed slowly into the shade.

"You come with me to the railway. Watch me buy the ticket."

"That won't be necessary. We have trusted you."

"I would be in pain for ever. I would suffer if I had misused Baba's name. I am no cheat."

"We believe you, truly," reassured Jack.

"I was your penance, Swami said, Swami said." And with this he retreated into the shadow.

Jack was deep in thought, exploring the possible extent of his generosity or his stupidity. He and Hari were walking slowly, painfully, in Jack's case, towards the ashram gates to meet Hari's mother, who wasn't waiting but a paid messenger was.

"Are you Master Hari Sarnhi?"

"Yes," replied a nervous Hari. He didn't recognise such an important sounding set of names.

"I am here for your mother." The aged, well-dressed, semi-official spoke with the gentle but firm tones of the elderly junior civil servant, a stamp seller of some standing, a man whose unchanging position in both office geography and career had finally marked him out for distinction.

"Is there anything wrong?"

"Not at all. Be reassured. That is my first message. I am to say, 'Do not worry, for there is nothing wrong.' That is my first message." He paused for encouragement or permission, gently fawning, his nodding head wobbling from side to side.

"What was your second message?"

"My second message is to ask you, with your permission, to proceed to Sai Deep Café and wait with patience there. Your illustrious grandfather . . ."

"Was that part of the message?" interrupted Jack.

"No, sir. I embellished." Faltering, the messenger had lost all his momentum.

"Is that it?" Jack's question set the messenger going once more.

"Your grandfather, my employer," he bowed towards Jack by way of excuse and explanation, "has opened an account for you at the café. The proprietor will recognise you and never again will demand money. When necessary business is concluded at your grandfather's new house all the family will fetch you from the Sai Deep Café. Eventually." He paused. "That is the end of my message."

"Thanks." Jack went to give the messenger some loose change for his trouble.

"That will not be necessary, sir. My employer has paid me. Twice. It was my proper employment. Excuse me now." He withdrew.

"Would you like a cup of tea, Jack?"

"No. But I could drink something."

"Jack?" Hari had already fallen into a natural place a few feet in front of Jack, offering a shoulder, occasionally an arm, for balance. He wasn't asked to and it was never to be acknowledged.

"Go on, I'm listening."

"Did you neatly fold any of the rupee notes in your pocket?"

"Harry, as far as I can remember, I've never folded anything that you might call 'neatly' in the whole of my life. Was that it?"

"Yes. Thank you."

"My pleasure." Jack's answer left Hari deep in thought.

The tables at the Sai Deep Café were full. This was the time for the regulars. Most of the day trippers had gone, whether Western and wealthy and already returned by taxi to comfortable hotels; or Indian and poor, spilling out of buses in the empty countryside into the dark interiors of mud-made houses.

All the spaces in the café were taken. Undaunted, Jack stood menacingly by one of the larger tables, looking down. Pressed close together, the tops of the heads of three women were visible beneath Jack's stare. One was Western, recently shaven, with a soft covering of downy hair growing back. Another sported an unruly quiff, upright in defiance of the rest of a neatly combed head of glossy black hair. The final, youngest head was close-cropped into wiry stubble.

Jack heard something of their squabble and indentified English, South African and Australian as the accents shared.

"Is there room for us?" asked Jack, not waiting for a reply, making his awkward intrusion irresistible.

"Sorry?" The Western woman spoke, the other two looked up in surprise.

"Hey, budge up." Jack forced himself onto the edge of their bench and invited Hari to squash in beside him. Proprietor arrived on the instant, grinning with foreknowledge.

"Hello, Master Hari. You are welcome. Whatever you want is yours."

"Who's this, Harry, your genie?" asked Jack, charmed.

"No, this is Proprietor," explained Hari. "I would like lime soda and cake. Jack?"

"Sounds great to me. I'll have the same. What's the cake?"

"It's as it comes, Jack." Hari guessed at all sorts of complications. "All the cake is nice."

"I'll trust you. Would you ladies like a drink? The boy's genie is paying. My name's Jack. I'm doing all right. What about you?"

Jack held out a universal hand that was taken first by: "Joan. I'm called Joan."

Hari recognised her as the woman who had named Lunasha.

"Pleased to meet you, Joan. Are you visiting?"

"No. I have a house here. I've been here many years."

"Really?" Jack was surprised.

The youngest of the three, with sad, owl eyes, introduced herself.

"I'm Sam. I'd love a cup of tea, please." She spoke to Proprietor, awkwardly inserting a few words of the local language into her usual Australian.

Maddy

"Are you from here?" asked Jack, accentuating the 'you'.

"No. Melbourne. Did you think I was Indian?" Sam looked at Jack with eyes that hurt and questioned simultaneously.

"Yes. I guess I did."

Sam laughed nervously.

"No. I'm a visitor. A long term one, but a visitor nevertheless. Maybe not for much longer." Sam mouthed her words. She seemed surprised to hear them emerge. Jack instantly recognised the careful enunciation of a deaf speaker. Hari hadn't yet realised.

Jack waited for a response from the third. She appeared to be Indian but Jack wasn't going to assume so.

"I've no time for tea. I have to get to Bangalore. I'm busy."

"Hello, Busy," said Jack, pushing on regardless.

"I'm sorry to have been rude. I'm Maddy. We have a rather urgent problem that must be solved. That I must solve."

"It's Sam's problem, really," Joan explained above Maddy's sigh of disapproval.

"Is it a secret?" asked Jack, sardonically. "Can it ever be told?"

"Of course." Maddy was a bustling swirl of energy that couldn't stay still. Jack sensed her impatience with him and the tardiness of the world. She was on edge, fidgety, somehow hunted. Her metronomic gaze scanned the scene before her, looking for opportunities, not wanting to be baulked. She needed to rush through the obstacles that the world put in her path. Perhaps she saw Jack as the latest hindrance or: changing instantly to an optimistic persuasiveness she decided: "You could help."

"Could I now?" Jack responded, wryly. "With what exactly?"

"Her visa has run out," Maddy declared, pointing towards Sam. Sam nodded, acknowledging this truth, clearly ashamed.

"She can only stay for one more day then she must leave the country for twenty-four hours and then she can come back for another six months. If she doesn't, then . . ." The consequences were left unsaid. "We all have to do it," Maddy added, with a hint of reassurance for Sam.

"Not you, of course." Joan made her remark in all innocence. It was greeted with a fierce scowl by Maddy.

"Oh, I'm sorry. I didn't realize . . ." Joan was embarrassed.

"Go on! Tell him my business! All my friends know my plight, my enemies aren't certain, so, lets involve every passing stranger, shall we?" Maddy spread her arms in universal invitation.

"Hey, keep your secret," said Jack. "Though it would have been safe with me."

"It's not . . ." Maddy was quieter now. "I was careless. I'm in no position to judge Sam or anyone else. I forgot to renew my visa. Nobody came. The months went by and then the years. My own South African papers ran out during that time, so now I have no nationality. I am a stateless person. I don't exist. The principal at the university said he would help. I have the protection of Baba, so the police keep away. But I have no right to stay and I don't have the means to leave. So, I am stuck."

"Can you ever go back home?" asked Hari, concerned.

"Sure. Why not? It's a better place now. Mandela is free. Everyone votes. Perhaps they'll welcome you with open arms and you can resume your old life again." Jack smiled and clapped his hands in confirmation of this happy thought just as a genie-born tray of drinks was being placed into the centre of the table.

Whilst the others sipped their drinks, Maddy was deep in thought. The images in her mind were anything but nostalgic. Her family had lived in District Six of Cape Town. They were part of a small Indian community, displaced from other parts of Africa. Her father had run an import/export business down by the docks and she had helped in one of his offices, keeping records and printing labels. Although she had never set foot there, she knew the names and places of all the major cities in India. Then, twenty years ago, the white authorities had forcibly removed her and her family as part of the state of being apart. Their house was bulldozed. The whole district was levelled and left. It was decided that interaction between the races would breed conflict. It was the opposite: it had bred understanding. District Six had never been the slum the authorities claimed but now it was derelict. As far as she knew, it still was. The area was never redeveloped, just destroyed and abandoned.

Her family was moved to Cape Flats. The 'Flats' as they called them, were a wasteland of Aeolian sand. What a pretty name for a windblown desert where antelope and gangs were free to roam. Her father died that first winter of the cold wet weather. The family dispersed. Maddy shipped to India, looking for ancestors and a place to belong, weary of being institutionally set apart.

"What will you do?" Hari asked, waking Maddy from her musing.

"I keep busy," was her clipped reply. She hadn't enjoyed her memories. "I won't be going home," she informed Hari, and herself.

"Maddy does everything," Joan claimed, hoping to make amends. "Airline tickets, trips, reservations, all that needs organizing."

Instead of responding, Maddy slipped once more into a deep reverie. The others knew to be quiet. Jack and Hari held their breath. Something odd was happening.

"You. The boy. Yes, you. Is your name Hari?" Maddy demanded, abruptly, now awake.

"Yes." Hari felt oddly nervous.

Maddy beamed a huge, forgiving smile. "Ah. Then it is not you but your older friend I have a message for."

"What, me?" asked an intrigued Jack.

"No. Not that old. This friend is blond with beautiful eyes."

"Jean Paul. I think she means Jean Paul." Hari touched Jack's arm in reassurance. "He's another friend of mine."

"Okay. Okay." Jack was satisfied.

"There is a message from Baba. Tell him it is time to leave. When Swami goes to the mountains your fair friend must go to his mountain."

"Which mountain?" asked Hari.

"Arunachala."

"Ara where?"

Sam helped.

"It is beautiful there, Hari. Is your name Hari?"

"Yes." He liked Sam.

"It's truly beautiful."

"What's there?" asked Jack.

"It is a divine magnet that will turn his scattered mind towards the Self," intoned Maddy, most oddly.

"Pardon? Is she serious?" Jack asked of Joan.

"Oh yes. Swami often speaks through her. They will be Baba's words for Hari's friend."

"But, what am I to say?" Hari was lost.

"You are to say", continued Maddy, "he must go to the Sacred Red Mountain of Arunachala. That he is far beyond this place. That spiritually, this is for children. He has finished here. It is now time to go."

"When? When must he go?" asked Hari, trying to remember every word of the message.

"When Swami leaves for the mountains."

"When will that be?"

Now in her own voice, Maddy adopted her usual businesslike manner.

"My friend at the university says the Wednesday after next. There is so much to be organised. Coaches, taxis."

Hari was deep in thought. Jack was full of questions.

"Let me get this right. You're telling me Baba is leaving here in a week or so?" Jack was concerned.

"It is normal," Maddy assured him.

"The hell it is. I only just arrived."

"Who are you with?" asked Maddy.

"Sven. I joined his group from . . ."

"Denmark and Holland. Yes, I know. He has already ordered six air-conditioned taxis to take your party."

"Take it where?"

"Kodaikanal."

"Ah." The spoken name jogged a memory in Jack.

"It is a cool place, further south but much higher up. Swami has an ashram there. He goes after European Easter, normally. We all like it there. It is small. Interviews are easier. It is less frantic."

"You go too?"

"We all go," explained Joan.

"You mean you follow him around? Wherever he goes?"

"We follow. Yes. That is our life."

"For how long?" Jack persisted.

"That is up to Swami," Joan answered.

"No, I mean, how long have you been doing this?"

"Eight years," offered Joan.

"Seventeen years," topped Maddy.

"Eleven months," said Sam. "I may not see my anniversary."

"What does this girl have to do, Maddy? You seem to have all the answers." Jack was interested. Perhaps he could help.

"Unless she fills in the necessary forms by the end of today that prove where she is and where she still hopes to be, she's out. Even then we've got to get her in and out of the country. It's so difficult. I'm still not sure about the train, Joan." Maddy was clearly anxious.

"I know. But the air fare?" Joan frowned.

"What's wrong with the train?" asked a persistently rational Hari.

"India is a country that shouts, rings bells, pushes buzzers, generally likes to make a godawful noise to let everyone know what they've left and where they've arrived. Every bus and train is announced over the tannoy. Sam cannot hear the shouted instructions. She has missed her destination more than once. We managed to pair her with another traveller on one occasion. It's too late to organize anything now. Sam kept the problem quiet for too long."

"It will have to be the plane. I will find the money. Arrange it, Maddy,

90

please." Joan lowered her eyes. Worried.

"If you're sure." Maddy touched Joan on the arm as a gesture of thanks.

"What is decided?" asked Sam. Joan and Maddy had spoken face to face. Sam could read nothing of their shared words.

"Joan will pay your airfare. We'll fly you out and back in tomorrow, or the next day. I can arrange it all. The stopover, the tickets but, Sam, you must follow all the instructions exactly. Make sure you know the times and the whole schedule. Yes? Okay?" Maddy's attentions only seemed to alarm Sam. She was disturbed and anxious.

"I am a burden to you all and myself. You are so kind. I left Australia to find a family, a home and a place to be. They are proud to be outspoken in Australia but I couldn't hear them speak, so I couldn't belong. India is a land full of beautiful sights and wonderful smells. I can't hear its noises so I can't follow any instructions that are spoken without a face. One day, if I wait long enough, Baba will let me hear once more and I will be able to travel and be less of a nuisance to my friends. I apologise."

In the silence that followed Sam's humble speech, Joan remembered their forgotten urgency.

"What about today?" she whispered.

"Where in Bangalore does she have to go?" asked Hari, still on the trail.

"It's just off Mahatma Gandhi Road. But, none of my taxis are here. They're all there. It's a bad time." Maddy was clearly frustrated.

"Grandfather can take her. We will have room. It is near for us."

"That was quick. Your quickest yet." Joan spoke to no one.

"I'm sorry?" prompted Hari.

"I was just thanking Swami. You have become the answer to my prayer."

"I have?" Hari was pleased.

"Yes."

"Does Baba know I'm here?" he asked, bewildered.

"Of course. And, he's let you help."

Hari felt proud.

"You have become one of the unheralded miracles he works every day, Hari. That's quite a privilege." Sam beamed happiness. She went to tidy Hari's hair but stopped herself.

"Do you believe Baba can work miracles, Sam?"

"Of course he can. I've seen them myself."

"You have?"

"Yes. I didn't want to believe them at first. I was very difficult when I came. I was angry." For the first time Hari noticed something strange in Sam's speech. The word 'angry' seemed to annoy her jaw in its saying.

"I am deaf, if you are wondering."

Hari blushed.

"I am all right with this now, I wasn't then. I wanted to blame Baba and at the same time I wanted him to cure me. I needed many interviews."

"You've had an interview?" Hari still saw this as a rarity.

"Five. I had five, pretty close to each other. I was very antagonistic. I was shameful, really. It is only the really hopeless cases that need interviews. And I was hopeless."

"What did He say to you in your interviews?"

"He knew I was angry, so he called me to him, rested his hands on my head and said, 'Bless your anger.' Another time I asked him to let me hear again. He shook his head. I asked him again. Still, he shook is head. Finally, I walked right up to him and looked him straight in the eye … Oh yes, Hari, don't be angry with me."

"I'm not angry, Sam, I'm amazed. You stared God in the face?"

"I did. I demanded: 'Why will you not let me hear?' and he replied, and I heard the reply:

"'Because there is nothing you are prepared to hear. Only when you are ready will you hear. Bless your anger.'

"'But I want to be at peace!' I shouted and I fell to the floor. 'When will I be at peace?'

"And Baba said: 'You will be at peace when you remember me in the precise moment that you forget the world.'

"And then something truly amazing happened.

"Baba said: 'Watch. You will recognise this.'

"In the interview room there was a group from Australia, my home. He called them to him. One man lingered.

"'It is you I have called,' said Baba. The man came forward, reluctantly.

"'You are not with me here. You would sooner be somewhere else. Is this true?'

"'Forgive me, Baba,' the man said, 'my mind is elsewhere.'

"'Where is your mind?' Baba was smiling.

"'With my wife. She is ill.'

"'Ah! Is she here?' Baba waved the waiting pilgrims away from the back wall of the interview room. He opened his palm and a beam of coloured light was suddenly projected from it. On the wall was a picture of a street that I recognised.

"'That's Melbourne. I reckon that's Melbourne.'

"Baba chuckled. He was obviously very happy.

"'That's my house,' shouted the sad Australian, 'that's a picture of my house!'

"'No, you are wrong,' said Baba, 'it is your house. Go home. Step into your house.'

"The man walked towards the wall. He turned to his other Australian friends. He was bewildered and I bet, just a little bit afraid.

"'You mean?'

"He pointed at the wall.

"'Go to your house. See your wife,' instructed Baba.

"The man walked to the wall. There was a flash. He disappeared and the picture vanished. That same afternoon, his friends telephoned his wife to tell them what had happened. And, do you know? Her husband, their friend, answered the phone. He'd no idea how he got there. Isn't that amazing?"

"The version I heard was Venezuela."

The gentle male voice was Andreas the Dane's. He was sitting with his twin sister, Freja, on a nearby table. It seemed overhearing and threading into other people's conversation was acceptable in the Sai Deep Café. Other chairs shuffled half-round so their unknown occupants could share.

"He sent someone to Venezuela as well?" asked a delighted Sam.

"Yes. But I think it was a daughter that time. There was a particularly good vibhuti miracle this afternoon. Back lit. It was really fine. Did you see it? If not, well, I managed to film it." Andreas was very excited.

"I'd like to see that," Jack said.

"I can project it back through the camera. But of course you would know that. I'm Andreas, by the way, and this is my sister, Freja. We met you once before, in Copenhagen. We're also part of Sven's group. We came ahead, the advanced guard, as it were. It's an honour to meet you . . ."

"Jack." Both outstretched hand and sudden interruption forestalled any further information concerning Jack coming from Copenhagen.

"I thought he was a cobra today," Freja suddenly declared. "Did you see that?"

"No," Andreas replied. "And anyway, I couldn't have filmed amongst the women. I shouldn't even be filming amongst the men, but . . ." He was a little shamefaced.

"I'm sorry to have missed that," Maddy said.

"You weren't there, today?" Jack asked.

"No," she replied.

"Nor me," added Joan.

"Neither of you?" Jack was surprised.

"No. I no longer go to the ashram," Joan explained.

"Not even for darshan?" asked Hari.

"Not regularly, no." Joan confirmed.

"Why is that?" asked Andreas, keen to be involved.

It seemed the whole café was listening.

"I don't find it necessary. I no longer have the daily need of his physical presence. I feel his spirituality is contagious. It reaches me without the need of his actual touch." Joan was measured in her response and Maddy nodded her agreement with Joan's explanation.

"You mean, you never go?" asked a disbelieving Freja.

"I didn't say that. I go when I need some special reassurance, or a specific answer."

"Such as?" asked Andreas.

"To confirm a decision. To see a sign," Joan explained.

Jack requested an example and Sam immediately suggested, "Tell them about the taxi. You went to darshan then."

Joan was clearly reluctant.

"Well, I'll tell them," offered Maddy.

"No. It's all right. I'll say. There was a local family. One of my neighbours. I rent a small house, down the way, you see." She pointed. "I began as a spiritual tourist, like most people here, but now I live a permanent life with Baba."

"You don't have to do this, Joan," interrupted Sam, conscious that she might have embarrassed her friend.

"It's okay. It's not Baba that I avoid. I should make that clear. It's the ashram. Don't misunderstand me. I do not complain of my life. I am happy to be here. After all, Baba came all the way to England to fetch me."

"I thought he never left India," Andreas remarked.

"He bi-locates."

"What?" asked Jack.

"He can be in more than one place at once. How on earth do you think he can stand the life he leads? No one could be here all the time. I should think bi-location is his saving grace," Joan explained.

"Is this right?" Jack needed convincing.

"How else can you explain what happened to me? I was walking in Arundel. That was my home, in the south of England. I glanced up at the sky and saw an impossible vapour trail. The clouds pictured a perfect nought

94

and crosses grid, but with a trailing squiggle . . ." Joan imaged this squiggle with a wiggle of her finger, " . . . curving away at the bottom of the grid. It was at the bottom right, or left, depending on how you looked at it." She moved in her chair, changing point of view. "I thought 'God is playing noughts and crosses'. There is no point. I can put a nought", she drew a circle in the air, "at the centre and he can never get a line of crosses."

"That's tick-tack-toe." Jack declared.

"Yes. And God had lost. I forgot all about it. A friend had become interested in India and she sent me a magazine with a photograph on the front cover. It turned out to be that of Sai Baba. He held out his hand and there on the palm was a noughts and crosses grid. The trailing skyline I didn't understand was the lifeline of his palm. But the face I knew. In my mind, in my dreams, Baba's face was the face I recognised as God. Then he came to me. In my room, or in my dream and invited me to India. I left the next day."

"This is all very interesting, but what about the taxi miracle?" reminded Andreas.

"It wasn't a miracle. It was just a lot of money."

"How much?"

"Fifty thousand rupees."

The sum of money brought a hush.

"But that's only fifteen hundred dollars," Andreas had figured.

"Maybe, but it was all I had. There is no mystery here. My neighbours came and said that Baba had sent them, that I was to buy them a new car because their old taxi car had finally disintegrated and that without my help all the family would starve. And, I just wasn't sure. So, I went to darshan and Baba came right up to me, nodded and smiled into me, so I knew, and I gave them the money."

"You gave them fifty thousand rupees?" asked Jack, just to be certain.

"Yes, I did. And I don't regret it."

"Makes our two hundred look like a good deal, hey, Harry?"

"What's that?" asked Andreas.

"Oh, nothing." Jack winked at Hari.

"Of course, we give considerable parts of our income to the ashrams," Andreas explained, twiddling with his God-made jewellery and glancing at his divine watch. "We seek no reward."

"Other than nearness to Baba, hey darling? Can you remember . . ?" Freja giggled endearingly, ". . . when Baba asked that young Belgian why he had come to the ashram and the boy had said 'to get closer to God' and Baba had sat right next to him and said, 'How much closer do you want to be?' and we all laughed. It is for people like that Belgian that we give," she explained with sudden earnestness, "and can you remember when Baba materialised the monkey?"

"Excuse me. We're going," interrupted Jack. He'd had enough. "Would you walk me back to my room, Harry? I'm getting a little tired. It's been a long day."

"You won't forget Sam will you, Hari?" reminded Maddy.

"I'll be right back," Hari replied.

As they were leaving, Jack wondered, "Could we go the long route? I'm not fond of those narrow bridges.

Hari led Jack along the road, past the ashram gates and to the southern tip of the bazaar. He had just noted the end of the ditch and a solid place to cross when Jack fell down, heavily.

"Jack!"

"Ooooh! How did that happen?" He tried to get up, too quickly, so stumbled again.

"Don't rush. Wait a minute." Jack turned onto all fours, ready to rise, when he saw something.

"Harry! Look at this, Harry. If I'm not mistaken, this is the exact spot where we gave that man his train money."

"Yes. I think it is." Jack's body was masking what he was seeing. He rolled sideways, onto his bottom, pointing for Hari to see, first, his bloodstained right knee, and second, drawn clearly and precisely in the dust, the perfect shape of a heart.

"I guess we got it right. What do you say?"

"What does it mean, Jack?" He was still sitting on the ground. Hari was staring at the heart drawing and with increasing alarm at the growing bloodstain around Jack's knee.

"That we weren't tricked."

"Could Baba be a trickster?" asked Hari.

"I didn't mean by Baba. Anyway, it wouldn't make any difference if he were. We were happy givers."

"Is that what counts?"

"Sure it's what counts. In the United States, when we talk about a 'Con-Man'—you know that phrase, Harry?" Hari nodded. "Well, what he steals is trust, not things. You gain someone's confidence and then you take something from them and every victim says, 'Hell, I liked him so much I would have given him what he took!' You see, they were willing; they so wanted to believe that whatever story they were told was true. But if you gain someone's confidence and you believe you have been given something. Is that stealing? Is that a crime, or wrong? It's like a burglar breaking into your house and leaving all kinds of gifts there. Could you help me up, I'm feeling a little stiff."

"You shouldn't walk on that leg. We should get a rickshaw, Jack."

They did.

The major benefit of Jack's pessimistic packing was that he had brought an excellent First Aid kit. Hari carefully and rather nervously dressed an alarming wound below Jack's knee.

"You must get a proper doctor tomorrow. It looks terrible."

"I'm sure it will heal. You have kindly hands, young man. You must rush. Your family's expecting you. Goodbye now."

There was already a taxi waiting with its rear doors open as Hari came into view.

"He's there. I see him. Hari! Quickly now!" Hari's father called out.

"You are late. You should have been here. Grandfather doesn't like to be delayed," explained Hari's mother in a whisper, leaning out of the open taxi door.

"Who's this?" she leaned back to reveal Sam, sitting silently on the other back seat.

"She's ..."

"Who is that woman?" Hari's grandfather asked.

Hari remained calm, outwardly, glancing towards an already empty and unsupportive café.

"She is Sam. She has problems with her papers. Could we drop her at the Immigration Offices on our way to dinner? As a favour? Please, Grandfather?"

"Why is this our problem? Do I have a choice?" Ramu Sarnhi didn't seem too cross.

"Of course." Hari dropped his gaze.

"Might I have been consulted before the favour in question took root in my taxi?"

"Yes, Grandfather, you should have been, but it was urgent and everyone was in a rush. She was in difficulty and needed help."

"Can't she speak for herself?" Hari's father asked.

"She can speak but she can't hear. Being deaf makes travelling very difficult for her. Her friends will help her tomorrow but they couldn't get to Bangalore tonight and I said that we could. I'm sorry if I did wrong."

"Of course I will take her, Hari. What you did was very decent and laudable. I'm sorry if I was cross. You are clearly a young man to be reckoned with."

Grandfather Sarnhi patted Hari's head in praise and sitting energetically in the front seat of the taxi, ordered the driver to:

"Drop her, then to my house. Quickly."

CHAPTER SEVENTEEN
A house for a saintly beggar

Ramu Sarnhi was sweating even though the air conditioning was working at full blast in his morning taxi. The family was travelling to Whitefield, earlier than usual, with an extra passenger squashed nervously between the chairman of his company and the driver of the taxi. The dapper undermanager, small in stature and significance, did his best to keep himself separate from those beside him and was quick to apologise as any unexpected bump in the road nudged him into touching.

"Sorry, sir."

"Stop saying that. It is annoying and it is not necessary." Ramu Sarnhi was irritable. He turned to his son. "You must understand the importance of these visits, surely?"

"Of course, Father."

Ajay, Esther and Hari sat in a line on the bench seat in the rear. It was with some difficulty that Ramu Sarnhi tried to twist around to look at his son. Eventually he stopped trying and, appropriating the rear-view mirror, twisted its view to centre on Ajay's face. It was oddly intimidating. Esther Sarnhi nudged her husband into speech.

"Esther is worried about leaving Hari," Ajay began.

"Leaving him where?" Ramu Sarnhi asked the mirror.

"On his own in the ashram."

"He's not on his own. The place is full of stray children."

"That's not a recommendation," Esther declared. Her father-in-law's reflected frown forced her to lower her eyes.

"It's an ashram, for God's sake!" Ramu Sarnhi smiled at his accidental witticism. "He'll come to no harm there."

"He goes out alone in Birmingham," Ajay mentioned, much to Esther's annoyance. She wondered whose side her husband was on.

"And that's a pretty godless place, by all accounts," Ramu Sarnhi claimed, with a wry smile.

"Not really, Father. Birmingham has too many gods."

"At home, Hari walks on known streets to his school or homes of friends. He is recognised and that protects him." Esther was anxious. Hari tried to attract his father's attention. Ajay was still transfixed by his father's mirrored stare.

"He is protected here. By me. I am known so he is known. In the ashram he is safe, clearly. In the village he has friends. We know them, nod to them and acknowledge their care. Beyond the actual village, everything is mine. I own the land, the houses and the people on it. No one would dare threaten my grandchild. Believe me."

They all did.

Finally, Ramu Sarnhi looked away. The taxi driver snatched back his mirror and once more could see where he'd been. Now Hari could be heard.

"Grandfather is right. I do have friends in the village. But why is it a problem today? What is happening?"

"Grandfather has arranged a series of visits for me. Shobhan . . .", at the sound of his name the undermanager sat bolt upright, ". . . is going to take me to some of the places our family own and run as businesses. It is necessary that the people there see me in person and I get to see them. It is important and urgent. Do you see?"

"Of course, Father. You mustn't worry about me."

"But it may be quite often now. There are many places to see." Ajay wanted to be clear.

"I don't mind, Father. I am very happy in the village with my friends and it is not far to grandfather's rented house. And mother ..." he added as an afterthought. He didn't mean to be disloyal but he was used to her. Everyone else was new and exciting. He didn't need an exciting mother as well.

"I want her with me," Hari's father began.

"Oh." Harry was perplexed and anxious, for a moment.

"She will take notes for me. I need to capture all the information I can on these lightning visits. Your mother will be an enormous help to me, especially looking at the accounts and ledgers and the minute details of the business. She does this for me in England. I value her skills. I need her with me." These last remarks were meant for his father rather than his son.

"I understand, Father," said Harry, willing to please.

"I knew you would." Ajay was delighted with his son's understanding and compliance.

Esther clutched Hari's hand. Her loyalties were torn. She enjoyed her status, knew it pained Ramu Sarnhi to hear her praised, but that pleasure alone could not dispel her anxiety at leaving her son unguarded.

"I will watch over the boy," Ramu Sarnhi decided. "He will be my special care. I will tell him some of the family secrets," he laughed, "and what it means to be part of a silk family."

There was a pause as he wiped the cold sweat from his brow with a neatly folded handkerchief.

"Don't be anxious, Esther. Ajay will be back for evening darshan. I will never send him away for more than half a day. Will that put your mind at rest?"

"Thank you. Yes, it will help."

"Good."

Now everyone was pleased, except the upright undermanager. How was he to fulfil the itinerary of the day now half the allotted time had gone?

Ramu Sarnhi kept his word. As soon as Hari had waved away his parents, his grandfather proposed, "Tea?"

Instinctively, Hari headed for the Sai Deep Café.

"No. Not there, Hari, not today. Come, I'll find you an authentic cup of tea, made by a proper chai wallah."

On the edge of the village, heading back towards Bangalore, there were roadside stalls, instant factories with men beating metal, plastic containers full of diesel that the seller fed into lorries and taxis with a thin rubber hose that was sucked into the transfer by the seller's own lips. He must swallow some, surely, Hari thought, worried at the danger of such a trade. Men sat in temporary shelters, sewing on foot-treadle machines; others were ironing beside piles of crumpled clothes. No matter how fast their skill, the returning dhobi wallahs kept adding to their task.

There were several tea sellers, some large scale, some small. They walked by one where two men struggled to strain a huge saucepan of tea on a roiling boil through a muslin sieve into a waiting bowl that was equal to its task.

Everyone acknowledged Ramu Sarnhi as he and Hari walked by. All knew Hari's grandfather; his was no hollow boast. Judging by the bows and genuflections, the tipped forelocks and cheerily raised hands, he was respected and revered; liked and feared, perhaps in equal measure. The men building his house were cowed by his sudden appearance. Certainly there was activity and endeavour at the site. Building was evident and fast, unlike Jack's house that still wasn't built.

"Come Hari, meet Santosh." A diminutive figure, with hollow cheeks and not an ounce of flesh to spare, stood by his stall, stoking the fire with a grimy kettle boiling on its coals. A miniature churn of creamy milk stood on a tray beside a row of small glasses tipped on end. There was an earthenware bowl full of sugar and a pestle with the crushed remains of a root of ginger.

Ramu Sarnhi ordered two teas and provided a commentary on what Hari saw.

"Tea will be a while. It is better not to be in a hurry."

Santosh, the chai wallah, made a frugal living mainly from the workmen at the site of Ramu Sarnhi's new house. There were other new buildings nearby. With those workers included, Santosh could feed his family.

"It is a sad but magnificent fact, Hari, that many simple events in India have become time-filling rituals. As you see, the making of a humble glass of tea is elaborate and energetic. See, Santosh begins with a muslin sock filled with leaves that infuse and drain in a steady drip . . . " He paused, waiting for the event to occur, then resumed, " . . . into a waiting jug. See its long handle?"

Hari nodded.

"Over there is another jug with milk warming. He'll match the milk to the tea and pour one into the other."

Santosh began this elaborate interplay, ten, twenty times perhaps, cascading the mixing liquid from great, skilful heights, blending and cooling but never spilling. He poured the dark, syrupy mixture into the two glasses he selected from his tray. Hari was mesmerised. Grandfather Sarnhi handed his grandson his tea and Hari sipped the sweet, sticky emulsion with nervous trepidation.

"Is it good?"

"It's delicious, Grandfather. Thank you."

Ramu Sarnhi paid the chai wallah.

"It cost tuppence, Hari. All that effort for so little. It saddens me."

Suddenly, Ramu Sarnhi stumbled. He recovered quickly. He made no comment, sipped his tea and told Hari a secret.

"I was a chai wallah once, Hari. Not on the roadside like Santosh, but in the village where my parents worked producing silk. I made tea for all the family. I had an urn made of steel. I kept the fire alight so that always there was instant hot water. I could pour it into pots, cups or glasses from a tap on the side. I didn't toss it through the air. I hadn't the skill. But all day and every day, or so it seemed, I squatted over trays of individual cups or glasses. I sweetened every one with condensed milk from a can and ran around the huts with the tea on trays making sure it was still hot when I arrived. Santosh makes better tea than mine."

Ramu Sarnhi smiled despite this bitter memory. He disguised his resentment and indignation for his grandson's sake.

Returning to the village, he couldn't hide his breathlessness.

"Stop, Hari. Just for a moment. I must rest."

With nothing to lean on, Ramu Sarnhi chose Hari.

"Are you all right, Grandfather?"

The noisy gasping for breath frightened Hari. Gradually, enough air forced its way into Ramu Sarnhi's damaged lungs. His light-headedness passed. His breathing and composure were calm once more.

"I am sorry to have worried you, Hari. It happens often now. I just can't find a way to breathe. It looks worse than it feels. I know it passes so it concerns me less than those who witness it. Will you walk with me back to the rented house? I have a daybed on the veranda. I will go and lie down. I will not go to morning darshan. I hope you don't mind going on alone? Will that be acceptable, Hari?"

"Of course, Grandfather."

Hari didn't know what to say. He waited for his grandfather to move and, standing close, not daring to take a hand or offer a steadying arm, he walked beside the troubled old man until they reached the rented house. Servants rushed to assist, obviously used to these moments of distress.

As he was being led inside, Ramu Sarnhi called to Hari, "We'll be together for evening darshan but you must represent the whole family this morning. Would you do that for me? Oh, and Hari, if you are granted an interview, would you please mention me and ask Baba to let me live just a little while longer?"

Hari ran to darshan. He didn't want to be late on such a responsible day.

He needn't have rushed. Darshan that morning was short and joyless. Hari was saddened and disappointed. What was wrong with God? How could a powerless child help or intervene? At least he could be His faithful messenger. He must find Jean Paul and give him the message Baba sent via Maddy.

"What is this mountain?" Hari asked.

"The Indians believe that the gods placed it there to mark the spiritual centre of the world," explained Jean Paul.

"So, you already knew about the mountain?"

"Everybody does, we all do." 'All' was Borg and the Doctor. They each nodded. They were drinking tea at the Sai Deep Café, guests of Hari's genie.

"'Of all holy places, it is the most sacred, know that it is the heart of the world,'" quoted the Doctor.

"Whose are those words?" asked Hari.

"They were spoken by Sri Ramana Maharshi. His ashram is still at the foot of the Red Mountain."

"He's dead?"

"Yes. A little while ago," offered Borg.

"It might be to you, but it was over forty years ago to we mere mortals," added the Doctor.

"What was he?" asked Hari.

"What are our options?" mused an amused Borg.

"He wasn't an avatar, like Sai Baba, which is, I think, what you meant?" Hari nodded to Jean Paul.

"He refused that status. From what I have read, he was a beautiful and pure human being."

"It's true. He was. I visited several times," offered Borg.

"Of course," smiled Jean Paul.

"He seldom spoke," continued Borg, "and those of us in his presence always felt purified just by his gaze. Great eyes! Unbelievable eyes! But never said a dicky bird. It was deliberate, he used to say."

"I thought he never spoke," interrupted the Doctor.

"In his writings. I know he spoke sometimes. But, in his teachings."

"I thought he never taught?" interrupted Jean Paul.

"He wasn't a guru, not formally, no. Would you accept, in his thoughts? Would that pass your tests? It would? Good. He used to say that the highest teaching in the world is silence. And it sure is quiet at his ashram."

"I will enjoy the peace there, Hari. I too seek solitude to still my mind and in that stillness I may see more deeply into myself. I believe that is the purpose of Baba's message."

"It's a great place. The locals think the mountain is God himself," continued Borg.

"Baba?" asked Hari.

"No, son, Shiva," the Doctor explained.

"How many names does God have?" asked a deeply perplexed Hari.

"You must understand this, Hari," continued the Doctor, gently patting Hari's shoulder, sensing his anxiety, "in India we are not besotted by the idea of the individual. We don't need things to be unique, the only one of its kind. The fact that there are many, and that nothing is new but has probably lived or been thousands of times before is a great comfort and a strength to us, not a disturbance or a weakness." He paused to stare at the silent arrival of the beautiful beggar woman, already standing in the pit, preparing for her dirt-wash.

"A Western mind might think her life is vile, her mind unsound, her presence unneeded. But for all we know, she may be a saint. And even if she isn't, the suffering and penance of this life will make sense in later lives. Today is not hers but is the responsibility of her continuing soul. But the filth is real and her actions can make you retch. And I am aware that men of spiritual calm", he graciously acknowledged Jean Paul, "have come here and been offended, disturbed . . ."

"It's a mad house!" suggested Borg.

"And Arunachala is a place of peace," concluded the Doctor.

"And the food is great." Borg, necessarily, had the last word.

Hari caught Jean Paul's eye. They smiled in private conspiracy, sharing their special knowledge. Hari was delighted that someone as learned as the Doctor should also suggest that Lunasha might be a saint.

Hari left the café and crossed the bridge over the pit, staring at his feet. It was for safety, he told himself. He must not fall or fail. The accumulating filth beneath his gaze was repulsive and to be avoided; the quiet singing of Lunasha, heard some small distance off, was compelling but equally to be shunned. Tempted still, Hari glanced towards her, almost tripped, made an awkward, final stride that planted him safely on the other side and straight into the path of Maddy.

"I'm sorry," he blurted out.

"You must look where you're going," Maddy advised him sharply, then scurried away.

"No. Stop. Miss Maddy, please!" Hari ran after her.

Maddy was a small, round dumpling of a woman, with sturdy legs that could propel her forward with astonishing speed. She moved like a manic Victorian automata, a wind-up toy run amok. She wore a brightly patterned dress, not a sari, and seemed as preoccupied and as busy as Alice's White Rabbit in Wonderland.

"I'm late," she also declared. "It'll have to be a quick hello and goodbye. I'm late." But she did stop and face Hari for a moment.

"What is it?"

She had a wide, open face with coarse features and large, staring eyes. A mass of black hair framed her head, swept back, almost neat but, unruly and untamed, a magnificent quiff escaped skywards, pointing vertically in defiance of any taming comb. She held two mysterious baubles, one in each hand that she rolled deliberately in some private ritual of concentration or prayer. Hari wouldn't dare to ask their purpose. Maddy was a little fierce and, Hari understood, was not to be trifled with.

Hari came straight to the point. "I want you to help her." He turned and looked behind him. Lunasha had left the ditch and at the moment of his pointing was no more than a few feet away. She was gliding by the side of the road, unseeing as always, and holding some uneaten gift of food in her right hand.

"She is called Lunasha," Hari declared, breathless, nervous at his daring and the beggar woman's proximity. She could have heard him speak her name.

"She has been violated," Hari explained. He was eager to complete his mission in a rush. "And she is dying."

He had Maddy's attention. They both watched as Lunasha wandered away.

"No. I'm sorry. There's nothing I can do." Maddy had decided quickly.

"Please. You look after Sam." Hari hadn't meant to imply an obligation, just a comparison with an equal task of care. But Maddy knew she was obligated. Hari had helped her: she must help Hari. She wasn't interested in a moral equilibrium, a sense of justice or shared propriety; Maddy hated debt. She disliked owing and being owed. In debt, to or from, restricted her freedom of action and set awkward conditions on her terms of business.

Hari interrupted her silence, hoping it was indecision. "Couldn't she live in your compound? I doubt she'll be any trouble or expense. My family will feed her." Before he embarrassed himself by a promise he might not keep he added, "But then, she never eats. I give her food." Hari added as an afterthought.

"When?" Maddy was curious now.

"When she passes. I push bread or fruit into her hand. She doesn't seem to know it's there. She's careless. Lets it drop. It never reaches her mouth. The roadside monkeys scavenge her meals. She does not ask or beg, never stretches out a hand but people still give to her. Will you help?"

Maddy fell silent once more.

"My grandfather is a wealthy man," Hari began and as he'd guessed, this statement had alerted Maddy. "He's very ill and determined to get an interview with Sai Baba. He will be going to Kodaikanal. He has been told he will stand a better chance there. Is that true?"

"Yes, yes, it is true. Has he made arrangements?" Maddy asked tentatively.

"No, he hasn't. Or, I don't think he's had any success. He fears he might have left it too late."

"He has. The best accommodation would have gone." Maddy was thoughtful. Here was an opportunity for business. She wondered how much. Hari, learning from the dealings of the men in his family, clearly showing an aptitude for negotiation or simple deceit, added, "There will be a large party of family and business friends. He wants to be a group."

"Taxis are expensive and flying tedious, there are no nearby airfields but, I have a few seats on an air-conditioned coach that might interest your grandfather." The coaches were Maddy's most profitable means of transport, so her hopes lay there.

"What is Kodaikanal?" Hari asked, hoping to redirect their conversation away from his obvious manipulation.

"It is a beautiful hill station. The princess of its kind. There is a star-shaped lake, a summer forest and the Palani Hills. It is green and misty and damp and cool."

It sounded just like Birmingham, thought Hari.

"Swami has an ashram there. He tends to go after English Easter. It could be any time now. Your grandfather needs to make plans, urgently."

"Would you meet him at the Sai Deep Café before darshan tomorrow morning? I will tell my grandfather."

"Of course. I will bring all the necessary information. Papers and prices."

"And Lunasha?"

Maddy looked quizzically at Hari.

"The beggar woman," Hari reminded her.

"Oh. Of course. I'll give her to Om. They are kindred spirits. They each possess nothing but their souls."

"Thank you," said Hari.

"I'm late," Maddy reminded herself. "Too late." And without further explanation she sped away.

CHAPTER EIGHTEEN
Accommodating

"How much?" exclaimed Hari's grandfather, clearly alarmed at the figure Maddy had scribbled on the scrap of paper passing between them.

"I was considering staying there, not purchasing the place."

It was early morning in the Sai Deep Café. Maddy was waiting there before Hari and his family arrived. Instantly, she and Grandfather Sarnhi had moved to a separate table to begin negotiations. Hari's father had been pleased at his son's initiative.

"You see, son, it is never wise doing business in a buyers' market. The taxis are full, their prices immovable at best, even rising, and public transport is for the public. Businessmen must be allowed to wriggle."

Hari was perplexed. He couldn't visualise this ritual, especially if it was to be performed by his grandfather.

"Beginners always dream of the big deal: buy low and sell high. With experience, you come to realise it is the small margins, the little wriggles above and below, shaving a little here, adding a little there. That is where most money is made, quietly, cleverly, at the margins. There must be a turn in every step or it isn't business, it's just shopping." Ajay Sarnhi was pleased with himself, his advice and his son. He almost ruffled the boy's hair but thought it might alarm him.

"How did you meet your new friend, Hari?" asked his mother, pleased to hear her son praised. Ajay, Hari's father, was scant in his praise for anyone, including himself.

"Through Jack and . . ." Unable to lie directly to his mother or acknowledge his constant disobedience concerning Lunasha, the name 'Sam' came to his aid.

Maddy heard it, looked across to Hari's table and declared, "She's back. The papers are signed. She is safe. Thank you for your help. But the Carlton Hotel is one of the finest in all India," she explained, returning seamlessly to her dealings with Ramu Sarnhi. "It has five stars. You are paying for its reputation. And of course, it is on the lake."

Maddy thought she had played her winning card but was forewarned by the frown on Ramu Sarnhi's face.

"Which," he began, leaning forward and prodding the air between them with an accusing finger, "... is contaminated with mercury."

He sat back, looking satisfied. This information confused Maddy. It wasn't in the brochures and was beyond her normal brief.

"I wouldn't know, sir." She offered her ignorance politely, hoping to be excused.

"The thermometer factory dumps its waste there, so I'm informed." And so was everyone else. Ramu Sarnhi offered this damning news to the whole café.

"They make thermometers in the hills?" asked Hari, fascinated. Obviously someone, somewhere must make them. The discovery intrigued him, nevertheless.

"It's a scandal, my boy. Someone must pay." By his look, he seemed to expect reparation from Maddy who must be assumed innocent of any involvement if judged by the look of bewilderment on her face.

Undaunted, she pushed on. "I do happen to have a few bungalows that I manage and some cottages. You could take your own cook and servants. They are not by the lake." This was usually a criticism, a geographical failure that lessened their appeal. But not today. "They are beside Coaker's Walk. It is one of the most beautiful pathways in the whole region. Splendid for ramblers." Maddy could sense Ramu Sarnhi's aversion to the prospect of walking, whatever the prospect, and added quickly, "But it is still near to the ashram and the good restaurants in the town. We could house all of your party in, say, two cottages?" Maddy assessed the response to her 'say' instantly, "Or one large bungalow with wide terraces for the servants?"

"And that would cost?"

The price was written on a piece of paper. Such sums were best not spoken out loud. Ramu Sarnhi made a minor alteration. Maddy looked. Nodded yes.

"And combined with the costs of the coach?"

Another figure was written and trimmed to acceptance. With slow, thoughtful smiles, business was concluded.

Everyone relaxed.

"When will this be?" Hari's father asked.

"There are rumours. Always rumours," Maddy began, "but a week Wednesday is the favoured day."

"And there is no prior warning?" Ramu Sarnhi's tone expressed his disapproval.

"No. We wait. We find him gone. We follow."

CHAPTER NINETEEN
Jack and Joan

Jack was alone. When the Sai Deep Café emptied to go to darshan he stayed behind. He'd half-emptied the jumbled contents of his bag onto the table. Next to his camera stood a row of unused films standing on end. They were neat triangles of black plastic with 35 colour exposures in each. Jack was scribbling in a small red notebook. The writing was fluent but looked clumsy. He was clutching the stump of a well-used pencil that was grasped in a fist rather than held at fingers' end. He'd signalled for more tea earlier and it arrived, hopelessly late but just in time. Proprietor, expecting a rebuke was disarmed by Jack's smile of gratitude.

"Wait. Can I take your picture?" Jack asked the startled proprietor.

"It would be my honour, sir. What should I do?" He preened himself in readiness.

"Serve me my tea again. That would be in role, yes?"

"Of course."

With studied seriousness, Proprietor placed Jack's tea onto the table, with far more care than he ever showed in his normal way of waiting. Jack grinned and took a careful picture of the careful pose.

"Thank you."

"Will you let me buy a copy, sir? I have no pictures of me working."

"Is it such a rare sight?" asked Jack, sardonically.

"Very." Proprietor grinned.

"Sure. Be my guest. When it's ready it will be a gift." Happy, Proprietor withdrew.

The camera was expensive, small but very clever. The compact Nikon was lost in Jack's hand and looked far too elegant for his clumsy fingers to use. Jack swivelled in his chair and began to build a panorama, scrolling frame by frame, clicking the shutter with certainty as he focused on the imagined gaps and joins in his growing patchwork frieze. He was eager to capture the full scene that he met every day on his travels from his room— across the dangerous ditch—to the ashram. He was clearly a highly skilled photographer.

"Did you ask my permission?"

A gently enquiring voice stopped Jack in mid-click. It came from beneath the café stairs, an external addition of concrete steps with an iron balustrade that led to upstairs rooms. It was angled in such a way against the sun to cast a permanent shade beneath itself.

"Do even the walls talk here?" Jack asked the darkness beneath the stairs.

"Sometimes. Today it is only me. I'm Joan."

"You're the tick-tack-toe lady."

"You remembered."

"It was a memorable story."

"It was a little more than a story."

"I'm Jack and until you spoke, I was doing okay. Tell me, what were you doing under there? You scared the hell out of me."

"Glad to be of use. There's no mystery. It's cool. It provides shade all day and, during darshan, the café is empty and peaceful. Tell me, Jack, what are you doing here?" Joan wasn't accusing, just matter of fact.

"I was taking pictures." Jack made an obvious response but he hadn't answered the question asked.

"No. What are you doing . . . here? What's your reason for being . . . here?" Joan was persistent.

"I'm a pilgrim," Jack began.

"And what else?" Joan insisted.

Jack wasn't offended; he laughed instead.

"I was going to say that I'm here to investigate plausible liars and implausible truths. But I thought that sounded pompous even inside my own head."

"I see you watching and you're always listening. Are you from the ashram or the Rationalists, like that horrible man Bishnu?"

Jack shook his head in denial but made a quick note of the name Bishnu. He liked horrible men; they always knew dark secrets and could never keep them to themselves. "None of the aforementioned," Jack declared, amused.

"The immigration police, then? Are you a journalist?" She suddenly thought.

"That's a better question. Nearer the mark. I was once, but for most of the last years I've been a filmmaker."

"Ah!" Joan seemed pleased with herself.

"You guessed?" asked Jack, as if he'd been uncovered.

"No. Never crossed my mind."

"Does that disappoint you?" asked Jack feeling oddly deflated. Most people were impressed by what he did, at least they were curious.

"I thought you were a spy. There is at least a certain glamour in that," Joan added.

"I am."

"You are?" Joan seemed delighted.

"Yes, but I don't represent anyone or anything. I just watch and listen, as you noticed. I've planted myself in a group of Danes."

"Yes. Sven and his happy band of devotees, according to Maddy. They sometimes come here."

"True. Mostly I avoid them. We've travelled enough together, already. If my cover is blown then I can break free."

"I'll not blow your cover," Joan assured him.

"Can I buy you a cup of tea? Hey! I need another tea out here." Jack shouted into the alcove that hoped to be a kitchen. A quiet voice responded and Jack concentrated once more on Joan.

"So, what's your story, Joan?" Jack smiled encouragement.

"You haven't finished yours yet." Joan was determined.

"True. So, I am amongst a group of Western spiritual tourists who want a fast track to God and Enlightenment. They've been grouped and dispatched to the God-Man of their choosing, Sai Baba, and I'm going to make a film about an uncommitted pilgrim called Soren. His fellow travellers are all devotees, as you have seen. I want to track the change in him and his perception of their god. I also have an interest in those who manage Baba's ashrams. I've heard they can be jealous. I understand they criticise those who visit other God-Men. They demand exclusivity. They call those who wander spiritual prostitutes."

"Do you wander, Jack?"

"Endlessly. By their standards I'm a spiritual tramp. I've made films about ayurvedic medicine and Deepak Chopra. I spent hours taking pin-knob steps with a Vietnamese monk in a valley full of plum trees saying in all honesty: 'I am here. I am here. I am now. I am now.' I'm off to a red mountain that's a god. And a woman who's a god. And a man who sprays vibhuti ash from his mouth. And a yogi whose hands fused together in prayer and if I'm in time, I'll have lunch with the Dalai Lama in Pondicherry."

"Are you Soren?"

"No, I'm Jack, I've already told you."

"I meant in spirit?"

"I know you did."

"Does your film have a name?"

"Nearly. I thought I'd call it, 'The God Business' or perhaps, 'God Incorporated.'"

"Choose that last one. That's a clever title." Joan brightened.

"I'm a clever guy," Jack declared.

"Really?" Joan showed genuine surprise.

"Why so surprised?" Jack was offended.

"You're an American." He relaxed. It was only prejudice, nothing personal.

"No, I'm from New York."

"That's different?"

"Entirely. Look, Joan, can you help me? You've been around this block a lot of times. I may have a scruffy body and unpleasant habits but my brain is very tidy and I'm nobody's judge. I'm nosy, really curious, about everything from the superficial to the deep: Why does a white European dress like an

Indian? Why are the Indians complicit in this game? Why is this place a circus? I look around and feel no sacredness here and yet, when I'm stuck on the ashram marble and my bum is dead to this world, I sense something really special in that man. We nearly touched toes, you know, and I was thrilled. Help me answer these questions, Joan. Why are you still here? Why were you ever here at all?" Jack paused. Joan thought carefully before answering. Her face saddened as she reminded herself of her difficult past. She would be entirely honest with both Jack, the inquisitive stranger, and herself.

"Because of the death of my child. He was called Michael. He was twelve and even then young for his age. He was fair-skinned and fragile. He was always polite and so innocent no one bullied him. He had freckles, across his nose and the tops of his cheeks. He wore a brace on his teeth. It made him salivate so always he was wiping his mouth on his hand . . ." She made the gesture herself, intent on remembering. "Even when he was singing in the church choir, he would wipe his mouth. The boys let him be. If they tempted him to smoke a cigarette, after practice, by the shed where they left their bikes, he'd say, 'No, thank you'. And they left it at that. They wept by his coffin when they sang in their church. I thought it unfair to ask them to do that. I had to be there. I was his mother. But they said they had volunteered, because they liked Michael so much. I thought that was kind, don't you?"

Jack nodded. He wouldn't speak.

"It was meningitis. The doctor hadn't guessed. No one realized he was dying until he did. I could never accept his death." Tearless, she looked at Jack with a rekindled anger glowing in her eyes. "There were enough people to blame, but I focused on God. I asked questions that no one could answer. Why? Pointless. Why a child? Pointless. Why my child? Personal. Selfish. I decided to hate the Almighty. I wouldn't accept Fate. I scoffed at the inane remarks of our well-meaning vicar who swallowed and regurgitated more clichés than I thought existed."

"I'm sorry for you," Jack offered in a moment of silence.

"It got worse. My husband left me. My obsession with the unfairness of it all bored him. There was soon nothing more to say. It became the sound of a cracked record that stuck in the same scratch. It festered and went bad."

"So why here?" asked Jack, tentatively.

"Baba beckoned me from the sky and I accepted the invitation. I was exhausted with all the unanswerable Christian questions. It didn't help to think Michael was with God, in a happier place, taken early because he was pure. After all, only the good die young." Joan put on a wry smile.

"I'll make old bones then," Jack claimed, smiling in turn.

"If each physical life is only part of a greater and more complex journey then the impact of its loss is somehow lessened. Michael's death wasn't premature; it was on time. He wasn't taken; he left. I have a new explanation and a new experience. I came here in hope. I came in love. I dress like an Indian because my European clothes wore out and no one in the Home Counties can imagine the heat in India. I still love Sai Baba but He ignores my love. I dislike the ashram and everyone inside it except Him. It makes no sense any more and I've made a habit of waiting, praying one day He'll call me back and, to be ready, I need to be nearby. So I'll stay and I'll warn the others of the corruption and the evil inside there." She pointed across the ditch to the ashram walls. "I won't help you, Jack. Not because I don't want to but because there is someone else who might be of more use to you than me."

"Who?" Even if disappointed, Jack never lost the scent, however faint.

"Her name is Rita. She never goes out. Not now."

"Why not?" Jack was concerned and instinctively reached for his notebook.

"Give me that." Joan reached out a hand.

"What for?" Jack was cautious. His thoughts and ideas were precious and too private to be seen; on occasion, even he didn't like what he read.

"I'll draw you a map. It'll take you to Rita's house."

"Tell me something of her story." Jack watched as Joan, hand extended to receive his pencil stub, drew a simple outline map on a fresh page of the notebook.

"She'll tell you everything. Or nothing at all. She may not even open her door. Persuade her to come out. Do us all that favour. She mustn't give in to her fears."

"What is she afraid of?"

"What she knows. What she has seen. She was there on the day of the assassination attempt. She was a witness. Rita was really influential in the early days. She knows everyone, good or bad, mostly bad, in the Trust. She was a major organiser of the trips from England and Europe to here and Puttaparthi. She thinks she knows too much about the corruption. She has all the detail, Jack. She'll give you names and dates and tell of amounts of money, or she'll not speak to you at all." Joan gave back the notebook. Before letting go she looked intently at Jack. "Be kind, Jack. Don't rush her. Don't bully her. She lost everything to be here. All that's left is her life and she fears for that."

"I hear you," said Jack.

CHAPTER TWENTY
Finding Rita

Jack was reading his map. He was already lost and he'd only walked in a straight line from the ashram. He'd ask Maddy. If she didn't know the way then it wasn't knowable. Rita would never be found.

Jack grinned. He dithered outside the open gate and stared. Forming part of the entrance to Maddy's compound was a pillar built of red brick, capped by a concrete coping stone. Drawn clumsily in peeling white paint was a sign 'Way to Rita Conveni' with a bold arrow beside the 'to' pointing left. Jack laughed, automatically thanked Sai Baba and frowned instantly, annoyed that he too had been infected by the absurd habit of accrediting every accident and coincidence to some divine plan of the avatar.

He went left. Off the road his clumsy shuffling sent out clouds of dust. His map had a house number, 120 Main Road. Frustratingly, the houses he saw had no numbers. He would ask. He called to a young boy, festooned with bunches of flowers. He was helper to a busy Indian girl who was selling the flowers door-to-door.

"Hey, young man, I need directions."

The boy approached Jack but looked nonplussed. Jack began again and the boy waved the words over his head, signalling their lack of meaning. The boy pouted and 'pouffed' so Jack guessed he was French.

"Bon jooer," he began, but it didn't help and the Indian girl came to his aid.

"Isn't he French?" asked Jack.

"Yes, sir. But you're not. Can I help?"

Her English was good, her French better, as she dismissed her helper and pointed his way down the dirt road. Jack showed the girl his map and explained, "I'm looking for Rita's house. Is this it?" He pointed to the nearest building in hope.

"Yes," the girl replied and followed her flower carrier in a rush.

Jack banged on the door. No one came. He banged again and a strange-looking Indian appeared in the doorway. He'd snatched the door open so was suddenly in view. The speed startled Jack. So did the man. He was little and perfectly round with a long stubble of hair, dyed pink. He wore glasses with lift-up shades that carried lenses in both halves. Jack, top to toe, the Earth and the distant horizon would all be in focus simultaneously. It must have been confusing. And now he'd met Jack.

"I have a map. It doesn't work, see." Jack placed the open page in between himself and the man with the pink hair who snapped the lenses to and saw the enlarged image with some semblance of awareness. He nodded and smiled. It was misleading. He wafted the map away, shrugged his shoulders and slipped back inside, closing the door slowly. No words were spoken.

Further down the road, Jack saw the French boy but not the girl. He waved. The boy pointed with verve to the building that he stood next to. Then he turned and ran. Most of his flowers had gone. When Jack arrived he stood next to a humble hut with a corrugated roof. There was an untilled garden growing dead things, the semblance of a path and a solid looking door with a large brass knocker. To the side of the gateposts (there was no gate) was a bird box for letters. Nailed to the post was a sign that said 'Rita's' in white paint. Jack admired the apostrophe. Its use pleased him. Striding boldly to the door, he wrapped the knocker, not loudly but constantly; a regular beat that soon annoyed him, let alone anyone inside.

Nothing

Rap! Rap! Rap!

Nothing

Rap! Rap! Rap!

"What is it? What can you possibly want with me?" The voice was shouting but the wood of the door muffled its volume.

"Are you Rita? If you're Rita I'd like to meet you. If you're not, well, who knows? I'm Jack. I was told to say Joan sent me. That's my passport. Will it work? Will you let me in?"

Jack waited. He smiled at the absurdity of the moment. Across the way the French boy passed, all his flowers gone, and he gave Jack a cheery wave and a pair of confident thumbs, raised up in greeting. Jack waved back. There was a creak and dragging and the door opened.

"I'm Jack. Are you Rita?"

"Yes, I'm Rita."

She let Jack in, closing the door carefully behind him and indicating he should sit on the couch set against the back wall of the room. She sat on a nest of cushions on the floor. Changed her mind. Stood up.

"Can I make tea? I forget to be sociable. I rarely have a visitor, you see."

"So I understand," replied Jack, his normal voice sounding loud in the room. Rita's speaking wasn't muffled by the door, as he'd thought; her voice was naturally soft, not a normal volume suppressed into a whisper.

Jack liked how Rita looked. She had a mass of hair, parted to the side, wavy and full but mottled grey now and a little greasy. It needed a wash. She wasn't as old as she wished, Forties in years and style. There was a hint of the film star with her fine features: straight, elegant nose, high cheekbones, delicate chin, a mouth that might be pretty but was at this moment resigned, set somewhere between a smile and a scowl.

She wore a floral-patterned dress and a white cotton shawl. No shoes. She was pale, out of the sun, hollow-cheeked with dark, tired eyes. Jack imagined her in a Hollywood movie. This was before: he'd like to see her after. Dye her hair, refresh her skin, put on thirty pounds, she'd be a looker, in the sort of way Jack enjoyed. But now, there was no light in her eyes. She was emaciated and grey and nervous like a bird in a cage. Jack had time to stare. He could've drawn a sketch. She made him tea, handed it over, took none herself and sank into a profound silence on the cushions on the floor.

Suddenly she spoke.

"The storm is rising."

"It is?"

"There is no harmony here."

"Where?"

"The whole organisation of the God-World."

"I'm not following you, Rita."

"Others are."

She looked straight into Jack's eyes. The challenge of her stare was unnerving.

"Who?" Jack took her seriously right away.

"The Council and the leaders of the ashrams."

"Why?"

"I questioned their motives so they threatened me. I do not share their views so I was disaffiliated." The delicate 'f's' of the oddly chosen word, rather than being reassuring, sent a shiver through Jack.

"If you don't believe me, believe Baba."

She pulled a small metal box towards her. It was full of plain postcards. She flicked through them skilfully with the long nails of her fingers.

"This is Swami: 'Many people are collecting money in various places using My Name for various purposes. That is unauthorised and against My Wish and Command.' Now do believe me?" She stressed all the capital letters in her quotation.

"I already did. What's this about, Rita?"

"Power."

Jack was out of breath and he'd hardly spoken.

"Can we start at the beginning rather than the end? This is all too sudden for me and not a little bit scary, I tell you."

Rita seemed calmer after her outburst.

"Who are you, Jack? Joan doesn't have friends like you."

"I don't have friends like Joan. Not in normal circumstances no, but not much is normal here, is it?"

"No."

"To cut to the chase. I've come to you for detail. That's what Joan promised. I'm a filmmaker. I'm in India with a group of Baba-besotted Danes to make a film about the God Business."

"To expose it?" asked Rita, with the beginnings of an interest.

"Perhaps. That's not my job. I've come to find out. You know things I don't know. Will you tell me your story? Would you like to be in a film?"

Rita froze.

"Don't answer that. It's your information I need more than your face. I can hire any number of faces. It's your private story that matters and I don't need your name to broadcast other guilty names or to expose guilty faces. So, relax. You've a very quiet voice but it's not English," Jack added, hoping to build confidence in his frightened new friend. He needed a softer approach, less fraught, more inane.

"I'm an American," Rita revealed.

"I thought so."

"That's why I let you in."

"How did you know I was American?"

"You spoke."

Jack laughed. Rita smiled.

"Where you from?"

"Washington DC. In another life, when I owned a bookshop, had a husband and a daughter."

"Where's your husband? Do you mind?" Jack held two objects in his hand, surreptitiously smuggled out of his bag while Rita was remembering. The one was the red notebook, the other a micro-cassette recorder. Rita didn't speak but nodded to the notebook and grimaced at the recorder.

"I usually record myself. It's so darn hot here the pencil slips from my fingers. But then, I'm clumsy anyway. Is your husband . . .?"

"Dead. He died a while ago. Baba wouldn't save him."

"Did he try?" Jack asked carefully.

"Not hard enough, clearly. But that is . . . I met him in a 'New Age' community living around a man-made lake. He taught classes."

"On what?"

"The nature and cause of miracles."

"Unusual," was all Jack could think to say.

"He went on to specialise in Astral Travel."

Jack hesitated.

"Don't you want to write that down?" Rita asked.

"I'm not sure. I won't forget it."

"We went together to the Blue Ridge Mountains and lived in sleep-boxes. We weren't interested in the Orient then, just flower power and aerobics."

Jack had written none of this down.

"Then one day, a boy bought me a book on Sai Baba. I glimpsed big hair, a tight orange gown and a very small man."

"So it began." Jack concluded.

"No. I never read it. What I did read was *Autobiography of a Yogi*. That did change my life. It will change yours … anyone's."

116

"I'll get a copy," said Jack helpfully.

"I'll lend you mine." There was to be no escape, Jack realised.

"I met an exhausted friend in a diner in Colorado. Our daughters were at the same school. She was going to India to see Sai Baba. I expressed an interest. She was very touchy and defensive but gradually, one by one, she lent me books. Each one was a revelation to me. The sky opened. I used to sit and cry over those books." She paused and smiled at her memories. "I found a group of Indian followers of the great man. It was lovely. It was the sweetest experience. I joined their prayers and chantings, learned to call the hymns bhajans. They were innocent people. So was I then."

"When did you lose that innocence?" asked Jack, knowing guilt was far more filmic.

"Immediately." Rita was calm: Jack was perplexed.

"I met people who spent fortunes getting to Puttaparthi. One was a girl with the sweetest singing voice, dying of a debilitating disease. There was no interview, no cure, and no God interference. Baba never heard her sing. The mother of my daughter's friend, she stayed away months at a time. Her family went to drag her away. Baba visited her in a dream saying, 'You have very bad thoughts!' So she went on seven visits in seven years, to think good thoughts. There was no interview. I was always very sceptical. I am too analytical perhaps. I am after all, a practical person."

CHAPTER TWENTY-ONE
Sweatshops and Bondslaves

Hari was shepherding his grandfather towards their rented house. He had said goodbye to his mother and father. His father's parting words had disturbed him. Hari was revelling in his independence, reassuring his mother that he coped easily in her absence and marvelled at the extent of his grandfather's acquaintants, the main source of his security.

"But he doesn't know the beggars, Hari. I warn you again, stay away from the beggars."

Ramu Sarnhi was taking longer rests and only attended darshan once a day, not always in the evening, but mostly then. He sat on his daybed, comfortable with cushions and throws, and invited Hari to join him there on the veranda at the rear of the house.

"You look troubled, Hari. Is anything wrong?"

"No, Grandfather." Hari wondered if he should share his concerns for Lunasha and declare his disobedient involvement in the life of a beggar. Perhaps another time. He didn't want to add to his grandfather's difficulties. Ramu Sarnhi looked ill that morning.

"Grandfather, there was something you said that has been bothering me." Hari was much more at the ease with his grandfather now. It might be because the encroaching illness had made the self-important man a little less assertive or that Hari was more used to his ways. There was a growing intimacy that they both enjoyed. Ramu Sarnhi was keen to draw Hari into the family, and Hari was eager to feel he was welcomed and belonged.

"You said you owned all the land beyond the village and the people on it. Is that true? Do you own people?" Hari looked concerned. He knew more than he was saying. Immersed in the rag trade of Birmingham, he was aware of the terms 'sweatshop' and 'sweated labour'. He knew his father always questioned the origin of some of the cheapest garments he was offered. They might end up on his uncles' stall. Even they expressed concerns about exploiting children, keeping them away from school, stealing their childhood. He knew about child labour in India and hoped his grandfather wasn't involved.

"I have no bondslaves, Hari, if that's what you fear." Ramu Sarnhi was a little offended by his grandson's suspicions.

"I don't know what they are, Grandfather? Please explain to me." Hari recognised his grandfather's annoyance. He hoped his declared ignorance would restore the balance between them.

"I had two cousins who were bondslaves. I never was, but I could so easily have been." Bitter memories passed through Ramu Sarnhi's mind. "It's very seductive and so easy to be trapped."

"How can it happen?" Hari asked, nervous of what might be described.

"A kindly adult offers you 'sponsorship' or a small loan. I mean very small, just a handful of rupees. 'You can buy the tools of your trade,' they'd say, or, 'Don't pay me money, pay me with work.' They bind even children with debt. One of my cousins borrowed ten thousand rupees, two hundred and fifty of your English pounds. He bought a part share in a loom. It took twenty years to pay off his debt. I've seen children in debt-bondage, sold as indentured labour by their parents. They pay the children two, three rupees a day for twelve hours work. They will never be free."

"But you don't do this, Grandfather," Hari stated.

"Of course not. It is illegal. It was abolished twenty years ago, but still millions of children are enslaved, particularly in our business of silk." Ramu Sarnhi paused. His anger had animated him: his memories gave him energy. "I would never borrow. I was perhaps your age, no, maybe twelve, a little older than you, Hari. I was set free from sorting cocoons or sitting at the loom. I was going to sell. I was a pretty boy, can you believe that?"

Hari smiled, not daring to comment.

"I was slender and elegant and very persuasive. I insisted that I worked on commission only. If I didn't sell, I didn't get paid. I never needed to use other people's money and they could never use me. They still can't. I began by bidding for spoiled end pieces to sell to market traders."

"Like my uncles in Birmingham," Hari interrupted.

"Is that what they do?" Ramu Sarnhi asked quizzically. "But not your father, surely?"

"No. Father is high end." Hari never knew precisely what the term meant but he had heard it often enough to feel comfortable repeating the phrase.

"It didn't take me many years to move to the high end myself." Ramu Sarnhi paused, rethinking his past. Hari waited patiently.

"Tomorrow, I'll take you to one of my villages. I'll show you what I do. I buy the looms and roof the houses, bring in water and dig cisterns. But I don't enslave my workers. We have a co-operative. We share. I wouldn't see any of my workers' children with dye-stained hands or scalded fingers. I have set up a school with a teacher. It is kind of me, is it not?"

"Of course, Grandfather, most kind." Hari was somewhat abashed by these revelations.

"It is kind, but also, it is very good business. If all of the villagers can read and write; if they feel they benefit from the work as well as me—I am no hypocrite Hari, I and my family and you make far, far more than they ever will out of silk—then they are much better workers. You must go. Tell me about darshan when we meet later. Remember me in your interview."

... a group of itinerant beggars had set up camp

CHAPTER TWENTY-TWO
Sam

Hari was peering into Maddy's compound. The ornate iron gate was open and the barbed wire fencing was no longer attached to the tumbling concrete pillars that protected the front courtyard from the roadside. A male helper in European shirt and shorts was filling a bucket from a freestanding, blue water tank half-hidden beneath a row of palm trees and an incongruous conifer.

The furthest building had a concrete façade, stained with moss, dirtied with age, made cheerful by window frames painted lime green. The nearer building looked much newer. The roof tiles were neat and entire, the windows were shuttered and the paint was still white. People came and went but not Maddy or Lunasha.

Hari walked the lane from the ashram each morning, occasionally accompanied by Jack who seemed bent on some mysterious business of his own and veered away to follow the sign to Rita's house. Hari asked why, but Jack didn't respond. Next to Maddy's compound a group of itinerant beggars had set up camp. It was temporary and fragile: an awning strung beneath a tree, a stone for a hearth, a pile of twigs and kindling half-covered in rags to make fires for cooking. A couple of girls were staring into a metal cooking pot, its steam drifting in the early morning breeze. A toddler and a mangy dog stood guard over the mouth of the awning. Hari peered inside. He caught a glimpse of a pile of bodies, creatures, he thought of them as creatures, lying there as part of, as growing out of the dark earth.

He had been told that these were experienced professionals, followers of a crowd, from way up north. They were happily deformed, skilled in wretchedness. A young girl wriggled and turned at the edge of the pack. Half of her face seemed to rest on the floor after she raised her head. A dewlap of flesh clung to her left cheek and dangled to her shoulder with alarming ugliness. Another fold of skin had distended her eye and then grown down into a wrinkled goiter on her neck. She seemed very pleased, absurdly proud, to be able to point to such an unavoidable deformity. Hari looked away, ashamed of his horror and his fascination. In her sleep, another beggar girl whined "Sai Ram! Sai Ram!"

"Hari? It is Hari?" He was startled to hear his name but pleased when he saw it was Sam calling, the deaf Australian lady who he'd met in the Sai Deep Café and had helped with her papers.

"Come away, Hari. They are to be pitied but also, to be feared, I think. Come." She beckoned him close and to his surprise put an arm around his shoulder, held him tightly and ushered him through the gate into Maddy's compound. She sat on the steps in front of the old building and encouraged

Hari to join her. She was tall with large features, accentuated by hair cut severely to the shape of her head. Despite being close-cropped it was black and wiry. Hari guessed if left to grow it might sprout into a halo like Sai Baba's. There was a similarity, Hari realised, as Sam stared intently into him.

"What are you wondering about me, Hari?"

Embarrassed, he didn't know what to say.

"Am I strange to you?" Her voice was coaxing not antagonistic.

"No. I think you're very nice." His honesty was clear.

"Thank you." Sam was flattered.

"I was wondering where you were from. You said it was Australia?" Hari dared to ask.

"But I don't look Australian, do I? And I'm definitely not white. Don't worry, Hari. I am not offended. I have been as confused as you about who I am."

Hari hoped he hadn't awoken unpleasant thoughts or memories for Sam.

"I was born in Africa. My father was Indian, my mother half-white, half-African. I have little memory of Africa. We were expelled when I was still a young child. Most of my father's friends went to England. My father thought Australia might be more welcoming to my mother. He was convinced it was a tolerant country, more easy-going than the United Kingdom, more welcoming of foreigners. He was wrong. We were never entirely welcome, especially as he was to become a successful businessman. Somehow that made things worse. My mother pined for Africa. It made her ill and she died. My father and I stayed. He too became ill but not until recently. He also died. I am here in India because this is where his family had their origin. I came looking for somewhere to belong. I didn't find it amongst his family, no matter how extended. But I did find my home in Puttaparthi, in the ashram with Sai Baba. He became my spiritual father and mother."

'Sai Ram,' thought Hari.

"Sai Ram," said Sam.

'Sai Ram,' had called the beggar girl.

"I'm learning the language Swami speaks," Sam continued, "a language my father and his family also spoke. My father forgot the words. I'm relearning them on his behalf. I will speak his language even if I can't hear it."

Hari dare not ask her how.

"Do you have problems of belonging, like me, Hari?"

"No. I don't think so."

"Do you belong here?" Sam's gesture implied all of India beyond the compound.

"No. I'm from ..."

"Where?" Sam interrupted him.

"I was going to say Birmingham in England. I was born there but I suppose I belong here. My father was born here but grew up in England and my grandfather always lives here. He rarely leaves Bangalore."

"So where are you from?" Sam was persistent.

"Birmingham and Bangalore. I'm from both places." He was 'Hari' in India but usually heard his name as 'Harry', that was how all his friends in England pronounced it. And so did Jack.

"Can you span such a distance? Don't answer me. I was only wondering. You see you looked lonely to me, Hari. As if you or something were lost. Have you lost something, Hari?" She smiled. Hari liked her very much. She seemed full of kindness. Yet he didn't know what to reply. He couldn't deceive this woman. She was too open-hearted.

"I haven't seen Maddy for a few days. I was surprised. She's been so busy and bustling my grandfather and everyone. Or Lunasha." The afterthought came first. That much was obvious to Sam.

"Lunasha isn't here," Sam began to explain.

"But Maddy promised! She did promise." Hari had interrupted. He was concerned, worried, angry, confused.

"You must let me finish my sentences. I know they take time because I have to be deliberate. I'm sorry for that."

Hari felt a little ashamed but no less worried.

"I'm sorry, Sam. I didn't mean to be rude. It's just that, well, you must keep a promise or not make one." He was calmer.

"She has kept her promise, Hari. Lunasha has joined us here. She is sharing a room with Om."

"Is that a person?" asked Hari, wondering.

"Yes. Om is a young girl. She found us here a few months ago and is a natural friend for Lunasha. There is a difference, though."

"What?" asked Hari, momentarily distracted from his anxiety.

"The world rejected Lunasha: Om rejected the world. She wears the orange robe of the sanyassin. It signals a total surrender to the will of God. The robe is all she possesses. Together she and Lunasha might make one skeleton. They both forget to eat."

"Where is Lunasha?" Hari was determined. He followed only one trail.

"Maddy has taken her to Kakinada, on the coast. It is quite a way. They'll return very soon."

"Good." Hari paused, hoping Sam would explain why this sudden journey was so important.

"They have gone to visit Maddy's guru." Hari had not understood.

"I thought it was Kodaikanal, not ..."

"Kakinada," Sam completed the sentence. "Kodaikanal is Sai Baba's

123

destination. Maddy has gone to visit Shivabalayogi."

"Who?"

"That is her guru. He's very ill. He may not return to Bangalore so Maddy has rushed to him and has a special quest just for Lunasha, something quite precisely for her."

"What?" Hari demanded then added, "Precisely?" to lessen the urgency of his question.

"I don't know. She didn't say. You must ask Maddy when she returns. Of course, there would be no point in asking Lunasha." Sam didn't expand on this statement. She had a habit of speaking a sentence then pausing, perhaps to ensure all the words had escaped, made complete sense and were understood. But such a deliberate method only added to Hari's frustration.

"Why not ask Lunasha?" Hari asked finally after an interminable quiet.

"Because of her vow of silence." Sam's announcement astonished Hari. It was he who was suddenly dumbfounded.

"Would you explain please? I don't understand."

"You know that Lunasha has been mistreated?"

"Yes, I do."

"By both her families?"

"Yes."

"And by society at large?"

"Yes."

"She told her story to everyone concerned. Husband, father, mother, cousins, the police authorities and finally, anyone she passed on the roadside. But no one listened. Then one day she realised that her spoken truth and total silence were equal in the world. So she decided to speak no longer, to save her breath for prayer. She would talk to her soul instead."

Hari listened. Thought he understood but suddenly objected.

"How do you know?"

"Sorry?"

"How can you know this if she vows to be silent?"

"Maddy discovered this. Quite quickly." Sam smiled, trying to allay Hari's suspicions but surprised by his doubts.

"Maddy understands how bodies talk. The gestures of hands and the yearning of eyes are just as expressive as mouths. I'm sure Lunasha found ways to explain her plight to Maddy and I know Maddy would be quick and perceptive in her understanding. She responded to me at once and found ways to shape my lips and her own to let me know if my word-sounds were pure or not. She is a remarkable being, Maddy. You did well to bring Lunasha to her."

"Will she make her speak?" asked Hari, reassured but still anxious.

"No. I shouldn't think so. Only Lunasha can decide to do that. But we are concerned that she eats so little. We'd like to preserve her life, not dissuade her from her simple protest at the disappointing ways of the world."

"And will ..." Hari didn't even attempt the name, "Maddy's guru save Lunasha's life?"

"No. He is a yogi, not an avatar. Swami is a very different being to Shivabalayogi."

"Is it allowed?"

"What?"

"To have two gods." Hari was struggling with this concept.

"Like I said, one god, one teacher. Let me tell you about Shivabalayogi. His name is long but its meaning is simple. The boy yogi inspired by Shiva."

"I know about Shiva," Hari was quick to explain.

"Good. When Shivabalayogi was a young boy, a few years older than you, just fourteen, he was playing with his friends by an irrigation canal on the edge of the village of Adivarapupeta where he had been born and where he worked. He was with his young friends, playing, laughing and eating palmyra fruit that had ripened and fallen from the palm trees. He was about to bite into the soft, sweet flesh when the sound of 'Om' came from inside the fruit. There was a powerful light and suddenly he was holding a black Shiva lingam this long." She measured half a metre and Hari nodded his understanding so she would continue quickly with her tale. "It suddenly broke in two to reveal the future guru of Shivabalayogi. He was seven feet tall. His body was smeared with ash. It was Lord Shiva himself. He stepped forward and touched the boy between the brows, on the site of his spiritual eye and Shivabalayogi entered into a state of spiritual bliss. For twelve long years he sat in silence, thinking, growing more and more spiritual day by day, year by year. We call this state samadhi. Thousands of people came to see him. Then late one summer, he stopped. A divine light from the sky lit up his body. And he spoke to the people for the first time in twelve years."

"What did he say?" asked Hari.

"'In samadhi you can go to the Sun and you can come back. I am telling you from my own experience. Only the person who wants to bring peace to the world can visit the Sun.'" Sam spoke in, what Hari assumed, was an imitation of Shivabalayogi's voice.

"I don't understand."

"Nor me. But it is very beautiful." Sam laughed.

"Is he a good guru?" Hari wondered, out loud.

"Oh yes. He is simple and pure. He never gives lectures. He has written no books. And his message is so simple. 'Meditation is the light of the world'."

"Is it?"

"Yes. I think so."

"Is it hard to meditate?"

"No. It is very simple."

"But, twelve years is an awfully long time."

Sam laughed. "It is. But that is only for the holiest of the holy. Shivabalayogi recommends just one hour a day. That is plenty for people busy with the world like Maddy."

"Or me," said Hari. "What do you do? Exactly?" Hari was intrigued.

"We could meditate together now."

"Really?"

"Yes. So, sit comfortably." Sam flicked her supple legs into a Full Lotus. Hari didn't even try.

"Close your eyes."

He did.

"Do not move your eyes."

He had.

"Concentrate your mind and focus your attention in between your eyebrows."

Hari hoped frowning would count.

"Say no mantras, significantly repeated phrases, words or chants."

Hari didn't know any so he was safe.

"Name no names."

He wouldn't

"Imagine nothing."

He imagined nothing.

"Keep your eyes closed until the meditation is over."

Hari did as he was told and sat in dutiful but thoughtful silence for what seemed like a very long time. Fortunately Sam spoke after ten minutes.

"Well done. Were you peaceful?" Sam asked.

"Yes. I was, thank you. I don't know if I did it right. What's it for?"

"Meditation?"

"Yes."

"To bring about the realisation of 'That'."

Hari didn't ask any more questions.

CHAPTER TWENTY-THREE
Rita found

On his second visit, prearranged and less troublesome to complete, Jack was hoping for something controversial. He liked Rita. She was a nice person, full of troubles and sadness, but nice. Jack knew that nice wouldn't film.

Even though expected, Rita had made no effort with her appearance. Waiting for tea, Jack looked around the house she occupied. It was untidy and ruffled. Pillars of books stood on the floor. Postcards full of notes in an immature hand were spread in loose fans over the worn carpet. The kitchen area was as unwashed as Rita's hair. Jack felt at home. He knew his untidiness was innate. He guessed Rita's grew from her depression. She handed Jack his tea and again, drinking nothing herself, sat on the floor.

"I was thinking, when you left, I should've gone back to America." This was Rita's opening statement.

Jack had checked his notes before this meeting. A few quick glances in his notebook only added to his confusion.

"I didn't know you'd left. Last I heard you were in a diner in Colorado."

"It burned down."

"What did?"

"The diner. Isn't that strange? It served a purpose and was gone. Obliterated. Quite frightening, really. No traces left."

"Where the hell are you, Rita? I reckon you spend too much time alone. You seem to have lost the knack of conversation. You kind of jump bits, whole scenes, and it makes the narrative tricky. I need to pick up the thread."

"Oh." Rita was unrepentant and in no way fazed by Jack's controlled annoyance.

"Didn't I say?" She was still vague. Jack hoped it was drugs.

"Say what?"

"We moved to England. South of London. It's hard to keep changing cultures, don't you find?"

"Not really," Jack replied.

"We bought a house. I placed my daughter in a grammar school. It was a good one. I had forgotten all about Sai Baba. Then slowly, my house fell down."

"Was this 'Three Little Pigs' or for real?" Jack had taken no notes.

"It was very real. Subsidence. Our neighbour's house was leaning as well. And the one beyond that. There was no one to blame. At least, the blame kept moving from builder to planner to council; the mining companies, the holding company, then to the government. It was quite a trail. None of us could sell. We were trapped inside a tumbling world. It was very troubling, Jack."

"I can see that. So what did you do?"

"I joined a Sai Baba group."

"Ah." Jack was on the trail again.

"Where?"

"They were based in Suffolk."

"Was it a relief?"

"No. I was disgusted with the organisers right from the beginning."

"Right." Jack jotted down the phrase 'unpredictable witness' and waited.

"There were weird happenings. I mean, weird." She looked perplexed.

"I wanted to run a mile. I sensed vibrations. I thought I was governed by my common sense but I ignored it, even though my every instinct knew that the organisation was awful. The people who ran the whole of the Sai Baba organisation in England were corrupt. They were only interested in collecting money. They were from North Africa. They were called ..."

"Yes?" Jack waited, pencil poised.

"I can't name them. Nor can you. They will sue you, me, the world, God himself, given access. I kept wondering how had they managed to gain control of such a huge organisation when they didn't have enough money for their children's shoes? Was it a deliberate act of poverty? Or something more sinister?"

"You tell me."

"I will. I travelled with them to India. London-Bombay-Madras-Bangalore. It took thirty-six hours. We were a huge group. Many were well into their seventies. They were entirely off-balance, with no sleep. We were packaged like, I was going to say slaves but that's too extreme; each one of us was a commodity. There was no proper accommodation in Whitefield. We all slept in a shed. There were no toilets. Everything was communal. There were piles of rubbish everywhere. My husband, Tom, was very ill. He needed some comfort."

"Did you find any?" asked Jack, as Rita fell into silence.

"At darshan, yes. The whole group was granted an interview."

"Wow!" Jack was impressed.

"Baba didn't look at any one of us. We weren't individuals to him. But it was very seductive. Very beautiful. Breathtaking. Mesmerising."

She stared at the wall behind Jack's head, focused on the only image hanging there, a photograph of Sai Baba, looking the other way.

"I saw us all as gargoyles. Images from the unconscious. We were covered in pinks and blues. The vibrations in the room were very high. I tried to talk to Him about Tom. 'My husband,' I began, quietly, 'My husband!' I shouted. Baba didn't want to know he existed. He waved me aside. 'He's ill!

He's dying!' I told him. Still He waved me aside."

"I'm sorry." Jack tried to be sympathetic.

"I wasn't, oddly. Not sorry. I was besotted with His power. Why wouldn't God be indifferent to an insignificant man? One man. One man dying in millions dying in thousands of millions living?" She paused then, businesslike; in turn, she quickly continued. "I had another interview two days later. Baba spoke to me the night before the interview. He spoke to my subconscious. He has that yogic power. I sensed something. Someone. I remember being ill. Of what, I don't remember but I was near to collapse. Then the lights went out. I couldn't breathe. Then my breathing changed. I lay still.

"'Are you all right?' asked the voice.

"'You,' said the voice.

"The voice was inside my body. I was talking to me. The voice was my voice. His voice. My ventriloquist. I was his doll. I don't know how these things happened to me. He/I called my name four times.

"'Rita!'

"'Rita!'

"'Rita!'

"'Rita!'

"'You.'

"'I'm in your heart!'

"'The problem lies with the heart. You must open it wide. I've been knocking away at your heart for ages now.'

"It was as if I was struck by lightning. I got up. I went to a friend, a woman, I said, 'I really don't feel well. It frightened me.'

"'Go to the toilet,' she said.

"'There are no toilets.'

"I lay in my cot all night awake. I knew I would have an interview the next morning."

"Did you?" asked Jack, unsettled by Rita's account.

"Yes. I didn't want to go. Even before I went, I didn't want to go. But I went." She stopped.

"What happened?"

"Sai Baba talked about toilets. I've even got it on tape. Tom recorded it. I can let you listen to God, talking about toilets.

"'I know many of you are suffering,' Baba said.

"'I know that some of you need the toilets. But, I ask, why do you choose to come here at this time of year?'

"No one answered."

"Well, you couldn't, could you?' commented Jack.

"No. The inscrutable God. I didn't sleep after that. At most, two hours a night. I went to every darshan. I was scared. The nights were vile. The men were peeing in the night, into bottles and bowls, making obvious noises. It was horrible in the sheds." She shuddered.

"I used to walk to the Meditation Tree in the VIP building. There was a copper disk under the tree. It had magical powers to enhance meditation. I broke away from the group, knowing nothing. I was leaving the Meditation Tree when suddenly, in a quietly spoken voice, I was told or I told me:

"'You will have an interview on your birthday. Beware of it. You will hear words I don't use. Don't tell anyone.'

"On my birthday I cashed three hundred pounds worth of traveller's cheques. I felt well guided. I still wanted to stay. I had no reason to leave."

"Did you have your birthday interview?" Jack interrupted.

"Yes. It did happen. It all came true."

"What were his words?" Jack asked, concentrating hard.

"'You will leave tomorrow. Your body is sick. You will return next time to a comfortable room.'

"That's what Baba said, out loud. I told Him myself that I wasn't ill. That I wasn't leaving.

"The next morning a taxi arrived that I hadn't ordered, to take me home. I looked at myself in the mirror as I washed, hurriedly, annoyed by the impatience of the taxi driver and my own reluctance to leave. I saw I was covered in a vile rash. I was suddenly in agony. I was bundled into the taxi and flown home. It took several weeks of clever medication to heal me. I was suddenly back in England."

"That must have been really difficult," Jack suggested.

"No. I didn't really place my feet on the ground. No one felt like I did." Rita smiled

"Disappointed?" Jack suggested tentatively.

"No. Not at all. I was on, perhaps Cloud 8 if not 9. I felt calm and placid."

"Why?" Jack thought this woman was really confusing.

"I wanted to start again. I wanted to get away from Tom."

"How was he?" asked Jack.

"Still dying. But I'd lost weight. I slept. I was blissed out. It wasn't bhajan bliss. This was an overdose. I'd had all those interviews. I wanted to go straight back. It was an addictive drug."

"But . . ."

"Tom deteriorated. He was in agony. He lost his job. He would never go back."

"How did you feel about that?" asked Jack, nervously.

"I still felt calm. There was so much peace in me. I felt like a magnet magnetised. I had to return. Had to."

"So you did," Jack concluded.

"So I did. I left my dying husband. He was unemployed. I was unemployable. I abandoned my daughter. She had become a catholic and I hated her for it. She refused to believe in Baba. So I left."

"Did you feel any remorse, guilt perhaps?" Her matter-of-fact selfishness shocked Jack.

"No. Not then. No. Absolute certainty. I belonged beside Baba. No one else. Nowhere else. I left and I would stay away."

"Did you?"

"Yes. For months."

"Was this visit better?"

"A little. My room, despite promises, was not comfortable. The darshans were good. I was pleading, powerfully."

"For what?"

"Just that, a good darshan. Proximity to my God. It was as if I was flirting with Baba. Not in a sexual sense. Perhaps a little. He makes you feel you are the only person important to him. Then he ignores you."

"Is he flirting back?" Jack wondered.

"No. I don't think so. He always seemed to favour the men. They are more concentrated. He will touch the men. Once, during darshan, he was amongst men and looked towards me."

"'Don't leave,' Baba said."

"Out loud?" Jack was quick to ask.

"In my head.

"'Change your ticket,' he said. 'Change your ticket!'

"So I did. It was a wonderful time. I worked in the garden, at the bakery. The sense of energy around the ashram was immense. It was a powerhouse. I dug the earth with hefty swings of a pickaxe I couldn't even lift off the ground in England. This access of energy began to alarm me. The words in my head became increasingly sexual. Sai Baba was my God. Sex was not on my mind.

"One evening during darshan, I was wearing a big sun hat with a sari-scarf over the top. Baba had his back to me. He was on the balcony with the boys, talking to the students, sat to one side. Inside my head I heard Baba sing:

"'Getting to know you'.

"Just those five bars. A song from 'The King and I'. Baba was laughing. Deborah Kerr was the English teacher; here was the King. Where was I? She found out that when the innocence goes it is not so nice. Her King was flawed. I was yet to see that. But it would come soon enough."

CHAPTER TWENTY-FOUR
Sericulture

Ramu Sarnhi had chosen the village where Hari once saw Lunasha star-spread and floating. His grandfather had built the cistern that was her refuge. The coincidence startled Hari and distracted him.

"Come Hari, I'd like you to see the weaving. We'll not disturb them, just take a peep."

Ramu Sarnhi held open the door to a large hut where three weavers in a row, surrounded by their looms, were concentrating intently on their task. There was an asymmetry to the rhythmical clang of the mechanisms but it was not annoying or unpleasant. The objects colliding were wood on wood through thread. It was a gentle cacophony. The weavers seemed hypnotised by the rhythms of their work.

They were distinguished in appearance to Hari. They were of an age, elderly, lean, all with sharp, neat features. Two had grey/white beards, trimmed to a length, and a mass of matching grey hair, parted at the side. One wore spectacles and all had staring eyes. Each face bore a tight-lipped determination.

"Silk is a business of extremes, Hari. Which is why I love it so. It will take these men more than a day to weave half a metre of silk, and over a month to produce one of our finest saris. Let's leave them in peace. They do seem peaceful, don't they, Hari? Not angry at my exploitation?" Ramu Sarnhi smiled. He was teasing Hari, nevertheless his grandson felt a little ashamed.

"I'd like you to meet the school teacher and her grandparents. They can tell you about the whole process of making silk. I remember it clearly but you need to realize that these village looms are only a small part of the family business. Your father is visiting a factory this morning where the weaving process is mechanised. The quality is poor, compared to this, but the market for it is big."

Hari remembered the girl, standing in front of her children, when he'd peered into the dark of her classroom. He and Ramu Sarnhi were outside her grandparent's house looking into a very simple, earth-floored room with a kitchen corner and a cot to lie on. An elderly couple was slumped on a bench just inside the open door. The young teacher, Aanya (she'd introduced herself, Ramu Sarnhi couldn't remember her name) offered to make tea for the adults but fetched a bottle of soda for Hari.

She prised open the metal cap and it made a fizzing sound, like champagne escaping around the cork. The old man chuckled and spoke to Aanya. She translated for him; he had no English and he spoke a type of Indian Hari's grandfather struggled with.

"He says that's the noise the silkworms make when they are feeding."

The grandfather hadn't finished talking.

"He claims they eat and breathe at the same time."

"How?" Hari asked.

"There are holes in the side of their bodies ..." Aanya paused. The old man was miming their location, prodding positions on his own gnarled finger with the forefinger of his other hand.

"They take oxygen straight from the air, he says. They must absorb it," Aanya concluded and looked as unconvinced as Hari.

"Why would they do that, Grandfather?" Hari asked.

"Let the old man tell you. He spent most of his life producing silk." Ramu Sarnhi rested a hand on Hari's shoulder, encouraging him to be patient.

"They are greedy beyond belief, he says. From the tiny egg that the moth lays the worms grow 'miraculously'. They increase in size ten thousand times and have four bodies, each one shed in turn. After the fourth they will spin their cocoon." Aanya raised her shoulders in a gesture of disbelief.

"Is this true, Grandfather?"

"Yes, Hari. I told you, it is a business of extremes. They are only four weeks in the nursery baskets and they grow before your eyes. They consume mulberry leaves as fast as you can deliver them. It would take as many pounds of leaves as I weigh just to make a single sari."

"What's he doing?" Hari asked Aanya, seeing her grandfather swaying his head from side to side in a curious fashion.

"It's how it weaves its web, he says. Swinging its head round and round and from side to side in the pattern of the number 8. I know the cocoon is made from a single filament and that when unwound the thread can be a thousand yards long. My grandmother told me that. That was her task, unweaving cocoons."

"What happens to the caterpillar?" Hari wondered.

"It is a pupa once inside the cocoon. It's not a caterpillar anymore," Ramu Sarnhi instructed Hari.

"What happens to the pupa, then?" Hari didn't like being corrected in front of Aanya. She was young and very pretty.

"They are immersed in boiling water," Ramu Sarnhi began.

"You kill them?" Hari was quick to realise.

"Of course."

"Why of course, Grandfather? Isn't it cruel?"

"You have to kill the grubs because, as soon as they hatch, in order to escape from the silk cocoon, they spit out a particular chemical that discolours the silk. It is red and nasty and the silk turns to slime. But their death is instant, like lobsters and crabs."

Hari didn't like that idea either.

"You think like Gandhi, Hari," Aanya began. "He preferred fibres spun after the silk moth was allowed to escape from the cocoon. It is called Ahimsa silk," she added.

"Do you make any, Grandfather?"

"No. The main strand is destroyed and the fragments that remain are far too short to process. I should say, Hari, we don't raise the silkworms any more. Others are more efficient, less labour intensive and cheaper so I start our silk processing with the fibres already made. I wanted you to meet the school teacher's parents …"

"Aanya," Hari reminded his forgetful grandfather.

"Aanya's grandparents, because they raised the silkworms in the traditional way. I thought you might find it interesting."

Aanya was explaining to her grandfather what the visitors were discussing. The grandmother mimed eating and rubbed her stomach in mock delight. Aanya laughed.

"What is she saying?" asked Hari.

"She said that the boiled bugs make good eating. They taste like peanut butter."

Hari grimaced.

"Hari, if I can put your mind at rest, a little at least, in the wild everything eats silkworms, including the Koreans, who think they are a delicacy. And if left alone to become moths, as many are, or else they couldn't maintain the whole process, they can hardly fly. They sniff out their mate. Look for her on foot, find her, and then die, in little over a week."

"It's not much of a life," Hari concluded.

"No it's not," Ramu Sarnhi consoled Hari, "But their legacy is magnificent. They give mankind silk."

CHAPTER TWENTY-FIVE
Shivabalayogi

"You've seen Maddy's guru?"

Hari was astonished, as always around Borg. He'd sought out Jean Paul and found the Doctor and Borg at the Indian Café after evening darshan. He was still full of the news that Sam had told him earlier that morning. He hoped the Doctor would be able to tell him more about Shivabalayogi. It seemed Borg was the expert, not the Doctor.

"He's a proper yogi, in the line of Ramakrishna, not a pretend god in the line of Elvis Presley."

"That's a little harsh," interceded the Doctor. He had found a seat for Hari and waved an order for tea that materialised as rapidly as any avatar's gift.

"What I find delightful", Borg began, leaning across the table and twitching the collar of his ashram suit free from his neck to let an imagined breeze cool his spine, "is that he had such grubby beginnings."

"Really?" The Doctor spoke, not Hari, in ironical disbelief, not wonder.

"His father died when he was a toddler and he was raised by an evil stepmother, like in all good fairy tales. He was an apprentice weaver, making cheap cotton saris for women and unspeakable undergarments for men."

"My grandfather makes saris," Hari offered, unashamed.

"In silk?" asked Borg.

"Yes. Over there." Hari pointed to the village he'd visited.

"Silk doesn't count."

Borg's look of disapproval silenced Hari.

"He was good at it. He organised the workers into a co-operative so they needn't co-operate with their suppliers. He undercut the competition."

"So does Grandfather," Hari interrupted, sharing a family secret.

"Do you mind?" Borg raised a pair of quizzical eyebrows that were so thin his whole facial mask twitched.

"He was an awkward cove." This remark was clearly addressed to Hari but was tempered by a grin. "And was nicknamed 'Against'. I suppose it means 'Contrary' or just plain awkward. I enjoy his transition from agent of weavers to agent of God. He made one hell of a sacrifice!" Borg exclaimed.

"Or a 'Heaven' of one," corrected the Doctor. "He was just a child, like you are, Hari, but he led the entirely selfless life of an enlightened being." The Doctor wore his usual doleful look, with sad eyes looking inward and lips pressed together not wanting to speak ill. His neatly trimmed, pencil moustache was his only vanity.

"I was coming to that," Borg interrupted, with customary arrogance, one of his many endearing sins. "It's just that he did it all in public so everyone could see. Normally, great yogis do tapas, a silent sitting Om-ing away the days, perched on a rock in a cave. Not Shivabalayogi. He sat for all to see. His hands were clasped together for so long they had to cut them apart. Skin had grown in the gaps between the fingers. His hands are still ugly and deformed, unless they've changed in the last few weeks."

"You've seen him that recently?" Hari wanted up-to-date information. He needed to know where Maddy's guru was right now.

"Yes. Just before he went to Kakinada."

"Is that where he is now?" asked Hari.

"Yes. And it's probably where he'll stay. He will not be back to his ashram in J. P. Nagar. Mind you, I used to visit him when he had the more modest place in Bannerghetta Road. Did you ever visit there, Doctor?"

"Yes. But I haven't seen him for a while."

"Where are these places?" asked Hari. "Are they so far away?" Hari needed to locate Lunasha in his mind. Where she was, where she might return to and when. He had no sense of the geography of India. Time was uneven, distances vast, events accidental and sudden. He feared he might be gone before Lunasha could return.

"No. They are ..." Borg waved absently over his right shoulder, as if the unlocated places might be within his sight. "In Bangalore. No distance but very slow to reach. There is too much traffic in the newly built parts of the city."

"I agree." The Doctor supported Borg. "I never visit. I don't recognise my way anymore."

Hari was frustrated. "When will he be back in Bangalore?"

"I doubt he will ever return." Borg was adamant.

"Why?" asked Hari, alarmed.

"Because he's gone home to die." Borg's abrupt reply shocked Hari.

"Can he die?" asked Hari.

"He's a guru, not a god. Of course he can die and soon. When I saw him last he was very close."

"To what?" asked Hari.

"Death." Borg softened his tone.

"What does he look like?" asked Hari.

"Yellow," Borg responded, and drew a look of disapproval from the Doctor.

"His kidneys have failed. He is also very anaemic, hence his faded colour. He needs dialysis twice a week but there is a much better machine in Kakinada. That's why he is there now. He can receive better treatment. I believe he also enjoys the sea bathing there. I'm sorry you are so concerned, impossibly young man."

"Does he have a hall like Sai Baba?" Hari asked.

"No. He is a very modest man. There is nothing of the faded rock star about Shivabalayogi. He is still pretty tubby so he must have an appetite. His hair is gone from the top of his head but still grows long down his back, and on his chin is a fine beard, that is all grey now.

"He greeted me and an annoying group of Westerners eager for answers that would transcend their miserable little culture and their spiritual limitation. He was sitting on a couch that resembled a four-poster bed. It was in a screened-off area with intense lights focused on him and creating a very theatrical space. It was like a one-man studio theatre. He sat beneath an elaborate bedhead supported on a couple of rather splendid cushions and his back was resting on a mighty red bolster. The covers were festooned with garlands of flowers and petals were scattered everywhere by his attendants. An earnest pair stood either side of him, punkah wallahs, gently wafting a pair of paddle-shaped fans throughout the proceedings.

"He was draped in a simple pink robe that covered his arms and hands but couldn't trap the smell of decay. He has an unfortunate injury. He burnt his right foot while travelling in a car. It has been infected for a long, long time. It is covered in a fungus and it smells. Oh, and he has diabetes for which he takes insulin. Apart from that, he says he has stomach pains and he was scratching invisible itches under his robe all the time I was there. He has not been well for many years. He has always wanted it kept secret so as not to distress his followers."

"Shouldn't you keep his secret?" questioned Hari, unsettled by the detail of Borg's account.

"It can't be concealed now. The man is too obviously sick."

"Did he speak to you?" asked Hari

"Not to me, no. I had nothing to ask him. But he did answer some of the questions set by the eager Westerners. He acknowledged their curiosity and their voices, but he kept his eyes closed. I found that oddly pleasing."

"What did they ask that annoyed you so?" asked the Doctor.

"'Is it possible to achieve samadhi with one hour of meditation a day?'" Borg asked his question in a mock American accent that whined and insinuated and made all of them laugh.

"Those damned Yankees, always wanting a quick fix."

"Isn't it possible, then?" asked Hari, concerned. Maddy seemed to think an hour a day was sufficient.

"I doubt one would gain full enlightenment on such a small ration of thought. Peace of mind, certainly. A sense of inner well-being—why not? But, the full escape into a spiritual reality, wandering the astral plane, free entirely from the illusion of the world permanently, no. I doubt that. Few would even seek it. You would need to relinquish family, wife, children, friends. Only a very few great souls dare make such a sacrifice."

"Would you?" Hari asked the Doctor.

"No," he replied with certainty.

"Would you?" Hari asked Borg.

"I already have," was his enigmatic reply.

CHAPTER TWENTY-SIX
Rita

It had never really occurred to Jack, until these meetings with Rita, what an oddly feminine place the world of Sai Baba was. The very first darshan had been described as a rock concert. It was similar; Jack could see that. He'd sat and waited on some uncomfortable seats to see great musicians play in New York and other cities. So, Sai Baba was the star and the Joans and Ritas were the groupies. They were getting old now, spurned and passed over. The jetsam of the god-loving jet set. There's a phrase, thought Jack. Cast aside, hurt, and bitter perhaps but still following, still hoping to be recognised. Put them together, even in a shed and their shared desire would border on the hysteria that Jack sniffed around the ashram. It was like an open-air nunnery with Baba as Christ. Jack had never understood why you'd choose to be a nun. What was the point? A life of silence, in prayer and celibate devotion, hidden from the world. That was the life these widows of Whitefield were living. That was another good phrase, Jack thought.

He visited Rita once more. He wanted to be brought up to date.

"Tell me, Rita, when did it all go wrong?" Jack was very matter-of-fact.

"Tea?" Rita rushed away.

"No. No tea. I've not long had breakfast. Look, I've heard the lovey-dovey stuff, the bliss and the joy. You've been honest and not hidden the power of your infatuation and the damage it has caused to your family and your life but, why are you in hiding?"

Like a child chastised, Rita slumped to the floor.

"It was towards the end of that long, long stay. Tom had died. My daughter was alone in England. But still, I stayed. Do I disgust you?"

"Not yet." Jack was kind. He knew he was opening unhealed wounds.

"I couldn't sleep again. I resorted to taking tablets. I don't take tablets. Then, late one night, a picture of Sai Baba flew off the wall and landed at my feet. I hadn't touched it." She raised her hands in the air in proof of her claim.

"I didn't like this kind of magic. It was actual, kinetic, unimagined. I began giving Baba leaving-letters at darshan. He wouldn't take them. My meditation ran out. Something changed. Everything changed. The whole place felt evil. There was tighter security. Less giving. It was shutting down and shutting out. There were fewer interviews and shorter darshans. All the managers were new. They were not religious men. They were business people. I had given the ashram four thousand pounds. It was all I had left. It was a donation. When these new faces came and the unpleasant atmosphere they brought with them, I asked for it back. They refused. I was meant to have better accommodation and better food. The slimy little creature I gave the money to denied ever receiving it. I could not produce a receipt. I never had one. They always wanted cash. I kept writing letters to the ashram. I might as well have written to the man in the moon.

"I accused the English trustees of corruption. I knew the actual cost of the trips. I should, I helped organise them. There were meant to be stop over hotels, proper rooms, proper food. There never were. I reckon they made over five hundred pounds per person per trip. Whilst the organisers had breakfast with Sai Baba and set up interviews for the rich, we lived in squalor. They would bring sixty to seventy people every other week, hundreds throughout the year. They have made a fortune. And then, there was the shooting."

"I know about that," Jack declared.

"Were you there?"

"No."

"I was."

"Good." Jack didn't disguise his enthusiasm. This is what he came for.

"Good?" Rita didn't disguise her contempt.

"Sorry to interrupt."

"I was there." Rita was remembering.

"You've said so already," Jack reminded her.

"Those boys were murdered." Rita looked Jack full in the face. The signs of alarm in her eyes unnerved him.

"What could they do? They had rushed to Baba to ask for forgiveness. They were with him, in his private room. They were trapped inside. There was nowhere to go. They wouldn't have harmed Baba. He slipped away and the police burst in and they shot them all dead. It wasn't necessary. It was too severe. They shot any one that could say or dared to say the truth."

"Did you actually see the shootings, Rita? I mean were you there?"

"Of course I was there. I was right outside the room. They wouldn't let me in. I could see the bodies through the door. I wanted to help. They grabbed me. Threw me to the ground." She looked up, tears filling her startled eyes. "They beat me asleep and carried me away. I wept and when I woke up Baba was standing over me and frowning. He glared and waved me down. I lay on my face, flattened to the ground, weeping, hoping he would walk on me. Then Baba spoke: 'You must go!'" Rita paused. The remembered rejection overwhelmed her.

"Can I get you anything?" Jack asked, concerned.

"No. Thank you."

"Can you go on? Should I come back another time?"

The intensity of Rita's frown let Jack know she must continue.

"They turned the place into a prison. The police treated the devotees like dirt. They didn't want us there and Baba didn't want me. He became frightening rather than kind. He stopped interviewing large groups. Men can conspire in large groups. He seemed afraid. At my very last darshan He gave me a disapproving look then clenched his nostrils to snort! I decided at that moment to leave the ashram. I ran. I managed to escape the officials on guard. As I left, I saw the body of a girl. She was a Westerner, murdered and abandoned. There she lay. White pigeons were pecking at her flesh. Their beaks drew trickles, minute flowings of red blood. I ran."

"And you'll never go back," Jack concluded.

"I will. Yes, I will. I still love Him. It's his ashram I hate. It's his people I hate and what they've done to him. Ashram! Cashram! That's our joke. Ashram! Cashram! The ashram is Anti-Christ." She spat the 's' in Christ. "As you see, the anger is not out of my system yet. I want to believe I've not been taken for a ride. I want to believe that what I did wasn't wrong."

"But it was, Rita." Jack was certain.

"Sorry?"

"Don't apologise to me, apologise to your daughter. Where is she?" Jack was stern.

"She's in England. She's grown up. I supported her, Jack. I'm not that wicked. Most of any money I have, any income, goes to her. I only pay 100 rupees a month for this house, a few pence a week. I have no expenses." She looked up to Jack then lowered her head.

"And no purpose. Hey? Who has? None of my business." Jack closed his notebook.

"Since you've been coming here, I've thought about her a lot. I've written and I've left telephone messages for her. I've invited her to come, to visit Kodaikanal. It is nice there."

"What's she called?" Jack softened his tone. He wasn't the world's best father and as he'd already said, it was none of his business.

"Susan."

"Will she come?"

"I've sent her the fare."

"If she comes and I'm still here, bring her to the café and I'll buy her tea and cake. Okay? Is that okay?"

CHAPTER TWENTY-SEVEN
The Indian Coffee House

"I have no intention of signing such a thing. Here!"

Ramu Sarnhi pushed the document case and its offensive, hardly glimpsed content back across the tabletop towards his son, Ajay. The Formica showed less resistance and the case slipped into Ajay's lap and then onto the floor. The magnificently clad waiter bent quickly, retrieved the half-zipped leather case and placed it back onto the table, securing it in place with a reassuring pat.

Father and son were sitting in the Indian Coffee House in Mahatma Gandhi Road in Bangalore. It was a magnificent place, traditional, outmoded, originating in the 1950s as a workers co-operative, once upon a time a meeting place for workers, intellectuals and political activists. Local businessmen used it now even though the Coffee House hadn't paid its rent in years. It was colourful and crumbling. The walls were painted blue-green, somewhere between turquoise and teal blue; the tabletops were bright yellow. The waiters were splendid fellows. They were dressed in white tunics and long white trousers divided in the middle by magnificent belts, dark red edged with gold and clasped with elaborate, ornate buckles. Their turbans were similarly swathed with a narrow sash in the same colours and a magnificent cockatoo crest rose proudly from the side of each turban.

The elaborately turned legs of the tables couldn't disguise their poor quality. Formica always was a shoddy topping. Bench seats created alcoves for privacy and even the smallest table had a crowd of intent customers seated around it. A sign above Hari's father's head supported a picture of an elderly man, turban and whiskers in white, above two mounds of coffee. Each was described as: 'A fine type', 'A fine coffee' and, 'Both are Indian'— but of course.

Ramu Sarnhi defiantly ordered rose milk. "And sweet cakes," he added, seeing none on the menu.

"There are none on the menu, sir," his patient waiter confirmed but before even the beginnings of a complaint, the waiter clicked his fingers. A young boy appeared from behind the distant counter and was sent immediately into the noisy street in search of the missing items.

"They will be here shortly, sir."

"Thank you." Ramu Sarnhi smiled. This was the kind of deferential service he valued.

"Why must you always be awkward, Father?" asked Ajay Sarnhi, embarrassed.

"Not awkward, decided." Ramu Sarnhi leant back in his chair. He was wearing a crisp, white cotton short-sleeved shirt and white cotton slacks.

The clothes had been ironed into sharp edges rounded by a small belly that signalled a contained affluence rather than any indulgence. He fiddled with a pair of thick-framed sunglasses. They were American and expensive. All his ornaments were gold: watch, rings, bracelets, chain.

Hari's father was a gawky figure. He had a long neck and slicked-back hair. He had thin, wire-surround sunglasses that he was still wearing. They faded in the dark, darkened in the light. His long, elegant fingers zipped and unzipped his document case. His bulbous nose detracted from a feminine face. His eyes shone with an intense energy.

"If you are truly going to die, Father, shocking as it is, sad as it will be, in terms of business, if you don't sign these forms there will be a catastrophe."

"You exaggerate." Ramu Sarnhi was dismissive.

"A disaster, then?"

"Still too extreme. A nuisance, for you, perhaps."

The son was ready to appear frustrated but would continue to disguise his extreme annoyance and genuine fear. He and his father had met in Bangalore, in secret effectively, to try and unravel the complex web of deceit that his father had woven so elaborately around his business affairs.

"If you are lucky enough to live a longer life, most of it, in all likelihood, will be spent in prison." The anxious son made this declaration with such careful intent that he finally grabbed his father's attention.

"What are you talking about?"

"You don't pay your taxes, Father. It seems you never have."

Ramu Sarnhi smiled. "That is not a problem. Tax evasion is a national sport. It is not even illegal."

"It is!" The son was baffled and exasperated. "Why do you and your associates keep saying that? Tax evasion is against the law everywhere. Including here."

"Would you pay such extortionate rates? Our top level of tax is 93%. That is ridiculous. No one will pay. For two years, in the early 1970s, the rate was one hundred and seven and three-quarters percent. Can you believe that? They don't deserve any tax when rates are so impossibly high."

"You could pay something."

"Why go it alone? No one I know pays anything. We are organised. We pamper the officials. They know when we buy a property at least 40% is paid in cash. The prices are tempered. The taxman doesn't need to be involved. Our bureaucracy is suffocating, you know. Some states are kinder than others. They offer tax holidays, especially from manufacturers and exporters like us. There is no tax to pay in the state of Uttarakhand, did you know?"

"No. But I guessed there might be something dubious about us having such a large subsidiary there, seeing as we have no staff or factory or office."

"We have an office," Ramu Sarnhi asserted.

"We do?"

"Well, an office address. It is a service open to such enlightened companies as ours."

"Your cakes, sir." The delicacies arrived on a high-sided tray and were deftly slipped onto the table as Ramu Sarnhi placed a few rupees into the hardly extended hand of the bowing waiter. All that was done was seemly and in perfectly good taste. It pleased the old man and softened his mood.

"Let me see your form." He proffered his free hand; the other seemed reluctant to set down the sticky-coated cake held at fingers' end then suddenly popped into an open mouth. Ramu Sarnhi chewed ruminatively.

"I doubt this Power of Attorney will hold sway in India." He handed the form back.

"I'm sure it will," replied his son.

"I will think on it."

"Don't take too long. There is still a lot to do."

Ramu Sarnhi was now thoughtful and serious. His dismissiveness was not unusual but intensified by a delayed breakfast. The sweet cakes calmed him.

"I think only the *karta* may decide. You, as *coparcener* don't even have the right to inspect the accounts. It was my indulgent gift to allow you access to them."

"I don't understand these terms, Father. You will need to explain them to me." Ajay Sarnhi reluctantly slipped the documents back into his case and zipped them inside with a disappointed swiftness.

"For many years now I have been establishing a Hindu Undivided Family, an HUF for short."

"Short or long, what is it?" Ajay was suspicious. He was nervous whenever his father mentioned one of his difficult financial creations.

"Well, don't trouble yourself. It is perfectly legal and quite commonplace."

"What is it?" Ajay was losing patience.

"It is like a Family Trust. All successful Hindu families create them. It is a common pool for the joint ownership of property and monies. It is very tax advantageous."

"What have you been up to, Father?"

"You should not speak to the *karta* of an HUF in this disrespectful way. Give me a piece of paper. A plain sheet, not one of your dangerous forms. Thank you." Ramu Sarnhi produced his own pen from the briefcase open at his feet. He began to draw a diagram.

At its centre was a box with *Karta* written in it and, each one labelled, a series of circles emerged laterally: 'spouse', 'sister', 'brother'; and above and below, 'brother's spouse', 'daughter of spouse', 'mother', 'mother's brother' and so on until, spreading from the centre like a street-seller's clutch of balloons, a complex genealogy was drawn.

Returning to his briefcase once more, Ramu Sarnhi placed a framed photograph between himself and his son, then turned it away from himself so Ajay could see the picture clearly.

"That was taken at a recent family wedding. That is your Indian family, Ajay. Aunts and cousins, wives and spouses, few of whom you know. I, as *karta* am the unchallenged head of the HUF, the trust I have been building for many years now. After this wedding, I made a gift of fifty thousand rupees to the fund. For me there were no ancestral properties but all the agricultural land I have acquired and those huts and bungalows on the land, they are assets of this trust. All gifts to the trust are tax-free. The trust has its own tax allowances separate from the income of family members. We can reinvest all profits from property sales back into the trust and buy new land with the money. We have holding companies and subsidiaries and a delightful maze of framework agreements. This is all done by line of descent. You will be the next *karta* and Hari after you. Then it ends. After three generations the trust can be dispersed amongst its male members, the *coparceners*. Which is what you are now."

Ajay Sarnhi listened to this tale with increasing alarm.

"What have you done?"

His father failed to see any cause for concern. "I thought you'd be delighted. This means we are an established family. The Sarnhis are important for the first time in their history, Ajay. Don't you see?"

All Ajay saw was immense complication. It seemed to him that a trap had been set that was intended to keep him in India. He had yet to make it plain to his father that he had no intention, none whatsoever, of living again in India. His plans were the exact opposite. He intended centering the Sarnhi textiles empire in Birmingham, using the Indian village workers and the Bangalore Emporium as supplier and showcase of a modern, Western business. He had no idea he was to be made responsible for so much unknown kin nor that his imagined family wealth was to be scattered amongst so many, divided so thinly it must disappear. That was his capital, dissipated and squandered in little parcels, owing something even to the spouse of the son of some distant aunt's spouse.

"What have you done, Father? What on earth have you done?"

CHAPTER TWENTY-EIGHT
Eating at Maddy's compound

There was a tea party in Maddy's compound. It was a celebration of safe return. Hari was the first to be invited. His constant vigil was rewarded with an early sighting of Maddy as she rushed around the ashram and in and out of the bazaar. She was frantically confirming all her business contracts, ensuring her absence had let no one slip away or any rival take her place. This whirlwind of commerce had no time to sit, chat, or explain, certainly not to drink tea at breakfast.

"Come to the compound after darshan," she shouted over to Hari, too fast moving to answer any of his urgent questions. Even when Hari set out in hot pursuit, he knew it was pointless. Maddy was as uncatchable as time and as inexorable as fate. Hari would have to wait.

There were only a few people flanking the central courtyard. Maddy had baked some sweet cakes and piled them on a steel platter. They were elegant pastry parcels, shining in the sun after their dip in a sugar-syrup glaze. They contained no more than two mouthfuls of roasted cashew nuts, raisins, shavings of coconut and a hint of cardamom once swallowed. Hari chose one shaped like a Cornish pasty, a crescent with plaited edges. Others were round; some looked like envelopes or a small girl's purse.

Maddy made more cups of tea than people as one after the other of her strange guests emerged from their rooms, took a few of the sweet cakes and withdrew to eat alone and out of sight. There was one exception. Seated in a far corner, leaning against a closed door, Lunasha sat on the threshold, tea in one hand and a cake in the other. Without focus or undue fuss she put the cake to her lips and ate it in two greedy bites.

Hari turned to Maddy, his face full of surprise.

"She's eating," he whispered. "How?"

Maddy touched his arm to silence him.

"Come. I'll tell you about our wonderful journey and how this lovely miracle came to be. Tea? Cake?" Maddy shouted these last two words and startled Hari. But nothing could shock him from his delight.

Hari wandered towards the gate and sat where he had talked to Sam earlier that week. He waited a long while. Maddy was a bossy host and insisted everyone should join the party. She found him eventually, still bearing sticky gifts of the very sweet cakes. Hari knew not to decline but set his aside, uneaten as yet. Soon the ants would know and it would disappear in minute, determined bites.

Maddy slumped beside him, happy to be at rest.

"Isn't it wonderful, Hari, Lunasha is eating. We must thank my wonderful guru, Shivabalayogi and his generosity of . . ." she paused to swallow her cake, ". . . soul."

"What happened?" Hari was suddenly subdued. He knew he must not rush Maddy, she moved at her own chosen speed, but he was so relieved he felt oddly exhausted.

"I knew we must visit Swamiji and it could not be here in Bangalore but in his own village of Adivarapupeta. I also knew what might happen at the consecration, so Lunasha must come too." Maddy resumed eating. Hari thought to offer his uneaten cake but as he prophesied, the ants had already found it and a clever column was dismantling it and carrying it away to a nest somewhere beneath the foundation of the building behind him.

"What was being consecrated?" Hari asked finally, having waited patiently for Maddy to finish her tea.

"The new Dhaya Mandir."

"What is that?" asked Hari.

"It is where Swamiji's spiritual life began. You know about his meeting with Lord Shiva and his momentous twelve years of tapas?"

"Yes. Sam told me all about it."

Maddy seemed a little deflated but continued her story undaunted.

"You know, at first, Shivabalayogi just sat on the open ground at the edge of the village. He was unprotected. I think the other boys thought he was pretending, seeking attention for himself. Wanted money, perhaps, for being so devoted. They beat him where he sat."

"No." Hari was shocked.

"They poured sugar cane juice on him so the ants would bite him."

Hari glimpsed towards his cake and nudged it further away.

"One boy doused a rag in kerosene, lit it, and threw it at him."

"Why?"

"I don't know. They were jealous perhaps. Swamiji waited until the middle of the night and moved into the village graveyard. He chose the part set aside for unfortunate infants, those who died before their lives had properly begun. It was rumoured to be haunted, so the nasty boys kept away but not the worms, or insects, rats, snakes, scorpions. They tormented him. The villagers took pity. They knew by now that the boy yogi was serious. They built him a gunny-sack hut for shelter. Eventually, they acquired a square of land in a graveyard and built his Dhaya Mandir, a miniature temple for his silent prayer. It was twelve feet by twelve feet and made of stone. He now sat on a tiger skin that would become glued to his body."

Hari winced in sympathy.

"At least he was safe now. He could be protected by lock and key. He turned East, North, West and South during those twelve long years. His body was covered in sores and boils. At times blood escaped through his pores in a scarlet perspiration. He was even bitten by a king cobra."

Maddy's ghoulish narrative quite unnerved Hari. In her enthusiasm, Hari feared she might bite him herself.

"But the walls of the Dhaya Mandir are cracking. It was built in a hurry all those years ago."

"Will they knock it down?" asked Hari, relieved there would be no more tales of suffering.

"No, they are going to build around it. They want to leave the Shivalingam and the statue of Devi in situ. They are the only blessed possessions Swamiji lays claim to. We saw the foundations laid. Twenty feet by twenty feet. Once the new outside walls are built the internal walls can be demolished. There is so much building."

"Is it like here?" Hari nodded towards the ashram and the massive monuments built in Sai Baba's name: Sai Ramesh Hall, the hospital, university, and administrative buildings. He hoped Maddy's guru would keep things simpler, less grand.

"No. Nothing like this. They're still digging the foundations. It is all very small and humble compared to here. The whole of the Mandir is smaller than the gateway to the private drive that leads to Baba's quarters. But there will be a new building for the Weavers' Society. It is a place of weavers, you know."

"Yes. I do. My grand . . ."

"Long loops of cotton are washed in the canal and four-sari-length pieces are stretched on racks all along the village streets. It is amazing. But I must tell you about the night of the consecration."

"Please." Hari nodded.

"Lunasha and I were in attendance at Swamiji's residence. It is a life she enjoys. It is a life she may lead. We had been singing bhajans, she loves to sing, and praying for the building's success. I think the builders were pleading that we would leave them in peace. Apparently the water table is very high and the soil, even if fertile, is unstable so the foundations keep flooding. Suddenly, in the middle of the night, Swamiji came downstairs. We had been told he was too ill to move but, there he was, full of life and giving orders.

"'1:47 a.m.!'

"He shouted to us all. The builders were fetched.

"'You will lay the foundations at 1:47 a.m. exactly.'

"He was smiling. We were clapping. The builders were cursing. But Swamiji was serious. We all went outside. There was a concrete mixer and a ceremonial first brick. At the appointed time the builders pushed the wet concrete into the corner of the pit and dropped the brick in place. There were other offerings. Lunasha and I threw in sand whilst others poured in coconut milk and water. After the dedication, Swamiji shouted:

"'I have returned victorious!'"

Hari was caught up in Maddy's enthusiasm. This was holy work and her eyes sparkled with spiritual delight, not business cunning.

"The following morning people began to enter the village in their hundreds. They lined the entrance, beside the wide, peach-coloured road. It is a very poor place, Hari. The houses are simple. The rice paddies lay all around. Every school emptied of its children. Bands of drummers made them shriek and laugh and then there were fireworks." She paused, looked to the sky, remembering. "The girls swayed, entranced, dancing wildly at times, not quite out of control. Some of the men were. They were in noisy trances, shaking their heads violently. Police began arriving to keep everything in order.

"Then he was there. His car nosed a pathway through the people. They could see him through the window. We couldn't yet; he was too far away. Eventually he reached the centre and his attendants helped him from his car. He looked weak. They put him in an armchair and lifted it onto a platform to save him from the crush of people. They were excited, full of spiritual fervour, desperate to touch his holy feet.

"We did touch them." She smiled at the thought. "It was frightening at times but then, before he was taken away, he blessed tray after tray of food. This became prasadam, holy food, the manna the Christian God gave to the Jews. This is what I went for, Hari. This is why I took Lunasha. There was to be a mass feeding and I wanted her to take part.

"By now there were thousands present. But it was calmer, especially after Swamiji had gone. Little trucks and dozens of rickshaws started to share the blessed food. Swamiji would say eating in a restaurant is simply food. If food is offered to God and it is blessed it becomes prasadam. We had been close to Swamiji as he left. Lunasha was amongst the first to be offered the blessed food and to my great joy and even greater relief, Hari, she ate it, immediately."

Hari overcame his natural shyness and his genuine fear of Maddy and her surrounding bubble of energy, to wrap his arms around her neck and whisper, "Thank you, Maddy. Thank you for saving the life of Lunasha."

CHAPTER TWENTY-NINE
Hari and his mother

"Will we have to stay here, Mother?" It was the first time Hari had voiced this fear. For several days now, especially with his father increasingly absent, he began to realise that this visit might be the rehearsal for a future life based permanently in India. If it was, he feared he'd fluffed his lines already for, on several occasions recently, he'd invoked an impatient response from his father when asking: 'How much longer will we be here?'

"Would that bother you, Hari," asked his mother, "if we were to stay?" She was nervous, the question tentative. Hari was quiet. He wasn't sure what to say. He looked around the empty tables of the Sai Deep Café. Everyone else seemed to be busily and purposefully engaged elsewhere. He too wanted to be away from here, near Maddy's compound, with Jack, even alone on his bridge.

"Do you want to stay, Mother?" Hari returned the question unanswered. Esther Sarnhi was clearer in her mind than her troubled son.

"When I married your father, Hari, I made a very determined choice. My family were working-class English, self-employed, happy go lucky and, fortunately for me, very tolerant. They liked your father for your father's sake. The fact he'd come from India and an exotic sounding city called Bangalore and not from Wordsworth Road on the edge of Small Heath Park, like the rest of us, well, that just didn't matter. We were surrounded by Indian families, ate in Bangladeshi restaurants, shopped at the Asian supermarket on the Warwick Road. We were neighbours and friends and comfortable with our different cultures. I vowed to be wherever your father was. I trust him, Hari. If he thinks being in India will be best for us, well, then it will be. He would do nothing to hurt us. He cares for us so much." Even Esther Sarnhi sensed the hollowness of this last assertion. Her husband had been absent in every way these past days: distracted, preoccupied and distant. She cast her mind back to happier times.

"Can you remember The Fancy Silk Store, Hari, just outside the market? The big, red-brick building on the main road."

"Yes, of course I can, Mother."

"It may have looked dull and ignorable from the outside, but inside it was an Aladdin's cave."

Hari was intrigued, wondering why his mother had asked. Then she explained.

"I used to meet your father there before we were married. He courted me amongst the silks. It was a feast for the eyes. The bales of cloth, in pinks, limes, yellows and magentas were stacked floor to ceiling like a thousand bookends of a library lying on its side. There was a cabinet with silk threads on bobbins and every shade was available in the shop as a woven fabric. There were strange displays, five-foot metal cones, draped top to toe in brocades and patterned silks. They looked like women, completely veiled, standing quietly, huddled together to whisper gossip and to wait. Can you remember, Hari?"

"Yes, I can. They frightened me a little." He smiled. He enjoyed seeing his mother happy, even if the source of her good humour was the past.

"On the first floor there were fabrics for the brides. Your father led me to a special shelf and began to unravel a most delicate material. It was like gossamer. On it was a peacock design in silver and gold. The neck of the bird was pale green and its crest silver. The markings of its tail were like pearl droplets. It was stunning. I remember it so well, Hari, because your father promised me that one day he would buy it for me to make a veil for our wedding."

"Did he?"

"Yes, of course he did. He keeps every promise."

"Father isn't the same here, Mother." The second he made this statement, Hari looked away. It pained him to say it but he was worried. He must share these feelings with his family, at last. He knew Jack knew. Jean Paul guessed everything. Borg could see into his brain and Maddy could organise the universe. He felt disloyal. He wasn't sharing his being with those closest to him. He felt alienated there, welcome elsewhere. The strangers had become friends and his family had become strange. It had to change.

"I know," said his mother.

"You do?" Hari was so relieved. "You do?"

"Of course I do." She smiled and reached for one of the hands Hari had trapped beneath his knees.

"Why is he so different?"

"This is a strange land to him too, Hari. He left here a long time ago. He will always be Indian but he is forgotten here. A whole generation of his family has been born, grown up and married since he left. He showed me a photograph Grandfather Sarnhi had given him. He kept pointing to young faces in the front and second row of a huge wedding group. 'Who is that?' He kept asking me. 'And this?' 'And that?' I could only say, 'I don't know.' 'Neither do I,' he said, as if ashamed. I said, 'How can you know? You've been elsewhere.' 'How can it be possible to be the head of a family I don't know?' he asked."

"But Grandfather is head of the family, isn't he?" asked Hari.

"While he lives, yes. But then, perhaps soon, it will be your father and then you."

"But ..." Hari paused, deep in thought. "This is only one part of us. What about Grandma and Grandpa in England? What about all my funny uncles and annoying cousins, aren't they family? Would I be head of that family too, one day?" Hari was overwhelmed by the very thought of it.

"No. No you won't." She patted her son's hand in an attempt to reassure him and herself. "Your father is a gentle man but very strong and very stubborn, when he needs to be. He is also very clever, Hari. He thinks a great deal. He is cautious. People might misjudge him. My brothers seem full of confidence, even brash sometimes, especially in the market where they feel known and utterly at home. But your father is the strong one. His confidence is quiet. I think he is being made nervous and a little baffled by his own father's ways. Grandfather Sarnhi is a very impressive man, isn't he?"

"Oh, yes," Hari agreed. "I wouldn't dare contradict him." He grinned.

"Few would, but your father must. I think at first he thought he should copy his father's rather", she thought for a tactful word, "imposing way. He tried to be bossy and a little controlling with the managers he will one day manage. He felt the need to impress them. It must have seemed rude at times."

Hari nodded, a little embarrassed.

"I think he was trying to impress Grandfather Sarnhi."

"Yes." Hari could see that.

"But it's not your father's way. I'm sorry we've neglected you." She cupped his head in her hands to steady his look.

"I've been fine, Mother. I have made friends. I've not been lonely. I ..." He turned away. He was not yet ready to tell his story of Lunasha.

"I've been helping your father with his paperwork. It is all very dull but very important. Things will be decided soon." She was matter of fact rather than reassuring.

CHAPTER THIRTY
A spiritual life

"Won't she be so terribly lonely?" Hari asked Jean Paul. They were eating supper together in the Indian canteen. At the moment of Hari's question, Jean Paul popped a ball of neatly rolled rice into his mouth so there was a pause before he answered.

"Not at all. It will be a wonderful and companionable life to live in the ashram of Shivabalayogi. To attend him and be close to his being constantly will be a magnificent way for Lunasha to live her life. Do you understand what a privilege this is? What an honour has been granted her? How on earth Maddy has brought this about, I don't know. But be thankful that she has. It will be a triumphant end to a troubled life."

Jean Paul began to arrange his food for eating and uninterrupted by a thoughtful Hari, continued to the end of his meal.

"What is wrong, Hari? You look troubled."

"I am," Hari confirmed.

"About what?"

"The whole idea that she will disappear from the world; not be seen, not to be part of the rest of us. She'll be like a nun." Hari brightened at the sound of his perfect choice of word. "A nun," he repeated, to be certain of its value.

"Precisely."

"Is that a good thing?"

"It's an entirely good thing, especially for a sometime beggar woman who has been spurned and silenced by the world. You must recognise that it was a vile life she was leading."

"Not in Maddy's compound," Hari quickly replied.

"True. But, Maddy's people are only passing through. They are refugees and she cares for them until they are repaired enough to return to the world. There was never anywhere in the world for Lunasha to return to."

"Why not here?" Hari persisted. "Why wouldn't she stay in Sai Baba's ashram? It is only up the road. Why would she choose Maddy's guru instead of Sai Baba? Why choose a teacher instead of a God?"

"It is a choice I would make." Jean Paul's remark startled Hari.

"You would?"

"I would. And since my choice seems to have alarmed you, it is on a similar journey that Sai Baba has sent me. I will sit in an empty, silent room, full of the spiritual memory of the great guru called Sri Ramana Maharshi, and I will be content and filled with his peace. I cannot be comfortable here in all this noise."

Hari tried to digest these astonishing declarations from the man he considered his guru, his wise teacher and friend. What he had said had confused him utterly.

"I know what Maddy's guru did was amazing, quite wonderful, I'm sure. All those years, all that suffering. But . . ." Hari's thought ran out. Jean Paul completed it for him.

"What purpose could such an act serve? Is that what you are wondering?"

"Yes. I suppose. It was brave, it was . . ." Hari meant no disrespect.

"Pointless?" Jean Paul confirmed what Hari had dared to think.

"I can't know. But, may I ask, what was the point? How are people who shun the world and ignore it entirely serving God's purpose? I can understand good deeds. I grasp the idea of saints and sacrifice and selfless courage. Men who win the Victoria Cross, posthumously." Hari was secretly proud of knowing the word his history teacher had lent him. "Men who give, yes. Men who died bravely, yes. Men who serve others, yes. But men who hide from the world wrapped in the silence of their own thoughts, no. I don't get that."

Jean Paul took his time. He wanted to be clear in his own mind before trying to explain this process to his baffled young friend.

"Those years of silence are only one part of the process. Shivabalayogi, and all other such divines who have undergone tapas, eventually re-enter the world. The guru I am to visit, Sri Ramana Maharshi, sat on a rock in a cave on a mountain for seventeen years. He said not a word. And even though long dead, his followers still hear his voice. It is a voice that travels through Time and Space. His silence wouldn't have been loud enough if he hadn't withdrawn from the world first. It was during those years that he acquired the power to transmit."

The modern word, whilst incongruous, caught Hari's attention.

"A man like Shivabalayogi, seemingly inactive, becomes for those whom he teaches, those who choose to follow him and his spiritual ways, a beacon, a lighthouse. His very being emits a power that inspires and energises others. He is the prayer-battery, the source, the engine room, I don't know, the furnace that purifies and gives strength to less intense beings. Such a teacher is uplifting, enlightening. He can act as effectively and as extensively in the world through his silent transmission as any other great philanthropist or statesman can affect the physical world through charity, change, gift or endowment."

Hari was overwhelmed by Jean Paul's enthusiasm. What he could muster as a question already seemed inconsequential, even in his own ears.

"What part can Lunasha possibly play around such a being?"

"She will be part of the prayer," Jean Paul explained calmly. "She will add to its force so it can expand beyond the ashram and enter other minds far distant from here. Lunasha gives up nothing, Hari. She embraces everything.

Shivabalayogi will guide her to the infinite. She might be entirely pure by the end of it all, like Ambapali, if you remember, who gave a tea party for the Buddha and finished her life in the same way."

Hari was quiet but not satisfied. He struggled to make some kind of sense of all the ideas and experiences that he confronted each day. He thought he had established a clear hierarchy in his mind and, in terms of God-Men, Yogis, Gurus, Monks, Beggars and Saints, the top man, the most significant in all these was Sai Baba. He was the god they'd come to worship, the man who might save the life of his grandfather. Surely, such an experienced and wise man as Grandfather Sarnhi wouldn't make such a wrong choice. Surely Sai Baba was best.

"What did you say, Hari?" asked Jean Paul.

"I . . . nothing. Well, surely, Sai Baba is best." He allowed his last thought a voice, even not entirely sure of its truth but needing to be reassured.

Jean Paul smiled. He would never make Hari feel foolish, and had understood from his very first acquaintance that the young boy was sincere and meticulous in his search for the truth.

"It may be true, Hari. It is so for many."

"I saw him perform a miracle. You saw him as well. You said it wasn't a trick. The Doctor had an explanation. I didn't entirely follow, but it was about power and gift, not deceit."

"Yes, I remember our discussion. Let me try to explain these 'miracles'. We are asked to believe, by Science and not Religion, in fact, not in faith, that this table that I can smack", he did and startled Hari into a nervous giggle, "is not solid but made up of minute, unseen entities. Not just unseen, but unseeable. We are told there are particles so much smaller than atoms; you probably know some of their names. Protons and neutrons with quarks inside them: up, down, bottom, top, strange and charmed. There are electrons and photons, muons and taus, gravitons and gluons and Higgs bosons galore. But that is not how we experience this table. If we did and the skeleton of matter was visible to us, our food would tumble into the gaps in the table and we would fall to the floor through the wood of our chairs and onwards to the bottom of the universe. That doesn't feel real, but it is. Most scientists now believe that there is more 'nothing' in the world than 'something'. That less than five per cent of the universe is made of ordinary matter and all the rest consists of Dark Matter and Dark Energy that we will never see, never monitor, never be able to prove, but need to accept as the truth. How does that sound to you, Hari?"

"Crazy!" He laughed.

"I agree. I was once a science student and the more I learned the more I agreed with you. It was crazy. I thought, finally, that it was a much more rational choice to believe in God." He paused. Hari was relaxing.

"It is argued that some enlightened beings, using methods secret to them, can manipulate matter at this sub-atomic level. They can 'make' or 'materialise' anything they want; and some claim to do so. One gifted guru, the 'Perfume Saint' materialised smells."

"Smells?" Hari wriggled his nose in anticipation.

"Yes. The scent of flowers. He could produce them at will and place them anywhere, even in the palm of your hand."

"Why?"

"A good question. Why materialise an odour when you can experience the same scent in the petal of a flower? Some people demand to be amazed. Sai Baba creates theatre, spectacular moments with his vibhuti ash and silver rings and stainless steel watches, gifts from the ether for his needy Westerners who expect a miracle on demand. That is their proof of his godhead. But more thoughtful people find such acts of no use at all spiritually. They are entertaining but distracting. They are not serious. Not to me. They get in the way. The mysterious link between a pupil and his teacher is based on love and trust. The guru is the link between heaven and earth. His presence, even absence, should put us in a state of grace where we might sense the presence of God, not an excited state of nervous wonder when we shout 'Wow!' instead of whispering 'Om'."

CHAPTER THIRTY-ONE
The Indian Coffee House again

Ramu and Ajay Sarnhi had deliberately squashed into a corner table, almost out of sight in the Indian Coffee House. They were by the 'No Admittance' sign on the kitchen door where the waiters passed in and out in a silent stream. The highly trained waiters knew never to rush, so they weren't disturbed. Years of passing, leaning and brushing had worn a discoloured patch at elbow height along the high counter opposite.

"We need to talk, Father," Ajay began.

"Why all this secrecy?" countered the father.

"Because secrets are threatening, Father."

Ramu Sarnhi sighed.

"Not taxation again, surely. I've told you, it is not a problem. The government is under siege from much bigger players than us. National Governments, International Corporations, huge Finance Houses. We are a modest, private company. We inhabit the forest floor. All official eyes are on the canopy." He raised his eyes to the ceiling to illustrate this thought. "They fly and catch the eye, we walk by unnoticed." He lowered his gaze to look on his son.

"It will take weeks, perhaps months to legitimise the Trust. Perhaps the tax position is not irretrievable after all."

Ramu Sarnhi laughed out loud. A few eyes looked his way. A waiter paused in passing.

"Is everything satisfactory, sir?"

"Perfectly, thank you. Perhaps a refill would help settle my son's nerves."

"Certainly, sir."

"You are in India, my son. If you choose to unpick the Family Trust it will take you most of your life. It might be completed in Hari's time and by then it would not be necessary, so why bother? Thank you. Not for me." The coffee pot had arrived sitting in the exact centre of a high-rimmed steel tray. Ajay accepted a fill-up. It might help his concentration, he thought, but it would not steady his nerves.

"Let me try, just for a moment, to explain. You have made many gifts to the Trust personally and so have other relations. You have all, no doubt, claimed the tax back on your annual submissions."

"Naturally."

"But where are all the deeds of gift?"

"The what?" Ramu Sarnhi changed his mind and steered a returning waiter with a useful coffeepot towards his empty cup.

"Every gift must be accompanied by a piece of paper that makes it legitimate," Ajay explained, exasperated.

"I hate pieces of paper, especially your sort that would steal my power." The father assumed a sullen face that annoyed the son.

Ajay Sarnhi placed a pile of papers in the centre of the table and, roughly picking from the top, slapped down each sheet in turn with an angry description.

"Gift taxes—not paid. Consumption taxes—not paid. Sales taxes—not paid. Property taxes—partly paid." The break in the rhythm allowed his father to interrupt.

"No, you're wrong. They are fair and proper amounts."

"But the property values have been estimated by the owners, that is, you." Ajay pointed accusingly at his father's chest.

"No," was the calm reply. "You are wrong. They were individual valuations. That goes for the land as well. I don't have to pay anything on what can be described in any way as agricultural production. I don't understand fields and cows and rice. My knowledge is in silk and textiles. I employ an agent for all that. The prices are sound."

Ajay was both alarmed and starting to sense the beginnings of relief.

"They are? Truly?"

"Truly."

"But . . ." Ajay Sarnhi began to herd numbers into columns and whispered an urgent counting beneath his breath. He arrived at a final sum that he covered with his hand. All the cash sums he divided by fifty, a conservative rate of exchange and, after a breathless silence, he looked up from his conclusion and smiled. "And you claim this is an accurate valuation of all that the Trust owns?"

"Are you still doubting my word?"

"No. Of course not, Father. God forbid."

"He does."

"I know. And I agree with God." Ajay Sarnhi fell silent and sipped his coffee. He peeked again at the sum under his hand. He began to intone his private mantra: 'pennies for pounds', 'pennies for pounds'. The total of all the land, huts, barns and sheds, livestock, equipment and carts (even including the cash deeds of gift) came to a relatively modest sum. His father's life was insured for a greater amount. The whole of the Family Trust couldn't buy the modest house he owned in England. It was a nice area in which he lived, he remembered happily.

"Are you satisfied now?" Ramu Sarnhi was relieved if unapologetic. His son relaxed and gazed absentmindedly at his father's gold watch.

Something was missing.

Directed to the minute detail of the Trust, Ajay had been skilfully manoeuvred away from the herd of golden elephants that were crowding the room. Ramu Sarnhi guessed his son might realise his oversight and had come prepared.

Frowning, Ajay started to focus on what was missing from the H U F. The fine house in Bangalore. The flats his father was building in the outskirts. The house in Whitefield. The emporium in Mahatma Gandhi Road, et cetera. The real wealth of his father and the family business wasn't implicated in the trust. At all. The income declared there, taxed or not, could not possibly sustain his father's lifestyle.

"Father . . ."

"You'll need to see this." Ramu Sarnhi handed a small notebook to his son. It had red card covers that were worn with use. The inside was lined like a simple ledger. It could have been mistaken for a petty cash book but the sums Ajay saw inside widened his eyes. They were far from petty.

"What is this, Father?"

"I believe it's the traditional 'Little Black Book' that all clever men write their secrets in. For some it is mistresses, others horses or gambling debts. Mine is for offshore holdings. Take your time. There are a lot of entries."

"And this one is red."

"Yes. It shares my blushes." Ramu Sarnhi, despite his ironical tone, did blush.

"Good God," Ajay exclaimed.

"He has been. And he will need to continue to be. It takes a little time to sort this kind of thing out. I pray he will grant me that time. There are ways. I know them. We will need to begin the process today."

"I don't understand. Where has all this money come from?"

"The family business. Honest trading. I've been quite good at it."

"I don't doubt that. Well, let me try this question. Where is it?"

"A wiser question, my son. All these deposits are in a variety of institutions on the beautiful island of Mauritius. Have you ever been? You should go, and soon." Ramu Sarnhi was delightfully capricious.

"Mauritius?" His son was bewildered.

"Yes. And before you start to panic about imposts and prisons, we have a tax residence certificate from Mauritius. We are not obliged to pay any taxes in India on all our holdings there.

"Why?" asked a bemused Ajay Sarnhi.

"Because for a while there was a 'Double Taxation Treaty' with Mauritius. Any company, our company for instance, could only be taxed in the country where it was domiciled. Even if all operations were in India, it was possible to use the Mauritius Offshore Business Activities Act—M O B A for short— to create Postbox Companies there and escape all Indian tax liabilities."

"Why?"

"Stop saying that."

"But why would the government do such a thing?"

"It was keen to attract foreign investment and any sensible overseas company wasn't going to allow itself to be taxed in India. It is all to do with capital gains. We have the capital: we gain." Ramu Sarnhi grinned and opened his hands in a gesture of honesty. The son shook his head in disapproval but couldn't take his eyes off the figures in the little red book.

"Stop being so outraged, Ajay. We may deprive the government of income tax but we invest in India. We create jobs and opportunities here. We pay excise duty on imports and exports. We pay sales taxes and other duties. We do actually pay a lot of tax, indirectly, we just don't pay any tax directly." Ramu Sarnhi was very persuasive.

"But how …?" Before Ajay Sarnhi could finish his question his father began the answer.

"How do we transfer all this into your name?"

"Yes. Just how do we do that?"

"Fortunately, Mauritius is not so cumbersome as India. There is a neat way. Not with the Hindu Undivided Family. That will linger but, I like to think of it as a decoy, a symbol of good intent and it matters to me. It matters a lot. Don't tamper with it, please. All the real wealth is elsewhere and the Trust is about trust. It is about my family. I am its head. I will act decently and responsibly towards it. Is that clear?" Ramu Sarnhi's assertions were draining him of energy. His breathing was becoming shallow and he was starting to sweat.

"Crystal clear, Father. I will leave the Trust as it is." Ajay Sarnhi was concerned but didn't draw attention to his father's apparent weakness. He knew it would frustrate and annoy him.

"No you won't! You'll add to it at every wedding and every funeral. It will be your responsibility and you will shoulder it."

Ajay Sarnhi paused. His father was anxious and looking deep into his son's eyes.

"I will, Father, of course. You mustn't trouble yourself about any of this. I will do everything you wish. Calm yourself."

Ramu Sarnhi was rushing to end this meeting. He needed to rest but not until he was satisfied.

"Draw up papers to that effect. I trust your word but you like paper. Put it into words, the sort that will make it legal. I assume you won't be staying in India."

The sudden change of subject startled Ajay Sarnhi.

"I . . ."

"We won't discuss this now. I fear I'm guilty of my own success. I was not careful of what I wished for. I wanted a son who would be confident in the ways of the West. I seem to have succeeded all too well. But this is not for now. I want no apologies or explanations. This current business is urgent and its time is short. Your future will be long, I hope."

"You were going to tell me what to do about Mauritius," Ajay reminded his father.

"I was." Ramu Sarnhi said this to himself. Having voiced his fear and apparently come to terms with it, he still hoped his son might contradict him and declare his intention to stay in India. He hadn't. It was a bitter disappointment.

"There is a mechanism we could use. We transfer all the shares in the company but not the capital assets. They will remain intact and safely hidden on their paradise island. You will then have the right to dispose of those assets as you see fit. They are yours after all. Use them wisely and pass them on carefully. Hari's life should be easier than yours as your life has been easier than mine. We must contact the institutions and generate paper."

"How many shares are there?"

"One."

CHAPTER THIRTY-TWO
Where was Jack?

Jack was missing. Hari was looking. By the late afternoon he was deeply concerned. Jack had not even turned up to evening darshan. True, little had been missed. Baba was again distracted, avoided the people and went straight to his throne. But darshan was the centre of things and Jack had been absent. Hari had been to his room several times, Sai Deep Café as many. He had tried to retrace Jack's guessed-at day. He discovered he had been to Maddy's compound.

"He left a long time ago," Maddy explained to Hari, "just after lunch. I gave him grilled rice. I didn't see which way he went. He stayed with us here most of the morning. I think he found us amusing."

Jack had visited Maddy out of curiosity. She seemed to be involved in most of the happenings at the edge of things. The concerted avoidance of the ashram by the Whitefield widows interested Jack. He would investigate. Maddy might enlighten him. He also hoped to enlist her help in socializing Rita, coaxing her back into the world she'd shrunk from in fear, a justified fear, perhaps, Jack thought.

Beguiled by the impressive modern house, standing well back from the busy road, he'd wandered across the courtyard of hard mud and lingered beside the string of terraced cottages that formed the three sides of the rectangle of enclosed space. Knocking on or peering into a succession of doors he had been accosted by round-bellied dogs, screeching children, an angry goat and a wandering cow that, to him at least, looked menacing.

"She's harmless," Maddy was quick to explain but Jack was hard to convince.

"I wanted to talk to you about things to do with the ashram, if I may, and to enlist your help or advice with Rita, the recluse down the road?" Jack was unnaturally polite.

"Perhaps later. You must excuse me. I am most sad, my guru left his body today."

Maddy was distressed and dull.

"I'm sorry. Is that dead?" Jack needed to be sure.

"That is dead." Maddy left him alone.

Jack decided to leave and almost tripped over a strange object on the floor. He looked down and saw a shaven-headed, sunken-eyed girl who was perhaps in her twenties and who usually wore the orange robe of the total renunciate, the sanyassin. Today she had washed that only possession; it was hanging rather magnificently on Maddy's clothesline at the edge of the compound and she sat with her back pressed to the wall, totally naked, even of flesh. Jack had stumbled on her outstretched legs.

"I am not here!" she intoned with fiercely intelligent eyes.

"Okay," agreed Jack.

"This is not my body. I am dead."

"There ya go!"

"You must sacrifice, but not surrender."

"Maddy?" Jack was running out of pleasantries.

"Who are you?" asked the girl.

"Won't be a minute," shouted Maddy from inside her toilet.

"I'm Jack and I thought I was doing all right. Now I'm not so sure."

"You need only ask 'Who am I?' and then you will be sure. Jack, I cannot persuade you, I can only reveal."

"What's left?" asked Jack.

"Total Surrender. I have to sit here because I have a bad back. Total Surrender."

"My back is bad too," offered Jack, hoping to share.

"We cannot make contact in the body. The act of surrender has to be repeated endlessly." Jack glanced with thinly disguised distaste at the intoning skeleton.

"If you'll excuse me."

A telephone was ringing. Maddy, not entirely re-dressed from her ablutions ran through the courtyard untidily.

"Be right back. I see you've met Om. Will you have some lunch, Jack? Coming!" She was gone. Jack and Om stood in silence.

Maddy returned, smiling.

"Good news?" asked Jack, glad to end the silence.

"I enjoy silence," observed a remarkably perceptive Om. "Your relief betrays a lack of spirituality. You want to know but you don't know how to know. What is the use of knowing about everything else, when you do not yet know who you are?"

"I'll get you both some lunch," offered Maddy, by way of answer. "He's not dead!" she added, by way of excitement.

"Who?"

"My guru!"

"There is no such thing as death, only Total Surrender," explained Om.

"He was out of his body. He just looked dead. He managed to get a message to the mortuary assistant. In thirteen days he will return to his body. Isn't that wonderful news?"

"Where is he?" asked a bemused Jack.

"Six inches above his own head. He never goes far," explained Maddy, as a matter of fact.

"Has he done it before?"

"Oh yes. For twelve years. He sat in a graveyard for twenty-three hours a day for the first eight years and twelve hours a day for the next four. The rats ate his thighs and flesh grew between his palms and fingers because his hands were clasped together for so long. Lunch?"

"Er . . ."

"I'll grill some rice. It's my speciality."

"What did he think about for twelve years?"

"Nothing. He listened to the sound of 'Om'."

"Total Surrender!"

"Not you dear," Maddy patted Om on the shoulder.

"Lunch?"

And that was the last anyone had seen of Jack.

Hari had gone to his bridge for inspiration. The noisy squarks of squabbling red kites convinced him that Jack had wandered into his grandfather's village.

"He's there!" Hari declared and ran down the baked roadway shouting, "Jack! Jack!"

He clambered up an embankment and ran along a raised causeway

that shadowed the course of the river. Immediately to his right, Hari could see the edge of the village. Outside and clearly defined against the white side of the hut, Hari saw a child wave. He slowed. No, it wasn't waving to say hello; it was beckoning him to come. He ran. The child still waved. As he approached the hut with its collapsing roof of matted palm fronds and woven reeds, Hari stopped.

"I'm looking for my friend, Jack," he explained. A finger pointed. Hari crept from the sunlight into the dark interior and heard a groan.

Jack sat exhausted

"Jack?"

Silence.

"Jack?"

"Is that you, Harry?" Eyes adjusted, Hari could see his friend. Collapsed in the corner, back to the far wall, Jack sat exhausted. His orange bag lay crumpled between his legs; his mouth hung open; his eyes stared in pain.

"What's wrong, Jack? What's happened?"

"I'm fine. I got a little lost. I needed to rest up. The boy lent me the hut. I'm afraid there's no furniture. They've been very kind. They carried me in."

"Did you fall again?"

"Well, yeh, I guess so."

"Why do you keep falling down, Jack?"

"I'm not sure, Harry. Maybe the soil doesn't like me." He grinned. Hari felt better.

"Are you in pain?"

"A little. It's my back. My knee's fine. But, I hurt my elbow." There was blood and brown earth stains mingling on the left forearm.

"Would you like some water?" Hari started to be busy.

"In my Baba bag. I just ran out of energy. It's so damned hot."

Hari bathed Jack's face, gave him a drink, took one himself and started to ease the sleeve away from its bleeding.

"Tell me if I hurt you."

"You've kindly hands, Harry, I told you once before."

Hari went quiet.

"I was worried, Jack."

"That's good of you. I just kind of knew you'd come. Harry?"

"Yes."

"Where the hell am I?"

They both laughed.

"You're on the edge of the village where Grandfather's silk is made. It's a long way from the bridge. What were you doing down here?"

"I didn't intend to be here. Maddy said that she and Joan and the Om woman often went swimming. Not in the river, that's public, but in a well. It sounded amazing. A huge, walled well with steps down into it. Sounded a great idea, so I went to find it. I knew it was by the river but not exactly where. Then it was hot."

"When was this, Jack?"

"Around midday."

"It was in the forties today."

"I think it was the sun. Melted what's left of my brain. Anyway, I was trying to reach a raised pathway and I must have tripped on a furrow or a hole in the ground, whichever, I went a hell of a tumble and I woke up here. Can we go now?"

"Yes, of course." Hari welcomed Jack's normal impatience. He knew he was on the mend.

"Now, I'm too heavy for you all alone. Let's get some help here. Hey! You boys out there!"

Within seconds, Jack had organised the whole junior population of the village. As if he were a silent Pied Piper, ten or twelve shoeless youngsters supported and carried any vacant part of Jack. The rest of the village followed in their wake, noisy for their turn.

At the bridge, Jack distributed rupees like a liberating general and destroyed the local economy within seconds. As he and Hari re-entered Whitefield, the suddenly rich peasant boys fought to divide notes that all their fathers would have found difficult to change.

"What you need is a hat," realised Hari.

"Right!"

Within the hour, Jack had tried on every headpiece in the bazaar. He drank tea to reflect, returned and dithered and finally settled on a splendid white one with huge flopping brims that would bounce away the damaging rays of the sun.

"Is it me?" He yanked at the brim and turned in profile. "What do you think?"

"I think it's perfect. Promise me you'll wear it. And don't lose it."

"That's up to the hat."

CHAPTER THIRTY-THREE
The death of a yogi

It was early morning. Ramu Sarnhi had called a breakfast meeting for a dozen of his managers at the rented house. There was a new urgency to these proceedings and Hari's presence as a social nicety was both irrelevant and a nuisance. Hari was happy to be absent and waited at the ashram gates for morning darshan. He looked across to the bazaar. Jack was hovering indecisively on the other side of the ditch, wondering if he should cross. He was testing the edge of the wooden bridge with the outstretched toe of his trainers. Even from as far away as the ashram gate, Hari could see the danger. Laces trailed, the shoe dangled, the plank-bridge wobbled and all Hari could do was shout.

"Jack! Wait for me!"

Absent-mindedly, Jack looked up, waved to Hari and sank straight onto his bottom; his knees had refused to bend. Before Hari could arrive others came to Jack's aid. By the time Hari had tripped across the bridge, Jack was upright and blissfully unaware of the danger he'd been in.

"Hi, young friend. Could you lend me your legs for few days? I'd love to be that nimble again. Can you believe I was once nimble?"

Hari said, "Yes, Jack, I could. Let me . . ." Jack took Hari's arm and rather than cross the bridge, steered him towards the Sai Deep Café. There was still a while before darshan.

"No. I lied. I was never nimble like you and I don't ever remember being so young."

Jack winced and even by his standards, was unsteady and an awkward weight.

"Are you all right, Jack?" Hari asked. "After yesterday?"

"Yesterday?"

"The fall, the heat, the hat?" Jack had stuffed the hat in question into his disintegrating Sai Baba bag. It was not hot enough to be needed yet.

"I think your bag is dying, Jack. Should I run and get you another one, while we are waiting for our drinks? And perhaps a walking stick?" Hari suggested this tentatively. Even now he found it hard to judge Jack's mood and possible reaction. He was only ever certain of being surprised.

Jack frowned ominously. "Just an idea." Hari began to retrench.

Jack smiled.

"And a brilliant one. But, I must change the word as well as the bag. Call it a walking cane and I accept. That's elegant. That's class. That's a style choice, not a necessity. I don't have to admit I'm decrepit. Not yet. Oh, and get a bigger bag so I can put this one inside it. I've grown rather fond of it and I feel kind of responsible. Okay? Understand?"

Hari nodded his understanding, fished amongst a mess of crumpled rupee notes that Jack had grabbed from his ashram-trouser pocket and offered to Hari in a clenched fist.

"Get a good one," Jack added to Hari's retreating back. "I'm hard to please." He laughed. Unashamedly.

It wasn't easy to find but somehow, from somewhere, the trader had materialised a splendid specimen fashioned from ebony and topped with an elegant disc of silver. At least that's what he claimed. Hari was a seasoned trader by now and guessed nothing was genuine but it looked the part and cost little, pennies for pounds, of course, and the handsome bag he'd bought was a sturdy version of the original and might withstand Jack for a few days longer.

"Now that is a gentleman's cane." Jack had prised himself upright immediately when Hari had presented his prize to his friend. "I could be a Southern swell if I didn't smack so much of New York, hey? It's the price I will always pay. Thank you, Harry. You're a good friend and you have to pay for the drinks because I gave you all my money."

Hari was still baffled by Jack's complete ignorance of the value of the local currency. Without a word, he returned most of what he'd been given and, because two traders had managed to split a high value note, Jack thought he'd actually gained on the trade and laughed with delight.

"Drinks on me. I'm rich again and I have a walking cane to prove it."

Maddy passed by without stopping. As so often, she greeted no one, she was too engrossed in the rush of business.

"It's sad for her right now," Jack commented.

"Why?" asked Hari, expecting no news of note.

"Her guru's dead. Shiva something." Jack drank his tea, as unaware of his noisy slurping as the impact of this casually mentioned fact.

Hari went white.

"Is she cursed?" he asked the sky, looking upwards to glimpse a traditional god, forgetting Sai Baba across the way.

"What you say, son? Who you asking? You asking me?"

"No. Sorry, Jack. That's such bad news."

"Hey, I'm so sorry. I didn't know you knew the guy. Did you know the guy?" Jack leaned towards his young friend and placed a reassuring hand on top of Hari's.

"No. No, I didn't know him."

"Good. That's a relief. I wouldn't have been so," he paused, "matter-of-fact."

"It just makes things really difficult for a friend," Hari stated.

"You have so many friends, Harry. I envy you that. I have very few, but then I don't deserve to. I'm not as nice as you."

Jack meant what he said and Hari was instantly distracted from his circling thoughts.

"No, Jack, you're really nice. You're so much more important than me. I'm honoured that you're my friend."

"Thank you for the pretty speech, young man. Hey. Cheer up. I forgot the phone call."

"Pardon?" Hari was lost in Jack's confusing thoughts.

"Maddy had a phone call to say her guru man is not dead."

"I thought you said?" Hari was unsettled.

"Let me finish."

"Sorry." Hari had forgotten that Jack must not be interrupted. It was a game they played.

"Let's say that in any other place he'd be buried by now. We tend to think that when hearts stop and breathing ends then perhaps we have a corpse on our hands. But not in India. Apparently, he sent a message to one of his followers to say he'll be back in his body next week, the week after next, perhaps."

"Where is he, then?" asked Hari, totally baffled.

"Six inches above his own head, so he claims. Gone on an out-of-body holiday it seems. Watch this space, hey, Harry. Let's hope he can get back in. Stranger things have happened."

Throughout the long wait for Sai Baba, Hari wandered through the conflicting thoughts milling in his mind. After his talk with Jean Paul, not only was he reassured, he was convinced that life with Maddy's guru would be a good ending to Lunasha's story. He'd not wanted that at first. He'd hoped she could be normal. She was so beautiful; perhaps she could marry a wealthy man and be safe in the world. Then she could talk once more; her voice would be heard. If this was a good choice and at its centre was worship, and prayer and purity, why take it away from her? How long could she stay with Maddy? Would she become a beggar woman once more? He couldn't face the idea of her continued humiliation. He'd wanted to erect screens around her to hide her from the world's eyes when she stepped into the pit for her vile cleansing. He'd shouted at the washer-men by the river and delighted in her spinning bathe on the surface of the well, hidden from the world, private and safe. He'd ask Sai Baba for help, perhaps. He hoped he'd come near. But he didn't like to make any demands. He didn't wish to be like the others. This was a problem for the world. Perhaps Maddy could solve it. He apologised for his lapse into need. It wouldn't have mattered that morning. Sai Baba had come nowhere near him. His time amongst men was becoming less and less. Perhaps he'd lost interest at last. Hari was pleased that he had not added to God's burden.

CHAPTER THIRTY-FOUR
Lunasha

Hari ran from the ashram, dodging traffic, stepping on and off the road, and startling the monkeys. He rushed inside Maddy's compound, calling her name.

"Hi, Hari!" Maddy replied. I'm on the phone. There's tea. I have news. Come in." She placed a guarding hand over the mouthpiece of the phone and nodded Hari towards the tea. She gestured to herself so Hari poured two cups. "That's wonderful news," Maddy was saying. "Thank you. Same time tomorrow. I'll post the messages on the board so everyone can read them. Goodbye." She put the phone down and began an instant search. She returned clutching a large sheet of cardboard. She pinned a scribbled note on it that read: 'I am not dead. I am in *yoga nidra*.'

"What's *yoga nidra*?" Hari asked.

"No idea. No one at the ashram knows either."

"But who said it?"

"Swamiji," Maddy answered as if Hari had asked an absurd question. "Shivabalayogi himself, of course."

Risking Maddy's patience, Hari asked, "How?"

"Through the voice of a child at the Mandir in Adivarapupeta. He does that, you know. It's how we experience Swamiji when he is not with us." She sipped her tea. "We can call the ashram in Bangalore on the phone in Swamiji's room, any time. There will be people there to answer."

"What is happening, Maddy? Please explain." Hari was calm, reassured by Maddy's certainty and always in awe of her organising skills. Perhaps she could manage her guru's resurrection. There seemed to be few things beyond her power to arrange.

"He appeared to die at 1.47 a.m. yesterday. That was the time we laid the stone at the Mandir. Did you remember, Hari?"

He had, and the coincidence made him go a little cold.

"His body began to glow and his moustaches stood on end."

"Why?"

"I don't know. Strange, isn't it?" Maddy's wavering between authority and bafflement did little to lessen Hari's confusion.

"His body is in the ashram in Adivarapupeta. They seated him in a yogic posture, in an armchair, facing north. He is clothed and settled on a platform, in the shade, just at the front of the building. He looks for all the world at peace, relaxed and alive. So I'm told."

"But not breathing," Hari stated.

"No. But Swamiji is going to communicate with us through written messages. These are the ones he's sent so far."

"Who to?" asked Hari, bewildered by the strange happenings.

"Well, this one came from a Miss Yashoda, in Bangalore. 'Sri Swamiji will wake up at two o'clock early Tuesday morning'."

"That's today," Hari interrupted.

"I know. Clearly, it hasn't happened. Let me finish the message. 'The devotees have to do bhajans, fold their hands to mimic his'," Maddy clasped one of her hands on top of the other and entwined them in an awkward union. "And, at 2 a.m. pray and ask for Swamiji to wake up and he will."

"But he didn't."

"No. Perhaps not enough of us prayed for his return. Here is the latest message. 'The devotees may wait a maximum of 386 hours. If the body starts decomposing and emits a foul odour, I will be in *madasamadhi*'."

"Where or what is that?"

"It's a 'where' and a 'what'. It means to be in a perfect state of bliss. The body will have been relinquished entirely."

"What's it like now?" asked Hari, embarrassed at his own ghoulishness.

"There are no signs of decomposition. They are fanning the body but it is outside in 40° of heat and there are no signs of rigor mortis and apparently, it is cool to the touch."

"That's impossible, isn't it?" Hari suggested.

"Not for Swamiji."

On each of the next three mornings, the message was the same and unfulfilled. On the fourth night, Hari was out late. His grandfather was entertaining and Hari had wandered towards his bridge of respite after a quiet supper with Jean Paul, who had done his best to reassure Hari that all would still be well for Lunasha. As he returned from his walk, refreshed by the gentle noise of the flowing river, Hari saw lights in Maddy's compound and heard the sound of chanting. It was repetitive and as far as he could discern, the words were 'Om namah Shivaya'. He didn't know what they meant but their rhythmical insistence suggested they contained a powerful message. Then there was the distant sound of a conch. It invited Hari inside.

In the middle of the courtyard were a few familiar faces but most were unknown to Hari. Perhaps they were devotees from Bangalore. To his delight, right in the middle of the chanters, Lunasha was singing with a gentle smile on her lips. Her eyes were closed.

There had been no more messages. The body was still 'fresh', according to Maddy's last bulletin but the skin of the face was darkening. When would this stop, Hari wondered?

Then it did. The chanting ended. There was a sudden and intense silence. The crowd stepped quietly away, their vigil complete. Only Lunasha remained. Suddenly, she opened her eyes, entwined her hands in the awkward shape Maddy had achieved, and declared in a strong and certain voice:

'Wait until 3 p.m. tomorrow. Bury me then. It is time.'

She closed her eyes, stumbled and was stopped from falling by the pair of devotees closest to her. Hari was amazed. The silence ended. The devotees crowded around Lunasha, cheered and clapped and knew something special had occurred in their midst and that the messenger was as special as the moment.

"She has been chosen," Maddy declared and shooed everyone away, so Lunasha could breathe freely and recover herself.

Hari kept to the shadows until everyone had gone. He was reluctant to leave but as he did so, with one hand on the open gate, sensing a presence but hardly daring to move, a voice spoke to him.

"Don't worry about me, Hari. No. Don't turn round. It is Lunasha. I want to thank you for all that you have done for me. I will comfort Maddy for her loss. Swamiji has said he will return to his body but he will not. He can't. It doesn't matter. He will still talk to us all, silently, in our heads, privately. It will suit me perfectly, Hari. Truly. I know of your concerns. I will talk without speaking and hear without listening. I can be at peace. I have no need to be part of the world. I will sing holy songs and help the followers of Swamiji. That will be a good life for me. Thank you for guiding me to it."

Hari sensed her close. Lunasha reached out and touched Hari gently on the arm.

"Goodbye, Hari."

He froze.

When he dared to turn around, Lunasha was gone. Hari knew he would never see her again.

CHAPTER THIRTY-FIVE
The business of dying

"What are they doing here?" Hari asked himself, whispering even inside his own head. He ducked out of sight behind a neighbouring wall. His grandfather was there, shaking hands, being friendly, being completely false, surely.

"I thought he hated them," Hari said. He must have spoken this out loud. All three men peered in his direction, saw nothing and parted company almost immediately afterwards.

Hari watched the two ashram officials walk away. Were they deliberately chosen because they were tall, he wondered? Certainly their straight-backed, deliberate stride added to their air of self-importance. They swaggered. They seemed beyond reproach. Hari thought they were also beyond approach but clearly Grandfather Sarnhi had found a way.

The two officials still wore their all-white uniforms: neatly tailored, long-sleeved jackets and slacks with the distinct triangle of their kerchiefs obvious even in this half-light. During darshan, Hari would stare into the starburst effect of the two shades of blue in their design. To secure their badges of office, most wore gold clasps where a boy scout's woggle would be. Hari feared these men. They were rarely helpful, instantly gruff and clearly all powerful. He thought them sinister. He would watch them orchestrate the day's events. They would usher most of the peasant pilgrims roughly and autocratically to their sitting spaces. Hari had even seen one official kick a sad little man back into place when he trespassed into the corridor where Sai Baba might pass.

The wealthier visitors, the VIPs like his grandfather, were treated with greater care but still scant respect. Hari watched carefully as one or two of the officials who stood closest to Baba would pull a small but significant bundle of papers from the breast pocket of their jackets. Having quickly consulted their notes, they would peer around and appear to nudge or guide Sai Baba their way. One had access to God's ear. He was a privileged whisperer and Hari became convinced that he was making Sai Baba go ways he didn't choose and greet people he would avoid. The 'whisperer' was also the 'tapper'. He was the one who made the all-important gesture that meant you had been chosen. You, and a few like you, would then leave and prepare to talk to God.

Why did the official have this right and not God? Had he and the others taken charge? No wonder Sai Baba looked so unhappy during the most recent darshans. Hari wondered if God's sudden exits surprised the whispering official or were they part of a carefully managed plan? He hoped not. He hoped God was still free to choose. Surely those officials hadn't taken charge of Him?

"Hari, you're so late." Esther Sarnhi was waiting just inside the door of Ramu Sarnhi's rented house.

"I'm sorry, Mother. I saw people, official people, in the doorway and didn't think I should push by them."

"No. That was wise." She closed the door. "Have you eaten?"

"Yes, thank you. I ate with Jean Paul."

"Did you use your grandfather's account?"

"I was in the Indian Café. He doesn't have an account there. But I spent my own pocket money. I played fair."

"Good boy." The mother patted her son's head. She was distracted and clearly anxious.

"What were those people doing here, Mother? I thought Grandfather hated them."

"Your grandfather hates no one, Hari. I think their power frustrates him, that is all. He is used to success and usually people defer to him. He is rarely expected to do the opposite."

"Except before Sai Baba," Hari suggested, hopefully.

"I believe that was the purpose of the visit."

"To see God?"

"If it can be arranged."

"Can it be?"

"I'm not sure. It's none of my business. It might one day be business of yours but I believe the Sarnhi Family Trust has just made a significant donation to the ashram."

"How much?" was Hari's instant, if inappropriate, question.

"I've no idea, Hari." His mother laughed. "They were served meat at dinner."

"Did they eat it?" asked Hari.

"Oh yes. So you see, Grandfather still doesn't like them."

They both smiled.

"Those men frighten me, Mother."

"They are a little frightening, I agree with you. Sai Baba leaves so much to them. I think the shooting and the invasion of his private world unsettled him. I suppose all great men, and who can be greater than an avatar, need some protection, bodyguards and men who shield them from danger."

"They are so rude. I've seen them push people and say cruel words. One even kicked an older man." Hari's eyes were wide in disbelief.

"You should see the officials in the women's area," Hari's mother began, cradling Hari in her arm and guiding him further inside the house. "They are far worse than the men."

"Surely not."

"Surely so. Some even have sticks, like army sergeant majors. They never use them, at least I've never witnessed a beating, but they whip them from under their arms and swish and threaten." Esther Sarnhi pushed Hari away and mimicked the threat she was describing. Hari laughed; the angry faces were meant to amuse not frighten him.

"There have been complaints, directly to Sai Baba."

"What did he say?"

"'Who else will employ them?'"

Hari laughed. It was a very clever reply.

"But the other women are pretty alarming too," his mother continued. "They won't queue like in England. They bustle and wriggle and elbow their way through." She waddled into Hari and made him giggle.

"Shush!" She hugged him close. "I'm sorry, that was my fault. Grandfather is not at all well, I'm afraid. We must be quiet and not disturb him."

The household rose early. Hari's father had already been to the temporary Post Office in Whitefield.

"It is so old-fashioned, it is absurd." He was complaining to his father. They were breakfasting early at the Sai Deep Café. No one else was awake but them. Their business was urgent.

"It would be troublesome to phone Mauritius from our office in Bangalore, let alone from here." Ramu Sarnhi was trying to console his son. It was obvious to all his health was failing. The anxiety surrounding his business affairs was certainly accelerating the decline but he now blamed himself for leaving everything to this last minute. He had signed every form his son had presented to him recently, without question. This was the endgame. It was entirely possible that all his secret wealth could be trapped in its carefully concealed hiding places for all time. He'd heard of such things. Some of his friends had chosen very obscure places, Bermuda, and the Cayman Islands, places he couldn't point to on a map. The key man had died and provided an endless living for the trustees with no funds ever transferred to the intended benefactors. This was his worst nightmare. He must have enough time. Everything was in place but not in one place and not in the right place: here in Whitefield or Bangalore. The faxes and following papers could even be routed to Birmingham but only after having passed through India and all these processes ate into the time he didn't have.

"Do they have a fax machine here?" Ramu Sarnhi asked his son, between calming sips of tea.

"Yes. They do. I'm not sure they know how to work it. I offered. They were happy to let me but they've no electricity this morning. I swear the phones are working on wind-up batteries, like in the war. God, it's primitive."

"It must work for us, son. Or God must." He looked knowingly at Ajay. Nothing needed to be said.

"How did that go?" Ajay looked down. He was an honest man in his dealings with family and friends and matters religious. The world of business involved a morality all of its own and misbehaviour there didn't trouble him. Bribing officials in what amounted to a church or monastery did.

"Who knows? I made a bequest. They might help. They might not. It is up to God, they tell me. They cannot lead, only follow."

"Do you believe them?"

"Not a word. They are as corrupt and untrustworthy as any men who have access to those who truly wield power or control great wealth. Swami does both, I suppose. I'm sure I'm of little interest to Him but He is of great interest to me. He is my only hope, right now."

For a moment, Ajay pitied his father. He suddenly appeared weak and vulnerable, even afraid. But only for a moment.

"Come. We have work to do." Ramu Sarnhi pushed away his chair and stood briskly. The son was relieved. The natural order was resumed.

Darshan didn't start well. Even the VIPs were inconvenienced. There was a rumour that the prime minister was going to appear again so security was tight and obvious. The exact positioning of such an important political figure seemed to take precedence over the needs of the religious potentate the ashram officials were meant to serve. The ballot of the lines was abandoned. A space was cleared and cleaned and the rest of the insignificant earthly mortals were streamed around it, ushered and placed with less ceremony than usual. Ramu Sarnhi sensed his opportunity was gone, his money lost and an investment made that would pay no return.

Sai Baba's entry was delayed. Even the most devoted interrupted their contented 'Oms' with the odd 'tut' of disapproval. The politician didn't arrive. His space stood empty for a while but once the distant rumble and hum that signalled the arrival of Sai Baba was heard, the space was seamlessly filled by encroaching bodies that nervously hoped their spot was sanctified and might afford them special privileges over all the rest.

They were wrong. Spitefully, as they saw it, Sai Baba avoided their area entirely. He lingered instead just inside the Great Hall. His officials buzzed around him, collecting letters, presenting placards woven with names and messages of good intent. Small boys offered bowls of sweets that Sai Baba scattered absent-mindedly, with no apparent aim.

The whole party shuffled closer to the Sarnhi family and passed by. The Whisperer whispered, took three paces back and without bending, tapped Ramu Sarnhi on the shoulder. The whole family rose but the grim-faced official scowled them seated once more. Only Grandfather was chosen. Abandoned, so it seemed, in the centre of an empty aisle, he wasn't sure what to do next. From the wings a fussing official beckoned him outside. He joined a small group of half a dozen people. A tall, angular woman with a Germanic bearing stood next to a much smaller, rotund lady who must be her mother, for she fussed and directed so. This was not her first interview; that much she made clear. There was a hollow-cheeked man separated from the Iranian party, still wearing his green kerchief. Of the ill and halt in his group he was the healthiest and his anxious pallor wasn't promising. There was a distinguished, aristocratic man, grey-haired, self-important. He stood alone, impressive in European clothes. A rather startled middle-aged woman, Dutch perhaps, dumpy and jolly with a very round face and inappropriate plaits of grey-blonde hair pinned to the side of her head was keen to make conversation but didn't know what to say.

The happiness and instant elation of being chosen had now waned into a nervous apprehension. Called forward as a group they were led through the arched doorway that led down the drive towards the private quarters of Sai Baba. They were going to a meeting with God.

CHAPTER THIRTY-SIX
Meeting God

A door opened into a small room. The light from outside cast a few defining shadows. The walls were empty, the floor bare. There were no ornaments except for a single chair. Sai Baba sat there alone, waiting, as the select group of his apprehensive followers was ushered inside. The boldest was the Dutch lady. She rushed forward and fell at Baba's feet. He was not alarmed by the suddenness of her coming.

"Forgive me, Swami, I have failed you. Don't be angry with me." She was immensely sad and wracked by sobs that tormented her body. Baba touched her head and spoke softly and slowly to her.

"Neither you nor anyone can disappoint me. I expect nothing from you, so whatever it is you have or have not done it was not contrary to my wishes or my hopes. I can therefore never be angry with you. If I made plans for you to follow, then I would be using you for my own ends. That I do not do. I can only be made happy by witnessing the happiness of others. Can you be happy, for yourself and not for me?"

"Yes, Swami, I can, Swami. Forgive me."

"Then be happy so that I can be."

Whatever it was that troubled her was lost in private whisperings between herself and her God. The others stood in awe. Ramu Sarnhi lodged himself between the walls that made the corner by the door. He resolved to be last. He felt the least appropriate there.

The tall lady with her mother and the elderly European were revealed as a family unit. They had wisely split to prevent comment. They were clearly known to Sai Baba and the rumours of the ashram. This was the Russian family. They had been involved from the start and were huge benefactors to the ashrams of Whitefield and Puttaparthi. They all wore Baba-made jewellery. The daughter was nursing a fractured specimen in the palm of her hand. She signalled that the stone had cracked. Baba covered the pieces with his hand, swirled his fingers in the air and another silver ring fell into the open palm to clink next to its imperfect neighbour. Everyone gasped in wonder except Sai Baba, who giggled at his act. It was charming, thought Ramu Sarnhi, and defused the discomforting bafflement that humans feel when witnessing something they cannot explain and, in Ramu Sarnhi's case don't want to believe.

The father bent and the mother knelt, awkwardly. Only the tall daughter had the suppleness to sit cross-legged at Baba's feet. They talked and smiled. It was a natural seeming conversation that Ramu Sarnhi caught snatches of. The mother was asking about a lost child.

"You did not lose him. He lost himself," Baba was explaining.

He leaned forward and touched the old lady gently on the shoulder. She was expensively dressed and probably proud. Kneeling before anyone or anything was not easy for her, Ramu Sarnhi had guessed. Baba knew also.

"This is hard for you, I know. But if you bow to nothing, honour no power beyond yourself, you will never bear the burden of this guilt. Even God would not intercede. Man alone chooses. There is no fate, only history. The sum total of all former actions taken by the past incarnations of our souls may determine what we are but not what we may become. The stars think nothing, good or bad. Your child was a soul that had a body that was destroyed. The soul lives on. It is always free. It wasn't ever born. It will never die. Speak to the living soul. Free yourself."

"What is he saying?" asked the husband, irritated by the whispering beneath him.

"He still can't hear anything, Swami," the troubled woman explained.

"I know."

"Can you help him?"

"No. Not yet."

With the smallest of gestures, Baba flicked his fingers to drive the mother away. He signalled the daughter should rise. She towered over him, clearly in awe and almost overwhelmed by being in such a presence. Baba raised his eyes and smiled.

"I will look after you. Always. There is no need to be here. I will reside in your heart." He touched his chest as a sign of confirmation. "Tell your mother to be happy." The lady nodded, unable to speak. Everyone listening envied her the promise He'd made.

The sallow-faced man from Iran inched forward. He wriggled along the ground as if approaching some jealous potentate, a caliph or an emperor from the past. Baba lifted his chin and told him to rise.

"Please stand. Stand tall. I will look up to you."

The Iranian couldn't obey but fell to his knees in shame.

"I cannot make you do that, Swami. It is too humbling."

"Nothing can humble me. I am not. I am. Please, stand."

The Iranian did so.

"Swami, I'm not here for me."

"I know."

"Of course you know." The Iranian was on the verge of tears. He hit himself hard on the side of the head to indicate the level of his stupidity.

"Stop that, please." Baba took both of the tortured man's hands into his and calmed him.

"My uncle is very ill," the Iranian began. "He is the head not just of our family but also our clan. We need him to lead us and to guide us. We need his wisdom. Could you please spare his life?"

"No. I would not if I could, and I can't."

"Oh!" The poor man was crest-fallen.

"Do not despair. You are wrong, so wrong. You will lead the family now. You will have the wisdom and strength. I promise you that. The things you fear are false. The weakness you chastise yourself for, you don't have. Go. Prepare your family for their loss. Be ready to lead them."

Even as Baba spoke the words, the man seemed to gain in both strength and stature. He was different. At that moment, he seemed to become the prophecy.

It was Ramu Sarnhi's turn. Last and least, as he saw it. He approached Sai Baba and squatted in an awkward bow.

"You must stand also. For you it is natural. You don't need to learn how."

"Thank you, Swami." He lowered his head, in awe, certainly, but immensely curious also, to stare God in the face.

"You've been a benefactor to the ashram, I understand."

"Yes, Swami. A modest donation."

"Very modest."

Ramu Sarnhi was embarrassed. He couldn't very well assert that one hundred thousand rupees was an appreciable sum, or that God was ungrateful.

"Do I shock you?"

"I . . ."

"Good. You know why it was modest. It was a careful amount. Calculated. A wise investment, you thought."

"I can hide nothing from you, Swami."

"Yet you still try."

Ramu Sarnhi was silent. He couldn't second-guess this Being.

"Tell me what you want from me, Swami."

"Nothing, or everything."

Ramu Sarnhi was confused. What was being referred to here? Money, goods, material wealth or spiritual matters? He could and would offer any amount of things unseen and unseeable.

"You wish to live a longer life. You want a bed in the hospital in Puttaparthi. You think my facilities will give you those years."

Ramu Sarnhi was about to agree but a raised finger stalled his response.

"These are in my gift, perhaps. But what is in yours? I offer you a choice: all that you possess in the world of matter for all that will be given in the world of spirit. There could be clever surgeons and care but only to give you time to prepare your soul."

Ramu Sarnhi fell silent. He didn't know how to respond. His wealth wasn't his. He held it in trust. He couldn't give away at this particular moment what belonged to future generations. How could he explain to Ajay and Hari and sons of future sons, that he had exchanged the fortunes of his whole family merely to prolong his own, selfish life, for a few more years? He smiled, wondering how many years he would need to first find and then tutor his soul for a spiritual end.

"Your choice is made. It will be easier than you think. Here, take this with you."

Baba swirled his fingers, stirring the air and made a silver ring with a pale opal stone that he placed carefully in Ramu Sarnhi's hand.

"Thank you," he said, bewildered.

"Go with my blessing," said Baba.

CHAPTER THIRTY-SEVEN
Grandfather

Within the hour, Ramu Sarnhi collapsed across the threshold of the house he'd rented for business in Whitefield. He had suffered a massive heart attack. His servants ran in all directions, seeking help. The youngest arrived beside the Sai Deep Café where Ajay Sarnhi, Hari and his mother were anxious to hear the outcome of Grandfather's interview. Even before any words escaped from the breathless messenger they were all standing, ready to respond, pre-prepared for the news.

They arrived at the same time as a young doctor from the temporary Field Hospital nearby. She was leaning over the body of the grandfather and pronounced him living.

"Thank God he's alive!" Hari's father exclaimed, and he pushed the nervous young doctor aside to make certain for himself.

"He's had a massive heart attack, I would guess," she began to explain.

"Guess?" The son was aggressive. He was nervous and afraid. The young doctor looked vulnerable and uneasy.

"I know he has. So do you. There is the danger of an aneurysm, a blood clot," she added, seeing the confusion on Ajay Sarnhi's face. "He can be moved. He survived the worst but I don't know what further damage may have been caused. No one would, not without further tests, an angiogram for example," she asserted, technically defensive. She knew she was young, almost certainly inexperienced but she was more than competent, near the top of her class. She needed to be, to justify her family's spending on her education. "He needs to be in Bangalore, in intensive care."

"I'll ring for an ambulance," Ajay Sarnhi offered, more polite now.

"I wouldn't if I were you. It can only come from the hospital. Take him by taxi. It'll be quicker. I'll come with you if it would set your mind at rest."

"You will?" Esther Sarnhi rushed forward and took the young doctor's hand. "Thank you."

"Yes. Thank you. I'm sorry I was . . ." Ajay began.

"You were anxious. It's a frightening moment, thinking someone you love might have died."

"Yes. That was it. Thank you for understanding."

They commandeered the largest and fastest taxi they could and laid the grandfather across the back seat. The young doctor sat with him, squashed into the corner. Ajay Sarnhi sat in the front with Hari on his lap. The mother stayed behind to organise the house and be prepared for any of the possible outcomes.

He was still alive when they reached the hospital. Ajay and Hari stood by the bed in quiet expectation. As Ramu Sarnhi's body tensed and relaxed, the ring still clenched in his hand fell onto the bed sheet. Ajay picked it up carefully and instantly recognized its provenance.

"It's one of Baba's rings. He made this for him. Look Hari, God made this ring for your grandfather."

Ajay toyed with the ring, fitting it on his own finger when he noticed something strange.

"It's too small."

"I don't suppose you can know in advance the size of everybody's finger," Hari suggested, excusing Baba's error.

"But he does. The ring always fits. Look." He gave the ring to Hari. It slipped onto the middle finger of his left hand and fitted perfectly. Both father and son stared in amazement.

"Baba intended the ring for you, my son. Or at least, once Grandfather could no longer wear it, it was destined to change to fit you."

Simultaneously they drew in deep breaths, bemused and unsettled by these divine happenings.

By the following morning, Ramu Sarnhi had been moved to a side ward. He was conscious but was desperately weak and his speech was slurred.

"What are you saying, Father? I don't understand." Ajay Sarnhi bent close to his father's face. It was an intimacy and a proximity that made them both nervous.

Making a great effort of will, forcing a shape to the words in his mouth, Ramu Sarnhi whispered, "Baba's hospital." His eyes were filled with fear before he closed them, exhausted by his effort to speak.

"I'll see to it, Father. Immediately."

Before leaving, Ajay spoke to the consultant in charge of his father's care.

"I think he has suffered a silent stroke," the doctor explained. He was squat, middle-aged and used to the responsibilities he carried. "His speech is slurred and he has lost some motor skills. It annoys him. He is a proud man, I think."

'Yes, he is. You know, he is a follower of Sai Baba and might be offered a bed in the hospital in Puttaparthi. Would that be of any use?"

"Perhaps. They have all the equipment that money can buy. But you must understand, your father is very ill."

"Could he be moved?"

"Perhaps."

"'Perhaps' is enough, wouldn't you say, Esther?" They were talking at the very end of that difficult day in the family house in Bangalore.

"I don't know, Ajay. Isn't he comfortable where he is? Is Baba's hospital so much better?" She was concerned for her husband. He was pale and overly worried.

"I must at least try," Ajay concluded.

He did. He lingered around the ashram offices for several hours, seeking the officials they'd already dealt with, hoping to acquire a bed that might prolong his father's life. By late afternoon there was agreement in principal and in cash.

"A hundred thousand rupees?" Esther was astounded.

"That's what we paid for the interview," Ajay offered as a flimsy defence.

"I thought the treatment was free?"

"It is. It's acquiring the bed that's expensive," Ajay replied with some bitterness.

CHAPTER THIRTY-EIGHT
Messages from beyond the grave

Written messages ascribed to Lunasha appeared over the next few days on the notice board outside the compound. Maddy informed Hari that Shivabalayogi had been buried on 'Good Saturday' at 3 p.m., just as Lunasha had prophesied. The still perfect body was washed in hundreds of pots of milk, curds, coconut water and a myriad of perfumes. A pit was dug inside the Mandir and the body seated on a bed of salt, vibhuti and rice. His body was smeared with turmeric, sandalwood paste and other precious oils. He was covered in unhusked rice. He faced north. What excited Maddy was that as he was being buried, the sky darkened and released an unseasonal drizzle of rain, and then suddenly, an unexplained light coming from deep within the clouds lighted the whole ashram.

"How's Grandfather, Mother?" Hari would ask each morning

"There's no change, Hari. I'm sorry."

"Can I see him?"

"Not yet. I think your father is hoping to move him to Sai Baba's hospital in Puttaparthi. The arrangements are being made."

"That's good news, isn't it?" Hari was confused by his mother's sadness.

"Perhaps," she replied.

A few days later, Maddy and Lunasha attended a ceremony in the ashram in Bangalore. It had once been Shivabalayogi's intention to be buried there in his principal ashram. But then, as Maddy reflected, he was equally convinced he would live another forty years. There was a newly planted grove of rudraska trees that encircled a mound made sacred by a statue of Lord Shiva meditating.

Instead of his body, a small portion of jata, the knot of matted hair that once grew down his back, was placed in the symbolic grave, along with the cloth he was wearing just before he died, a Shivalingam and a bed of vibhuti. Maddy claimed it rained in Bangalore on the day of the ritual and a bright light suffused the whole of the site. This was a kind of miracle, she claimed, and proved the sanctity of her precious guru.

Ramu Sarnhi had been moved into intensive care and plugged into a variety of machines by the time Ajay Sarnhi had arrived at the hospital.

"What's happened?" he asked the nurse guarding the door and preventing his entry.

"The aneurysm struck. It was only a matter of time. It's found its way to his brain. He's suffered a massive stroke. I'm sorry."

"Can I see him?" Ajay asked, breathlessly polite, winded by the news.

"The consultant would like to speak to you. We've been carrying out tests

184

most of the night. He'll tell you the results. He's by the desk over there." She pointed his way.

The consultant met Ajay and explained the situation as clearly as he could. He had been invited and licensed to tell the truth. He did.

"There is a double difficulty here. The heart is weak and beyond repair. The blood pressure is so feeble that without the machine he would die. But also, the massive stroke has destroyed a large area of his brain. The scans suggest little or no activity. He will never regain consciousness, I'm sorry to say. Even if he could, there is no possibility of a self-sustaining, independent life. Your father has effectively died." Despite his familiarity with the situation, the consultant seemed genuinely compassionate and understanding about the son's dilemma.

"Can I take some time to come to terms with this?" Ajay asked the consultant.

"Of course. It is your decision. Could I just add, hoping this will not seem insensitive at this impossibly difficult moment but your father's is a hopeless case? Those machines that keep him alive might just save another, more viable life. Please bear that in mind as you are making your decision. Excuse me."

"Of course." And as he left, Ajay Sarnhi whispered to himself, "Please excuse me too."

When everyone had gone, Ajay Sarnhi sat beside his dead father's bed, soothed by the plinking rhythm of the machines that kept the corpse alive and confessed.

"Father, please forgive me. When that young lady doctor said you were still alive I was delighted and relieved. It meant more time to complete our business. It meant a stay of execution. That's what went through my mind. Those exact words. I am so ashamed, Father. Please forgive me. I've lost my way, somewhere. If only I knew what Sai Baba said to you. He gave you the ring, for yourself or Hari. I'm not sure. The doctor says you are not aware so I can only talk to your body. If your soul hasn't gone, perhaps it hears me now. Wasn't that a special gift? Does he bless our work? I need a little time. For everything. Not just the papers from Mauritius and the transfer of the Family Fund but to understand a little more about what this means. With your permission, I will make a donation to the hospital here to help purchase more of these machines. I'll feel better about keeping you here, suspended between life and death, while I settle our affairs. I'll stay in Bangalore. Esther is very competent. She will close down the Whitefield house. The one you're building there, I'll donate to the Family Trust. Let all the members of the family use it to pray for you and us in all the future years. Forgive me, Father."

"How's Grandfather, Mother?" Hari asked each day.

"There's still no sign of life, Hari. He hasn't awoken yet."

Hari understood his grandfather would never wake.

The last of Lunasha's messages, the final contact Hari was to have with his beggar woman, was in the voice of Shivabalayogi:

'Did you get the part about the rain in Adivarapupeta?'

'Did you get the part about the rain in Bangalore?'

'Did you get the light?'

CHAPTER THIRTY-NINE
Jack has fallen again

As early as breakfast and long before darshan, two of the workers who regularly leant on the scaffolding still surrounding Jack's house, found him collapsed on the floor. This time he'd caught his head on the lintel and spilled himself into the roadway. He rolled over once, perhaps twice because he'd managed to open the earlier wounds to his knee, leg and arm. Jack was woozy and vague so offered little resistance as a skilful group, one at each limb, carried his awkward body across the dangerous bridge above the ditch and sat him in a bicycle taxi that sped him to the General Hospital nearby. It was a small facility that had originally been opened to offer basic medical care to women and their children.

Jack's needs were beyond their skill and messengers were dispatched to the ashram to authorise his movement to the Super Speciality Hospital in Puttaparthi.

Permission was granted.

He was led to a taxi, held upright between two helpers. His clothes had not been changed and like a latter-day Christ, the blood of his wounds stained his body with secular stigmata. He clutched his bag to his chest. Seated in the rear, he slumped to sleep but was prodded awake. The taxi couldn't start without an advance fare, it seemed. Jack fumbled for the six hundred rupees and, spurning further attention, lay across the back seats and slept the whole of the three-hour journey through rural India. He missed the nervous moment when a group of villagers had placed stones across the road, tentative highwaymen, hoping to demand a ransom to pass by their string of huts. The taxi driver shrugged. Jack snored. The villagers weren't too menacing. Suddenly in reverse, the taxi outran them backwards then stopped and ran forward, the vehicle tilted into the ditch to angle the offside wheels over the smallest of the rocks. The highwaymen didn't wave or shout. They seemed to be prodding each other in recrimination when one of the group kicked the stones aside, as the taxi disappeared from view.

"Jack, where have you been?" Hari was delighted to see his friend. He'd missed him these past two or three days, whenever he visited the Sai Deep Café.

"I've been to paradise, young man. I've been to a hospital made of pink icing that makes the Taj Mahal look shoddy. It's vast. It's so modern it hurts and spreads like a giant palace all around its ornamental gardens. Your genie would love it. He'd feel right at home."

That must have been Grandfather's hospital, Hari thought. He was unlikely to visit it now. A pity. It would have impressed him too.

"How are you?" Hari asked, truly concerned. There was a dressing beside Jack's eye. Despite the best efforts of the bandages, hints of blood stained the outside of his white clothes.

"Well, I'll start with the back. It's not critical. It's not urgent but it's more than cosmetic. They want to cut small pieces off five vertebrae to let my spinal cord move more freely. They've given me a dose of 2 x 10 milligrammes of morphine sulphate tablets for my breakfast and an extra one for supper. They cut more than half the pain but they keep me groggy and detached." He was going to say sexless but that was too much information for a ten-year-old, however wise.

"I still have my diabetes, so in this heat, I suffer! Now, Harry, listen up. You must never sound sincere when you ask someone 'How are you?' Don't do it again!" Jack grinned. Hari was uncertain what to say.

"My friend, I need your help. No one else will do. It must be you, okay?"

"If I can, of course I'll help you." Jack always made him feel special.

"Good. You see, I've been making phone calls and making decisions. I don't mind a few stitches and a few bits of lint and gauze but when it comes to major surgery, well, I'd sooner have that done back home, not here in India. I've sent a number of faxes and all seemed fine. I have insurance. Denmark is kind to its old men, of any nationality, but I made a mistake. I told them I'd fallen and hurt all these bits of me, particularly my back, because of the heat of the sun."

Hari was about to declare it was true but Jack prevented him.

"Take a pause there. I'm not quite done and I've not reached the punch line yet. Where I was walking, there were loose and broken stones. If I can say they caused my fall, they'll pay all my expenses here and back home. Did you see those loose and broken stones, Harry?"

Hari hesitated.

"I . . . there was the hard, baked earth."

"Yes?" Jack encouraged Hari, expectant with raised eyebrows.

"There could have been stones."

Jack smiled.

"Yes?"

"There must have been stones." Hari was beginning to understand the game.

"Now we're getting somewhere. Proprietor!" Jack called. "Do you have paper and a pen?"

"Yes, sir. Right away, sir." He didn't have either but sent a messenger into the bazaar to see what could be purloined.

"So, Harry. I propose using you as a witness, as described in the enclosed."

The enclosed was a fax, folded to illegibility. Hari returned it to Jack to read to him.

"If you agree, I would appreciate a statement from you based on my reported facts. In which case I will owe you endless lime and sodas, good friend. And incidentally, I hope it's okay since my test is always, whether I would do the same for you."

Hari understood the challenge and was certain Jack would do the same for him, not that he could imagine any circumstances when such help might be needed.

The paper and pen arrived. Hari waved the cost to his genie and on one of the three white sheets he made the list as dictated. The hurt was 'serious'. He was to mention the knee but most of all, the back.

"Tell them I was really in trouble," Jack added.

"You were, Jack. I was very worried."

"'Very worried' is good. Mention the stones!"

"I will."

After a few minutes of careful thought, Hari Sarnhi made his first official witness statement.

"Don't mention your age."

"I wasn't going to."

"And say we were travelling together in South India."

Hari really liked the sound of that and began with it.

"'My friend Jack and I were travelling together in South India. We were away from the normal roads. He had a nasty fall. The earth was hard and there were some loose stones. They made him slip. I thought he might be seriously hurt and I believed he was really in trouble. He was bruised. There was a large open wound on his knee. He was eventually tended to by a doctor and me. He had damaged his back and was in considerable pain.'"

"Sign it!" Jack commanded. Hari wished he had a signature. He printed his name.

Jack picked up the paper and was about to fold it. In a moment it would disappear into his bag.

"Jack. Let me keep that. Perhaps we can get it faxed and copied while it's still fresh. What do you think?"

"I think you take good care of me, Harry. I'm grateful. Hey! One lime and soda over here! That's my first payment."

"I don't need any payment, Jack. I'd do it for nothing."

"Hasn't anybody taught you about business yet?"

Hari just smiled. Unbeknown to Jack, few days had passed since his time in India when he wasn't taught about business, in particular, his position in the future generations of a silk family.

CHAPTER FORTY
Last Rites

"Whoever said God moves in a mysterious way hadn't had dealings with the Indian Post Office. Look." Ajay Sarnhi placed a small array of precious documents on top of the sheet of his dead father's bed.

"I received these last night. They are the official documents, signed, sealed and obviously delivered confirming the transfer of title to all the investments in Mauritius. They are in my name now. This one confirms the consolidation of all the separate investments into a single financial entity. That was complex. That was efficient. They were very quick. There are various certificates of ownership and title deeds to a number of our properties. This fax arrived at the same time as the deeds saying they couldn't be transferred." He showed the sheet of paper to his unseeing father. "This one came this morning reversing that decision. And only a few minutes before I left to come and see you, this fax informed me, with great authority, that the documents I requested will be forwarded in the near future." Ajay fumbled with the papers. His hands were shaking. "So, they came before their time. And I come before yours." Ajay was chattering inconsequentially because he was about to make a momentous decision.

"It is time to say goodbye, Father. I told the doctors, Hari and Esther what I intend to do. They agree. They support me. It is my only choice, it seems. I hope this weird and uncomfortable gap between dying and death hasn't been too difficult for you, Father. I do know you understand the reasons for the delay. All our scheming is over. It is finished.

"I'm going to call a nurse and with my authority and permission she will switch off these machines that give you this false life. Please, come in." The nurse, elderly and thankfully self-assured was quickly briefed, nodded to Ajay Sarnhi, and walked briskly to the tangle of wires by the side of the bed. She removed drips and pipes with startling speed, wheeled the metal gantries that dangled the once pulsing bags of translucent and blood red liquids quickly out of sight, behind a screen. She flipped a switch that made one monitor squeal, silenced that and, bowing to Ajay Sarnhi, left the room to the officially dead father and his son.

Clumsily, Ajay Sarnhi found a glass phial in the corner of his jacket pocket. It contained water taken from the River Ganges. He poured the blessed water into his dead father's mouth.

"There are no sacred rivers in Bangalore. There are hardly any rivers at all. But of course you know that, Father. This was the best we could do."

Ajay glimpsed nervously over his shoulder. A crowd was beginning to gather. Uncertain what to do, hopelessly out of place, Ajay had delegated all the last rites and funeral arrangements to a committee of cousins. They were eager to begin. Ramu Sarnhi was to be cremated at dusk that very day. They had chosen an electric crematorium to the north of the city, close by the Bangalore-Hyderabad highway. The son stepped aside and let them begin their ritual tasks. Suitable mantras and rhythmical hymns were already being sung. Ajay watched them perform: detached, a little overwhelmed, hoping to learn.

Hari remembered a crematorium by a lake dotted with wooded islands alongside a giant and noisy highway full of traffic. The whole day was manic and rushed. At times his cousins seemed to panic, pushing the day's events to the edge of chaos.

A firm's van, gaudily disguised, was used to carry Ramu Sarnhi's body through the busy streets. A tented superstructure, covered in flowers, wobbled unsteadily throughout the process. At the four corners, angled rods dangled flower chandeliers, and fronds of flowers woven onto threads hid the sides of the vehicle, creating a floral beaded curtain of primary coloured petals. Bolsters of flowers, in red and white blooms, curled above the wheel arches and festooned the bonnet.

In the very centre, lying in a vestigial coffin, the exposed body of Ramu Sarnhi was clearly on show. The physical presence and unholy parade troubled Hari. Jogging alongside, he peered at his grandfather, wished him more privacy, more delicacy at this time of his death.

There was a hammock of flowers dangling by the van's side. It contained dozens of bouquets, still wrapped, overspill from the body of the dead man. He was already clad toe to head in scatterings of flowers. The only neat array was the garland that circled his neck and a small shrine beside his head, littered with petals, around a portrait of Sai Baba, lit by an oil lamp that reflected on its glass.

On arrival, more family members crowded round and Hari was ushered inside. As the *karta*, the head of the Trust, his father had a specific role to play. He was nudged into compliance by a pushy priest in an orange scarf and the excited attentions of the young men of his family.

The actual machine that would burn the body was too obviously on show. The latticed panes of a semicircular window cast reflected light onto the shiny tin surface of a giant metal box. At ground level, in the centre of the base, another semicircle that mimicked the window above was cut into the side. This was the entrance. A pair of rails over a sunken track pointed to this entry. A tray, a sort of crude platform, rolled on the rails. It would let the coffin pass with a certain ease up to and through the interposing wall of tin.

Hari saw his grandfather carried inside, as seven or eight young men clutched the flimsy substructure that bore the body in a precarious balance. They jostled with a crowd of relatives who chatted and pushed with no sense of occasion, so it seemed to Hari, and no obvious respect.

He was relieved when the shallow stretcher, litter, whatever the platform was, hidden out of sight beneath the dead man's clothes, balanced at last on the rail platform and was wheeled a little closer to the hole that would swallow him soon.

His father carried an earthenware pot that was full of water. It had been blessed, an unknown uncle explained, and Ajay Sarnhi began to spill its contents onto Ramu Sarnhi's head. Others rushed forward, cupped their hands and scattered the blessed stream to all parts of the dead body beneath.

An elderly man knelt by the feet—Hari noticed the big toes were tied together—and began massaging some kind of oil or paste into the soles of the feet and further, reaching beneath his grandfather's white robe, to anoint the lower legs. Hymns were being sung. All the men joined in.

Hari's father bent down and gently rubbed some of the same ointment on the forehead. Hari noticed the man, who was dispensing this opaque oil, squeezing it from a plastic container.

Hari was beckoned forward and the busy priest, who pointed to the dead man's head, spilled a rain of vibhuti ash into his palm. Reluctantly, Hari stooped and rubbed the holy ash across his grandfather's forehead and forced himself to look once more at the familiar face. Grandfather Sarnhi looked oddly content. He was more serene in death than Hari ever remembered him in life.

Bustled aside, other relatives performed similar acts of this strange ritual washing. Stepping back, Hari saw that a row of long twigs had gradually been insinuated beneath his grandfather's body. A lattice was created, a kind of symbolic kindling, Hari thought, to help the fire that needed no help at all.

The sound of the singing grew. The cousins gathered, and after two false starts managed to drape Ramu Sarnhi's body with a white sheet. Incense was burning. Its smell began to fill the hall. The mean little orifice in the metal wall opened and the stooping and kneeling cousins manoeuvred the body through. They pushed gently and steadily until it was completely inside. With a clunk the opening closed. The burning would begin. The ceremony was at an end.

"I hated it, Father. It seemed so clumsy and public. Is there no privacy in India?"

Ajay Sarnhi comforted his son. They had been staying in Bangalore but they would return to Whitefield and give thanks to Sai Baba for his care. The ashes had been collected and in a few days they would be scattered in a special place Ajay Sarnhi had chosen for this act.

"Hari, as I understand it, and it had to be explained to me, I need teaching too, you know, I've not experienced these things before, there is little respect for the remaining body once the soul is gone. It seems callous, almost, the way they bundle the bodies about but the soul is all that matters. It will have many bodies in its existence, possibly thousands; so one particular incarnation has no significance. The body is burnt according to all the rituals. You saw those. They were very particular to get them right, to encourage the soul to migrate. They make certain there is nothing of that life to come back to. Only Holy Men are buried. Their soul is already detached from their body so they don't need to encourage it on its way. I like that idea."

"Will you miss him, Father?"

"Yes. I will. He was a strong man. I can never follow in his footsteps and I've no intention of trying."

Hari was puzzled by this remark.

"I don't understand, Father. I thought you were to be the head of the family now."

"I am, in name at least. But I'll not lead it from here."

Hari brightened.

"Do you mean . . .?" Hari let the thought of going home begin.

"I mean we will go back to England. Not for a few weeks. There are things I must do, rituals the *karta* must perform."

"Thank you, Father." Hari contained his excitement and relief.

"It is as much for me as you, my son. And your mother."

"I do love India, Father."

"So do I, Hari. I just don't understand it."

"You went there?" Maddy was astounded.

"Yes, I went there." Jack began to explain, slowly, hoping to reduce Maddy's amazement.

"I'd already made an appointment with him long ago, before setting out from Copenhagen. He couldn't keep it but I kept mine all the same, because I could."

"He's dead and buried," Maddy offered as an unnecessary explanation.

"I do know that, Maddy. I'm not dead or buried. My life goes on. But I'm telling you, he was there, not just in spirit but in body also."

"This is nonsense, Jack. I was present at both of Shivabalayogi's burials."

"So, this guy gets to be buried twice?" Jack was incredulous.

"Show respect, please. Swamiji is my guru. In death all he has dropped is his impermanent and unreal physical form."

"So, he can die, at last?"

"Of course. If you prick him, he will bleed, just like Shylock."

"He was Jewish?"

"No. What I'm trying to say is that for his followers and me, he lives on, despite the corruption of the body. After initiation into meditation his physical presence isn't necessary." Maddy was forcing herself to be patient. Jack was upsetting her. "What do you want from me, Jack? This is my house. I welcome you into it. I will make you tea and I will give you cake. I will be hospitable and good mannered. You must be too. Your steps are clumsy. They crush precious things. Please, tread with care."

"I'm sorry. I came for answers and explanations, that's all. I'm pretty confused. Un-confuse me. Tell me about this meditation business and I'll tell you what I saw." He nodded and smiled in a conciliatory way. He was all deference and charm. His notebook was at the ready.

"Shivabalayogi practices dhyana meditation. It is meditation without an object." Maddy was calm now.

"Okay. I don't quite get it but, moving on, what happens when you have these objectless thoughts?"

"I get bliss, like anything." She smiled.

"Do you go into a trance?" Jack was intrigued.

"Sometimes. Many people do." Maddy was trying to be matter-of-fact about a mystery.

"How can you be sure people in a trance are not pretending?"

"There would be no point. No one is watching. There is no one to deceive. When I meditate my mind becomes controlled by Swamiji's presence."

Jack underlined the word 'controlled'. Maddy noticed and added, "He gives us power but doesn't force anything on anybody."

"No instructions?" Jack asked, always appearing suspicious.

"The power he gives can be used for anything," Maddy explained, patiently.

"Even business?" Jack asked, knowing of Maddy's many ventures.

"Of course, why not? The basis of the knowing is still spiritual. I'm not burdened by your doubts or endless suspicions. When Swamiji is with me I enter a fearless state."

"I'm not suspicious or doubting, Maddy, just nosy. Put it down to professional curiosity."

"Rita tells me you're making a film." Maddy hoped to surprise Jack with this knowledge.

"Yes. How great. You've visited!" Instead of surprise or embarrassment, Jack was genuinely delighted.

So was Maddy.

"Better still, she visited me."

"That's great. She needs to be free."

"So do you, Jack."

"Oh, I am. This is freedom to me. This is what I do. It's important to me."

"And it makes you feel important?"

"Perhaps."

"When I am free my personality is so vast I am no longer the little being associated with my small physical body. When he leaves, all that is left is a disappointing Maddy. I'm not as content with me as you are with you." Maddy wasn't challenging Jack.

"What I am is of no value here. Think of me as a pair of eyes, the dog's sniffing nose and the sneak behind the door overhearing all that is said. I'll make something of all these fragments. If the bits are sincere and honestly told then the picture I make will be true." Jack was confident and professional.

"Do you hold the camera, Jack?" Maddy was interested, happy to deflect the conversation away from the problems of the personal.

"No. I put everything together. I have no individual talent. I bring in the writer, the cameraman, the actors and presenters, the director and the moneymen. I have the idea then they make it real. I get all the worry. They get paid, whatever the outcome. And, at the end of it all, if it's good, I get all the praise. So it's worth it!" Jack laughed.

A truce was called over tea and cake. Jack was a messy eater. Most of his cake broke between his fingers and fell as crumbs to the floor or freckled his chin in pastry stubble.

"So, can you explain what's going on in Shivabalayogi's ashram, in

Shivabalayogi's name?" Jack began, scrubbing his face clean with the sleeve of his crumpled ashram suit.

"I'm not sure what you mean. What happened to you?" Maddy guessed at some of the problems Jack had uncovered but wasn't prepared for his next statement.

"There was nearly a riot. I was pushed around and shoved out of the hall."

"What? Why?" Maddy was shocked.

"So, I arrive. I introduce myself. Tell them I'm expected. They tell me they're new and things are changing. They ask if I'd like to make a donation, I say no, but they can be in my film, if they are interesting and I am invited to darshan."

"But how can that be?" asked Maddy.

"I'm telling you. Be patient. So, I'm led into this hall and sitting on the platform, in a trance, is a guy dressed up as Shivabalayogi. I know this because he's sitting right next to a huge photograph of the real thing and he's dressed in identical clothes. So, there is this copycat, sitting on an antelope skin, complete with head and two huge horns and, worse still, he's speaking in the voice of Shivabalayogi and giving the other people in the hall instructions. Suddenly, a bunch of people rushes in and starts shouting at the bogus guru. The guy who asked me for money claims this character on the stage is speaking in the authentic voice of their teacher. Well, anyone could tell this is not quite true. The one on the stage is obviously aware of what's going on and is looking pretty shifty. It starts to get ugly. Someone tugs the antelope head. The horns are pretty scary. The ventriloquist guru quits the stage followed by half the crowd.

"I get bustled and knocked into. I say 'Hey!' Or 'Watch out!' Whatever. Suddenly, the rest of the intruders turn on me. Call me an American devil or some such and frog march me out of the hall. Well, my legs barely walk, let alone march, so I fell and was heaved up and so on till I was in the ashram gardens. What goes on, Maddy?"

"I'm not sure, Jack. It's very worrying."

"Tell me what you do know." Jack was insistent.

"Throughout his life, Swamiji had two protectors, his birth mother and the Maharini of Patna. They were strong women. One cared for him physically: the other was his worldly educator. Remember, Swamiji had no proper education. He spent all of his developing years in a state of deep meditation. His protectors are gone. He is gone and others who surrounded him want to take control of the Bangalore Trust."

"So, it's money again, is it?" Jack sounded disappointed.

"Partly, perhaps. I think it's more to do with power. Swamiji is nothing like Sai Baba. His Trust is very small but influential and prestigious. If you asked Swamiji 'Is there wealth in the Trust?' he would say his only assets

196

are his devotees, whom he loves very dearly. But I know, while he still lived, that he accused some devotees of only being interested in being seen and recognized in the ashram. Certainly, substantial donations had been solicited from unsuspecting people but the money had disappeared and was unaccounted for. Certainly, I know that two disciples, influential men close to Swamiji, tried to persuade him to sign over to them his powers in the Trust. Swamiji was very ill but he had the strength to refuse. There were rumours there was even an attempt on the life of my guru. He nearly died after a failed dialysis. People close to him spoke of black magic. Others, more rational, thought they'd tampered with his medicine. Fortunately, Swamiji was able to choose the exact moment of his own death. It was not decided by jealous followers."

"But there is no proof," Jack concluded.

"There never is," Maddy decided. "I do know that Swamiji was shocked at these threats to his life. 'What have I done that they do this to me?' He said that. It was a question that spread to his devotees. He asked it during my meditation. It is the sort of question all great spiritual leaders are forced to ask. Swamiji knew there would be doubters. Always, profound spiritual experience will clash with human frailty. No one can ever be a complete mouthpiece for Shivabalayogi or beings like him. The man you saw had too much of his own ego left to even begin to approach the spiritual levels of Swamiji."

"You are very accepting. Shouldn't you be outraged?" Jack was hoping for a more extreme response.

"It is just another moment in the history of spiritual men. Always the follower will try to kill the God or his messenger, if nothing else, to test his authenticity. They always need to ask, 'Are you really who you say you are?' A lowly worker who prepared his last meal poisoned the Buddha. It might have been pork or the pig's favourite truffle but it poisoned him and triggered his death. The Buddha didn't blame his man Cunda, just as Christ didn't hold Judas responsible for his fate. The leg of the goat he was eating forewarned Mohammed that he would be poisoned. And he was. And today, everyone would discredit Sai Baba, a being who is the complete embodiment of love and selfless service to humanity yet they would kill him." Maddy clenched her teeth on the pain of her disbelief.

"Why?" asked Jack, subdued by Maddy's wisdom.

"To see if he can die. Do you know your Bible, Jack?"

"Only the Old Testament," was his enigmatic reply.

"Then you won't know the whole verse of this quotation, even if you recognise part of it. It might answer all your questions. 'Give not that which is holy unto the dogs, neither cast ye your pearls before swine, lest they trample them under their feet, and turn and rend you.'"

CHAPTER FORTY-TWO
Ashes

Hari was standing at the roadside, looking out for his father's car. Ajay Sarnhi had rented a vehicle and driver for the day. He had been mysterious about the trip but Hari knew it was special, if for no other reason than the chance to spend a whole day alone with his father.

Ajay Sarnhi had been busy in Bangalore. He had assumed the role of *karta* and just as quickly dispersed its power through as many relatives as he could. They were delighted: he was relieved. The managers would be left to manage. They were to keep in touch. He'd arranged monthly phone calls, quarterly reviews and twice-yearly visits. Cleverly, he appointed a team of secret monitors, each assured of their unique role, to watch and report privately to him, to him alone. He saw it as a kind of self-imposed industrial espionage. It appealed to everyone involved and ensured some vestige of control over his distant business interests. His real excitement concerned the holdings in Mauritius. They would enable him to expand his business in England in such a way and with such speed it would quickly dwarf all that happened in India. He would keep his word and maintain and add to the Family Trust: undivided in India but divided from his enterprises elsewhere.

"Father!" Hari shouted and waved. "Father, I'm over here!"

Settled in the rear seat of the car, Hari and his father were separated by two splendid objects. Nearest the father was an opalescent green urn with a matching lid, elegant and simple in design. It was large, ten, twelve inches tall perhaps and half as wide. It was also heavy, much heavier than Hari anticipated as Ajay Sarnhi lifted the precious object over to his son. Hari almost let it go but landed it carefully in his lap.

"Are Grandfather's ashes inside?"

"Yes."

"They're so heavy."

"That's because they're not really ashes. They're cremulated bones."

Hari hadn't understood and wanted to peek inside to see what was meant but had no need.

"They explained to me at the crematorium that all that is left from the burning are the bones of the body. Small remnants, larger fragments, I understand. They grind the pieces into fine sand so that they will disperse and sink when scattered in the air over water. Believe it or not, there's over two kilogrammes in there and nearly half a kilo in yours."

"Mine?"

Ajay Sarnhi reached for the urn on Hari's lap, put it safely beside him and handed Hari a miniature copy coloured pink and white.

"They're made of rock salt. They will float, sink and dissolve. That way all will merge with the water. That's very clever, isn't it?"

"Yes, Father," Hari replied, absent-mindedly. He was in awe of the delicate object in his hands. He daren't let himself imagine the origin of the contents.

"Why have I been given this?"

"Because you will be the next *karta* and you must choose where you disperse the ashes in your care. I thought that might be a nice gift and an honour. If you are to spend most of your life in England, I thought this important and unusual privilege might forge a special memory for you, something indelible that will link you to India and the family you may never entirely know. I thought that the weeks spent with your grandfather should be crowned in some way. And, well, this is what I've arranged."

Hari did feel privileged and kept spinning the delicately made urn in his fingers.

"Put it down, son. I'm not sure how robust they are."

"Sorry, Father."

"Something else I was told I found interesting."

"What was that, Father?"

"Well, I didn't realise the significance of the question at the time."

"What question?"

Ajay Sarnhi was looking anxiously through the window. The driver was middle-aged and meant to be competent—he actually owned the taxi and car hire company—nevertheless, his movements in and out of the traffic, most of it slow and inferior, pulled by animals or powered by men, was better unwatched. Every miss was near, the cursing and shouting muffled by the window dividing front and rear, keeping the paying passengers air-conditioned and cool while the driver could rage in the heat of the front seat and his front-line battle waged with every impeding object that lined the roadway from gutter to gutter.

"Sorry. That was close."

"I close my eyes, Father. Even when I'm walking by the road." Hari smiled.

"What was I saying? Oh yes. Because your grandfather had a heart condition they asked me if he had a pacemaker, you know, a device implanted in his chest to keep the heartbeat regular. Of course, I said no, but apparently, that's the one foreign object that must be removed before a body can be cremated."

The father waited patiently until his son asked, "Why?"

"Because they can explode and damage the inside of the cremator."

Hari was thrilled by the idea and wondered how they discovered the problem in the first place. It must have been quite a shock to the poor family whose dead relative broke the machine.

"Where are we going, Father?" Hari asked once they were free of the city and driving less frantically along a main highway signposted Mysore.

"We going to a town called Srirangapatna. At least, quite close to it."

"Is it a long way?"

"No, about eighty miles. It's so slow in the town. It will only be an hour or an hour and a half from here. I wanted something really special for my father and my son."

Ajay Sarnhi took Hari's hand. It startled the boy. His father wasn't a tactile man. He was formal and restrained in his ways. All Hari's hugs came from his mother. Hari preferred the formality he always observed when in the company of his father. It created a comfortable distance between them that, Hari believed, offered more freedom, not less. He thought his English friends were often smothered by the intimacy of their families. They were accorded no privacy and questioned endlessly about their thoughts and intentions. Hari was left alone and he in turn didn't pry. Father and son lived in separate worlds. One was full of worry, the other full of play. He was allowed the freedom of childhood by the distance preserved between the generations. He could never see himself jump onto his father's back or roll across the lawn in a pretend fight. He didn't want a 'dad' you could shout at, or who was happy to play in goal. He preferred a father. It was more dignified on the whole.

"Bangalore is a modern city and it embraces Western ways. I didn't like the crematorium and all the noise and bustle of the place. I let the family organise everything, rightly or wrongly, but today I chose. There are no serious rivers in Bangalore and the Ganges is much too far away. We are going to a place called Sangama where three holy rivers meet. The Kaveri, the Kapila and the Hemavathi. See, I've written their names in my diary. The greatest and holiest of the three is the Kaveri. Its waters surround the really holy island town of Srirangapatna. It is full of temples and saints and ancient religious sites. It purifies the water. It is nearly as blessed as the Ganges, and a lot cleaner, I believe. The river Kaveri flows towards Bangalore. The city takes its supply from the river to fill its lakes. Small tributaries enter the city, finally. But there are no ghats and nothing holy is left. I thought if I were to scatter my father's ashes where these three rivers meet, it would be a beautiful thing to do for him. And in time, his ashes will find their way home."

Ajay Sarnhi was visibly moved. He remained silent for much of the journey, always holding on to Hari's hand.

At the edge of a promontory, built on solid rock, an elegant shrine filled all of the corner space. It was no more than ten feet high, coloured red and green, the tones muted yet glowing in the midday sun. There were three tiers, the bottom plain with green sides and red borders. Photographs and epitaphs leant against the structure, the final farewells to the remnants of bodies cast on the wind. The middle tier was carved and ornamental. Writhing deities danced in a frieze. The females in relief were garlanded with flowers, dried and faded now in the persistent heat. The top had a miniature battlement, decorated with simple, face-like images, carved in stone and painted a dusky pink. The crown was a plant pot with a purple shrub growing in it and trailing the remnants of the flower petal garlands that adorned the wriggling deities beneath.

Beyond was a vast expanse of water, a basin of moving rivers with rock shoals proud of the water and wooded islands separating the flow. The hills in the flat land beyond added distance to the scene.

"It is so beautiful here, Father. What a wonderful place to choose." Hari was peaceful and relaxed. It was a while before he noticed his father's distress. With an instinctive wisdom, Hari withdrew.

"You'll need to be alone, Father. I'll come back for you soon."

Hari didn't see his father's farewell to his father. He still clutched his grandfather's ashes and, whilst walking along the banks of those shining, flowing rivers, he came to a decision. He wouldn't scatter the ashes there. He had the right to choose. He would go to another river with a bridge, and explain to his grandfather why he chose such a place.

When he returned his father was calm and welcomed Hari with a tired smile.

"Look. Can you see him floating?" Ajay Sarnhi turned Hari's gaze to the bobbing green object that was vanishing from sight. It was like a teasing fishing float, not gaudy being green and almost invisible next to the water in which it was afloat. Within minutes it was unseeable and father and son turned away.

"If we hurry, we'll make evening darshan. I'd like to visit Whitefield. I've had enough of Bangalore. I wish to see Sai Baba once more. I've missed my father's God."

CHAPTER FORTY-THREE
A Meeting

Children were giggling and scuffling in front of the ashram. Hari and his friends were drinking tea at the Indian Café.

"What are they doing?" Hari asked the Doctor, as a happy child with bright green hair, a half-red face and yellow back, leapt the ditch to avoid another coloured attack.

"It's a festival, for the children. It is kindly and fun. They shower each other with coloured powders. They all hope to be entirely covered in as many colours as can be. They become rainbows, like Baba."

"What on earth for?" remarked Borg, disapprovingly.

"It is a tradition," the Doctor explained, patiently.

"But what does it mean?" Borg was insistent.

"It means itself."

"But, I would have thought . . ."

"In India, what cannot be thought is still permitted a reality." The Doctor hoped he'd silenced Borg.

"Well said, Doctor," Jean Paul declared in support.

"What has he said that had any rational connection with what was said before? This is a madhouse. I've said it often." Borg was disgruntled.

"We know," agreed the Doctor.

"It becomes more like a circus every day. Now we even have clowns." As proof, another knot of nearby children burst coloured bombs into each other's laughing faces. For Hari, the word 'circus' was pleasing. He giggled sympathetically with the playing children. But otherwise he was sad. He still had to scatter his grandfather's ashes but at that moment his thoughts were on Sai Baba.

"Don't be so sad, little one," Jean Paul had sensed Hari's grief.

"Does everyone always want something from Baba? Is that why He is so unhappy?"

"Is he unhappy? Possibly. I'm sure we must disappoint him. No one ever does what is expected. Nor are they rightfully grateful. Even when Baba threw a banana at a beggar, the beggar threw it back."

"Can you blame him? I wouldn't like food thrown at me."

"You see, Borg is a good example of ingratitude," Jean Paul smiled.

"Does no one want to give?" Hari almost whispered his question. It didn't need to be heard.

"Men are selfish and unpleasant."

"And God made them," offered Borg, unhelpfully.

"True. But is what men do in God's name the work of God or the work of men?"

"I'll need time to answer that one," stalled Borg.

"We all do," agreed the Doctor.

There was a breeze that morning. Darshan was slow starting, quick to end and oddly unsatisfying. No one seemed at ease. Hari wanted to walk alone. He had a difficult task to complete. Jack joined him.

"You okay. Harry?"

"I'm doing all right, thanks, Jack." He smiled, as Jack rested his hand on his shoulder. "Still like the hat?"

"It's a great hat." Jack swaggered.

As they slowly left the village, people began to emerge from their houses to line the roadside.

"What's happening?" Jack asked, of no one in particular.

"Baba will pass in his car. He is going for a drive," answered a voice.

Jack and Hari walked on in silence. Jack kept glancing over his shoulder and staring intently at Hari. This was a dangerous manoeuvre and Hari feared a fall.

"What's wrong, Jack?"

"Not a thing, not a thing." Jack smiled at some secret knowledge. He even chuckled. Hari shrugged his shoulders.

"Hi!" Joan called from in front of her house.

"Hi!" Maddy called from in front of hers.

In the far distance came the muffled cry of "Total Surrender!"

Suddenly, Jack stopped.

"I'm going to stay under this tree, Harry. You go on alone. I'll be here when you get back. Enjoy your walk."

"If you're sure." Why was everyone so mysterious this morning?

Hari had lingered on his bridge and watched the river flow, invisible and slow, on its quiet journey beside the paddy fields that stunted its power, to enter Bangalore finally as an intermittent stream that fed a man-made lake. The river was wide and full of morning light. The flatland beyond, with its frieze of trees, added to the stillness. Hari wandered to the water's edge. The dhobi stones in the river next to the bank were thankfully unused, their obstruction signalling the minute passing of the river's flow in understated eddies and swirls.

In the far distance, beyond a patchwork of fields, a lone ploughman followed a brace of oxen in an unchanging biblical scene. A congregation of herons, menacing and still, waited for the frogs to breathe that had sunk beneath the surface at their stilted and almost silent approach. Red kites circled overhead and a fish eagle struck in slow motion in a waterlogged field but flew away with talons empty.

Hari was holding the elegant pink urn that housed his grandfather's ashes. He walked along the riverbank, bathed his feet in an irrigation channel and

sought the exact spot that Lunasha had used, away from the shouting washer men, to cleanse herself of the guilt of the world. He found it, stepped into the water and spoke to the ghost of his grandfather that he'd hoped he'd released when he gently removed the lid of the urn.

"I chose this river, Grandfather, because just here, I think it might be blessed. A lady once bathed here who I, and some of my friends

… a lone ploughman followed a brace of oxen

think might be a saint. I hope she is. I hope she made this spot sacred and a place worthy to scatter these, your last few remains. Goodbye, Grandfather. Godspeed."

Hari shook the urn gently and the grains of sand spilled evenly in a dusty cloud on the surface. The river spread them wide and, imperceptibly, they sank. Hari replaced the lid on the urn and put it gently into the water, nudging it with his hand towards the centre and away from the grassy edges of the bank.

It stayed upright for a while and, very slowly, moved away. As the river turned the distant object sank. Hari didn't linger. His attention was drawn to the bridge. He clambered up the bank and stood in the middle of the roadway. He turned to look back towards the village and sensed that something was approaching from behind him.

Steadfastly, he stared ahead. Quietly, imperceptibly, he heard the hum of an engine. As he turned, inching slowly onto the bridge came Baba's maroon Jaguar car. It stopped in front of him. For no reason, he raised his hand in greeting. He didn't wave, but opened his palm and stretched forward his hand in salute towards Baba, who at that moment wasn't really looking.

Then, something remarkable happened. Baba leapt, as if hit, stunned by a sudden access of energy released from Hari's being, guided by his palm towards Baba. The effect was electric, astonishing. Baba's eyes burst wide open. He stared in disbelief, amazement, deep, deep into Hari's being. A wave of recognition seemed to flood Baba. He relaxed, went to return the salute but instead, the beginnings, the middle and the delightful end of a huge smile filled his beaming face and suddenly sparkling eyes. The car jolted forward but Baba turned, eagerly. He greeted Hari, not with a regal salute but an eager, vigorous wave, an energetic wave and Hari heard his laughter as slowly the smiling face and waving hand, framed in the rear window, inched from view.

Hari burst into tears. His whole body collected in one gigantic sob of relief as he laughed and cried at once.

And all he could say was thank you. He had found a way, he had been shown a way of giving and for the first time in his seeing, God seemed happy. And so, Hari wept. How could he tell anyone? All the languidness had gone and Baba shone. There was beauty and generosity, an overflow of joy as Hari gave back joy. Who would ever understand what happened on that happy Tuesday?

It was a long time before Hari felt calm enough to go back. What could he say? He shuffled towards Jack, who greeted him cheerily.

"Well? How was it?"

"Jack, I . . . " Hari burst into tears again. Jack hugged him.

"You don't have to explain. Baba was still smiling when he went past here. Everyone noticed and everyone cheered. They'd never seen him so happy. Whatever you said to him, young Harry, sure did the trick. Come. I'll buy you tea and cake."

"But, I . . . I . . ."

"It's okay. There's no need to explain."

At darshan that evening, Baba seemed happy and relaxed. He stayed among the people, blessing and reassuring, laughing and chatting, at his best there. He didn't go to his throne.

At dawn the next day he left for the mountains and his followers followed according to their means.

CHAPTER FORTY-FOUR
Jack thinking out loud

Jack sat on the edge of his bed. His sheets and pillows were scrunched into a corner against the freshly plastered wall. The room was empty. Jack had transferred its contents, in no apparent order, straight into the huge canvas bag he travelled with. He couldn't lift it, wondered what to shed, thought he'd lost enough things to lighten its load, but mysteriously, it seemed even heavier. All that mattered to him was in his Sai Baba bag. He'd find a porter once he had decided on a destination. He was taking note, summarising himself, speaking into the hand-held recorder that heard his private thoughts.

"So, Jack, are you still okay? I think I'll leave Kodai Kanal to the Brides of Baba. That's a neat phrase. I'll use that somewhere. The beggars have left already, to be sure of a good pitch. All the talk is of exit: later today or tomorrow first thing. I've had enough of this circus. There is nothing new to learn by following along. As Rita said, this place is not auspicious; it is just full of temple-baggers. I wish they'd smile, these grim-faced Westerners. Makes me ashamed to be one of them. At least I smile. You know, the Indians love their touchable god. You can see it in their faces. The Europeans, men who think they are calm and full of God claim they've been robbed, offended even. There's no challenge, they say. We've been insulted, they say. Not enough abstraction, I guess, no theological conundrum. But when I interview the simple folk, they're happy. He's gonna fix the roof, milk the cow, let the grandmother die and the baby son live. I think the avatar is perfect for India. The rest of us are far too smart, so we think.

"Is Baba a fake? Don't know. The jury is out. I'm not even sure it matters. I've listened to his accusers and had his crimes listed. Sleight of hand, sexual abuse, money laundering, murder? He makes Seiko watches. Infringement of copyright? Guilty. He pulls gold from the ether. One clever guy sued him under the Gold Control Act. Not guilty. Case dismissed.

"I've seen the film, conclusive evidence of his cheating, producing a gold chain from his flickering fingers. The accuser, Bishnu, kept shouting in my ear: 'There, did you see it? There!' 'Where?' It was a fuzzy film, unclear and uncertain. I preferred the miracle-maker to the unmasker. There was a scholar at the university, he insisted on being named, who challenged the truth of Baba's godhead. 'He is not omniscient' was the fault. 'There are discrepant readings of historical accounts.' I suppose people in history have been burnt for less.

"Then a young boy from Denmark accused Sai Baba of touching him inappropriately. 'He rubbed my genitals with oil', he claimed. That was after he was refused compensation. Not Guilty. The boy with the shiny privates was discredited.

"It's not much of a case, Jack. I wouldn't risk my shirt on it. The shooting and the money and the corruption, well, that was the minions and the usual authorities are sorting that, it doesn't need one of my films. But, despite the sitting and the waiting, maybe because of it, he and I nearly touched toes and it made me feel good. I asked for a direction and I've been given one. I want to go east with Jean Paul. I'll see a silent teacher and a noisy vibhuti spitter, the exiled spiritual leader of Tibet and a God-Woman called the Mother. I'm following the trail of the gods and that's okay."

CHAPTER FORTY-FIVE
Farewells

The followers in Whitefield were breaking camp. The tented homes, roadside squats and tree shelters of the beggars were empty. They bought little, left nothing, just the ashes of their fires. The red Jaguar of Sai Baba had been spotted leaving the ashram at first light. It was heading to Kodaikanal for the respite of the hilltops and a calmer community for the more affluent or persistent of his devotees.

Neither Jack nor Hari had realised just how temporary this place was. The earth boundaries of the ditch were already disappearing as a busy group of workers buried the filth beneath the earth of its own making. Hari thought of Lunasha and smiled. She was safe now.

The bazaar was a façade, nothing more. The wooden frameworks of the stalls collapsed in minutes. The lines that stole electricity from the cables overhead, dangled free. The piles, racks and rows of goods for sale were already bagged and stowed, ready to reappear beside the ashram in Kodaikanal, anywhere Sai Baba stopped long enough for them to trade.

The Indian Café was boarded up. It was only ever a rented room with a terrace. There was a chest freezer, padlocked now, and a couple of hot plates, disconnected from their illicit supply. It ran on enterprise and good will and would be in business again the second the Whitefield ashram revived.

The Sai Deep Café was always there. Proprietor was a fixture. Jack was hoping to meet Jean Paul there to conclude some business, he'd explained to Hari. It was still busy when they arrived. Hari was to wait to meet his parents there later. They knew he had to complete his farewells.

Jean Paul and Borg sat together. The Doctor was in Bangalore. He'd said goodbye to Hari a couple of days before and, much to Hari's delight, had praised him for his spiritual understanding.

"Jean Paul. Just the man. Let me buy you tea." Jack sat himself at the table, shuffled uncomfortably close to his quarry and announced to Hari and Borg and anyone else listening: "I'll be the genie today and buy everyone drinks."

Tapping Jean Paul gently on the shoulder, Jack announced, "I've come to a decision, young man. I'm going to miss out Kodaikanal now and go with you to this Red Mountain of yours." Jack smiled happily.

"No, Jack," was Jean Paul's gentle but firm reply.

"Did you hear what I said?" asked Jack, genuinely baffled.

"Every word. The answer is no."

"Why?"

"I travel alone."

"So do I. We can travel alone together." Jack was pleased with his solution.

"I am seeking peace. I am seeking solitude. I am intent on being alone."
Jean Paul was serene even when being contradictory.

"Can't you do that at the end when you've reached your Red Mountain?"
Jack was less ebullient now.

"I could."

"But you won't. You still haven't said why." Jack sensed a weakening in
Jean Paul.

"Tell the man the truth, J.P. It's more your style," Borg suggested.

"You're very noisy, Jack," Jean Paul said quietly. "You create a disturbance
all around you."

"He means you're a nuisance," Borg explained.

Jack was unperturbed.

"Of course I'm a nuisance. I was born to be a nuisance. It's my destiny."

"You're a hard man to be around," Borg continued.

"So are you, my friend," Jack replied. Borg laughed.

"I understand you're making a film," Jean Paul began.

"Yes. That's what I'd do. I'm a documentary filmmaker."

"I don't want to be in a film," Jean Paul declared.

"You haven't been invited. Now Borg here, he's very photogenic and he's
as big a nuisance as me and I've documented all the wonderful stories from
his wonderful life, so he can be in my film because he's strange. There is
something dark about Borg." Jack sounded sinister.

"Thank you," Borg said, clearly delighted.

"You let in the light, Jean Paul. You're so good you can hardly be seen.
Look. This is the deal. I travel alongside you to the Red Mountain. If I get
on your nerves, say so, don't be polite, follow my example, say, 'Get gone!'
and I'll go. But, whats in it for you? Well, I'm a real good listener. I think
you're a pretty thoughtful man in search of other thoughtful men. There's a
crazy yogi there called Ram Surat Kumar I want to greet. I want to see the
room where Ramana Maharshi used to entertain his disciples. There is a
chaise longue and a photo, I believe."

"You're very well-informed, Jack. I didn't realize . . ."

"No. Part of the skill. Listen, don't tell, else there's no film, just
propaganda. Let me overhear what the teachers tell you. I'll be your Boswell.
I won't interrupt. I won't say a word. Not at the time. Then afterwards, we
can compare notes. It'll be more of a challenge on the Red Mountain. You
might welcome a smart-ass American filmmaker as a friendly confidant. You
just might."

"I just might." Jean Paul smiled.

"Great. I'll arrange a taxi."

"No."

"What is it this time?"

209

"I travel by bus," Jean Paul explained.

"Bus? Have you seen their buses? They . . ." Hari nodded 'no' to Jack.

"Fine," he said through gritted teeth. "The bus it is."

"It's a long journey but it's among the Indian people. It will be ordinary, Jack, not a separate breathing of conditioned air. It's part of the belonging."

"I'll belong, my friend. But for how long?"

"Most of the day. There is a meal. It will be served on banana leaves," Jean Paul remembered.

"Do I eat the leaves?" asked Jack.

"No. That's not necessary."

"Neither is the bus." Jack was persistent.

"It's up to you. That's the deal." Jean Paul smiled.

Jack shrugged his shoulders. "Everyone cuts a deal, it seems."

"It's a pity you're not coming to Kodaikanal, Jack," Borg began, "You could've visited me in my temporary splendour." Borg glanced at his fingernails and smiled mischievously.

"Go on. Tell me of your splendour." Jack was gruff but really amused. Borg fascinated him.

"I will stay at the Carlton Hotel on Lake Road. I have commanded full board. I will play the Raj," Borg explained. It was the first time Hari had heard the forbidden phrase used.

"How do you do that?" Hari asked.

"With great aplomb, young man, and a ridiculous spending of rupees. The British, in their prime, built a wonderful lake in the hills to distract their memsahib when fleeing the heat of the Indian plains. For a few days, I will rule the roost. I will be an arrogant Britisher, lord of all I survey, because I will pay for the privilege. I will paddle boats on the lake, drink tea on the terrace and dine in the hotel or, when I'm bored, choose amongst the finest eateries in Hospital Road. Once sated, I will repent of my folly, my brain cooled by altitude, my belly rounded by excess then, I will flee north to my Tibetan masters and do my indulgence by fasting and prayer. You might have dined with me at the Carlton Hotel, Jack. Such a pity."

"It is a great loss to me, Borg. I'll try and get over it."

"Good man." Borg smiled and passed his quiet time counting the eyes in the death's heads on the rings of his fingers.

Rita, was approaching slowly, navigating the last plank over the disappearing ditch, guided there by a distracted Maddy, who was seeking missing clients for her coaches and cars.

"I'll fetch you in fifteen minutes, maybe ten. Don't stray. I've enough to do." Maddy was about to rush away but delayed by Hari's call.

"Bye, Maddy," Hari shouted. "Thank you for . . . everything."

"Oh. Yes. No need to mention it. But . . ." She suddenly remembered the empty coach seats she'd managed to fill. "So sorry to hear about your grandfather. It was a great loss." But now the loss was recouped. Ajay Sarnhi had to forfeit the deposit he was sure he didn't owe, but was ready to compensate Maddy for any potential losses. In her rush, Maddy had forgotten about the empty bungalow. So much to do.

"Can't stop. I'm late. Hello, goodbye. I'm late. Safe journey to wherever you go. Forgive me." And she was gone and Hari, and for that matter everyone else, always forgave Maddy.

Rita looked nervous, sitting in the open. She was used to and probably preferred the seclusion of the shadows.

Jack shouted over, "Good to see you out and about, Rita. Any news of your daughter?" Jack remembered to ask.

"Yes, Jack, yes." She was shy and nervous.

"Is she coming?" Jack asked, smiling encouragement.

"No. She's not."

"Ah. Sorry." Jack was annoyed with himself for asking so publicly.

"It's all right, Jack. Not this time but soon. She will come. She has promised. She has kept the fare and I'm going with Joan and the others to Kodaikahal. I didn't follow Baba last year. We're all going. We're sharing a taxi. There's to be no charge. It's a thank you."

"Who from, Maddy?" Jack would be surprised if it was.

"No. It's the one Baba told me to buy. The driver came to me. Baba told him to come. I think I'm forgiven. I'll ask at first darshan. Then I'll know for certain."

"You take care, Rita." Jack was pleased to see her in the world again but was anxious for her. The continuing faith of Baba's Brides, as he happily called them, puzzled him. He was nervous on their behalf. Rock stars aged and their music faded and the groupies finally grew up. Gods live forever. Their acts are timeless. Jack was concerned that these good women might be wasting their lives.

A small man, sinewy and improbably strong, came into view balancing Jack's bag on his head. He wouldn't cross the ditch and beckoned for Jack with one hand and towards the bus stop with the other.

"That's my man," Jack declared. "How's he do that?"

"Hunger and anticipation of a huge tip, I suppose," Jean Paul suggested.

"I'll see what I can do."

Jack and Jean Paul rose to their feet.

"Don't you want to fetch your things?" Jack asked.

"They're here." Jean Paul patted the small canvas holdall slung neatly over his shoulder.

Jack laughed.

"What's not in there?" he asked as he ushered Jean Paul away.

Graciously, Jean Paul leant down to Hari, who prevented his stooping by standing himself. Instead of a handshake Jean Paul hugged Hari close.

"Thank you for your friendship, Hari. I've enjoyed our talks. Here." Jean Paul handed Hari a small envelope. "In there you'll find my parents' address in France and a few thoughts we've shared. Write to me. Stay pure. Visit Arunachala one day. The Red Mountain will bring you peace."

Hari tried not to cry. Jack helped him out.

"Goodbye young friend. Shake my hand." Hari did. Jack waved his arm up and down in an exaggerated way that made Hari laugh.

"It's been a pleasure. Thank you for picking me up off that marble floor. I've learnt a lot from you, my young friend. Here's my card. I've got your address in Birmingham, your father gave me his card, so, there's no excuse. We will continue to be friends. Guide me over the bridge once more and set me on my way."

For the last time, Hari led Jack across the wavering bridge. On the other side he stumbled away, shooing the wiry porter before him beneath his impossible load. Jack never looked back. He waved over his shoulder until consumed by the crowd. He was taking the bus and a lot else besides.

Now Jack had gone, Hari was bereft and ran towards his bridge for a final look.

Hari and his father and mother were the last and only occupants of the Sai Deep Café. They were waiting for a taxi to take them to Bangalore.

"It looks so empty now," Hari remarked. "And small," he added.

"And sad," Hari's mother concluded, "now all your friends are gone."

"I'm sorry I've neglected you, son. So many arrangements had to be made," explained his father.

"I understand, Father. I don't feel neglected. I've been amongst my friends and I've been busy."

"You've been wonderful." Hari's mother smiled and reached for his hand.

"Where are we going now, Father? There's no reason to go to Kodaikanal now Grandfather has died. And I'm too young to go to the Red Mountain with Jack and Jean Paul and at least a century must pass before I go to Tibet looking for Borg!" He laughed, enjoying the thought of his friends.

"Lunasha is safe now," he added, without explanation.

"Who?" asked the father.

"Another friend," answered the mother. "One of Hari's particular friends." She looked meaningfully towards Hari. Did she know, he wondered? Had she known all along?

"Good. I'm glad she's safe," Hari's father commented, absent-mindedly. "I've a surprise. To honour the ritual of mourning the loss of Grandfather, we need to return to Bangalore in ten days or so. Rather than stay here,

I thought we might go on a special trip, a distraction for you Hari, after all of this upheaval."

"Where to, Father?"

"Mauritius. I understand it is a very beautiful island. I've never been. Maddy booked the hotel and the flights. She seems infinitely capable."

Proprietor interrupted Hari's father.

"Your taxi is waiting, sir."

"Thank you."

As they left, Hari's father gave Proprietor a handsome tip. Hari shook his hand. Proprietor bowed his head in thanks.

"I will guard your genie until you return, Master Hari."

"Thank you, Proprietor. Thank you."

There was a bridge at the edge of a village and a village at the edge of a town and a town at the edge of the continent of India. The town was Bangalore, the village Whitefield and the bridge had a name. It came to be called Hari's bridge. Hari was the name of the boy who made God smile.

Sai Baba

Hari's Bridge